'Without fear or favour...'

Book three in
'The Borough Boys' series

By

Phil Simpkin

Copyright Information

This novel is intended as a work of fiction.

All characters and events in this publication, other than those clearly in the public domain, are fictitious, and any resemblance to real persons, living or dead, is purely coincidental.

Acknowledgements

This novel would not have been possible without the help and support, yet again, of my willing and able band of helpers.

Thanks to my long suffering wife for her willing eye and critical perspective, and often constructive criticism and feedback. At times I may not have been as readily receptive to that perspective as I should.

Also to Dave, Mel, Lian and Colin for their proof reading and critiques.

Not forgetting my loyal band of readers and contributors to my blog and other social media pages, for their encouragement and support in getting book three into circulation.

Cheers guys!

Foreword

As a young Police Officer in 1970's Leicester, I was to experience the delights of walking assorted beats of what was then, Leicester Central Division.

These included old parts of the City Centre, those on the Highfields, and those on the Hinckley Road side of the town.

Each section opened up to me the beauty and intrigue of Victorian Leicester, from the architecture and small streets of the Friars and St Martin's areas, to the narrow terraced streets across the Highfields, and the most deprived areas of the city abutting the River Soar around Bath Lane, Great Central and Highcross Streets.

My imagination would run wild considering what it would have been like to have Policed Leicester in the early days of the Borough Force from 1836, with cobbles, gas lamps, and fogs, and crime fighting was in its infancy.

This, my third novel in my 'Borough Boys' series, incorporates an element of history with fiction, as in researching this book, I have discovered so much about Victorian Leicester, that I dare say many people were unaware. I have lived myself within a few miles of the Centre for most of my life, and was oblivious of so much of the history of the old Borough.

I want to convey some of that history and at the same time delve into Leicester's darkest depravities.
Some of the characters in this novel are real, and I hope

I have portrayed them in the light of research available, and demonstrated their part in the development of Leicester, in context with the time period I cover.

I have tried hard not to go beyond the realms of what is known or can be reasonably established about those who are real, and apart from some license to imagine what they must have been like (where no records to that effect exist) but they are all (in the main) some of the good guys.

Most characters are totally fictitious, and are created to bring this novel to life.

Some are my villains, however, and reflect the sort of persons who were also wandering around the streets of the Borough, and who challenged and brought of age

'The Borough Boys'

*For many of you who are unfamiliar with the streets of Old Leicester, **maps** and information may be found on my website at Http://www.1455bookcompany.co.uk/ the-borough-boys.html*

*A **Glossary** of unfamiliar terms contained throughout this story can be found at the rear of this book.*

Prologue

The year is 1852, and the Country is entering the first days of a general election.

A disillusioned people and an unhappy and suspicious (if not paranoid) Monarch, Queen Victoria, await change.

This is a dark and murky Victorian England, with a transient population, and London housing foreigners of every nationality and description.

Secrecy, lies, and talk of spies and spymasters permeate the Government and Her Majesty's offices and departments.

Assassination attempts and foreign power struggles have made Victoria and her minders increasingly nervous.

The Capital, towns and boroughs are setting up for the hustings, and politicians busy writing and checking their speeches, in their bid for power. Nationally, the police are looking at the increased risk of public disorder and demonstrations.

For most of the population, life goes on as normal, with the poor getting increasingly poorer, the rich richer, and the dissatisfied increasingly agitated.

The last thing any police force currently wants now is a serious crime or crimes to investigate, but as the poor state - 'Life stinks!'

<u>Westminster - 28th June 1852</u>

'We really are for it now. When our Lords and Masters know what has happened, they will have our guts for garters,' said the shorter man, visibly shuddering. 'What is it with you and your temper?' His fair skin flushed with anger.
'I thought we were undisturbed. Where did he appear from, and why did he need to challenge us like that?' said the taller, collecting his thoughts.
Beneath his feet lay the body of an elderly man, regaled in the dress of some high office. Blood pooled beneath his head.
'He is old. What threat did he offer?'
'He would have raised the alarm.'
'By the time he had realised, we would have been out of the window and disappeared into the night.'
'Have you got the papers?'
'I have them safe. Little wonder she wants them back.'
'Did you take the other things, as instructed? It must look like a regular house burglary.'
'A regular house burglary, in this area? These are all important diplomats and from foreign embassies all over London. They would have to be rich pickings in such a case.'
'And are they?'
'I have a nice haul, and outrageously expensive, by the look of it.'
'And the old man?'
'Just leave him. We have taken too long already. '
The two men dropped, confidently, from the first floor window onto the lush grass at the rear of the property,

landing like cats, with no sound whatsoever.

Not a single guard dog barked, and most houses here had at least one.

Out over the high wall and off into the shadows, their sacks strapped across their chests. The full face masks they wore were quickly removed and pocketed.

The taller man slid a small weighted pouch from a strap around his wrist, and dropped it into his own sack.

He was glad he had one with him, but had not realised how dangerous it could be. It felt good in his hand, reassuring and empowering.

'We take the papers to the drop and leave them where we were instructed. We keep the jewellery and hide it. I want it somewhere it can't be found. It must never be seen, else we are further connected.'

'I fear we are dead men, now, my brother. He will not be happy, and you know his past threats.'

'We need a reason to stay alive.'

'I might just have that, in this bag,' said the taller man.

*****

A few hours later, a shadowy figure appeared on the quiet lane.

The culvert was dry from the long hot days, and the bag was left exactly where he had instructed. A hasty look at the papers brought about a look of pure evil.

The information was purportedly to be of either great use, or more likely, embarrassment to his masters, all the way to the top, but these were not the papers he had demanded.

He had been betrayed.

Rumour was already filtering back that an occupant had disturbed them and was now well and truly dead. That would result in far more police attention than his masters would have appreciated.

Metropolitan murder detectives were becoming very adept at their work. How long before they saw through a botched burglary and made the connection?

Heads would roll, and he had no intention of one being his. He had to work fast. When he caught up with them, he would reap his vengeance, swiftly.

Transferring the remaining papers into the leather bags which he had strapped across his saddle, he roughly mounted his stallion and set off, hastily, to the safe house.

A hot summer night - Friday 2nd July 1852

'Why is it, that everything sounds so much louder in the dead of night?' he cursed, conscious that something unusual had disturbed him.

Their bedroom window had been deliberately left ajar, the humidity at the level it currently was, which heightened the sounds coming from the normally quiet, exclusive, edge of the town.

Edward Paget and his wife Maria had found the heat of the day too much, and on retiring to bed at about ten thirty on the evening prior, Edward had opened the sash window within the front bedroom of the three storey townhouse to allow in any slightest breeze, and give the couple some hope of cooler air.

'Did you hear that, too?' asked Maria, nervously, also stirring. 'Is there somebody on the roof?'

'It's probably just a cat or a bird that's roosted for the night,' Edward reassured her, stepping down onto the bedside rug.

His bare feet brushed the plush pile, as his toes sought the slippers he had left at the side of the bed. The air felt warm on his bare white legs, below and beneath his billowing nightshirt.

The room was bathed in a soft, silvery light, considering it must have been after midnight, a consequence of the clear moonlit sky.

As he arose, the door to the bedroom opened inwardly before him, and he caught first sight of a small, dark, figure. Edward made out some sort of mask worn by the intruder.

'Back away, I have my pistol,' Edward heard himself

saying, bizarrely, as fear now drove his response.

'Doesn't look like it to me, my friend,' said the intruder, also benefiting from the moonlight, moving confidently towards the man of the house.

Such a young voice should not sound so menacing, Edward considered.

'What do you want? Take anything, but leave us alone,' whispered Maria, pulling the loose bed sheet up, thus protecting her modesty.

'Where is the money you collected from the bank, earlier?' enquired the intruder.

Some form of an American accent, perhaps tinged with European, Edward noted.

Both he and Maria had spent some earlier years in the colonies, on business.

'We have little money here at all. There is only a small sum on the premises,' said Edward, concerned as to how the man should have such knowledge.

'Open your safe, then, and let me see for myself,' demanded the intruder, raising his voice, assertively.

Edward suspected this was a young man, perhaps in his early twenties at the most. His profile in the moonlit room was small and wiry. He briefly considered whether to try and overpower the intruder and protect his wife, as a husband surely should, but his moral courage failed him. Bullied at school, he was by conditioning a timid man.

'I suggest you leave, before a local constable hears the commotion.'

Edward shouted 'help,' optimistic that it might attract some form of attention, else frighten the man off.

Before another word could be uttered, the wiry figure in front moved deftly forward, raising a small object in his right hand as he closed in. He swung it, purposefully, striking Edward across the left temple - a small leather sack or cosh, no bigger than the width of a man's hand, clearly weighted and efficient as a weapon.

Edward Paget fell to the floor, stunned and painfully aware that he now bled freely from aside his left eye. Warm blood trickled over his face and onto his hand. His temple throbbed and he felt overwhelming nausea. Oddly, He was concerned that it would stain their new Chinese carpet.

'You want more, or are you going to open the safe?' the intruder taunted, calmly, the weapon clear in Edward's view.

'Open the safe, Edward. Do as he says before we both get hurt,' Maria directed, timidly, cowering behind the sheet.

'You will hang for this,' Edward spat, incensed that he had been taken down by so slight a fellow. He rose, gingerly, to his feet and unwisely, or unwittingly, clenched his fists.

'Foolish man!' said the intruder, bringing down the weapon again with frightening speed, striking hard to the same part of the head as before, knocking Edward Paget senseless.

'Madam, I suggest you open the safe yourself, now, else you will never speak to your husband again.'

Maria Paget slowly climbed down from the bed, stepping over her husband's prone body, to a wardrobe standing just inside the door to the room. The menace in the intruder's voice disturbed her.

'Put down the sheet, for goodness sake,' the man urged. Opening the door, a large metal strongbox, about 5 feet tall and 3 feet wide and deep, with a heavy lock, and a plate on the door, stamped 'Hurley and Stanton: New York & St Paul' was revealed.

A motto, 'Feel safe in our hands' embossed on the doorplate struck the intruder as both amusing and ironic. Edward Paget had this safe brought back following a recent trip to Boston.

'The key?' demanded the intruder, lighting a small lamp from the side of the bed. The recessed cupboard was dark and unlit by the moonlight filling the room.

'A chain around his neck,' replied Maria.

With his foot, the intruder roughly pushed Edward Paget over onto his back, grasped the chain in his left hand, and snapped it from his neck. Paget moaned, quietly and pitifully.

'Get back onto the bed, and don't make a sound.'

The intruder pushed the sturdy key into the lock, levering the chunky brass handle. As he pulled the heavy door, a sound like a gasp of air could be heard as it opened. A dog barked, close by. The intruder placed the small lamp to illuminate the contents within the safe.

A small pile of white, £50 bank notes, held together with narrow ribbon, sat prominently at the front of the upper shelf in large denominations, and of high value, as the intruder anticipated.

Several heavy bags of coins, including gold sovereigns, half-crowns and other, smaller denominations, no doubt for wages, sat on the floor of the safe.

A selection of assorted velvet jewellery boxes and bags were visible behind the bank notes.

The intruder calmly opened each jewellery container, eyeing their contents in the light of the lamp, selecting an odd item, discarding most onto the bedroom floor, before placing his rewards into a large canvas bag, which he had strapped across his chest. The notes followed into the bag in similar fashion. The coins were left untouched, too heavy to conceal or easily remove.

He walked towards Maria, slowly climbing onto the bed, kneeling next to her, his body over hers, his left arm crossing her chest.

Slowly and deliberately he moved his right hand, tracing over the parts of her body that only a husband should have right of access, and placed it onto Maria's trembling throat, squeezing gently.

'Don't make a noise!' he whispered, menacingly, before calmly climbing down, crossing to the open window.

He whistled, lightly, and then threw down the bag from his chest, suggesting a waiting accomplice, below.

Maria noticed he wore no gloves, and his hands looked small, yet strong. She realised she had not noticed them before when he had grabbed her throat, only seeing the two small holes in the mask or hood that he wore. His eyes were the most strikingly vivid pale aquamarine blue, emphasised in the flicker of the lamp which he had carefully placed back at the side of the bed.

She also noticed he wore what she could only describe as men's ballet shoes, which she thought strange. He had such small feet.

Edward let out another low moan, as the intruder cautiously peered out through the open sash window, before sliding out and dropping from sight.

She was mindful that the bedroom was quite elevated, and the drop to the ground would have been fifteen to twenty feet, yet there was not a sound.

She sat, stunned, and cradled her prone husband.

Minutes must have passed before she found the strength to utter a scream. A Long, curdling, terrified scream, quickly drawing the attention of a nearby constable.

The dream

Shepherd sat bolt upright in bed, the flimsy cotton sheet around him clinging to the damp film which coated his naked body; his breathing rapid, for a moment, as he struggled to separate dream from reality.

His mouth felt uncomfortably dry. His heart would surely burst within his tightened chest. His head throbbed.

He stared, blindly, at his hands, watching Perkins' life blood ebb away. The stench of discharged gunpowder filled his nose.

He must have called out, and woke Sally in doing so, as he had so often, recently.

Sally opened her eyes and drew herself up onto her elbow, dragging the clinging sheet away from Shepherd as she turned to him, bringing her slim hand to rest on his outstretched arm.

'You're having that dream again, Samson. The poor boy has gone, and there was nothing you could have done to change things,' trying hard to reassure him, as she had done on an almost daily basis since the tragedy.

The dream had become a daily burden since the event in Cock Muck Hill, and she watched the terrible guilt of a survivor exposed.

'I heard, yesterday, that old Mr Williams, the man that shot Archie, had been found hanging in the borough Gaol. Couldn't live with his guilt any longer, I suspect,' Shepherd reflected, as he came to his senses.

Tears wet his cheeks.

'It's a hot night, Samson, and you've to be at work at six in the morning, so back to sleep with you,' she whispered, holding him in her arms until he could sleep again.

Grumpy old men

Shepherd entered the small office, not expecting to encounter the seated occupant.

'Morning, Sergeant Beddows, up bright and breezy today. What brings you in so early?'

Shepherd felt fresh, awake, temporarily free from his nightmares.

'A nasty burglary on New Walk,' said Beddows. 'Little bleeder went in whilst the occupants were asleep. Assaulted them both, one way or another, then, made off with rather a large quantity of money and some jewellery, leaving the owner unconscious and rather poorly.'

'Any ideas?' said Shepherd, scanning the room, which always looked dark and grimy, with pointless old candle stubs seemingly covering every recess.

Beddows had papers scattered across the small desk. An oil lamp still burned above them, suspended from a hook above the desk. Thickly overlapping rings from previous tea mugs glowed in the dim light against the desk's dull surface. Other miscellaneous marks reminded Shepherd of past encounters and 'difficult' interviews.

'The reporting constable says that the occupants thought the burglar might be an American, or at least someone who has settled and lived in America, although they also detected a European accent of some sort.'

'Do we have many Americans in Leicester?' said Shepherd.

'I've no knowledge of any residing within the borough. Seemed to know quite a bit about our occupants though, including the fact they had a safe, and that it was full, as of last night.'

'Someone connected, you're thinking?'

'Seems our victims have had a regular trade in the Americas, and travel quite a bit, so quite possibly.'

'Sounds like a thorough statement, for a change?'

'The statement is awful. I had to drag teeth from Constable Hobbs. He knew far more than he wrote down. Nigh on illiterate, I suspect, and the writing is dreadful.'

'Isn't he one of the original older ones, Beddows? Most struggle with their paperwork, but they can prove to be good interviewers, and those that can be bothered get good detail, in my humble opinion.'

'If they can't write a decent statement, they should be made to learn, or bugger off. Makes my piss boil, so it does, rewriting statements for the stupid or the lazy.'

'Doesn't Mrs Beddows get fed up with these early starts?'

'Mrs Beddows rarely speaks to me anymore, young Shepherd. Mind, she hasn't really for years. Probably doesn't even know, or care, for that matter, that I've gone out, yet.'

'I realise you've never really spoken much of her.'

'I haven't, for good reason. If you knew her better, Mr Shepherd, you would understand. She has little time for me these days, and even less time for this job. We no longer fit.'

'Surely it can't be that bad?'

'Me and Mrs Beddows make for good examples of what not to end up like! Be warned. Make the most of what you have today, because this job will take it from you, given half a chance.'

'How long is it that you have been married?'

'Haven't you got a job to do? I have spoken, nauseatingly, enough of Mrs Beddows for today,' growled Beddows, waving Shepherd away with a dismissive flick of the hand.

Beddows settled back in the old chair, in a further attempt to make sense of reporting Constable Hobbs' confused scrawl, and his own copious scribbles. Shepherd sauntered back towards the parade area, in the main station office, becoming aware of tell tale pipe smoke that signified the Charge Sergeant's presence.

'When is Mr Charters going to make sure this bloody lot can read and write?' Beddows slammed his fist, hard, onto the small desk, knocking over his half empty mug of cold tea, and the contents of a small inkwell. A wet, inky stain began to spread across the pages of the already illegible report, and miscellany of other papers, as Beddows struggled to move them out of harm's way.

'You seem in an exceedingly bad mood, Mr Beddows,' came the gravelly, Geordie tones of Head Constable Charters. 'Who has upset you so early?'

'Didn't know you were up and about, Sir. My apologies,' said Beddows, cursing under his breath.

'So, is it the lack of quality of report, or your dear wife who has brought about such anger?' said Charters.

'Mrs Beddows is the same every day, so I suggest it is the incompetent who completed this report. Why do we tolerate such men, out there on the street, dealing with matters that they are not capable of?'

'That is rich, from a man who courted his own fair share of controversy?'

'That was a very long time ago, Sir, and I thought my indiscretions were now expunged?'

'I never forget, Beddows. I forgive, or I tolerate, which is what I would implore you to do. Many of our older constables are still, sadly, not much better learned than the old Night Watch men they replaced, or from which they were selected by my predecessor.'

'Even when we get reports like this?' said Beddows,

pushing the soggy, stained report towards Charters.

'Even then. Most of our population are totally illiterate, and we have to make small allowances. Hobbs at least tries.'

'Well, now I've got to go and speak to these people again.'

'Isn't that what you get paid to do?'

'Well, it would have been better for a detective to have been sent in the first place.'

'I have five of you available to me. I have to defend your special status at a cost to patrols, to our Watch Committee. I want this crime resolving, so take somebody with you and get on with it.'

Charter's face had turned a boiled beetroot colour. Beddows recognised the sign and reluctantly backed off.

'Kettle's not in yet, and Smith and Haynes are still out on another over-night gang infiltration, somewhere down Carley Street.'

'Take Shepherd. He is in early, so make use of him. He will probably let you take it out on him, with that thick skin of his, but find a way of managing your anger. We are a team here, remember that. I will inform the morning Inspector regarding Shepherd.'

Beddows grunted, as politely as he could muster, picking up the damp papers, stomping towards the kitchen at the rear of the police station to alert his chosen companion for the day.

*****

Just after seven o'clock, Beddows and Shepherd set off across the dusty streets which separated the police station from New Walk.

The town was already alive with traders opening up their array of little shops, and a myriad of delivery carts of all shapes and sizes scurried around. Most of the factories had early shifts start at six, so their pitiful masses were already gainfully employed, young and old. The odd constable stood in a shop doorway, having a crafty smoke, or was seen shuffling down an alleyway for some gratuity or other, no doubt. A breakfast or a drink was favoured on the early turn, and free was best. Many favours were still 'owed' that allowed the old sweats to hold control. Butchers, bakers and grocers all gave their local constable frequent free goods 'in lieu' of a blind eye.

'Lazy, scrounging, toe-rags, your uniformed colleagues, Shepherd. I had hoped those days were over. Little wonder we have such a crime rate,' grumbled Beddows

'Most of them are of your era, Beddows, as you remind me, are they not?'

'Was that a statement or a question?'

Beddows was always careful as to where he placed his feet. Dried mud or dried excrement of some description layered the roads and pavements, but an odd fresh 'turd' was always a daily hazard underfoot, sometimes of human origin.

'Not seen you this annoyed for ages. Can I help?'

'You can best help by not asking me anything more about Mrs Beddows for a start.'

'Sorry, Sergeant.'

'You don't need to get all formal on me, either, or have you gone all funny on me now?'

'Sorry, Beddows, I'll not mention Mrs Beddows again.'

'I should be well rid of her at present. I should never have married her. Oh, for a bout of Cholera, or a speeding growler clearing her up as she shuffles across Welford Road.' Beddows looked to the skies in vain hope that the big man was listening, and then kicked out at a scruffy looking 'ratter' that crossed his path, hissing back as old cats do. A crow, picking at some foul scrap in the road, flew off at the sight of the cat.

'Surely you don't mean that?'

Beddows glared, but said nothing. More than once, particularly of late, he had wished his wife dead. Divorce was impossibly complicated, expensive and worthless, and he would probably end up with nothing. So complicated indeed, that it was rarely practiced. He knew, however, a myriad of places where bodies would never be found, and a number of people who would willingly remove the nuisance for him, at the right price. But, reality was that he had to be content with his suffering for the moment.

Crossing from Market Street, over Belvoir Street and into King Street, the town felt fresher. The breezes from the South Fields and Freeman's Common blowing across the narrow streets definitely helped, blowing the noxious smells from the middle of the town out towards Belgrave and The Abbey. Saffron Lane could often be smelled, in all its herbal glory, when it blew from that direction. Today it revitalised Beddows' ailing senses. Shepherd could only smell the chimneys and oil or dyes from nearby factories.

'Smell that fresh air already, lad? No more sausage stuffers or knackers yards for miles in this direction,' observed Beddows.

'You always say that as we leave the town. Ever think about joining the county force, Beddows?'

A lot of the originals had done just that, and went off with their new Chief Constable, Frederick Goodyer, for promotion, better pay and better conditions.

'Every day I thought about it, but I watched them all, following like sheep. Someone had to stay behind and look after this shit hole!'

'But why you?'

'Who else was going to look after your Uncle George, God bless him?'

'And after he died?'

'By then my name was mud! Charters had seen to that,

and Mr Goodyer wouldn't have wanted a drunk, as he already had enough of his own, so I never thought about it again.'

'Personally, I'm glad you stuck it out, Beddows. The town is a safer place for the likes of you, and Sergeants Smith and Haynes.'

'Why can't your other uniform colleagues be as sharp to learn as you?'

'Some are all right. Perkins would have been a good copper.' Shepherd swallowed, as his voice wavered, momentarily.

'Perkins is gone, lad, just like your Uncle George. All you and me can do is keep going after the buggers that do these wicked things. Send them away for as long as the courts allow, or better still, neck them.'

Shepherd started to feel more at home, himself, as he neared the edge of the town, with the countryside and open views more pleasing on his eye than the grime of the invasive Industry off to the left.

'I could think about a job in the county. It's definitely more like home,' said Shepherd.

'You'd make a stuffed bird laugh. Then who might actually find out who killed your Uncle George? We never found out, although there were rumours.'

'One day, Beddows, I will avenge Uncle George. That is my ultimate ambition. Some evidence will throw new light on his final moments.'

Beddows had never doubted that Shepherd would do just that, and see George's killer brought to justice.

How the other half live

New Walk was a welcome provision for the people of the town, and gave a pretty, tree-lined walkway from the bottom near King Street, passing the new museum, to the top of the hill at the racecourse, where borough met county. It followed the route of the ancient Roman *Via Devana* from Leicester to Colchester, and originally known as *Queen's Walk*, or, more locally as *Ladies Walk*. In more recent years it had become the site of some of Leicester's most prestigious housing, and those between King Street, up to the museum were predominantly owned and inhabited by the bankers and industrialists. Many owned the large factories that had sprung up in the streets surrounding Holy Cross Priory, Wellington Street and Granby Street, their limits defined by the old toll bar, just prior to the railway, and that filled the town with the sounds, smells and smog of the machine age.

Edward Paget was one of the latest of these industrialists. He owned a modest, but rapidly emerging, hosiery factory in Wellington Street, and procured the finest cotton he could import from America.

Most of his products were sold in markets outside of Leicester, particularly Birmingham, and London.

He had travelled regularly in recent months to 'quality assure' that his supplies were of the best raw material. American cotton was seen as superior over Indian, due to the longer, stronger fibres of the two main domesticated native American species, *Gossypium Hirsutum* and *Gossypium Barbadense*.

He had gained a liking of things American, and admired the population's determination to grow and prosper, which matched his own hunger. His factory manufactured excellent garments, and he gainfully employed one hundred and fifty machine operators; men, women and children.

His wife, Maria, was a local girl, the daughter of William Harrison, the owner of a similar business enterprise. She had met Edward at a cotton millers' dinner hosted by producers in Florida. Maria's family business was significantly larger and more established than Edward's, but their products similar.

The two families tied a strong allegiance and in doing so, secured an apparently healthy business empire, through the marriage.

The door to number 62 was a lush dark green, with a heavy brass knocker and what seemed like an over-sized lock mechanism of a similar polished brilliance. In the middle of the door was a matching letter box, identifying the status of the property and its occupants. These were still somewhat a novelty, unknown in most parts of the borough.

At the side of the door was a further brass handle, which appeared to be some form of bell pull, alerting the occupants of somebody's presence at the door. A gas lamp was fixed over the door with a heavy bracket, the gas pipe running into the house. Domestic gas lamps were also quite rare, although the borough's street lamps had been gas powered for some years.

Beddows could not resist the urge to try the device, pulling on it twice, robustly. A bell could be heard ringing inside the house.

'Cow bells,' thought Beddows, now mildly amused.

'Trying to wake the poor buggers up, Beddows, or trying to pull the house down?' Shepherd smiled, reflecting on how new fangled inventions still tickled Beddows.

Movement inside affirmed that someone was up and about, if they had even gone back to bed at all, after such an ordeal.

A young woman, dressed in a sturdy blue silk gown, opened the door. She looked pale and gave the appearance that she had been crying, her eyes red and puffy.

'Mrs Paget?' The woman nodded in acknowledgement.

'I am Sergeant Beddows and this is Constable Shepherd. We are here to ask some more detailed questions about events overnight.'

'Please, come in. My husband is in the drawing room with the doctor.'

Entering the house via a hallway which itself was bigger than the total of both constables' homes, an impressive dark hardwood staircase with heavy, carved, banisters dominated the space. The floor was colourfully tiled in red and cream.

To the right, another large polished door, through which, Beddows and Shepherd were ushered. Expensive polish and leather was the prevailing smell.

Inside, a man was sat on a leather chair of considerable proportions. Stood over him, applying a bandage which now covered most of his head, was Surgeon Thomas Hamilton.

Bloodied rags, in a bowl, sat at the doctor's feet.

'Good morning, gentlemen,' said Hamilton, glancing back over his shoulder as he worked.

'Mr Hamilton, glad to see you out and about at such an early hour,' said Shepherd, toying with the doctor.

'I am not yet *out and about*, Constable Shepherd, as I have not yet been in, or to bed.'

A large painting sat in an ornate gold frame above the fireplace. Clearly a representation of the seated man. A statement of his importance or self-importance?

'I'm sorry, Sir, I take it you are Mr Edward Paget?' said

Beddows, gesturing to the man being treated. The man raised a hand in acknowledgement.

'We apologise for such an early visit, but Constable Shepherd and I would like first-hand knowledge of the events of earlier today, and a chance to look around the house and grounds if we may, before any evidence of value may be lost?'

'I have finished now, Mr Paget. I will send you my bill. Is there anything else you require of me before I go?' said Hamilton, rising to his feet.

'No thank you, Mr Hamilton. I appreciate your attendance at such an ungodly hour,' said Paget, grimacing, his hands feeling their way around the bandages. The man spoke slowly and slurred slightly, and was clearly unwell. Pain showed on his face with every word uttered.

Shepherd considered the pain he must be in, cringing at the thought of how he had felt, himself, after a serious assault two years earlier.

'Mr Hamilton, we will need to speak later, if you are available,' said Shepherd.

'I shall be at the infirmary, in my rooms, all day today, Shepherd. You can get me there. Knock loud, as I may sleep, God willing.'

'I take it you are happy that we talk to both Mr and Mrs Paget and that there is nothing that should prevent us?' said Beddows, *not that anything would stop him from asking questions, in any event, but best be sure.*

'No, but be gentle though. Mr Paget has some rather nasty swelling and needed some sewing back together.'

'Not your impressive blanket stitches, I hope?' said Beddows, winking, a comment reflecting the good Surgeon's post mortem dexterity.

'My finest, most delicate of stitches, Sergeant, as you well know. However, his head will hurt like the blazes. He is extremely lucky to be with us still. The temple is a

fragile area. Mrs Paget is rather distressed and shocked.'
Mrs Paget left the room and showed Thomas Hamilton
from the House.
'I would like to talk to each of you individually, if I
may?' said Beddows, addressing Edward Paget.
'Constable Shepherd would benefit from examining the
house. Perhaps, whilst I am talking with you, Mrs Paget
could accompany him through the house and gardens?'
Beddows settled himself into a most comfortable
leather chair, directly facing the injured man.

*****

'Are you sure you feel well enough to go through this,
Mrs Paget?' asked Shepherd, as they walked through the
hallway, to the foot of the grand staircase.
'I am perfectly fine, now, honestly.'
'What can you recollect?'
Shepherd's hands lingered over the finely polished
handrail. *How could anywhere be so clean, he mused?*
Sally was thorough, as was his aunt, within their little
abode on Twizzle and Twine Passage, but this was
something else. How the posh lived, astounded him.
The pair started up the wide treads towards the first
floor landing. Shepherd awaited the customary creak of
timber, but the hardwood remained solid and silent,
except for the rustle of Mrs Paget's silk dress on the
leading edges. He worried that his hobnails would
damage the fine wood or the carpet running up the
centre of the staircase. 'Should I remove my boots?'
'Just stay on the carpet and you should be fine,' Mrs
Paget said, but her expression was, clearly, of some
concern. 'We can always have that cleaned.'
Shepherd decided removal of his boots was appropriate,
and was glad he had chosen a well darned pair of socks,
earlier in the day. Sally had been taught well by his

Aunt. He placed the boots at the top of the flight, and observed the marks his cleats had left. He hoped his feet did not smell, and felt conspicuous amidst the opulent smells of the house.

'It had been so very hot when we retired, and Mr Paget left the sash window in our bedroom open a little, in an attempt to give us some much needed respite.'

'At about what time did you retire to bed?'

'It would have been about half past eleven. We sat reading, due to the heat, for a while. We were in the house on our own last night, as normally our house-keeper, Eleanor, would have been present and locked up, but Mr Paget had to do so himself.'

'Tell me more about Eleanor.' The pair stopped on the landing, momentarily. Ornaments and artwork adorned the walls and sat upon a range of fine furniture and within recessed alcoves. All spoke of the couple's apparent wealth.

'She has been with us for several years, now. She worked for my Father first, and then came to us when my Father went off to America for a year or two. She is a wonderful and trustworthy lady. She has recently lost a close family member, hence she is out of town for a few days, making the arrangements for the family. It was sudden and came as a shock to her and her family, so we allowed her some time away.'

'Have you ever had concerns about her, or suspected her of anything?'

'Never.' She noticed Shepherd's eyes watching every word and every facial expression, for any glimpse of doubt. So studious, she considered, for a young man.

'Where has she gone to?'

'To Welford, in Northamptonshire, where her family lives.'

'Does she have access to any keys to this house?'

'Only when she is here. Then, she has access to all the

house keys, and has her own back door key from the lower ground-floor yard, which only gives access to the part of the house where her rooms are located. She has left the keys to the main part of the house with us. We have them all whilst she is away.'

'Does anyone else have keys to the property?'

'No, only Mr Paget and myself have keys. Oh, and my parents have a set, for emergencies.'

'We will need to talk to Eleanor at some stage. What is her surname?' Shepherd reached into his tunic pocket, removed and opened a small notebook and started to scribble notes with a short pencil.

'Skinner. That is her maiden name. She has never been married, to the best of my knowledge.'

'When are you expecting her back?'

'Tuesday or Wednesday, giving her time for any funeral rites and travelling back after all matters are concluded.'

'Please let us know when she returns.'

'I shall be pleased to.' Maria Paget felt concerned that Shepherd should even consider Eleanor a suspect. Nothing left to chance, she supposed.

'Setting Eleanor aside for a while, when you retired to bed, did either of you notice anything unusual?'

Mrs Paget moved towards the bedroom where the crime had occurred, Shepherd following close behind, still making notes.

'I certainly didn't, nor Mr Paget, else I assume he would have said. He went around and made sure everywhere was secure, and turned off the lamps, after checking the windows and doors. As far as I know, our window was the only window left open.'

'And the drapes?'

'We only have heavy lace drapes up, presently. Normally we would partially close the shutters, but it has been too warm.'

'So, after reading, you went off to sleep at the same time?' Shepherd took a long look around the room. His socked feet left a damp trail on the polished wooden floor, before they sank into the plush pile of the bedroom carpet.

'Yes, although we tossed and turned fitfully with the heat. We read a little as I said, and then extinguished the bedside lamps.' Mrs Paget felt embarrassed, recalling the man's close contact with her, earlier, on the matrimonial bed.

Her face reddened. *What would the constable think of her blush?*

'Did you hear anything beforehand?'

'There were the usual noises we hear. There are quite a lot of owls that roost nearby; the odd dog fox or vixen; the cattle from the farms on the High Fields, so nothing unusual, no.'

'So, when did you first become aware of the intruder?'

'Mr Paget was stirring, and said he had heard a noise. He thought we might have got a cat or fox on the roof. I thought I had heard something, also. He sat up and had just started to move to the bedroom door as the man walked in.'

'What could you see?'

'My eyes were adjusting to the moonlight. At first he was just a shape. He looked small, almost child-like in stature. It was only when he spoke that he sounded older, but not by much. A young man I believe. It was a few moments before I realised he had a hood or mask of some form over his head and face.'

'And?'

'Mr Paget told him that he had a pistol, for some foolish reason, but the man laughed and struck him.'

'And what did the man do next?'

Mrs Paget closed her eyes as she considered the response. A pained look broke upon her face. A tear welled.

'It all happened rather fast. He seemed to know we had a safe and that there would be an unusually high amount of money in it, which surprised me. We normally only keep money here on the day before we pay the staff. Mr Paget had considerably more than usual as he was to pay for some new Machinery we were to buy, from .'

Shepherd noticed the 'we' in the response. She obviously considered herself to have a vested interest in her husband's business.

'Who would know you had so much money?'

Shepherd's pencil paused above the paper. He must have stepped a bit close to the furniture, as a wash basin and jug rattled, causing him to take hold of the jug, and stop it falling. The noise echoed around the cavernous room.

'I am surprised anyone did. For all they would know, the money would come from the bank and be paid out, more or less straight away. Perhaps the Manager or Head Clerk at the bank who would have signed the notes? The company we were paying for the machinery?'

Shepherd sensed a frustration appearing at the extent of his questioning. Either that, or Mrs Paget was fearing for her fineries with his apparent clumsiness.

'When Mr Paget was struck again, you told the man about the safe and the key. How could he see sufficiently to gain entry to the safe?'

'We have an oil lamp on each side of the bed, and he lit one of those. He must have had his own Congreve's, as I remembered smelling the match strike, just like when my father lights his cigars, at home.'

'Do you mind if I have a look around at the things he touched?'

Maria Paget nodded, obligingly.

Shepherd started to closely inspect the lamp that Mrs

Paget had indicated. He placed his notebook and pencil down, temporarily.

'Did he touch the glass funnel?'

'He must have taken it off to light it. Yes, of course he must.'

'And he wore no gloves?'

'No, apparently not, and he certainly wasn't as he left.' Shepherd held the lamp up at the window, and in the increasing sunlight, a number of marks could be made out.

'Please be careful, that was a gift to us,' Mrs Paget looked on, anxiously.

'I'm sorry, Mrs Paget. I shall be very careful. Do you or your husband or house-keeper have any scars on your fingers?'

'Not that I am aware of, why?'

'There is an interesting mark that looks rather like a crescent moon. Was the man definitely not wearing gloves?' Shepherd looked her firmly, eye to eye. *How reliable a witness was she, in reality?*

'No, definitely not, nor was he when he touched me,' she replied, blushing again.

'I shall need to check the hands of anyone who may have touched it. It may be of some importance.'

Mrs Paget looked puzzled.

Shepherd reached down, once again, for his note book and pencil, taking out a short ruler from his tunic breast pocket. He dutifully measured the marks he was observing, drawing them in his book, to scale, with precise measurements from the ruler.

Shepherd inspected the safe, and then the sash window. On the outside of the window were two apparent lines of finger marks, as if someone had pushed it up, and on what appeared to correspond to the right thumb, the same crescent shaped mark.

He repeated his measurements and sketches into his

note book. Identical in all respects.

'Do you clean the windows, Mrs Paget, or rather, does someone clean them for you?'

'We have a tradesman who does them for us, once a fortnight. Mr Allardyce, from Cramant's Yard, off King Street. He does many of the houses along here, well, he and his son, actually.'

'When did they last clean them?'

'Tuesday, I believe it was, as every other week.'

'Then the mark becomes even more interesting,' said Shepherd, studying his artwork and measurements. 'I think it might be a scar, or a wound.'

'You seem very observant, Constable Shepherd. More so than many people.'

'My artistic bent, I am afraid. An enthusiastic observer of fine detail.'

'Yet you pursue a job in the police?'

'I have good reason for such a choice, I assure you. I like catching criminals, and my observation skills have certainly been advantageous.'

'I'm sorry, I have distracted you,' Mrs Paget apologised.

'You told the first constable that responded, that the man whistled, dropped his bag with all the stolen property therein, and then dropped from the ledge, himself? It is about fifteen feet to the ground, I would think.' Shepherd peered down from the window.

'He looked very lithe, reminiscent of an athlete or a gymnast, I would say.'

'Did you see who he was with when he dropped?'

'I dare not move for a few minutes, other than to scream, and saw nothing more.'

'You said to my colleague, earlier, that you thought the man may have been American?'

'He sounded American, they have developed a distinctive tone. But he had a different accent, behind it. Scandinavian, perhaps?'

'I should like to look at the outside of the house now, if I may.'

Mrs Paget led the way downstairs and to the front door, which she opened for Shepherd. Shepherd remembered to pick up his boots on the way down, and slid them on, lacing them up quickly, by the front door. Both walked outside.

'To get around to the back, you have to come through the house, else we have an entry and a locked gate at the rear of the garden behind us, that leads out onto Wellington Street,' said Mrs Paget. 'There is no alleyway between front and back within the property.'

'The front is my main interest,' said Shepherd, walking down the short flight of steps, onto the area below the front windows, looking back up at the bedroom, above. Shepherd considered that to gain access to the upper first floor window, it would be easier to climb *down* from the flat roof.

'You say when you first saw the man, he was walking into the room, rather than already in the room?'

'I think so, but I was still quite disorientated.'

'Have you checked the rest of the upstairs window locks?' said Shepherd.

'Your colleague did earlier. He said they were all secure.'

'May I have a further look?'

'Please, help yourself,' said Mrs Paget, 'I am feeling a little light headed, and think I shall sit down for a moment.'

Shepherd went back into the house, yet again removing his boots, before he ascended the stairs and strode to the window directly over the front door canopy. This window opened onto the landing outside the bedroom. The sash was now fastened, but there was a dirt smudge on the floor beneath it, on the wooden floor. He concluded that this was the most likely point of entry and that the burglar could have closed it and re-secured it, himself. No obvious instrument marks could be seen. *What if it was actually open, and Mr or Mrs Paget had left an opportunity to gain entry, inadvertently? What if Hobbs had closed it, whilst making the place secure? Shepherd was perplexed.*

*****

Whilst Shepherd had been examining Mrs Paget's recollection of events, Beddows questioned Edward Paget. The comfort of the chair was distracting, and Beddows had felt himself dropping off, at one point. 'So, Mr Paget, who might have known about your safe and its contents, sufficiently well enough to put you through such an ordeal?'.
Edward Paget considered Beddows unconvinced of the story that he had originally heard.
'I really have no idea,' said Paget. 'Your colleagues in uniform have been telling us to be wary, as we are allegedly such prize targets, living up here. It is somewhat more remote than the wealthy houses of the rest of the borough.'
'Don't you think it suspicious, that not only did someone know about your safe, but also that you had more cash than of normal, last night?' Beddows' eyes fixed on the response.
'It is normal on one night every week, when I withdraw my cash for wages to be paid on the Following morning. Yesterday, it was just a higher sum than normal.'
'Which Bank did you withdraw the money from?'
'I use the National Provincial Bank on Granby Street, for all my banking business.'
'And when did you pay that money into the bank?'
'A day or so ago, but I can't recall exactly, in present circumstances.'

'And where was the money from?'

'I would rather not say. Business requires discretion. Sound investment is the key, and new investment would have set me ahead of my peers.'

'I understand the coins for paying the wages were left untouched, but the man took high value bank notes and some jewellery. Is that correct?'

'That is so,' said Paget, feeling almost accused by the tone of questions.

'So the money taken was additional to the normal wages, by several hundred pounds?'

'That is so, I am afraid.'

'So why did you have so much more, last night?'

'I am, or rather was, going off to this week, to settle my account for some new machinery. That is the investment of which I speak.'

'How much are these new fangled machines we keep hearing of?'

'A large rotary frame is costing me £200; a smaller rotary frame £100. I had two of each on order, to be settled in advance of delivery.'

'With bank notes?'

'I prefer to do it that way. Most businessmen I now have dealings with prefer bank notes to cheques, if at all possible.'

'Much to the annoyance of The Revenue, no doubt?'

'What are you implying, Sergeant Beddows?'

'Implying nothing, Mr Paget,' said Beddows, grinning knowingly. 'Not being personally familiar with such large denomination bank notes, am I right in believing that they are drawn to pay a particular named person, completed and signed by the bank cashier?'

'These particular notes are also endorsed with the caveat *or pay the bearer on demand,* at the payees chosen bank or at a branch of National Provincial Bank.'

'Why is that?' Beddows had not heard of this before.

'It means that banknotes can be exchanged between recipients, and whosoever wishes to finally bank the note may do so, not necessarily a named payee.'
'So who was named, specifically, on the missing notes?'
'Mr H. Stringer of Manchester.'
'But, they could be of great value to anyone coming into their possession?'
'Absolutely. This makes them more attractive for businessmen moving money and goods around quickly. It does, however increase the risk, if stolen. I hear tell that next year they will not require a named payee at all.'
'So they may still have been the true objective of the burglar?'
'He seemingly knew of the money, so there appears some connection.'
'And what of your new machines, now?'
'No money, No machines. Mr Stringer will have a queue of pending orders, so somebody else will benefit from my loss.'
'What of the jewellery?'
'There is little missing. One or two pieces belonging to my wife. They are sentimental, as they came from her family.'
'And we have full descriptions and values?'
'My wife gave them to your uniformed colleague, earlier.'
'You and your wife say that the man sounded American. How can you be sure?'
'We have spent a lot of time in America, between Boston, New York and Florida, seeking trade and the highest quality cotton.'
'Do the Americans sound different, depending on where they come from, like we do?' said Beddows.
'Somewhat, Sergeant, but many still have an underlying accent from their country of origin.'

'Could you say where you would think the man's accent was most likely from?'

'No, I'm afraid not, they just have this tonal difference that makes you know they are American. Perhaps there may have been a hint of Irish, or European origin, I'm not sure. My wife may be better suited to answer that, as he spoke more to her, I understand.'

'How many Americans do you know in or near Leicester?'

'A couple of Businessmen in the borough may have previously traded in America, I believe. I occasionally have American business clients who visit and stay, but nobody has been for some months,' said Paget.

'What about your safe. Isn't that American?'

'I had it imported after an earlier trip. An American associate had one and recommended it, so I shipped it back with a cotton consignment, and my own factory engineers installed it.'

'I will need to know who they were, of course. Have you had any trouble with any of your factory workers that might bring them to suspicion?'

'I have the usual labour troubles that every factory owner has, Sergeant. I pay my people well. Skilled workers are on 28 shillings a week, and unskilled on fifteen, the same as the women. The children get between three and five shillings. I pay as much as anyone else in Leicester, but there is always someone who thinks I should pay them more. However, I do give everyone Sunday as a day of rest, and occasionally, on a good week, some may finish early on a Saturday. That's at least twelve hours work I'm losing, yet paying a solid wage.'

'I was told that the children do the really unpleasant or dangerous jobs. Is that correct?' Beddows both looked and sounded disgusted at the proposition, Paget observed.

'They are small and lithe, so getting under the machines

and cleaning out the blockages, fluff picking, is suited to them. Sadly, working in this industry is difficult. The dust can be a killer to all of us. Children seem to succumb more than adults, or so it seems.'

'It's a good job that the borough has surplus of them, then. Easy to replace them, I assume?'

'There are always children queuing at the doors, so yes, Sergeant.'

Beddows thought Mr Paget was starting to look a little pallid. Fresh blood had seeped into the bandages that Hamilton had so recently applied.

'A nice portrait, Mr Paget,' said Beddows, looking over the fireplace.

'A wedding present from my Father-in-Law.'

'Very grand it is. Somebody likes you.'

'He is a generous and wealthy man. He commissioned it to a Royal Academy friend of his whilst we were in London, some months ago.'

'Royal Academy? Constable Shepherd will be impressed. A bit of an artist himself, you know.'

'Really? I didn't know constables were that bright?'

Beddows sensed Mr Paget had an increasing dislike for their presence.

'Do any of the workers have American connections?'

'Not as far as I am aware. Most of them are local and thankful of work. The old frame knitters came in droves when they realised they would be better off. Poor families sent the children, of whom twenty percent of my workforce is made up, to help make ends meet.'

'That is very charitable of you, Mr Paget, I'm sure. Must make you feel better knowing that you are helping out the poor families of Leicester?'

'Are you deliberately trying to offend me, Sergeant? I shall be talking to your Head Constable about your inferences.'

'I'm surprised you think me capable of such skill, Mr

Paget. He will tell you that I am like this with everyone. If I was nice all the time, I would never get everyone to tell me the truth, and I am good at getting to the truth. You may thank me one day.'

'Well, I'm not comfortable with it. After the distress we've suffered, I am not prepared to be insulted in my own home,' said Paget, holding his head in both hands.

'I probably have asked enough for now, anyway. I do hope your head gets better soon. I shall be trying hard to apprehend your intruder, as much as you may not like my manners.'

Beddows had made his point, but was becoming increasingly concerned with Paget's condition.

The inner artist

'So, what have you got for us, young Shepherd?' said Beddows.

The two men strolled back in the warmth of the late morning sun, amidst the dappled light of the trees along the bottom of New Walk. Birdsong filled the canopy of leaves, as growing numbers of squirrels scurried across the low branches.

'There are some interesting marks on a window and on the table lamp in the bedroom, both of which appear to suggest a scar or something similar on somebody's hand. The windows had recently been cleaned, so it looks like only the burglar could have made it. We need to see the window cleaner and have a look at his hands. I have taken measurements and drawn the marks to scale in my note book.' Shepherd pulled out the book and showed Beddows his observations. A few loose sweets dropped onto the floor, much to his annoyance.

'Ah, the mind of the artist at work is so rewarding. Where would we be without you and your little drawings and measurements? Not quite Royal Academy standard, though!'

Shepherd looked puzzled.

'As for the window cleaner, is he American, by any chance?' said Beddows.

'Sadly, neither he nor his Father are. Look like local tradesmen, from Cramant's Yard.'

'That's a shame,' said Beddows, tongue in cheek.

'By all I can make out, whoever did it has climbed up or down onto the ledge above the front door, and opened the sash window at first floor level, before gaining entry. Not an easy climb, either way, for most people,' said Shepherd.

'Doesn't sound like any of our resident burglars,' said Beddows,' who don't seem to climb well. Caught a few who couldn't get back down, over the years.'

'Strangely, there are no instrument marks on any window.' Shepherd slid his book back into his tunic. 'I suspect that the window was left ajar, and gave easy access.'

'Unless it had been deliberately left so. What else did you glean?'

'There is a house-keeper, Eleanor Skinner. She is away at present dealing with a family bereavement in Northamptonshire. She is back on Tuesday or Wednesday and we will need to talk to her, obviously.'

'Is she suspected of any involvement by Mrs Paget?'

'Absolutely not, it would seem. She has been with the Parents of Mrs Paget for some years, and then with the Pagets themselves.'

'So, we are just left with the burglar at present. He is someone who doesn't mind climbing, but also doesn't mind dropping some distance to get out. Very agile it would seem, and possibly American,' said Beddows.

'Seemingly, we are looking for an agile American with a European accent; possibly with a scar on his fingers or hand, and with vivid blue eyes. Shouldn't be hard to find in Leicester,' said Shepherd, consolidating what they had learned.

'When we get back, I shall get Sergeant Kettle to sort out some additional door knocking for us. See whether anyone else saw or heard anything, and to make sure this was a one off,' said Beddows. 'Bet the night shift all had their heads down, shagging or sleeping, or were tucked away having a wet in the back room of some local hostelry.'

'Old habits die hard,' said Shepherd, unable to defend

the majority of his uniformed colleagues.

'I rarely see anything of interest on reports of overnight activity from some constables. We all know that there must be loads of our villains walking about, at it, right under their noses.'

'Constable Hobbs, who attended says he saw nothing prior to hearing the screams,' said Shepherd. 'Can't remember a soul he passed. They all need to be told to stop, question, and record who they see, like us new boys have been ordered.'

'The arrest rate on night shifts should have gone up over the last couple of years, but sadly not all of your colleagues have your nose for finding villains in the dark.'

'Many of my colleagues don't consider that challenging anyone at night is worth the risk. Shaking door handles is one thing. Finding one open, or challenging a criminal on their own, is another.'

'Depends where you are. Can't blame them down the Rookeries or along Wharf Street, but up here, there's good criminals for the taking if they have their eyes and ears open,' said Beddows. 'Then again, they're probably more ruthless with the money that's involved. How very odd is that?'

'What, that they are more ruthless?' said Shepherd, confused at the change in conversation.

'No, I've just seen yonder billboard,' said Beddows, indicating a poster opposite The Kings Head.

... Sunday 4th July 1852 - for seven days - The greatest American Touring circus ever, will exhibit at Barker's Ground, Wharf Street. Incorporating exotic animals from George Wombwell's menagerie. Performances at 11, 2 and 7 o'clock daily. Admission: one shilling rising to seven shillings and sixpence for

box seats. A Grand Parade through the borough will commence at Midday on Saturday 3rd July...

'Well, that's tomorrow sorted,' said Beddows. 'Let's go and start turning some stones, see what our criminal brethren are talking about.'

A circus comes to Town

Saturday broke hot and sunny, once again. It was turning into a glorious summer. By eight o'clock in the morning, Beddows and Shepherd were in the station, ready for the arrival of the circus, and the enquiries that it would bring.

The building smelled rotten, and was full of flies, for some reason. It felt claustrophobic in the heat. The ancient plaster and laths were rotting, year by year. Lowlife prisoners didn't help matters, with cells brimming too frequently, Beddows considered. The floors to the yard reeked.

The salt-peter men had been banned by a string of Mayors, as the old building had started to crumble, and the old stale urine permeated in the heat.

A much welcome walk down to Barker's Ground revealed that the area was, presently, clear. No cricket games this weekend, and as yet, no signs of circus folk.

Shepherd had never seen a circus before, although he had been taken as a child into Nottingham, and visited the Goose Fair on Market Square. He thought a circus might be as grand if not grander.

Beddows stated he had known of circus parades arriving in the borough in previous years, but as never having children, he had no cause to attend, so had never seen performers or circus animals.

By twelve midday the streets were filling with an assortment of the population, many who would be up to no good, given half a chance.

The honest working classes were still toiling away in the factories, and might try to take the opportunity to peer from their small windows, before their foremen and managers would threaten them with violence, loss of pay or the sack for shirking.

Consequently it was the volatile mix of those who did not have to work, and those who chose not to work – or the destitute who could not work.

'Pick-pockets will have a field day today,' Beddows considered, not sharing his thoughts. He carefully ensured that his own valuables were secreted in the innermost pockets of his suit, and beneath the waistcoat he wore.

It would be hot, mingling with the crowds, and the streets were already chokingly dusty from the persistent heat of the previous weeks. A strange, musty, brownish-pink haze filled the air at street level, coating everybody and everything.

A full market was also running in Market Place, and stallholders and traders had been busy since early morning, setting up their trestles and baskets.

It would be a busy day for Borough constables and street crime be would be prolific as it always was on market day, but today would likely be worse with the arrival of the circus.

The route, Beddows had established, would see the parade enter the town from the top of the London Road, past the racecourse, then by the gibbet at Evington Lane, and passing the farm tracks to the right hand side, prior to the railway lines, before it would enter Granby Street, Gallowtree Gate, and turn right into Humberstone Gate, turning left into Wharf Street, and arriving at Barker's Ground, off Wheat Street, round about two in the afternoon.

It was too hot to walk the route, and uniformed colleagues were already on duty along the route, at set points on each beat that it would pass through.

Shepherd and Beddows settled themselves into a

vantage point at Cole Hill, in the shadow of the Assembly Rooms, where they could see it approach and then turn into Humberstone Gate, this being a point where there was not a lot of room at the best of times. Nothing and nobody should escape their scrutiny. Shepherd was in his *only* suit for the day, and his matching bowler, rather than his normal and restricting uniform, but he was by now well known amongst the miscreants of the borough, as was Beddows. They both received knowing looks from local thieves and toe-rags who scurried off when seen. A pair of constables not to be messed with.

Beddows had spoken to Tanky Smith and was keen to see how he and Shepherd might gain from his expert advice on disguise, and increase their ability not to be so easily spotted.

'The place is buzzing today, young Shepherd. Haven't seen so many of our locals out and about for ages. See them for miles off, all deathly white compared to the posh who have had their days soaking up the sun, all pink and sore above their collars.'

'They know we're here. They are like mice, scurrying back into the obscurity of the crowd when a cat comes close,' said Shepherd.

'Cat and mouse is the name of the game, Shepherd, and this fat old cat will have his rat or mouse by the end of the day! Leave all the others to our colleagues.'

The levels of cheering began to rise, indicating the approach of the parade. Young children were elevated onto their fathers' shoulders, or helped to the front of the crowds to marvel at the spectacle.

One or two local 'flimpers', the more aggressive snatch pickpockets, moved in close on such an occurrence, sensing that the man would be otherwise engaged and, hopefully, not realise they had been lightened of their property.

Tanky Smith and Black Tommy were mingling, in their most suitable disguises, and would no doubt take a few prisoners as hands delved into others' pockets. There would probably be a little 'summary justice' dispensed, for their foolishness, on the way in to the cells, if ever they got that far. Many would *just* receive summary justice, and would sooner be 'nicked'.

Tanky was in a foul mood. Black Tommy just sat rolling his eyes, knowing what would be the outcome of anyone upsetting Sergeant Smith today.

The dust was the first thing that struck Shepherd. Thick and clawing, rolling ahead of the parade, blocking any clear and early view he might have hoped to get.

'You're not here to enjoy yourself, Shepherd. Blue eyed American tumblers, with scars on their fingers, that's what we're here for.'

'I know,' said Shepherd, 'but it is a first for me, so I hoped to get a feel for both.'

In the distance the sound of a marching band could be heard, long before they could be seen. Drums beating and brass instruments tooting, and what sounded like hundreds of cow bells.

As the dust cleared, two rows of brightly uniformed musicians first came into view, instruments glinting in the midday sun, reds, blues and golds of their outfits in stark contrast to the dust, and otherwise dull, surroundings.

Shepherd took a deep breath as he first set eyes on two large elephants, the first of George Wombwell's menagerie of exotic animals, encased in straps and feathers, their trunks waving, ridden by elegantly dressed women.

'Beddows, look, elephants. I've only ever seen them in paintings and drawings.'

'Do any of them have blue eyes and scars on their hands?'

'I hope not...'

'Well in that case, I'm not bleeding interested.'

'Point made, Beddows.'

Next came a large procession of horses, similarly ornate, with feathered head-dresses and gold coloured saddles. The riders were mainly female, but on the odd one or two, scantily clad men and women in acrobatic garb, who tumbled and somersaulted on horseback, raising cheers from the crowd.

'That's more like it,' said Beddows. 'Possible suspects!'

Then clowns with strangely painted faces and costumes mingled with the crowd, shaking hands and rubbing the heads of the children at the front.

Shepherd noticed the air change and the smell of animals and dung, mixed in with the dust in the choking cloud, seemed strangely appealing, in contrast to the normal putrid stench of the town's narrow streets.

Next came the acrobats the constables were waiting for. Young and middle aged men, women and children, all performing a variety of tumbling tricks, in their bright costumes. It would be impossible to pick out one, from the numbers present, that might represent the best suspect, if at all he was to be found from within the circus.

Beddows' intuition told him that this is amongst whom they would find their burglar, and find him they would!

Next came, a large ornate cage with strong metal bars and a solid roof, and colourful cloth, gaudily draped across the top.

Inside were a pair of Lions, large and prowling, their roars heard over the crowd. Shepherd looked on in awe. Animals he, and no doubt many others, had heard of before. Women and children screamed, a confused mix of fear and delight.

Behind the parade came a host of well worn and bedraggled men and women, with carts that appeared to be holding ropes and folded canvas, no doubt the tents for the entourage, and probably the performance tent, which again, Shepherd had only seen in pictures. It reminded him of the columns that followed the soldiers off to war.

Slowly the dust and noise began to subside, and the parade moved off down Humberstone Gate towards its site for the next week, the cricket ground off Wharf Street.

'I hope they don't spoil the pitch,' said Beddows.

'Pardon?' said Shepherd.

'I'm on about the cricket pitch, Shepherd. I'm quite fond of cricket, but haven't been to a game for a while. I saw Midland Counties and Marylebone there, nine years ago. Amazing to watch, it was. Old Alfred Mynn himself, all 21 stones of him. Smashed the ball all over the borough, he did.'

'I didn't realise you had such interests?'

'There's a lot you don't know about me, and a lot more you would prefer not to know, I'm sure.'

'Have you played, yourself?'

'I have had the pleasure of knocking a ball or two about the ground, but I was never good enough to play properly, not like Mynn. Broke a couple of windows on Wheat Street and had to pay for them, which put me off a bit.'

'I'm sure they will have thought of any potential damage to such hallowed grass, particularly if it would upset our own Sergeant Beddows by doing so.'

'Don't know why they don't put them in the middle of the racecourse up the hill. Only gets used once a year to keep the Duke of Rutland happy,' said Beddows.

'Perhaps you could make that suggestion, Beddows. Pop in and see the Mayor and explain that you are worried about damaging the cricket pitch. I'm sure he would be sympathetic...'

'And I know whose balls would be the next two bowled on match day,' Beddows chuckled.

Eibhlin MacCormack

By three o'clock, Beddows and Shepherd were nosing around Barker's Ground, starting to ask questions. As much as it had been billed as 'The greatest American touring circus ever,' it was apparent that within the entourage were people from all over the world.
Many accents could be heard, including what both men assumed to be 'American'.
Shepherd would be guided by Beddows, as he had personally never, consciously, heard American spoken, and initially thought it was just another dialect.
'Where can we find the main man?' said Beddows to a passing clown.
The clown shrugged, raising his arms as if he didn't understand. With a sulphur-yellow horse-hair wig, white face, with painted tears, he looked bizarre. Shepherd felt quite uncomfortable, mentally questioning who, or what, lay behind the costume. Not the sort of disguise worn by Tanky Smith, but much more the stuff of childhood nightmares.
'I reckon Tanky and Black Tommy need to get down here. They'd have a great time getting their hands on some of this costume and fakery,' said Beddows.
'Gives me the creeps,' said Shepherd.
'Bleeding ignorant, though. Oi, you there, where is the circus organiser?' Beddows shouted after the passing clown.
'Look for where they're laying out the biggest tent, they'll no be far away,' said the clown, in a broad Scottish accent.
'Perhaps that is his own hair?' said Beddows.

Across the cricket ground, small groups of men, women and children were industriously employed putting up tents of all sizes, and unloading furniture and effects from the dozens of vans and carts that had materialised within the site. It was apparent they were used to rapidly setting up camp.

Beddows thought of military service, and stories of how long it had seemed to get a camp established in the British army. These circus types could show them a thing or two.

In the centre of the activity a much larger structure was taking shape.

The main arena was being erected, and a myriad of ropes and pulleys were being tied, pulled or wound, and tall posts used as a framework, for what Beddows could only consider to be the biggest tent he had ever seen.

'An American invention,' said a middle aged man, standing watching. 'They've been around a while in America, but not seen by many Englishmen outside of London; not of this size, for sure.'

'And that is where they all perform?' said Beddows.

'You bet,' said the man. 'How can I help you gentlemen? You want to buy tickets? I can get you tickets.'

'We're looking for whoever is in charge,' said Beddows.

'Not Pinkerton men, by any chance? Heard about those guys. Will follow you anywhere to bring you in,' said the man. 'I didn't do it, honest. Don't make me go back to her, whichever one it was.'

The joke was lost on the English constables. *Pinkerton men?*

'We are local constables as it happens, looking for some information, and that's why we need to speak to the man in charge,' said Beddows.

'I thought I recognised the mean look. You all look like hungry bloodhounds. Anyway, who says it's a man?'

'You mean it's a woman?' said Beddows.

'Not just any woman. You guys never heard of Eibhlin MacCormack and her travelling circus?'

'Can't say I have,' said Beddows.

'You mind what you say or do with our Eibhlin. Part American by residence, part Irish by birth and temperament, if you know what I mean! Punch your nose sooner than speak on a bad day, she would, and she has!' said the man.

'And you are?' said Shepherd.

'Henry Pensylva the eighth is my name, circus magician and necromancer. Why Henry the eighth? I've had six wives, and that's why I thought you were Pinkerton's men. Their husbands have all been chasing me too! You can find our leader stood next to the Lions' cage. That's her with the flame red hair,' he said, jovially.

'You are American?' asked Shepherd.

'An American, I am, Sir. Born and bred to Irish settlers, hence the accent, and the gift of the Blarney stone.'

Shepherd shook his head, as he heard the Irish, yet little else.

*****

Beddows and Shepherd strolled across to where Eibhlin MacCormack was standing.

Beddows noticed that she was exceptionally tall, with long, flame red hair, a much deeper red than Shepherd's ginger, and wearing a light, lacy blouse, tucked into what looked like riding breeches and long black riding boots. A stunning woman, in her mid forties, Beddows immediately considered her to be far too young to run an enterprise of this scale.

Shepherd saw an artist's model, with fine cheekbones, curves, and classical good looks.

'Might you be Eibhlin MacCormack?' said Beddows.

'Depends who is asking,' said the woman, avoiding any

eye contact. Shepherd heard an accent again, part Irish, but with something else mixed in. Feisty, too, by the sound of things, as suggested.

'My name is Sergeant Beddows of the local Borough Police, and this is my colleague, Constable Shepherd.'

'And what brings about such an early and ill timed visit?'

'Do you greet all policemen like that?' said Shepherd.

'I greet everyone like that, on days like this, and at times like this. There are too many people with too little to do but annoy me. I've got a circus to set up and have ready by tomorrow.'

'We're not here to annoy you at all,' said Beddows, moving to a point where eye contact became less difficult.

'Talk while I work then.'

'What may we call you?' said Beddows.

'I was given the name Eibhlin.'

'That's a very unusual name?' said Shepherd.

'Irish-American. My daddy was an early settler in New York. Hounded out of Cork, he was, and my poor mammy with him, and the rest of our people, and with somebody else's horses, so they say.'

'I'm surprised there are any horses left in Ireland, from what I've heard,' Beddows quipped.

'Very funny, Sergeant. You can always call me Mac, like this lot does, it's up to you.'

'Mrs MacCormack?' said Shepherd.

'There's no Mrs about me. I'm not the marrying kind; got too much on my hands with this lot. More like a brood mother, at times.'

'We are seeking answers to a burglary that occurred, here in Leicester, in the early hours of Friday morning past, and think you, or some of your people, might be able to help us,' said Beddows.

'Do I look like a burglar?'

'That's not what I mean at all. Is there somewhere

quieter we can go to talk?' said Beddows.

'No, I'm too busy today, unless it will wait a day or two, when I know everything is running smoothly?'

'That won't do, I am afraid,' said Shepherd. 'We need to ask you some questions today.'

'Well, here it will have to be, then.'

'We are looking for a very athletic young American, light on his feet, with vivid pale blue eyes,' said Shepherd. 'He may have a Swedish or German American accent.'

'We've got lots of very young, athletic, men, and some of them are what you would probably call American, and many are from Europe but have migrated to America.'

'We need to talk to them all, and as soon as possible,' said Shepherd.

'You say that this happened in the early hours of yesterday - Friday?' said Eibhlin.

'That's right,' said Beddows. 'Does that mean something to you?'

'We were in a place called Kettering yesterday morning, and everyone would have been breaking down and packing. We travelled to a little town called Market Harborough, where we camped overnight, last night. So, I doubt it will be anyone from this circus.'

'Do you have anyone who comes ahead of the circus? Who puts out the posters that we have seen appear around the borough?' said Shepherd.

'You're an astute young man, Constable Shepherd. And, yes, we do have people who come ahead of the circus and put out our advanced posters, but none of them are performers, just hangers on or performers' family, who I can normally spare. They came days ahead of us.'

'Who was given the job here?' said Beddows.

'I would have to ask, as I don't look after that side of things, I am normally too busy putting the show and our exhibition together.'

'Would those folk be here, too?' said Shepherd.

'I would hope they are in Nottingham, by now, with posters to place out for next week.'

'It must be hard work for a woman on her own?' said Beddows.

'Why do you think I am alone, Sergeant?'

'I'm sorry, but when you said...' Beddows visibly blushed.

Shepherd had not seen him like this before.

'Don't be embarrassed, Sergeant. I have my male friends and admirers. A bit like a sailor, I have the odd one secreted here and there, but nobody special... as yet.' She winked at both men.

'There's hope for me yet then,' said Beddows, regaining his composure, brushing his hair back from his forehead.

Shepherd's eyes fixed on Beddows. Who was *this* John Beddows?

'Perhaps there is, you never know,' said Eibhlin, smiling radiantly. 'Would you two gentlemen like tickets for a performance? It would be nicer to see you socially, as it were. Any little women to bring along?'

'I would love to bring along my wife,' said Shepherd.

'No, just me,' said Beddows.

'What about ...' Shepherd started to ask, before an elbow sank sharply into his ribs, making him wince.

'I will make sure that you have the best seats in the house,' said Eibhlin. 'Afterwards, you can ask me all the questions you like. In the meantime I have a large erection to resolve, and the daylight hours are shortening as we speak,' with a mischievous grin.

'That's very kind of you, Miss MacCormack,' said Beddows, chuckling.

'My pleasure,' said Eibhlin, gently touching Beddows' sleeve. 'We must help our new constable friends. Never know when we might need your help.'

'Do you attract much trouble, then?' said Shepherd.

'Me, personally, or the circus, Constable Shepherd?'

'I meant the circus. Sorry, I wasn't implying...'

'Constable, relax. I was teasing you. Such a shy young man, Sergeant Beddows.'

Beddows grinned. This was an unusual lady.

'Thank you Miss MacCormack,' said Shepherd. 'Now, if we may, we will leave you alone, and start talking to your people - provided they are not too busy.'

'Be warned, Constable Shepherd, they are not like most ordinary people. Some are artistic and temperamental, whereas some are secretive and elusive, and prefer to remain so. Some are dangerous and don't mix with anyone.'

'And which are you?' said Beddows.

'Wouldn't you like to know, Sergeant. Wouldn't you just?'

*****

'Beddows, that woman was flirting with you,' said Shepherd. 'In fact, I think you were both flirting.'

'Don't be so silly lad, she's a tease, and uses her attributes to her advantage. A bit more extrovert than we are used to in Leicester.'

'You blushed, Beddows, and you lied about Mrs Beddows.'

'I didn't blush and I didn't lie about Mrs Beddows. Anyway, have you any idea how are we going to winkle out possible suspects?'

'How about a little elimination exercise?' said Shepherd.

'How would that work then?'

'We gather them all together, and then get them all to hold their hands up. We ask various questions to eliminate those we don't want to pursue, until we have just a few with their hands still up. Those are the ones to look at closely. Like a party game, Beddows, only with a more serious purpose.'

'How many men are we talking about, altogether, do you reckon?'

'Fifty or sixty by the count I did on Cole Hill, excluding the elephants. See, I wasn't just watching the animals.'

'I can't count that high, Shepherd, so I will have to take your word for it.'

'Miss MacCormack won't like it. She wants her camp setting up and her circus to go ahead without disruption.'

'Leave Miss MacCormack to me, young Shepherd. I suspect I can get her to agree, if we do it at the right time... for her, of course.'

'We need a list, to make sure we do get to see them all. She must have a list, a payroll, perhaps?'

'That can be our next job, but not tonight. We'll start tomorrow morning. I want an early start. Mr Henry Pensylva may be a useful ally, as he seems to know a lot. Catch them in or fresh out of their beds. Not interfering with Miss MacCormack's business then, are we?'

'When will you tell her what we are thinking?'

'Let her have her beauty sleep.'

'What about the rest of this duty?'

'We need to start talking to our best eyes and ears. See whether there might be talk of this one by now.'

'Inside help?'

'Someone may have tipped off our American. Or has he just struck lucky? We still have to consider the missing house-keeper and also any link to Mrs Paget's parents.'

'If it's not one of the circus folk, it could still be somebody more local. We won't know until tomorrow, will we?' said Shepherd.

'Let's see if there's any talk in the usual places, anyway. Get that bit under way before Mr Charters asks. Let's head for The Globe. I'm gasping for a brew.'

The Globe Inn

The Globe Inn stood at the corner of Silver Street and Cart's Lane, and was the haunt of many of Leicester's emerging business men. Many a deal always there to be made, and more money exchanged hands over its floors, than in any bank in the Town.

Like the inns around the Market Place, generally, the inns were allowed to trade from early morning and throughout the day.

Drunken behaviour was endemic throughout the borough, all day and every day. Irrespective of where drink could be sourced, legal or illegal drinking houses profited from the urge to drink, with alcohol often the healthy option compared to the borough's water supplies.

The conduct of each legally operating inn was much more important, and that kept many official publicans in order. The Globe was amongst the best.

Traders, from small stocking knitters and frame workers, through to smaller emerging factories, brought in their finished wares and sold them to the bigger businesses, and the bigger businesses sold them on to widening markets, at a healthy profit.

Deals done over a warm ale or a large port, or gin were the norm, and cash transactions allowed the company accountants some discretion as to what was declared to the revenue men.

'Revenue exempt' profits were widespread and the inn had become the haunt of prying eyes and ears from Her Majesty's Government, looking for such under-hand dealings. Victoria's purse was suffering.

It was also, however, the haunt for a wide variety of local villains, looking for an opportunity. Careless talk gave burglars, tricksters and robbers attractive opportunities. Too much drink and some tart or molly could seduce a careless businessman, and keys and wallets lost forever.

Beddows could not rule out that such careless talk or action by Mr Paget had brought about his demise.

The Globe was busy by the time Beddows and Shepherd walked in. There was a noticeable drop in conversation, as they entered. Careless words and all that, not recommended in the presence of constables.

Many faces turned to consider an exit route, whilst others scurried into back rooms, or, strangely, upper floor rooms where they had only one way out.

Both men split up and went in opposite directions, taking in who was present, and who was seeking to make a hasty exit.

Beddows leant against the bar, with a good view of both doors onto Silver Street and Carts Lane. The coarse cloth of his jacket stuck to the swill drying on the wooden surface, brushing pewter and leather tankards to one side. The bar stank of stale remnants. It had yet to see a clean cloth or fresh water today, clearly. However, the tea was cheap.

'The usual please, Landlord.'

A few moments later, Nathaniel Hitchcock appeared with a battered earthenware teapot, a similar cup and a similar saucer, plus a small jug of milk, which he placed in front of the detective. Strange looks abounded from many who considered tea to be an odd drink for a policeman.

Nathaniel Hitchcock (pronounced Itchcock - as he would profess to his clientele) ran a well ordered inn - compared to many in the borough - in Shepherd's opinion. A large man, standing at over six feet four inches tall, and heavily built, Shepherd noticed the thickness of the man's forearms, which he considered were as thick as Shepherd's thigh. Lifting barrels on a daily basis, and manhandling errant drunks had served him well, and he was by sight alone, a man not to be messed with.

'Had any Americans in over the last week or so?' said Beddows, sipping carefully from the hot liquid. He swirled the tea around his dry mouth, clearing the residue of dust from the day's activity. Beddows considered it might sound a strange question to be asking.

'Not to my knowledge, Mr Beddows, we don't get many foreigners in here. Can't remember the last time I had a foreigner in. But then again, would I necessarily know somebody was American? I'm not so sure. Somebody once told me that they all sound like we used to in Leicester, some years ago.'

'Do you know Mr Edward Paget, by any chance?'

'The cotton goods manufacturer, the one that got bashed?'

'News travels fast within the borough, these days.'

'Quite a few been talking about it around the dealing tables. He comes in occasionally. Does quite a bit of trade with the Corah family. They sell on their goods in Birmingham markets. Strange that Leicester stuff sells better in Birmingham, I always think. But the Birmingham buyers can be a rum bunch, always looking for something for nothing.'

'Have you seen Mr Paget in here, lately?'

'Not that I can recall. Saw his wife in here more recently. She had a private lunch with her Father. He owns a factory off Granby Street. Now, he has a lot to do in the Americas.'

'What about circus folk?'

'They have only just arrived, Mr Beddows. They'll keep

their own countenance if they're anything like the last ones we had in the borough. Strange folk, much like the Romanies for sticking together and to themselves.'

'Anyone flashing more money about than they should rightly have?'

'Mr Beddows, if I was to tell all the dealing what went on in 'ere, the customers would lynch me. They move more money about at times than I dare dream I should ever earn in my lifetime. You want to talk to the revenue men that mingle. I'm sure you know who they are, as they're here for sure, but I'm buggered if I know who they are.'

'Even we don't get to meet the revenue men, Landlord. Our dear Queen has given them more powers than we have access. Laws unto themselves, they are. Clearly the rich are a greater threat to the stability of the Country than the criminals that we pursue.'

'They are certainly shrewd with their pennies, Mr Beddows. Mind, they don't like paying their dues. Always question my sums when they have eaten and drunk to excess, and accusing me of diddling them.'

'That's how to get rich, Landlord. Don't spend anymore than you have to, and don't tell The Revenue what you earn. Wish I'd had more insight as a young man. Might have made some money myself by now, instead of getting cold, wet, thumped and poorly paid for my troubles.'

'That will be a ha'penny, please, lest I forget.'

'The cost of tea is killing me. You're as bad as this dodgy bunch. Why is it cheaper to buy ale than a cup of tea?'

'Your mate at the King and Crown charges a penny, Mr Beddows. A ha'penny for a pot is the best price in the borough. Five shillings a pound they wanted at Sarson and Simpkin's, earlier today. And my price includes my costs, Mr Beddows. All that time brewing and serving it.

Cups and saucers don't come cheap.'

'Or clean, Landlord,' he quipped. 'Next time, I shall bring my own cup and drink from your well. I take it that is cheaper?'

'I shall have to remove the bodies, first, and warn off the ghosts,' said the Landlord, jokingly referring to the legends of long ago, when female prisoners spent their last night at the inn before the gallows, or worse, the bonfire stake. Talk of drownings from times when the well in the basement, like the one on Cank Street, caught out risk takers seeking fresher water than was available from the conduit in the Market Place. Tales of ghosts abounded around the pub and the local area.

'Right, now I shall have a nosey. Where has our Constable Shepherd got to?'

Beddows walked slowly and deliberately amongst the small tables, nodding on occasion, when recognised. Piles of notes and coins were swiftly and constantly changing hands, and handshakes no doubt sealing new business transaction. Many were unseen by those not skilled in observation.

He watched as one or two well-to-dos got up to leave, brushing past some of the less desirable of the borough who would otherwise have dipped their pockets. But Beddows had been seen and word had spread that coppers prowling. Sticky fingers remained concealed. Climbing the creaking stairs to the upper floor, Beddows spied Shepherd stood in a darkened corner, watching someone or something. Beddows held back, just in case he would interrupt something. Shepherd beckoned him to join him.

'What's going on then?' asked Beddows.

'They're having an auction for some new knitting machines. There are three Factory owners bidding, and you want to see how much money they are putting up. There's real money being talked of, or waved about under people's noses, far more than I've ever seen or heard of before. Not on show for long, but long enough.'

'And?'

'And I think that with this amount of money available in here, being waved about for new machinery, it wouldn't take a genius long to work out where that money might be going, later, especially if the man holding the money is known or followed. Surprised we don't get more robberies in the surrounding lanes.'

'The Highwaymen have gone. George Davenport is tucked up in his grave in All Saints at Wigston. The ones in the town don't need that much. At least Davenport put his gains to good use.'

'So, did Mr Paget do his bidding somewhere like this?'

'It's worth a thought, young Shepherd. We need to go and talk to our Mr Paget again, and see what he has to say for himself.'

A turn for the worse

At about 6 o'clock, Robert Charters was pacing up and down the public office, much to the annoyance of Sergeant Sheffield, who liked free licence to run the cells and public areas as *he* saw fit. Charters' presence denied him certain 'liberties' he might take, for people who annoyed him.

'I was about to send word around the borough to locate you both. Where have you been?'

'To make ourselves known at Barker's Ground amongst the circus folk, then back via The Globe and some observations, which may have shed light about how the burglar may have realised our victim's potential. More importantly, we have also got our snouts working.'

'Your concerns for your victim may be more of an issue to you now. Word has just come in of his collapse. Mr Hamilton has been summoned to the home address.'

'We'd best be on our way then, Shepherd.'

'Keep me updated, Beddows, I fear the worst, from what limited information I received,' said Charters, walking off.

Sheffield leant under his desk and emerged with his clay pipe stuck in his teeth, embers starting to glow.

'Thought he'd never bugger off. Got a drunk in the cell needs a thick ear, as it happens.'

Beddows commented on how the noise that followed, actually sounded like willow on leather, as he and Shepherd slid hastily from the station, striding off for New Walk.

*****

Wailing was evident from within the house. A less enthusiastic pull on the door bell was now in order. Mrs Paget appeared, tears staining her cheeks, and let the two men in.

'My poor husband is not long for this life, Constables. Mr Hamilton is resigned to his imminent and certain passing.'

As the distraught woman lead Beddows and Shepherd up the grand staircase, low, pitiful moaning sounds filled their ears. The whole house echoed to the pain.

'Good Lord, Beddows, that poor man.'

'Doesn't sound good. I have heard that moan before, too many times.'

Stood over the large bed was Thomas Hamilton. A brief, but telling glance and a subtle shake of the head confirmed the plight of Edward Paget.

'Mr Hamilton?' said Beddows.

'I am afraid that something is amiss within Mr Paget's skull. He has been bleeding from his ears, since he collapsed, about one hour ago. I suspect there is also brain fluid within the discharge. It is consistent with the effects some may sustain with a brain injury, from one or both of the blows he received. It can take time to show.' Hamilton shook his head, resigned to his prognosis.

Both Beddows and Shepherd nodded and waited. Hamilton placed his strange tubular stethoscope to his ear, and listened to the man's breathing, which seemed laboured and shallow. Shepherd always thought it resembled a dwarf hunting horn, and had, on past occasions, teased Hamilton as to whether he also played it, in dull moments.

A further low moan broke from the man's throat, his eyes widening, as if in terror. Then silence. The moan stopped, as Edward Paget breathed his last mortal breath.

Mrs Paget collapsed, sobbing, in a heap on the plush rug beneath the heavy marital bed.

'I am sorry, Mrs Paget, he is gone to a better place,' whispered Hamilton, sympathetically, closing the dead man's eyelids with well practiced fingertips.

'To a better place, Mr Hamilton? His place was here with me.' She looked angry. 'Sergeant Beddows, I want the man, or men, who did this caught and hung.'

'And so you shall,' said Beddows. 'No stone will be left unturned until we catch someone.'

A deep sigh, and the dead man's chest rose and fell, one last time.

'Doctor, he is still alive,' the distraught woman exclaimed, hoping for some miracle.

'I am afraid that he has definitely departed, and I am so truly sorry for your loss.'

'Do you have anyone we can contact to be with you?' enquired Shepherd.

'My parents should be told, I suppose. What shall I say?' replied the new widow.

'Leave that with us, Mrs Paget. We will arrange for them to be told and brought to you, if that is your wish?' said Beddows, nodding obediently.

Shepherd noticed this unusual act of tenderness from his normally abrasive colleague. A wry smile, momentarily, crossed Shepherd's face.

'Does Mr Paget still have parents?' said Shepherd.

'They both passed away, some years ago. He has no siblings.'

'I shall need to take your Husband's remains to the infirmary, Mrs Paget, to establish exactly what injury your husband sustained that brought about his death.'

'Please don't hurt him further, Mr Hamilton. Be gentle with him.' Mrs Paget had heard horror stories of what medical science demanded of a human corpse, for the furtherance of understanding anatomy and physiology.

'I shall treat him with the utmost respect, Mrs Paget, and return him to you for funeral rites, as soon as I possibly can.'

The three men could anticipate what the widow was already imagining of her husband's post-mortem examination, and each hoped she should not imagine too deeply. The release of the body would depend on the rulings of Coroner, Oliver Mitchell, following the necessary inquest, and the will of the jury.

Hamilton pulled the top sheet of the bed over the dead man's face, already swollen and distorting from the injury within his head, and announced that he would arrange for collection of the body, shortly.

Beddows and Shepherd made haste to the address of the parent's of Mrs Paget, to break the news, leaving the widow alone with her horrors.

'Shall I see you at the infirmary in the morning, gentlemen?' Hamilton enquired.

Beddows nodded and acknowledged Hamilton's intentions, and another post-mortem examination to stomach. 'Not too early, I hope?'

'Who will tell Coroner Mitchell?' said Hamilton.

'We will do that once we have informed the in-laws.' said Beddows. 'I will advise him that Mr Paget passed away at 7.15 p.m. as a result of his head injuries, if that is your observation.'

*****

'Poor woman,' said Shepherd.

'One minute you think you have everything, and then some moment of madness and it's gone before your eyes,' replied Beddows.

'She will inherit all his wealth, though?' Shepherd surmised.

'Assuming there is a will, Mr Shepherd. No doubt with a

rich family, she won't go short, I'm sure. Now, I should imagine that is the least of her concerns, what with Surgeon Hamilton planning to dissect her husband's cadaver.'

'What if he is worth more to her, dead? What if this has all been pre-planned? What if she left the landing window open?' said Shepherd, his own imagination working through a range of possibilities.

'A black widow, you mean? Time will tell us, Shepherd, but time is short in supply for us at present.'

The two men gazed as the immensely large white house came into view, the home of Mrs Paget's parents, Devonshire Place, London Road, just beyond the new houses being built along Prebend Street, encroaching into the High Fields and St Margaret's Fields of the borough.

'Very nice,' said Shepherd. 'Always impressed me, this house has.'

'Look at all the bleeding comings and goings,' said Beddows, noting a line of multi-coloured delivery wagons in the street, and delivery boys shuffling between their vehicles and the side of the house, where no doubt, the tradesmen would be allowed entry.

'I thought Mr Paget's house was rather swish, but his Father-in-law's premises are palatial.'

'That's poshest of the posh, Shepherd, and they are probably spending more on wining and dining today than you and I would earn in a whole year.'

'And we are about to spoil whatever it is they have planned,' said Shepherd.

'The joys of the job, young Shepherd. Never gets any better.'

An unexpected distraction

By ten o'clock, the two weary men entered the cooling confines of the station, to seek out and update Robert Charters.

Both had earlier commented on how the chimes of the parish church clocks were becoming harder to hear over the hustle and bustle of machines within the expanding Industry of the borough. However, sitting directly under the bells of St. Martin's, the police station was always a good place to keep an ear out for the correct time.

The heat of the day had diminished, slightly, but both men were still sweating, and their suits were far too warm for such weather.

Shepherd thought of similar summer days, back in Sutton Bonington, and work in the fields. A light and loose shirt would then have been the order of the day, and he could still imagine the feel of the seeds and dust from the fields sticking to his skin.

He ran a finger around the damp collar of his shirt, uncomfortable against the stubble at the nape of his neck. Beddows face looked reddened from the sun and heat, and Shepherd considered how it had looked earlier, when he had blushed at Eibhlin MacCormack's flirting. A day of revelations, he concluded.

'Does Mr Hamilton have a probable cause of death?' enquired Charters.

'He seems of the opinion that one or both blows caused damage to the man's skull and his brain, and a bleeding brain injury is the most likely cause. He will do a post-mortem examination in the morning,' said Beddows.

'And has Mr Mitchell been made aware?'

'We still have that to do, and warn him of the need for an inquest.'

'He will no doubt wish to get that out of the way. In this heat, he is not fond of decaying cadavers, and squeamish jurymen.' said Charters. 'Monday I expect, around a working lunch, no doubt. The Turks Head should be warned, also. One of you will need to lay an initial report with Mr Mitchell, tonight, and we can sort out the rest tomorrow.'

'Young Shepherd can do that. I have every faith in him in satisfying Mr Mitchell's requirements,' said Beddows. 'He's had plenty of practice.'

Charters and Beddows recognised the skills and maturity that Shepherd had acquired in his first two years, and considered him to be one of the better young officers, and promotion material, sooner rather than later.

As the men spoke, the large public door opposite to the station Sergeant's raised desk opened.

In walked an upright, thin, well dressed man of mid-thirties, wearing the tallest stovepipe hat Shepherd had ever seen, with a fine paisley band around the base, in contrasting brightness to the hat's material. The man's cravat matched the hatband, and the white silk shirt shimmered in the half light. A real Toff. His apparel made him seem much taller than he probably was.

The man carried a large, monogrammed, tan leather travel bag, and carried a smaller matching bag over his shoulder. Even in the heat he looked cool and sophisticated, apart from a fine layer of dust that had rubbed from his luggage and onto his apparel.

'Evening gents, my name is Nimrod Charles Hatter. Detective Inspector Hatter of the Metropolitan Police, no less.'

Robert Charters face turned to an angry scowl. 'The same Hatter I once had the misfortune to supervise at Westminster, when I was Sergeant?'

'My, if it's not Sergeant Charters. I heard you had done well for yourself, somewhere in the sticks. Didn't recognise you behind them Newgate Knockers you've acquired.'

'It is no longer *Sergeant Charters*, as you are no doubt well aware. I am now Superintendent and Head Constable, here in this borough. I am sure you would have been aware before you came. To what misfortune do we owe this visit?'

'I am in hot pursuit of some villain who I want for murderous deeds in the Capital. I have been close to him before, but now the suspect is in your borough.'

'I fear for anybody falling foul of you, Inspector. How you are even still in the job surprises me.'

'I hear tell my appointment and arrival sent shivers around White Hall Place. Don't think any of you old boys had ever seen anyone like me.'

'I'm sure if your Father and Captain Hay hadn't been acquainted, you would not have seen light of day by an honest policeman.'

'You should have found yourself a backer, Charters. But then again, what could you have done to impress Captain Hay? You're not our sort of policeman, are you?'

'Your sort?'

'A man that could be trusted to get rights wronged, no questions asked, all with Captain Hay's sanction, of course. Men that do, rather than the drunk and lazy, like most were, or rather still are.'

'What Captain Hay and your Father may have gotten away with on the Peninsular battlefield has no place in modern policing. Torture and lies.'

'The world is changing. People like me and Captain Hay will make England a safer place.'

'A safer place. I recall some of the beatings that were reported to us from the cells, and the blind eyes that were turned.'

'Sometimes we have to rewrite the rule book, Mr Charters. You might try it up here and sort out your squalid little borough.'

'Our squalid little borough is very well policed,' said Beddows. 'Mr Charters has been quite robust in getting the right sort of policeman since his arrival. He even managed to turn me around.'

Shepherd smiled, thinking back to the angry Beddows of earlier.

'Why were we not notified of your intended visit?' demanded Charters.

'Captain Hay gives me free hand to follow my nose, and trusts me to fulfil my duties in apprehending my man, wherever he might be. As it happens, I was told by a snout that my suspect would likely arrive in Leicester this weekend, so here I am, hot on his heels. No time to dither.'

'And the offence in question?'

'A burglary that went wrong and a man beaten to death for some foreign jewellery. A very capable burglar this man is. A real snakesman. He climbs like a monkey and is as fleet of foot over a roof as would a cat, and as ruthless as can be. I suspect he has done more, but on this occasion there had been a circus nearby.'

Shepherd and Beddows exchanged glances with Charters.

'And you suspect his agility is connected to the circus?' said Beddows.

'Doesn't take a genius to make a connection. My snout suggested Leicester, and normally my snouts are reliable,' he replied.

'We have not announced our offence to anybody, let alone The Gazette, as yet,' said Charters.

'You have had a similar crime here?' said Hatter.

Shepherd watched the man's face. There was no look of surprise.

'Yesterday. The victim died earlier today, so we now have our own murder to investigate,' said Charters. 'Fortunate I came along then, as I can have them both wrapped up for you, post haste, so to speak. Save you country boys a lot of grief that I am sure you can do without.'

'And why should you be so confident that these are connected?' asked Charters.

'My guts are telling me, so good enough for me.'

'May I remind you, Inspector, that as Head Constable of this borough I am in charge of any and all investigations here in Leicester. If you would care to work alongside my officers you will be offered all the assistance you may need. In the meantime I would like some assurance from Sir Richard Mayne or your Captain Hay that you are meant to be here.'

'Wasting your time there, Mr Charters, but if it will make you feel better, then that's down to you. You know Captain Hay.'

'You haven't changed much? Still a renegade with no respect for authority?'

'I get the job done, Mr Charters. Captain Hay would have something supportive to say of me. It was he, personally, had me promoted to Detective inspector, so he clearly recognises my talents.'

'Poor Sir Richard must cringe at having such a vile and ruthless man in his command, and must curse Captain Hay's influences?'

'Not sure Captain Hay would like your remarks, Mr Charters.'

'Then it is a good job that I am my own Head Constable, and not answerable to him.' said Charters, his face reddening further. 'If you do find your man, we will discuss where and how we will proceed, and I will decide.'

'Where do you put up your guests, Mr Charters. I take it

you have some pet Landlords nearby who look after your men?'

'I am sure we can find you some suitable accommodation.'

'Whatever you say, Mr Charters. So, who is going to get me settled in?'

'Beddows, would you take our guest and see him bedded down somewhere nearby?'

'Shepherd, you can bugger off and sort out Coroner Mitchell's needs, if you would. I will sort out Inspector Hatter. We will meet back here at six o'clock, tomorrow morning; bright and breezy.' Beddows cursed Mr Charters instructions. He had other ideas of what he wanted to do for his evening, or what was left of it. Shepherd gathered his paperwork for briefing the Coroner, relieved that he had not drawn the short straw to host the visitor.

'Come on then, Beddows, I hope the ale tastes good at this place?'

'I wouldn't know. I only drink tea.'

'A bleeding cat-lap? What sort of policemen do you have here, Mr Charters? A Detective that doesn't drink? Wouldn't last long in my office.'

'I used to enjoy my grog, Inspector, but I don't any more. I have learned the dangers of too much grog, but I am sure you will find our local brews agreeable.' Beddows walked Hatter across Town Hall Lane and through the front door to The King and Crown, directly opposite the police station, resisting the urge to take him straight to 'Manky Lil's' where the man would probably feel more at home. Dressed like a toff, but as rough as they come. Probably a nasty piece of work to the right girls.

'A bit close to home, this place?' said Hatter, looking out through the leaded windows, straight across from the police station.

'Mr Keetley runs one of the best inns in the borough, and is a strong supporter of The Police, which is more than can be said of many of our licensees. He will look after you. In return, look after him. He is a good man, and has many friends in the station.'

The inn was already busy. An alluring, heady mix of pipe and cigar smoke, alcohol, wood fires and hot food filled the air.

Joseph Keetley was busy serving, filling leather and pewter tankards overflowing with warm, frothing ale. One or two staff squeezed past his portly figure to get to the customers beyond him, at the bar.

A piano was being played to the rear of the pub, and a woman's singing could be made out above the chatter, but not even a sing song.

Around the tables, a few games of cards in progress were evident, but seems very civilised, by Hatter's normal expectations.

'No drunks. No fights. No Totty. No proper julking. What sort of a place was this?' Hatter enquired, cynically.

'A quiet and civilised inn, Inspector. The sing songs may be found in the gin palaces, should you prefer.'

Keetley nodded. 'With you shortly, Beddows'.

'I thought you didn't drink?' said Hatter.

'Only tea, and Mr Keetley has the finest tea in Leicester. We also happen to be good friends.'

'Good source to get some dirt on you then, hey?' Hatter smirked.

'Mr Keetley is also discreet.' Beddows was confident that not even Hatter could get Joseph Keetley to disclose anything. Anything would be old hat, anyway. He led a pretty boring and sober life compared to most of his colleagues - Shepherd apart.

'I bet you that within a couple of hours I'll know a lot more about you than you would like me to know,' said Hatter.

'Seems to be that I have a far better source in Mr Charters as to your antecedence, Inspector.'

'So, tomorrow, I want to catch me a murderer, Sergeant. Whether it's with you or without you, I want a quick result.'

'At any cost?'

'Scum should be hung, quickly. Once I've got him, it's inevitable. He'll squeal when I get my teeth into him.'

'So you know who you are looking for?'

'I know what he does and what he looks like. I have a name. If the name and all the other bits fit together I shall be a happy man.'

'What if they don't fit?'

'Then I'll go by my guts, Sergeant. A bit of common sense and a few extra strokes of the pen, if needs be.'

'A few extra strokes of the pen?'

'Little white lies never did us any harm, did it Beddows? Once the rope has done its work, no more harm to be done, hey?'

'Now then Mr Beddows, what can I do for you gentlemen?' said Keetley, edging down the bar, wiping his massive hands on a cloth, removing the residue of sticky froth from the last pint drained from the barrel.

'Do you have a suitable room for my colleague here, fresh up from London.'

'How long for, Mr...?'

'Shouldn't be more than a night or two. Get my business sorted swiftly and then I shall be gone from your little carbuncle of a town, and back to the Capital. And the name is Hatter - Inspector Nimrod Charles Hatter.'

'Nimrod? What sort of a name is that?' said Beddows.

'*And they shall waste the land of Assyria with the sword, and the land of Nimrod in the entrances thereof: thus shall he deliver us from the Assyrian, when he cometh into our land, and when he treadeth within our borders,*' said Hatter. 'It's Biblical, and it is the name given to a great Hunter, the Grandson of Noah. Very apt, for a detective, don't you think? Almost pre-ordained that it is what I should be doing, hunting down the worst of our country's scum.'

'A bit of a Poncey name for a common man?' smirked Beddows, looking to provoke some response.

'You think you are the first to try and wind me up over my heritage, Beddows? I learned from a master. My Father once had a corporal in the Peninsular, badmouthing him behind his back. Could have hung him with a field courts-martial, but instead my Father had his mark branded on the man's back, summarily. A reminder that he was always going to be not that far behind him. He never did it again. My Father was a hard man, trusted by Captain Hay. He taught me to be hard and reliable, resolute to the point that I am now as trustworthy to Captain Hay as he was. That being said, I haven't branded anybody. Not yet, anyway.' The man laughed haughtily.

'And that's how Captain Hay had his officers look after his troops?' said Beddows.

'Wellington had trusted men. He knew what needed doing, and let them sort it, God bless him. Crime is just another war, and the fight just as barbaric, if you want to keep ahead of the enemy.'

'I'm sure Wellington would have other thoughts,' said Keetley. 'My family was in Spain and France and said he was a fair and just man.' He took the key to Room three from a hook behind the rear counter, and scribbled something in a small ledger below it, presumably the Inspector's name, before handing it to Hatter. 'Room three should meet your needs - top of the stairs and facing you, when you're ready.'

Room three was the smallest, cheapest room in the inn, and sat directly over the stable yard doors, so was noisy all day and night. Keetley winked at Beddows.

'People see what people want to see. We have to see what others don't, isn't that right, Beddows?' said Hatter.

He snatched the key from Joseph Keetley, eyeing the number on the tab to ensure it corresponded with what he had just been told.

'True to a degree, Inspector, but there is fair, there is unseen, and there is downright illegal,' said Beddows.

'In years to come, Sergeant Beddows, history will tell which of us was right. Anyway, isn't it about time you bought me an ale?'

'A jug of your best for Inspector Hatter, and your best China tea for me, please, Landlord. And, by the way, your competition at The Globe is only charging a ha'penny a pot.'

'That's a lot of money for water and floor sweepings, Beddows. Mine's real tea.' Joseph Keetley grinned again, knowing he was not far off the mark.

'So, tell me about your quest, Inspector,' said Beddows. 'We had somebody crack a crib at a well heeled dwelling in Westminster. A large, four story mansion. To gain entry, he climbed up and in from an open fourth floor window. Went through all the rooms, top to bottom, but got away with only foreign jewellery and some private papers. He was disturbed by an occupant, and brutally stove the man's head in. Poor sod was dead before he hit the ground. A real pro. Left nothing at all behind at the murder scene. That's why I know he's a pro. Very agile he must be, also.'

And the circus connection?' said Beddows.

'There was an American circus on St. James's Park.'

'Was your man on his own or did he have any accomplices?' said Beddows.

'I've told you a bit about mine. Your turn now!'

'But you haven't finished. Why not answer my question?' said Beddows.

'Because it's your turn, Sergeant.'

'Mr Charters explained ours at the station.'

'What does your offender look like; what is his *modus operandi*?' said Hatter.

'A bit like yours. Climbs like a monkey and very agile. Cunning. Violent. Also assaulted our victim, clearly.'

'Is that it?' said Hatter.

'Why?' said Beddows. 'Your turn again, now, I believe.'

'I am the superior officer.'

'I don't recognise superior. Superior has no place in this job. Truth, skill, integrity and respect, perhaps...' said Beddows, 'although some may suggest otherwise.'

Joseph Keetley placed a jug of frothing ale and a clean tankard in front of Hatter, followed by a very fine china cup and saucer filled with dark liquid, in front of Beddows. 'Best of both, gentlemen. Temporarily out of milk I'm afraid, Beddows.'

'You're deliberately going to hold back on me, aren't you, Sergeant?' Hatter ignored the Landlord and made no attempt at thanking him, waving him away with a flick of the hand.

Keetley gave a blatant look of disgust at the visitor. Beddows shrugged and added a short nod.

'I'm wary of disclosing anything that may be untested, as yet. He was described as possibly having an American accent. What about yours?'

'I am following an American circus.'

'Your turn,' said Beddows, picking up his delicate cup, taking a careful sip from the steaming contents.

'I can see that you and I are going to find it difficult to work together, Sergeant. I think I may be better served working alone, if you're not prepared to fully brief me?'

'Your choice, Inspector Hatter. You're going to do whatever you want. But you're in Leicester, not London, and we have our ways of investigating crime.'

'Your point?'

'You and Mr Charters have some history?'

'Silly old bugger. Never been my sort of policeman. Too cautious. Too by the book. Everything takes forever. I don't work like that. Was a blessing to the Metropolis when he was dragged away to your little town.'

Hatter filled his tankard and swallowed the content, hard, and in one go, wiping his face with the back of his hand, before filling the vessel again.

'I actually took you for a whiskey or fine wines man, myself.'

'Don't change the subject.'

'Mr Charters has earned his reputation in Leicester. He is backed by the people, too. He is honest and a tough taskmaster, as several have found to their cost. Be wary not to push him the wrong way. And never think him a fool. He is a cunning old fox.'

'We'll see about that. You'll all need to have your wits about you to keep up with me.'

'I used to have a Detective Sergeant like you. Acted the same way, almost exactly, but he got his comeuppance and danced for Jack Ketch in the end,' said Beddows, 'as we are as accountable to the law as much as any man, and live under that threat.'

'Enough of work. You're clearly not going to give me anything else, tonight. Where is your local totty to be found?' Hatter looked around the inn for any young woman who might take his fancy.

'Depends what your taste is, and how much you want to pay.' Beddows considered that the seedier the better might be Hatter's choice, like his taste in grog.

'I don't pay for totty, Sergeant. A good looking woman; a few gins, then let nature takes its course. My charm obviously does the rest.'

'You'll not find many like that in here, Inspector. You might want to venture into the Town and to the gin palaces along Church Gate. Plenty of factory girls and tarts down there. Alternatively, there's Manky Lil's just down the road, our local abbey. Each will cost you, one way or the other.'

'Well what are we waiting for? Drink your tea and lead on. The gin palaces, that is, not the Abbey.' Hatter drained the last of his ale.

'I'll point you in the right direction, but I'll not be joining you tonight.'

'A little lady pining for you at home, a candle burning in the window?' Hatter sneered.

'A long day and an early start tomorrow, more like,' said Beddows. 'Good hunting, Inspector... Nimrod. I shall be in at 6 o'clock sharp, and I will better introduce you to Constable Shepherd who is working with me on this case.'

Beddows had no palate for spending a minute longer with the man. He sensed the Inspector was a liability to be around, irrespective of whichever side of the law a man found himself. A darkness emanated in his every word.

'Shall have to see if I get to bed,' said Hatter, licking the last froth from his upper lip. 'But first, some lady awaits.'

Hatter donned his Stovepipe, adjusted his cravat, and headed out onto Town Hall Lane.

'I guess I must be paying, then Joseph,' said Beddows, shaking his head.

'Mind yourself with that one, John Beddows. Strikes me as a nasty piece of work.'

Upsetting the locals

At five forty-five the next morning, Sunday 4th July, Beddows and Shepherd were sat in the back office, contemplating their day to come. The building reverberated to the sound of overnight drunks and whores, shouting and screaming. The bang of truncheon on cell door rang out, frequently, as was the norm. Much work was still to be done at Barker's Ground in any event, attempting to winkle out their potential suspect. Doubts reverberated in Beddows' mind as to whether Inspector Nimrod Hatter would throw early light on who that might be, or whether he really had a clue and was seeking Leicester's finest's efforts in identifying a suspect. Conversely, could he be wrong, and maligning the Detective on the words of Mr Charters? Something niggled Beddows, but he couldn't put his finger on it. Everything was happening too quickly.

'How did you get on with Coroner Mitchell, Shepherd?'

'He was his usual, inquisitive self, and is aware of Mr Hamilton's planned examination, later today. He wants the inquest at midday, tomorrow, subject to advice from Mr Hamilton. A free snifter for the jury and a prolonged Coroner's lunch in The Turks Head, it shall have to be.'

'We will need Mr Charters to allocate arrangement of the inquest and sourcing a jury. Probably a job for Sergeant Kettle, once again. We can't do it all.' said Beddows.

'How was your time with Inspector Hatter?'

'A nasty piece of work. Relished telling me about a soldier in The Peninsular who his Father had branded, as a lesson. Thinks that extreme violence is a means to an end. Dresses posh, but talks, drinks and behaves like an enlisted man. Strange fellow.'

'Mr Charters clearly has nothing but contempt for him?' said Shepherd.

'So it seems, Shepherd, but I would like to know more about why Mr Charters has such contempt?'

'Just ask me,' came the gravelly response, as Charters appeared in the doorway. 'Our Inspector Hatter was not a very honest or trustworthy constable. In the limited time that I had the misfortune to know him in Westminster, I had more complaints from both public and colleagues as to his unorthodox and cynical methods, and his allegiance to Captain Hay and the so called chosen men.'

'Corruption, are we talking?' said Beddows.

'Corruption and lawlessness. The man was best known for his violence and his lies. Yet he was seen in highest regards by Hay, yet loathed by Sir Richard Mayne. This led to all sorts of rumours about a rift at the top and influence at Government level due to Hay's allegiance to Wellington, previously. More like an old fashioned 'Runner' than one of Peel's modern policemen. Tales of torture for gaining confession for crimes that others could not clear up. Not a clip round the ear, or an appropriate thump where due. These Metropolitan officers are a volatile mix to this day, as I understand.'

'So we should be watching our backs?' said Beddows.

'I must suggest that you most definitely should have your backs covered. Sergeants Smith and Haynes will be taking care of that, whenever and wherever possible.'

'That bad?' said Beddows.

'That bad,' said Charters. 'They used to call him 'Mad Hatter' in the capital. One day he will be either famous or infamous. Tell Hatter as little as possible and be able to corroborate anything you establish. Protect your evidence and, more importantly, protect your witnesses, as Hatter will taint anyone or anything to gain a result.'

'And what about his Chief Constable?' said Beddows.

'I am waiting for a telegraph message in response to my earlier enquiry. I suspect he will be described as here legitimately. Hay will back him and his like, every time. The delay in response may be down to the time it was sent, or it might also indicate that questions are being asked within 4, Whitehall.'

Loud knocking at the main door to the station, audible above the cacophony from the cells, grabbed the attention of the three men.

'Where is Sergeant Sheffield?' yelled Charters, peering round the door into the main room of the station, which was empty. The cells went momentarily quiet.

Shepherd walked to the heavy wooden door, and turned the large brass key which locked it, pulling the door with all his strength.

The culprit for the early disruption was an irate Joseph Keetley.

'Is Sergeant Beddows about?' said Keetley.

'What is it, Joseph?' said Beddows.

'It's your visitor, Beddows. I'm not one to often complain, as you well know. Nor am I prudish. In the early hours, your Inspector Hatter and a number of dubious ladies came in, banging, crashing and causing a disturbance. Woke all the other residents with their shouting and screaming. Demanded drink for all of them. When I asked him to consider the other guests and for his ladies to leave or each would have to pay for a night's accommodation, he threatened me with violence.'

Sergeant Sheffield slowly appeared from the yard door, buttoning his flies.

'Can't a man have a much needed pony and trap without being disturbed?' he said, glowering. 'So much for a peaceful Sunday morning. Oh, sorry Mr Charters, didn't realise you were about...'

'What can we do to help, Mr Keetley?' said Charters.

'The man is a disgrace, Mr Charters. I want him out. He can empty his room and pay his dues, but I want him gone.'

A shadowy figure appeared in the doorway, silhouetted by the bright sunlight beyond. 'You snivelling little shit. Call your establishment an inn? If you can't allow for a bit of company and frivolity, you shouldn't be in the trade. What with you and a tea-total constables, what have I dropped upon?'

'I run a respected establishment, with good and regular clientele. I don't need your sort, and I certainly don't want a reputation as a bawdy house.'

'Fear not, Landlord. I wouldn't want to stay another night in your flea pit.'

'That's good news for both of us, then, Sir. You may settle up with me before you may collect your baggage and empty your room.'

'Settle up with you? I haven't stayed one night, as you caused me to leave. I spent more time at my new friend's little place.' Hatter crossed his arms, belligerently.

'One night's accommodation, Inspector. That's what you had, that's what I expect to see settled, else Mr Charters will be having my complaint of non-payment. Five shillings before you collect your property and depart.'

'Five shillings? You'll not see a penny from me, Landlord. I owe you nothing. Don't push things else you may come to regret it.'

Before Joseph Keetley could speak a word more, Robert Charters assured him, 'I will see that you get every penny the man owes you. If not, he may spend some time in our cells, himself, and Sir Richard Mayne himself will get notice of his demise.'

'God help the good people of the Capital if that is what their police are like,' said Keetley.
'God help them indeed,' said Charters, shaking his head. 'Inspector Hatter, my office, now!'

*****

'How many hours have you been here, Inspector? And how much distress have you caused in such a short amount of time?' said Charters, physically bundling Hatter into the small office at the rear.
'What I do when I am not on duty, is none of your business, nor of Captain Hay, nor Sir Richard bleedin' Mayne. It's my time, for me to exhaust as I wish. I also do not take lightly to being man-handled, either.'
'You are never off duty, Hatter, never, according to Sir Robert Peel's charter. And, as a guest in my borough, I expect you to behave like one of my officers. I expect them to be role models at all times. Those that can't or won't, quickly need to find other employment. Mr Keetley is a good man and you will settle your account, else suffer the consequences of arrest and confinement.'
'Wouldn't have chosen the place, myself. Your man Beddows stuck me there. Must have realised what the place would be like and that it was not what I was after.'
'Sergeant Beddows has no problem placing guests in Mr Keetley's care, as a rule. However, I am not disappointed that you will be leaving his establishment. Do you wish to be shown somewhere more suited to your *personal* needs?'
'I've got a bed sorted for the rest of my stay here, if I'm misfortunate enough to need to stay another night. Lovely girl she is. Very pleasing to the eye and she has something your Mr Keetley can't offer me.'

'You live a sordid life, Hatter.'

'Life is short, Mr Charters. Live like today is your last. Mind, at your age that's probably truer than you may care to imagine.' A particularly unpleasant sneer crossed Hatter's face.

'Is that a threat?'

'A threat? I'm just saying, you're getting on a bit these days, and you need to make the most of what you have left. That red face doesn't bode well for you. Looks like you've made a bid for this year's Admiral of the Fleet. Bad ticker?'

'I have survived to this good age, by guile, honesty, and godliness, Hatter, and will probably outlive you, at the current rate. And I don't take threats lightly, myself.'

'I shall have my fun, Mr Charters, whatever you may think. So, leave it there shall we?'

'Make your enquiries and, hopefully, your arrest. Then I can get back to living my life as I am accustomed. Let us hope that this is sooner rather than later.'

'Suits me, Mr Charters. More than you can imagine.'

'Sergeant Beddows is well suited to your needs, Hatter, as he is one of our best detectives, and very few escape his efforts.'

'Well, Beddows and Shepherd, I believe, should be accompanying me, post haste, to locate my man.'

'To find our offender, Hatter. If he is the one and the same, then we will decide who will have primacy, and the task of convicting him, first. Let's not get ahead of ourselves.'

'Your chaps don't know who they want, whereas I do.'

'Then tell us man, and make the job easier.'

'Play my cards close to my chest, Mr Charters. Don't know if I can trust your yokels to keep quiet until I have located him. A bit like the game your Sergeant Beddows is playing.'

'Don't tread on our toes, Inspector. Beddows and

Shepherd know who they are looking for. They may not have a name, but they have enough to identify him.'
'We'll see, Mr Charters. I know where my money is.'
'Get out of my sight and out of my borough as quickly as fortune may allow, Inspector. I am growing tired of your impudence.'
Beddows and Shepherd heard the last words, as Hatter emerged from the office. The door slammed behind him and the ancient walls of the building shuddered.
Sergeant Sheffield let out an audible grunt, 'That's buggered it for the rest of the day. Well done, Inspector.'

Differing priorities

Just after six-thirty, the three men strolled down Town Hall Lane en route to Barker's Ground.

The streets remained stiflingly warm considering the time of the morning, and the sickly air of the butchers, animal yards and knackers yards added a deathly stench to the sulphurous industrial haze which lingered from the working week just gone. Factory chimneys which normally belched smoke, lay unlit and the factories silent.

It was Sunday, the day of rest for most. Families shuffled off to church, sporting their Sunday best, albeit in most cases worn and shabby. Everyone would likely go at least once, even Charter's constables were entitled. Marriages, christenings and funerals would be taking place in every parish.

The better off would be considering a trip to the first performance of the American circus, with an afternoon and evening performance advertised on billboards throughout the borough.

The very poor and those who chose a life of street crime were starting to emerge from their drunken and squalid stupors, especially along the left side of Belgrave Gate, within the Rookeries, and from the dens in the newer slums around Wheat Street, Carley Street and Wharf Street, surrounding Barker's Ground.

Their business was the same every day. Steal and rob to live, or live to steal and rob, depending upon one's perspective. The circus would offer rich pickings.

Few words were initially exchanged. An uncomfortable silence between the men festered. Shepherd watched and waited as Beddows and Hatter stepped ahead of him. He was unclear how Hatter might influence their enquiries, but felt it improper to ask.

If it was just him and Hatter, he would seek clarity, perhaps? Then again, perhaps not. He was, when all said and done, the junior constable.

Shepherd was surprised that Hatter's fancy clothes were working attire, and wondered if his ejection from The King and Crown might have stopped him dressing more suitably for work. He looked more and more out of place as they neared their objective.

Beddows broke the silence. 'Who are we looking for then, Inspector?'

'Who or what are we looking for, do you mean?'

'If you know who we are looking for, might it not be a good idea to share the fact?'

'Now we are just three, the man I am looking for goes by the name of Michael Lenihan.'

'Sounds more like an Irishman than an American?'

'There are a lot of Irishmen who went off to The Americas. More went to America during and after the famine than came to the mainland. Irish or American, that is his given name,' said Hatter.

'And how can you be sure of that?' said Shepherd?

'Oh, the boy speaks,' said Hatter, spitting a great wad of phlegm onto the dry street.

'I do, Sir, when I have something purposeful to ask or something useful I can offer.'

'So?' said Beddows.

'I have had reliable information about the man. He has previously been of suspicion in our area, and was known to have left before the circus broke down and set off for Leicester.'

'What does he look like?' said Beddows.

'Tall and wiry, with a long, dark mane of hair, and with what is described as a 'strange, almost deranged glare,' said Hatter.

'That makes things interesting, then. We have our first possible problem,' said Beddows. 'We are looking for a young American, agile, slightly built, with vivid blue eyes.'

Nothing was said about Shepherd's proposal of a scar.

'They could be working together, in cahoots?' said Hatter.

'There was a suggestion that our man may have had an accomplice,' said Shepherd.

'Let's not make things fit,' said Beddows. 'Let's go and look at our suspect, first.'

The men reached the site, and Beddows led the men towards the brightly decorated caravan he now recognised as belonging to Miss Eibhlin MacCormack. Beddows was surprised at the levels of activity around the site, already, and a sense of animosity etched on the faces of the people milling about.

'The relevance of this caravan?' said Hatter.

'This is where we find the circus owner,' said Beddows.

'Is he to be trusted?' said Hatter.

'She,' said Shepherd. 'Quite a feisty lady, as you will no doubt observe for yourself.'

'She seems okay to me,' said Beddows, his mind wandering to their original exchanges of yesterday.

The door opened at the first knock. Eibhlin stood in the doorway, her long red hair hanging loose, shaking it and pulling it into some form of a knot as the men looked on.

'Why Mr Beddows and Constable Shepherd. You said you would be early. I was expecting you hours ago.' Her eyes locked on Beddows, a slight smile apparent.

'This is Inspector Hatter, from London.' said Beddows, introducing the man.

'From London. Why, we've not long come from London. Not a coincidence, I assume?'

'Not a coincidence, at all. I suspect it is far from a coincidence,' said Hatter, aggressively.

'Rather a rude greeting, I must say.' Eibhlin stepped down from the doorway, and joined the men on the scorched grassy area beneath, holding out her hand in greeting. 'I take it that it was your men that tried to turn this place upside down earlier, looking for somebody?'

'I don't know what you are talking about. Do you, Beddows?' Hatter offered, unconvincingly.

'What were these men doing?' said Beddows.

They woke up the entire circus, demanding they should look for somebody. They wouldn't say who, but knew who they were looking for, obviously. They said they were on official business, and were very rough and abrupt. I was going to report it to Mr Beddows.'

'How many were there?' said Shepherd.

'Just two,' said Eibhlin.

'They were certainly nothing to do with the Borough Police. How were they dressed?' said Beddows.

'Scruffy. They were big men, and had a military air about them. Hard looking fellows they were, and not very nice.'

'Inspector Hatter, does this mean anything to you?' said Beddows.

'If it was anything to do with me, would I be here now? I am here to represent the Metropolitan Police and to catch a criminal. Perhaps he has upset other people on his travels.'

'You do not seem very concerned, Inspector,' said Eibhlin.

'I'm not here to make any friends, I am here to catch a murderer, as are Beddows and Shepherd,' said Hatter.

'Murderer? I thought you gentlemen were looking for a burglar, Sergeant?' seeking Beddows' clarification.

'Since we spoke, Miss MacCormack, our victim has died,

so we are now treating our offence as a murder. Inspector Hatter is investigating a similar murder that occurred in London, some days ago.'

'Your circus is the common connection,' said Hatter, scanning the surroundings.

'My goodness. We don't want to be connected to a murderer. How can I help you?' A hint of sarcasm was clear to all.

'As we said, yesterday, we are looking for a slightly built young American, very agile, with piercing blue eyes,' said Shepherd.

'And I am also seeking a specific man, known to me by name,' said Hatter.

'And who might that be?' said Eibhlin.

'I am looking for a man named Michael Lenihan,' said Hatter. 'Do you know such a man?' Eibhlin appeared taken aback, momentarily, at Hatter's question.

'I do, but I have not seen him since before we left London, Inspector.'

Beddows saw the glimpse of concern in Eibhlin's eyes.

'That's convenient,' said Hatter.

'I have a large team of people and hangers-on, and I may be the owner but I am not their keeper.' said Eibhlin, venomously.

'Who is Lenihan?' said Hatter, unsatisfied with the initial answer.

'He is my son.' said Eibhlin, defensively. 'He is just one of the riggers. He is not what I would have called agile. He also is a little slow. His speech highlights a nasty stutter, which has developed since he was a a child. He is not a killer and he still has very child-like qualities,' stressed Eibhlin.

'Where will we most likely find him?' demanded Hatter.

'I have already told you, I have not seen him since before we left London.'

'Who does he work with, or spend time with?' said

Shepherd.

'My son is much of a loner, Constable Shepherd. His birth was somewhat difficult and consequently he is somewhat slow, at times. There are only one or two of the circus hands who he spends time with.'

'Has he been in trouble before?' said Shepherd.

'No, not for anything. Do you really think he would still be here if he had. Your justice results in hanging or sending men to the Colonies,' said Eibhlin, sharply.

'My information is that he committed the crime I am investigating, and in his panic, I suspect, left London before your circus did,' said Hatter.

'And you think he is smart witted enough to come to Leicester, under his own means, and yet stupid enough to commit a further hanging offence, here?' said Eibhlin, becoming more irate.

'As I understand, had he done this in America he would probably have been shot dead or hanged on the spot by your lawmen. You think our justice is harsh?' Hatter offered, cynically. 'If he is not here, and he left London out of panic, why should he do that?'

'Probably scared of what he might be accused of, by people like you, Inspector,' said Eibhlin, assertively.

'People like me?' said Hatter, snarling, eyes wide open. Eibhlin visibly shivered.

'Slow down, Inspector. We still have the information that *we* have. We should look at the possibility that somebody else may be responsible for one or both crimes,' said Beddows.

'I am confident that my son is neither a burglar nor a murderer, gentlemen. The fact he is not here, or that he left London early, suggests to me that he is scared rather than guilty.' Eibhlin shook her head in disbelief at Inspector Hatter. 'Anyway, who is your so called informant?'

'That is none of your business,' said Hatter.

'Who are the men he spends time with?' said Shepherd.
'They are brothers. Their name is Henson. They came to me in London, last year, and I needed tumblers at the time, so gave them a job. They left last winter, but came to me again in London, before this tour.'
'Henson - where are they from originally?' said Beddows.
'Sweden, I understand,' said Eibhlin.
'Where should we find them, now?' said Beddows.
'They should be in their tent, over in the performers camp.'
'Well, lets go and talk to them, shall we?' said Beddows.
'Where could your son go?' said Hatter, determined to get a response.
'When he gets scared, he would run to somebody he trusts. His Father still lives in America. He might try and get back there, if he really is that scared.'
'And how would he get there?' said Hatter.
'He could probably seek passage on a merchantman,' said Eibhlin, 'but he would get a message to me. He has run off once before when he got scared. He let me know and I fetched him back, myself.'
'Does he have money? ' said Hatter.
'He would work, Inspector. He is slow, mentally, but tall and strong. Ideal for labouring on the dock, or on board a working vessel.'
'Is there anyone else in England he might seek out?' said Shepherd.
'Only me. All our Irish family have died out or settled in America.'
'I need to get back to London,' said Hatter, impatiently.
'Are you not interested in these other men?' said Beddows, shocked that he did not wish to follow up other lines of enquiry.
'Your crime is your crime. I know who I want,' said Hatter.

'Even though he is not agile, has a stutter and is not mentally so bright?' said Beddows.

'Might as well see what your tumblers look like. See if my gut reaction changes things,' said Hatter, reluctantly.

Not a willing concession, Beddows speculated.

'Why should you not consider our descriptions?' said Shepherd, resulting in an unseen elbow in the ribs from Beddows.

'The Inspector must have good reason,' said Beddows.

'Easier to convict on the word and statement of a paid snout, than on good police work.'

'What are you implying, Beddows?' said Hatter

'You can go back and see your suspect hanged, and close your papers. Job done. We are not like that up here, and would sooner see justice carried out properly.'

'Not very efficient, Beddows. You don't sweep rubbish from one place to another, you bury it once and for all.'

'We'll do things our way, thank you. Miss MacCormack, when did you last see the brothers?' said Beddows.

'They were certainly with me in London. They performed down there,' said Eibhlin.

'Miss MacCormack, will you point these brothers out to us?' said Beddows.

'If I can save my son and clear his name, of course. I would do anything for that.'

The group walked beyond the main arena, to a far edge of the ground, where a ragged collection of tents, or assembled sail cloths draped over flimsy frames, were clustered.

People were already moving about, and some were already rehearsing.

A group began to form up, as they realised they were the subject of attention from the visitors.

'Where are the Hensons?' said Eibhlin.

'They haven't arrived as yet,' replied a pretty little

young woman, dressed in an ornate, short dress, and some form of performance stockings and slippers.

'What do you mean, they haven't arrived as yet?' said Eibhlin.

'They had gone when we started to break up at that last town, the day before yesterday. They said they had some business to sort out on the way here.'

Beddows ears pricked up.

'When are we expecting them? Their first performance is this afternoon,' said Eibhlin, anxiously.

'We expected them yesterday evening. Somebody thought they had seen their tent on the edge of the park we passed, coming into Leicester. The racecourse?'

'When did any of you last see them with Michael Lenihan?' said Beddows.

'They were talking to him in London, the night before we packed up. He didn't look happy and they were shouting at him. He looked distressed or upset,' said another performer.

'Did anybody hear him say anything about leaving the circus?' said Hatter.

'He was trying to borrow some money in London.' said the woman performer.

'So, he has associates that have gone missing too, and he was asking for money in London. They were all seen arguing. Looks like they're all guilty,' said Hatter.

'You are very quick to make assumptions, Inspector,' said Beddows.

'What are the chances of two very similar crimes being committed, one in London, one in Leicester, and three associates now at large, not being connected?' said Hatter.

'There is always a chance,' said Shepherd.

'Not in my book,' said Hatter. 'I will find them all, and see them all dead.'

'My son is not a criminal, Inspector. He may have been

an associate of these men, but what if it was these other men alone?' said Eibhlin.

'Who knows these brothers the best?' said Shepherd.

'Annie, the contortionist used to walk out with the elder brother,' said Eibhlin.

'What do you need to ask me?' said a very plain looking woman, with blond hair and skinny limbs, with a gown draped around her costume, announcing herself as 'Annie'. The woman appeared to be rubbing chalk from her hands, which she wrung, anxiously.

'What do the brothers look like?' said Shepherd.

'They are both young, slender and blond. Henry is a little taller than Peter. They are both on the sinewy side and very, very good tumblers. Like cats.'

'What colour eyes do they have?' said Shepherd.

'The most beautiful blue eyes. Like pale sapphires, gleaming,' said Annie.

'And what are they like, temperament wise?' said Shepherd.

'They are hungry. They need to be, but that makes them very aggressive at times. They look after each other and if anyone hurts one of them, the other will be there to protect him,' said Annie.

'And their relationship with Michael Lenihan?' said Beddows.

'Michael? He is just a play thing. Thy use him to run errands and tease him. They try to get him to do some of their acrobatics, but the poor man can't even roll over without banging into something or somebody,' said Annie.

'So, he wouldn't be very good at climbing a building?' said Shepherd.

'He's scared of heights, so I would very much doubt it.' said Eibhlin, interrupting.

'Do you know where they might be?' said Shepherd.

'I have little to do with them anymore. He betrayed me

with another, whilst they left the circus over the winter, and tells me nothing. He has no reason to.'

'Michael Lenihan is not a very likely fit for a burglar as adept as the one, or ones, that we are all seeking, Inspector?' said Beddows, addressing his observation at Hatter. 'However, the Hensons sound more likely.'

'I believe it sounds more likely that they are in this together,' said Hatter.

'It doesn't prove or disprove anything,' said Beddows. 'We need to find all three of them, and then we'll get to the truth.'

'We must start to make enquiries to track these brothers,' said Shepherd. 'If they may still be in Leicester, we must look for them. Perhaps on the edge of the borough, if they were seen beforehand?'

'And where are they going to catch a ship in Leicester? I need to get off to London, and quickly,' Hatter insisted.

'Especially if somebody else is looking for them, too,' said Beddows, who suspected Hatter knew more of the two earlier visitors than he would let on.

'And what do I do in the circumstances?' said Eibhlin.

'You will have to wait and see where your son finally ends up, but he will probably hang, if they are in it together,' said Hatter, sneering.

'We will speak to you on your own, shortly, Miss MacCormack,' said Beddows.

'And the circus?'

'You may wish to carry on with your performances?' said Beddows.

'You think I am a hardnosed woman, Sergeant Beddows?'

'Not at all, Miss MacCormack. There is little you can do until we find all three men, including Michael. Until then it is up to you as to what you would wish to do.'

'I have little choice, but I need to know that my son will be treated fairly and justly?'

'You have my word that we will do our best, Miss

MacCormack. But only time and evidence will tell.' said Beddows.

'Should I go and look for him, myself?' Eibhlin appeared genuinely concerned for her son's safe being.

'We cannot stop you, but we are probably best equipped to locate Michael and the Henson brothers,' said Beddows.

'This is not personal, Beddows, but police business, as your precious Mr Charters would remind you. We don't need interfering relatives getting in the way,' said Hatter.

'Of that I am very aware,' said Beddows.

'However, Michael Lenihan seems to have a head start over everyone, the brothers included, and must therefore be my priority,' said Hatter.

'in the meantime, we have many unanswered questions, locally, and then a post-mortem examination to attend. I take it you have no wish to join us, Inspector?' said Beddows.

'London beckons, and I can't wait to get out of this dump.' Hatter was definitely in a rush.

'Why the elbow, Beddows?' Shepherd whispered cautiously.

'I was deliberately avoiding that question to Hatter. Something is going on here and Hatter knows more than he is letting on. Either that or he is set on closing his crime with one hanging after a very short trial. The two early callers must be connected to Hatter.'

'What if Michael Lenihan...'

'No *what if's*, Shepherd. Let's find the Hensons, and quickly.'

Business first

In no doubt of the reality of the threat from Robert Charters, Inspector Nimrod Charles Hatter was escorted to The King and Crown to settle his dues with Joseph Keetley, before being seen on the first available transport to London by Beddows and Shepherd.

Charters wanted certain knowledge that Hatter was out of the borough.

Following a brisk walk through the town and to the Midland Railway concourse on Campbell Street, where Hatter was seen to purchase a first class ticket, before boarding and departing on the late morning Sunday train to London via Rugby, Beddows and Shepherd set off on their next, unpleasant task.

Their presence was required at the post-mortem examination of Mr Paget.

As they walked back along Campbell Street towards London Road, a figure stepped out from between the tall, ornate columns at the end of the concourse.

Mrs Paget's Father, William Harrison, now stood before them.

Harrison wore a wide black armband on his left arm. Even the silk it was made off reeked quality.

'Mr Harrison,' said Beddows, 'a surprise to see you out and about this morning.'

Shepherd suspected he had waited, deliberately, to speak with them both.

'Good morning, Constables. I hope you don't mind me enquiring, but who was the gentleman you were just with?' Harrison appeared anxious.

'He is a detective from London, following his own

enquiries into a similar offence which occurred there,' said Beddows.

'He seemed familiar to me,' said Harrison.

'In what way?' said Shepherd.

'I am sure I have met him, or been introduced to him somewhere, previously. I do have meetings in London, quite regularly, perhaps it was there?'

'He does move in high circles,' said Beddows.

'But something about him...' said Harrison.

'Probably a coincidence,' said Beddows.

'It will come to me, I am sure.'

'How is your daughter this morning?' said Shepherd.

'She will be residing with us for the foreseeable future, until matters are resolved. Not only is she distressed, quite obviously, but also unnerved about being alone at New Walk.'

'When does the house-keeper return?' said Beddows.

'She will be back any day now, and I know you wish to speak with her.'

'I must admit, I was somewhat taken aback to see you out and about, this morning. You are still off to do your business, Mr Harrison?' said Shepherd.

'Time and money waits for no man, Constable Shepherd, and as my wife is with my daughter, I would only be in the way. They can mourn together, as women do, and later, we shall attend church as God demands. In the meanwhile I need to check the factory and then I have lunch invitation with the Corah family.'

'Good day to you, Sir. We should not wish to detain you any further,' said Beddows.

Harrison was clearly another man who put reward over family. Beddows wondered at what cost to his relationship? His mind strayed to Mrs Beddows, but only momentarily.

*****

'That was strange, Beddows,' said Shepherd, strolling down the streets between busy factories running either side of New Walk, and towards the infirmary.

Carts of all sizes and descriptions, drawn by teams of horses, would normally be fetching and carrying goods and machinery in and out of the growing buildings. Teams of men would haul large bails of goods up and down by rope, from pulleys high up on the buildings, often hanging out of precarious and cavernous openings in factory walls to grapple with them. The old frame knitters must have looked on in wonderment at the size and scale of the new factories and machines.

Today, however, was the day of rest, and the streets were eerily quiet. Just a few watchmen or managers and owners checked on their assets. The cheerful sounds of church bells could be heard with clarity across the borough for a change.

The sound of the two men's hobnails echoed across between high walls of what Blake, some years earlier, had described as *dark satanic mills*.

'Mr Hatter looks like any number of toffee nosed, upper class, posh bugger, I would suspect. But strange the fact that Mr Harrison seemed to recognise him, and appeared disturbed by seeing him, yet he never asked us for his name.'

'Strange, but probably nothing, I would suggest,' said Beddows, not unduly concerned by Harrison's interest in Hatter.

'Inspector Hatter certainly makes me nervous.'

'You need to wise up, young Shepherd. He is just a mean and selfish individual. A bully. Stand up to bullies, in and out of the job, and you will go far. Fear them and they will crush your spirit.'

'That's alright for you, Beddows. But even you learned that the hard way.'

'Remember what I say. He uses his bullying to his own ends. Remember it well, and don't let people like him get in your way, but watch your back with Mr Hatter. I suspect we have not seen or heard the last of him.'

Shepherd spat something out, as they walked. The air was thick with small fibres that physically filled his mouth and nostrils, coating his senses. He let out an enormous and unavoidable sneeze. No doubt this matter was factory debris, picked up from the pavements and roads, blown up on the light breeze.

'How can anyone work in this stuff, for hours on end?' he exclaimed, blowing his nose, noisily, examining for fluff in the residue.

'Money, young Shepherd. Better live well and shortened a life, than live long and starve,' said Beddows. 'This is what life is becoming for us all, watch my words.'

'Mr Paget may have other enemies, then.' said Shepherd. 'Imagine how much a worker must hate such a life. Those poor folk. I would kill to get out of such a hell hole. A disgruntled frame-knitter? Someone who has lost a loved one? All grounds for revenge.'

'And that is something we also need to rule out. Inspector Hatter may think otherwise, thus, we leave nothing to chance. But a burglary? Doesn't that rule out revenge? Makes it more intriguing, young Shepherd, and something ain't right.'

'Money is a temptation, Beddows, for anyone who doesn't normally have it, however you get your hands on it. Revenge, on the other hand, may take many strange forms.'

'Mr Hatter may hang the three suspects if we don't find them first. I suspect he will shape evidence to fit his crime. Poor Miss MacCormack must be worried sick.'

'Well, we'd better get Mr Hamilton's needs met, and then do our best to outwit Inspector Hatter and his colleagues in London.'

Plate spinning

It was times like this that Charters felt let down by *'the borough', Mayor and all,* for failing to recognise the need for an expanded detective capability, or even an increase in the numbers of uniform officers with intelligence as well as brawn. It would be some years before this would occur, he feared.

A serious crime always left the borough painfully short of men for day to day policing. This crime was more complex, given the intrusions of Inspector Hatter.

A visit to the Mayor, or time with the local newspapers might be required again, and pressure for growth applied.

Charters anxiously awaited word from Sergeants Tanky Smith and Black Tommy Haynes, to reassign them to a task he would not be sharing with anyone else.

Precious time was needed to search the racecourse area and the fields surrounding to the south.

'Inspector Chapman,' Charters called out, loudly.

'Yes, Sir?' Heavy footsteps approached the office.

Bertram Chapman was newly promoted to the rank, having served Charters well as a constable and then sergeant, since Charters' arrival in the borough. He was a modest, family man, but confident and intuitive. He looked impressive in his superior uniform, and his confidence calmed many a difficult situation or irate public.

'I am running out of resources, Chapman. I need you to sort out an Inquest for our good Coroner, Oliver Mitchell, tomorrow at Midday at The Turks Head. We will need a jury, and the presence of Dr. Hamilton and the corpse of

Edward Paget available for viewing at the infirmary, opposite. Can I trust you to resolve that end of affairs, without delay?'

'I have just the man for that, Sir. He has organised them for me in the past.'

'And I need some constables to go with Detective Sergeant Kettle and make a start on transport providers, to see if our suspects may already have fled the borough.'

'I will double up the beats for remaining constables and take half of the early turn, if you are happy for me to do so?'

'Get them back here in the next hour to be tasked by Sergeant Kettle. He will require some to set up checks at the county borders. I have asked Mr Goodyer to have his county men briefed for checking main routes and crossroads in the south of the county.'

Southern borders of the borough, where it was felt the Henson brothers may have last been sighted, would be the likely route out of the borough and towards the safety of the docks in London, if that was ever their intention.

*****

Herbert Kettle sighed with relief. He had already a fair share of Coroner's inquests and post-mortems under his belt, courtesy of Beddows and Shepherd.

Kettle briefed his small section of uniformed constables and marched them off, up to the perimeter of the racecourse, before dispersing to where roads and lanes intersected. There they should stop and challenge anyone fitting the description of the Hensons or Michael Lenihan. They would not leave the points until advised to do so. One short stop was required on the way. Kettle himself started enquiries at the Campbell Street station, to establish possible suspects on trains that may have left for Rugby and onwards to London.

The telegraph message sent to Mr Goodyer's officers in the county with descriptions and details of the crime, and interest in routes to London would be scrutinised, particularly at Harborough, Hinckley and Lutterworth on the coaching routes, and to the railway station at Wigston. There, George Hudson's new Leicester to Hitchin Railway would take passengers to Kings Cross, via Harborough, Desborough, Kettering, Wellingborough, Bedford, and at Hitchin where the line joined The Great Northern Line to London.

After the Railway, Kettle would start on the coaching stands and the livery men in the borough for any clues. Had anyone bought fresh horses or enquired of any? Nothing could be left to chance. The Railway was an expensive means for most, so Shanks' pony or a real, four-legged one would be the most likely means of travel. Many roamed free around Freeman's Common and in the fields beyond.

A cause of death

Around half past eleven, Beddows and Shepherd walked under the ornate wrought iron gates at the entrance to Leicester's infirmary, where Thomas Hamilton awaited the men's arrival, before he would make an examination of Edward Paget's corpse.

The small operating room was located at the rear of the infirmary, in the shadow of the fever wards, looking out towards the River Soar and the fields of Aylestone and Westcotes. The ability to open a door and have some air in the room was greeted by the three men, as the heat and the sickly sweet smell of early decomposition was already unpleasant. Sawdust covered the floor of the operating room, and stuck to the soles of each man's shoes.

Shepherd was now less squeamish at the sight of a dissection.

Not all doctors were convinced of the need of such an examination, and some failed to report many suspicious or unusual / un-natural deaths. Coroner Oliver Mitchell had made it clear that he expected all such deaths to be reported to him, and cause the attending doctor to conduct a full examination, within his area of jurisdiction.

The sounds of the bone saw, and slithering precision of the scalpel in Thomas Hamilton's hand left both men fascinated.

As Hamilton skilfully peeled forward Edward Paget's scalp. exposing his skull, a clear indentation and catastrophic damage to the temple could be seen, even by the inexperienced constables.

'That is the effect of such a heavy blow with a weighted implement or instrument,' said Hamilton. 'A compression fracture with bone impacting on and into the soft matter of the brain, below.'

'How did it not kill him immediately?' said Shepherd.

'The shock would initially stun or confuse, probably causing a temporary loss of consciousness, as you saw.'

'And why the time lapse before he deteriorated?'

'You are in inquisitive mode today, young Shepherd. Looking for Mr Hamilton's job?' said Beddows.

'Keen to find out, Beddows, as I am sure this will not be the last time I see this sort of injury.'

'You see how the injury has swollen?' said Hamilton.

'Yes, I noticed the swelling when we returned to the house, later.'

'In response to the impact, the brain has swollen, and bleeding and fluid has built up inside, beneath the fracture. This has ultimately been what has killed him.' Hamilton deftly removed a disc of skull around the fracture, with a small, sharp, saw, and a little leverage, thus revealing the brain. A darker, damaged area was quite apparent where the blow would have struck. Clotted and liquid blood and fluid mingled and drained as the brain was examined by Hamilton.

'That is the damage to the brain. You can see for yourselves what such a blow or blows does to the delicate structure.'

'I take it that the pain would increase as the swelling increased?' said Shepherd.

'Rather,' said Hamilton. 'It would be the headache of all headaches for the poor man.'

'All in the pursuit of money,' said Beddows.

'How do you mean?' said Shepherd.

'If Mr Paget, here, had not been seeking to improve himself and his business, and had not broadcast his intention to spend it, I doubt that he would have been

targeted. The killer did it for the money, also. Sad, when you sum it all up. *Radix malorum est cupiditas.*'
'Pardon?' said Shepherd.
'You mean you have never read The Canterbury Tales?'
'Not yet, I haven't' said Shepherd.
'Sergeant Beddows is implying that greed is the root of all evils,' said Hamilton, 'a rough translation, anyway.'
'I am amazed at such learned and knowledgeable company.' said Shepherd.
'I heard it from our good Coroner, Oliver Mitchell, some years ago,' said Beddows. 'and it impressed me that much. It's the only bloody Latin I can recite, though. Thank you, Mr Hamilton. Most enlightening time with you, as always. Time we got back to catching the persons responsible,' said Beddows, who, unlike Shepherd, was always glad to leave this particularly unpleasant task.

*****

'What next then, Beddows?'
'Our priority must be to locate all *three* suspects.'
'But I thought that Michael Lenihan was likely in London?'
'That may well be, Mr Shepherd. We have some catching up to do with Miss MacCormack's son, and I just hope we are resourceful enough to find him before Inspector Hatter and his colleagues in the Capital do.'
'And the Hensons?'
'They are our immediate priority, and we need to get up to the Racecourse as soon as practicable, and make ourselves busy up there. A visit to the station and a conversation with Mr Charters and then out to the fields. I want to speak with Miss MacCormack again at some point. I suspect there is more she can tell us about her son that may help us locate him. She is quite astute

and has held something back.'

'What makes you think so?'

'Why tell Hatter about the boy's Father in America and getting a passage from London? I think she is rather cunning, and may be throwing us off the scent.'

'Us, or Inspector Hatter?' said Shepherd.

'She was no doubt horrified by Hatter's determination to see him hanged, almost without question.'

'So, you think he may be nearer?'

'I hope for his sake, he is bright enough to find somewhere safe. Miss MacCormack may be more inclined to believe us, and lead us to him.'

'Shall we see her next?'

'Not as yet. That is a job for later today. I want to find the most likely suspects as a priority, and we know they were likely here in Leicester, at least until of late. We are going to be pushed for time.'

'What help will Mr Charters have arranged for us, I wonder?'

'That is what we are off to find out. I just hope there are some of our brighter colleagues assigned to help us.'

The scavengers

By the time that Beddows and Shepherd had returned and updated Robert Charters, the extra men had been deployed to the road junctions to the south of the borough.

Herbert Kettle was rooting around amongst the rail, coach and livery companies, which would keep him out of the way for some time.

Inspector Chapman was doing his bit, attempting to tempt or cajole jurors for tomorrow's inquest with prospects of coin and a drink on HM Coroner.

Comfortable in the knowledge that the best that could be done was already in hand, Beddows and Shepherd set off for the racecourse.

'We need more eyes and ears than Mr Charters has provided us with,' said Beddows. 'Anyone we see along the way who has helped us in the past, might be worth tapping up. Snouts might have word for us.'

'Kids are normally good for sneaking around in the fields. I had a group of scavengers who helped me, recently. Those burglaries along Charles Street, where some of our Irish traveller friends were suspected. They found them for me rather quickly,' said Shepherd.

'Don't suppose you can point us in their general direction?'

'I might know where we can find them.'

'Lead on, Mr Shepherd, find us our bloodhounds.'

Shepherd led Beddows along Granby Street, and across London Road, into the new area along Conduit Street, over Sparkenhoe Street, into Upper Conduit Street. The roads led across to the county side of the workhouse and into the fields beyond.

'There are some spinneys at the rear of the workhouse, between here and the railway. Some of the staff who really care for the young waifs and strays risk their jobs and livelihoods by handing crusts and leftover vegetables to them. Not much, but better than nothing.'

'Better than living in there, too, I suppose, if living is even the right word to use. I hear tell that life is made so hard in these places, to deter too many people seeking the support of the institution and encourage them to find their own means. Little wonder we have so much crime.'

'Getting soft, Beddows?'

'Not me. Little buggers probably have a much better life on the outside. I wouldn't want to be cooped up. Prison by another name, and breaking rock is no better than the crank.'

'These little urchins make a few coins scavenging the waste in the tips along Belgrave Road, the other side of the cricket ground. Never ceases to amaze me what they find. I hear old clay pipes sell well at the moment, once they've been cleaned up.'

'So a ha'penny or two might help them along the way?' said Beddows.

'A ha'penny? They'll be after a bit more than that. Let's see what they say.'

The fields between the workhouse and the High Fields to the east of the borough were high with corn, and the air was thick with flying insects. Many folk told of stories of the night soil men dumping their human waste over the fields, which had encouraged crop growth. Care had to be taken as to where to stray, although it was not that much better in the streets.

Along common ground, the odd old nag roamed free - too old to work and too tough for most to consider eating. The farm fields, higher up the hill towards the Evington Lane were full of cattle and sheep, and the sound of the country prevailed, apart from the odd train whistle.

Sounds of children squealing and shouting could be heard as the men approached a turn in a footpath that had been worn through the vegetation.

A shrill whistle broke the other noise, and a small gang of young males, with one or two tough looking tomboys stood across the footpath.

'Where d'you think you're going, mister?' said a bigger boy, standing at the front of the group.

Ripples of laughter broke out within the group.

'Shit, one's a copper, run!' yelled someone in the group.

'No, hang about, we need your help,' shouted Shepherd, as the group dispersed in all directions. 'There's some coin in it for you.'

The youngsters all stopped dead, simultaneously, at the sound of some coin.

'How come?' said the bigger boy.

'Remember me?' said Shepherd. 'You helped me before when I was looking for some gypsies.'

'I weren't here, then,' said the bigger boy.

'Are you the leader of this merry little band?' said Beddows.

'Could be. Depends.'

'Depends on what?' said Beddows.

'Ain't had today's scrap, yet.'

'Today's scrap?'

'Best fighter on the day sorts out the leader. Then everyone else does what he says for the day.'

'Or her,' shouted a very boyish looking girl, tall and unhealthily bony, almost skeletal, with infected pustules all over her grimy face. Her hair had been chopped short and ragged. An old jacket was clumsily tied around her top, and half-legged breeches that had long seem better days covered her dirty legs. The girl jumped on the bigger boy's back and began to strike him with heavy blows, causing him to fall over, at which point she straddled him, not stopping the onslaught.

The group behind her wailed with laughter, and the boy on the floor began to bleed from his nose and top lip.

'Stop it, you win,' shouted the boy, crossing his arms across his face under the torrent of blows, tears in his eyes.

'I normally do, don't I?' she laughed.

'What's your name?' said Beddows, directing his attention to the victor.

'None of your feckin' business' the girl spat back.

'Do you want a smack from me?' said Beddows. 'I'm the Leader today, if you want some coin.'

The girl glared at Beddows.

'What's your name? I Shalln't ask again. I'll ask someone else and they can have the coin.'

'Smack a girl, would you?' the girl hissed, taking up a fighting stance.

'Oh, believe me, I would, if pushed.' Beddows said, straight faced.

'You don't behave like many girls I've met,' said Shepherd. He noticed the scars and calluses on her knuckles, and signs of fist fighting.

'And there aren't many like me, not up here anyhow. Some down in Green Street, but they're feckin' Mick's and that don't count.'

'You sound a bit like a Mick, yourself, to be sure,' said Beddows, grinning.

'Keeps most people off my back,' she replied.

'Now we have that established, what's your name?'

'The name is Queenie. I ain't got a real name. I got passed to somebody in the workhouse when I was a baby. Ain't got real family and never got told my given name, but Queenie is what this lot call me.'

'I've heard that name before,' said Shepherd.

'And so you should. I'm the smart one in this gang, as well as the toughest, and people around here steer clear of me these days. I can write, you know.'

'And where can we find you, normally?' said Beddows.

'Not very good coppers, are you? Thought you would know that.'

'Sergeant Beddows doesn't know you, but I do. How do you think we found you?'

'I know you, too,' said a younger boy from the group behind. 'You gave us a right good bit of coin, last time. Bought us some real bread and soup, it did.'

'Well, we need your help again. Are you going to help us? Do you want some more coin?' said Beddows.

'What do we have to do?' said Queenie.

'We need to find two men. Possibly three. We think they may be hiding, up in the fields beyond the racecourse. Anywhere between Aylestone on one side, and the London Road on the other, I would suggest,' said Beddows.

'That's a lot of places to look. There's lots of Romanies down there at the moment as well, for a wedding, and they don't like us going near them.'

'The two men we think we may find together are from the circus that arrived in the borough. They are very blond, younger than my colleague, here, and both have very bright blue eyes. They will talk with a strange accent,' said Beddows.

'And they are very agile, and can climb, so trees may be hiding places,' said Shepherd.

'What they done?' said Queenie?

'They killed someone,' said Beddows.

'Bleedin' hell,' said the boy with the bloody nose and lip. 'And I thought Queenie was dangerous.'

'We don't want you going near them. We just need to know where they are. They were last seen on the edge of the racecourse. They might be gone for all we know, but if they haven't we need to catch up with them.'

'That's worth more than bread and soup,' said the young boy, who had helped Shepherd, previously.

Looking around at the group, he noticed that they were all bare footed, and their clothes were falling apart. It was clear they had not eaten what many would consider a proper meal, for some time, and were pale skinned and dark eyed.

'We can certainly make sure you have full bellies for a day or two, but there might be some more, possibly some proper reward.' said Shepherd.

'That's confident of you, Constable Shepherd,' whispered Beddows, his face close to what was left of Shepherd's ear.

'I was thinking that some of the town's business folk may feel benevolent towards them, if they help us,' said Shepherd.

'Let's not get ahead of ourselves. Let's find the blighters first.'

'What do we have to do?' said Queenie.

'Find them for us. Look anywhere and everywhere. You lot can run further in a few minutes that we walk in a morning or afternoon, so you can get further than either of us. If you see them, or think you can, there are constables at each main road junction along the southern side of the borough. Some constables from the county may also be hanging around on roads. Let any one of them know, or send word to the borough police station if you can't find anyone else,' said Beddows.

'We won't be far away, either' said Shepherd.

'And how and when will you pay us?' said Queenie.

'We will pay you, either way, depending on if you find them or not. If you find them, the better the chance of a fatter purse,' said Beddows.

'Right you lot. You know what you're looking for? Get off

with you, and meet back here tonight. I got a pipe and some baccy for us for later,' said Queenie. 'Won't say how I came by it, not with coppers listening.' The girl grinned, wildly, winking at Beddows.

'And if you don't find them today, the same is wanted tomorrow,' said Beddows. 'Same arrangements apply. We will be back here later, too, if you don't get back to us first.'

A flurry of dirty bare feet and the scavengers disappeared into the fields and towards the county.

'What about us?' said Shepherd.

'The racecourse, first. See who is about and what is known. The early turn should have been asking questions of travellers, already, and I want to know what they've picked up.'

'And then?'

'And then, I want you back to meet this lot, later. I shall be off to see Miss MacCormack, as I said earlier.'

'You seem to have a thing about Miss MacCormack. Mind, young Queenie seems to have a soft spot for you, also.'

'Saying things like that could get me in big trouble, Shepherd. I have no thoughts for Miss MacCormack other than as the mother of one of three possible suspects for murder. Be wary about what you think and what you say, I don't want a falling out with you.'

'Sorry, Beddows. I didn't mean...'

'Just cut it out. Enough said.'

The two men set off for the racecourse amidst uncomfortable silence.

The Romany wedding

The mid afternoon heat continued taking its toll on the people of Leicester. Some of the richer residents had taken to an afternoon perambulation around the green area that had been provided, supported by the Duke of Rutland for the annual horse race week. The stroll up along New Walk provided shade from the tall housing that had sprung up or still being built, and the canopy of trees along its route.

The park itself was different altogether, and apart for a few ladies with parasols, and young children playing with their hoops and tops, few ventured out into the sun. Family pet dogs ran freely, stealing the toys and causing the children to chase them, to the delight of child and dog. An array of smart coaches and traps were stood around the perimeter, along London Road, and the coachmen and horses awaited their owners' return.

A small cluster of Romany carts and tents and a large caravan sat in an area on the fringe of the racecourse, down towards the rear of the asylum, out of sight of most.

This would be a good group to challenge, if their colleagues had not done so already. Not surprisingly, not one constable had been seen at the junction of the London Road at the old gallows by the Evington turn, or at the end of Occupation Road, where it joined the Knighton Mile.

Probably sat in a favoured hostelry, supping warm ale. Many could just not be trusted to follow simple orders, Beddows mused.

'I'll have their guts for garters,' bellowed Beddows,

ominously. 'If they let these men get away, they want stringing up themselves.'

'Out of sight, out of mind, Beddows. Lazy buggers and all will have a thought out excuse.'

'I'll see about them later.'

The two men approached the Romanies. Dogs barked at their approach, running up, sniffing or growling. Beddows hated dogs and kicked out at a scruffy brown mongrel which snapped at his trouser bottoms, sending it scurrying, before it got back to its feet and thought about another go. Saliva dribbled from its teeth.

'Mind that one, Beddows, you don't want a dog bite.'

'Had plenty of them over the years. Want to see my scars? Bleeding people always have dogs running loose. None of them bite, the owners always say.'

'Who is in charge here?' Shepherd asked, scanning the olive skinned faces staring at them.

'I'm the Rom Baro,' said an older man, sat on a small stool by the fire. 'The boss - that's me.' The man drew on a narrow, short pipe, embers glowing as he inhaled. Shepherd had always been wary of these people and their strange language and practices. He could never tell between the true Romany and the Irish tinkers who had come over in the famine. The Romany folk were often polite and helpful. The tinkers were rough and ready, and always seems to want to fight.

'What are you here for?' said Beddows.

'An Abiav,' said the man. 'A Romany wedding feast. This is *our* stopping place. Nobody dares bother us.'

'This is their normal stop-over place, when they come to Leicester' said Beddows, nodding to the older man.

'Seen any other strangers nearby?' said Shepherd.

'What do you want to know for?' said a younger man, hunkering next to the older man.'

'We're looking for two men, blond haired, with blue eyes, young and fit,' said Shepherd.

'Dickin,' said Beddows, pointing two fingers at his eyes.
'We're not stupid, Mister,' said the younger man.
'Who are you, anyway?' said the older man.
'Police,' said Beddows.
'Kushti, no problem for us then?'
'Kushti,' Beddows assured them. 'No problem for you folk.'
'Thought that was army speak?' said Shepherd.
'Our lads brought it back from India. Most of the Romany comes from Indian roots, I understand. The army liked some of the words.'
'You want some scran?' said a woman, dressed in black, with a scarf over her head and around her face, stirring a large metal pot. A stew by the looks of it. It smelled good. More than could be said of the woman.
The older man walked over to the caravan and came back with an earthenware jug and some small, well worn, drinking glasses. He placed the glasses on the grass, and poured clear liquid into each glass, before handing one to each of the constables and to his woman.
'What's this?' said Shepherd.
'Probably Poteen,' said Beddows. 'Fire water that they distil themselves. Learned off the Irish tinkers. Very popular and gives you a bloody great headache, as I recall.'
'But you don't drink,' said Shepherd
'Don't offend them, I'll manage,' said Beddows.
'Satismos,' called out the older man, smiling, raising his glass.
'Satismos' Beddows replied.
The glasses were raised all around, and the liquid drank. Shepherd coughed and felt instant heat in his mouth and throat, moving down across his chest. The Romanies burst out laughing and started pointing, giving Beddows time and opportunity to spit his onto the grass,

undetected. The warm liquid burned his mouth and gums, and for a moment he considered swallowing, but his past haunted him.

'God's teeth,' said Shepherd, regaining his breath. 'That's the devil's brew.'

'They're alright with us now, though,' said Beddows. 'Told you the Romany folk were okay. Just don't go upsetting them.'

'That's a nice caravan you have,' said Shepherd, eyeing up the tall, narrow wagon, complete with wooden walls and roof, windows and door. Pots and pans hung down off straps and twine under a canopy at the top of a short set of steps.

'My new Vardo,' said the older man, still laughing. 'A beauty it is. Cost me loads of gold, from my Brothers in Newbury. That's why I'm marrying off my Chavi - I need the gold back.' The man laughed even harder. ' A daughter a man can do without, but her dowry is worth having.'

'What about our two men?' said Beddows.

'They were here yesterday, yes.' replied the old man.

'How do you know it was them?' said Shepherd.

'We have a belief in fortune and fate, Mister. My old lady is what we call a Drabarni - a fortune teller. Soon as she saw them she started mumbling, as she does. Said they were outsiders, and in for some bad luck - she saw their ghosts.'

'She saw their ghosts?'

The Romanies laughed again.

'Mister, she says that they would be mullered by morning. She's not often wrong. That's why I hang on to her. Valuable to us she is. '

'Mullered?'

'Dead. Killed. She saw money changing hands. They've wronged someone, narky, they have.'

'And you believe all that?' said Shepherd.

'They'll all believe her,' said Beddows. 'They have strong beliefs, these folk.'

'But how do you know it was the same two men we are looking for?' said Shepherd.

'When she saw you, just now, she said you were in the vision she had, too. The Hunters are coming, she said.'

'Good job Nimrod Hatter isn't with us,' Beddows laughed.

'Where did you last see them?' said Shepherd.

'With another Mister. Tall, dark haired, scruffy, he was. Went off that way,' said the younger man, pointing towards the fields of the Freeman's Common.

The old man stood up and filled the glasses again. Beddows put his hand over his and winked, but Shepherd was too slow. The old man looked on in anticipation, and the Romanies broke out laughing again. The sun reflected off two rows of perfect gold teeth, and Shepherd grimaced as he tipped back the small vessel.

*****

'So, allegedly, all three men may have been together, as late as yesterday evening?' said Shepherd, excitedly, as they started off towards the common.

'Seems so, if we can believe their tale.' Beddows was open minded.

'Then we may have a chance of catching all three within the county or borough, if we are lucky?'

'If they aren't already dead - well, the two brothers, anyway.' Beddows sounded almost disappointed.

'What if they are?'

'Then it means that Eibhlin MacCormack's son, Michael, could now be responsible for more deaths. I hope to God he isn't. He just doesn't sound like our killer.' said Beddows, confidently.

Shepherd was surprised, again, at Beddows apparent

lack of suspicion towards Michael Lenihan.

'We'd best hope the Romany woman was wrong. I don't take with all that superstition, anyway,' said Shepherd.

'Never rule out what can't be explained, Shepherd. I've had dealings with these folk before, and they have a strange habit of getting things right. Would have hung as witches, years ago. Inspector Hatter would probably still string them up for it.'

'And you for putting him in The King and Crown...'
Shepherd winked.

'Probably right. If he gets his hands on any of this lot, I wouldn't hold a hope for any of them,' said Beddows.

'He thinks he has a head start on us by returning to London so quickly, but that may just have changed.'

*****

The two men left the campsite behind them, and reached the first fields at the rear of the asylum at the far end of Occupation Road, where the Knighton Mile, leading uphill to Wigston, crossed below and beyond the daunting building.

The pitiful wail of the inmates could be heard, clearly over cattle and birdsong. Shepherd often considered that both the asylum and the workhouse were so similar, that at times he confused one for another. Sad, lonely, helpless souls were trapped in each.

The people in the fields at this end of the borough began to change, and the well to do from the area beyond the racecourse disappeared, and farmers and farm labourers became more the norm.

Clouds of red dust sat high above some fields as ploughs were drawn through the dry earth, or beasts were moved from fields to longer grass.

The area was a difficult terrain to explore, and both men were glad of the assistance of the scavengers.

Thick areas of trees and high bush filled the vista. Stood at the corner, looking down onto the Knighton Mile hill, Shepherd spotted a constable, well concealed in the hedgerow, giving him a good view of passing pedestrians and carts.

Shepherd could see from the man's disposition that it was one of the better constables from the early turn, Daniel Dickens, sensibly keeping out of view and also out of the intense heat under the fragrant vegetation. Dickens raised his hand and touched the rim of his top hat, as to acknowledge their presence. He waited for them to come to him. In the hedgerow behind him, he had a small flask, and a pack of sandwiches, which was open. A bluebottle worked over the edge of the thick bread, licking at whatever filling ran onto the paper below.

'Afternoon, Dickens,' said Shepherd, slumping onto the grassy knoll alongside, taking the weight off his sore feet. Hobnails were heavy and rough and he felt the urge to remove his boots and rub his feet. Beddows sat down alongside him. A bee buzzed around his head. Beddows swiped out, but the bee was undeterred. It soon flew up into the canopy to join all the others, feasting on the flowers.

'Can you smell the elderflower?' said Shepherd, picking at a bunch of ripening black berries, which he put to his mouth, sucking in the bittersweet fruit.

'You and your bloody country habits,' said Beddows, who was not a fan of fruit.

'What have you got to tell us?' asked Beddows.

'Quiet for a Sunday, really. A couple of young scavengers came by, earlier, trying to sell me a dog. Said they were working for you, Shepherd.'

'That's right. Young hearts and legs, and extra eyes and ears.'

'A couple of carriages heading out to Wigston. One was

the stagecoach which drops off at the railway. Only one chap on that, off to his daughter's at Kilby for tea. The other - a haywain - had some farm labourers and was taking them to Knighton Fields for labouring. One or two travellers on horseback, off to the county. Nobody fitting the description of your men.'

'Seen any of our colleagues from the county?' said Shepherd, interested to see whether they seemed interested.

'Saw a sergeant in a horse and trap, a while back. Came up as far as the mile turn, by Knighton junction, then turned around and went back. Probably realised he was at the boundary. Didn't see me, which is how I planned it. See, but not be seen.'

'Good for you. Shame your other colleagues aren't so astute and considered,' said Beddows, aware of the fact that there were some other bright constables coming through. 'Hope for you yet, Dickens.'

'Anyone you've seen camped or signs of any camps?' said Shepherd.

'There was a clearing about 200 yards back, where someone had slept. A burned out fire and some bits of well chewed animal bone. Probably a rabbit been poached and turned on the fire. No signs of life, otherwise.'

'Anyone you've come across seen anything?' said Beddows.

'One or two vagrants that I know who come out here for a rabbit or two themselves. Couple of folk going to the asylum, but none had seen anyone fitting the description. I mentioned Americans or strange accents and they looked at me gone out. Don't think they've been further than around these fields and hadn't a clue what I was on about.'

'You came prepared then?' said Shepherd, eyeing the man's snap and flask.

'Sergeant Kettle told us to be prepared for a long day. Him and Inspector Chapman managed to get it for us before we left the racecourse. One of them has a mate in The Marquis Wellington. Made us all some snap and some lemonade. Sergeant Kettle stopped along the walk to pick them up and hand them out.'

'Bloody hell,' said Beddows. 'What is the job coming to? And still your colleagues will be filching whatever they can. Your mate on London Road has disappeared, so probably swigging ale, somewhere.'

'Shagging, more like. Has a girl at the farm cottages, just down the Evington footpath. Knew it was a mistake posting him there,' said Dickens.

'Drinking; shagging; bloody waste of time.' Beddows shook his head.

'Couldn't agree more,' said Dickens. 'Don't want to suffer the wrath of Head Constable Charters. I hear he can bring a man to tears.'

'Trust me, as one who knows,' said Beddows, 'you have the right idea!'

'Keep them peeled,' said Shepherd, 'we're off to the common.'

*****

Crossing over the Knighton Mile, as the bells across the borough struck five, Shepherd and Beddows climbed the slight rise above the common, to a point where they had astounding views of the south of the borough. From here, to the right, they could see the infirmary, The county Gaol and The Bridewell, sitting in front of the emerging factories.

In front of them they could look down to Raw Dykes, where the Roman settlement had allegedly extended, and to the river and meadows leading to Aylestone.

To their left the common extended beyond the Midland

Railway lines and to the Saffron Lane and Knighton. The sun, bright and high above them caused them to shield their eyes as they scanned the scene before them. There were small numbers of people everywhere, working, playing, poaching, fishing. The sun glinted off farm implements and scythes that could be seen, swinging in the workers hands, as far as the eye could see.

It also made it apparent that this was a harder task than they may have first considered.

Only two main roads, which should be monitored at both borough and county intersections, once the road split below the old gallows post at the point where Saffron Lane went off to the left and the road to Aylestone and Lutterworth to the right. However, the fields were a likely place of safety for the suspects, and it was in these fields that Beddows guts told him that they would be more likely found.

The scavengers would struggle, even with youth on their side, and a stroke of luck might be needed. It would unlikely be resolved in one day, Shepherd recognised. But if someone was to be found, the scavengers would find them, and he suspected they would also be growing in number, as one gang would no doubt be challenged by another and they would be attracted by the prospect of coin. So Shepherd hoped.

'Going to be a bugger for the scavengers,' he proposed. 'I bet the little sods aren't wasting any time,' Beddows replied. 'But you're right. We need to leave it to them or to our colleagues on the roads, to give us some news. In the meantime, we have other things to be doing.'

'What do you suggest?'

'I want you to go off and see the window cleaners. Then we need to start talking to snouts, and see what rumours abound. That's what I want you to get on with.'

'And what do you have in mind?'

'I am off to see Miss MacCormack at the circus. I want to know more about Michael Lenihan and I also want to have a word with some of the other folk down there. I need to know about Miss MacCormack and what and who we are dealing with. Can we really trust her?'

'I was starting to think you had already made up your mind about Miss MacCormack,' said Shepherd, cautious after the earlier response.

'Never assume, Shepherd. It takes a lot of instinct to get the most out of folk. I might seem friendly or sympathetic to her situation, but a suspect is a suspect, and a murder suspect is my main concern. *Without fear or favour,* Shepherd. Remember that...'

Cramant's Yard

The two men separated at the end of Granby Street, and Beddows set off eastwards through the little streets below the workhouse, towards Humberstone Road, and Barker's Ground. He was looking forward for some time away from Shepherd, who was becoming a little critical of his judgement. A break would do them both good. Shepherd in the meantime headed into the borough, and towards the shabby yards at the end of King Street, where he sought the window cleaners who had last been to the Paget's address.

Cramant's Yard was a small, dreary collection of shabby one up, one down dwellings, the most of which housed local workers and tradesmen. Tailors, cobblers, button makers and in this case, window cleaners. Some were Jewish settlers from Eastern Europe that were starting to make a presence in the area.

Entering the yard from King Street, a motley collection of children stood around looking in towards one of the communal privies - earth closets - from which loud grunts and yells were to be heard. The kids howled with laughter and one or two were on their hands and knees trying to look under the flimsy door, holding their noses. A couple of women were bringing in thread-bare washing from a criss-cross of lines, removing grey sheets and well worn clothing. Life seemed cheerful given the poverty they endured.

'What are you lot laughing at?' Shepherd asked the kids.

'Old Mr Williams has ate something bad. Must have a real bad dose of the shits. Been in there for ages, moaning and grunting, shouting out.'

'Perhaps he's really poorly.' said Shepherd, reflecting on the joys of sitting across the plank in his Aunt's closet, and having the squits. Didn't make for pleasant memories. How the night-soil men could do their jobs defied Shepherd's understanding? Digging out everyone's waste, pouring it into their little carts before tipping the contents on the tips along Belgrave Road, or as many did, in the river, before washing the carts down with the same foul river water.

'Mr Williams. Are you okay?' Shepherd called out, concerned, given how long the children said he had likely been there, and the noises he was making.

'I'm stuck fast.' came the strained reply.

'Open the door,' said Shepherd.

'Can't reach the latch,' came the reply.

Shepherd took a deep breath and peered over the top of the door. Below he saw the bald pate of a corpulent, elderly male. It became apparent in the limited light, that the plank across the closet had broken, and the man had fallen backwards into the hole. He was wedged, with his arms across the edges at shoulder level, and his legs poking out, forwards. Only his arms, legs and corpulence stopped him from falling in deeper, and probably to an unpleasant end, as had befallen many, over the years.

Shepherd leaned over and tried to reach the lock, but it was too low down. A simple wooden peg across two bent nails, simple but highly effective.

'One of you fancy giving me a hand, and if I hold you, to open the door for me?'

The kids took one look at Shepherd, realised the implication, and ran off in great haste. It seemed to be becoming a habit.

'What you doing frightening our young uns?' bellowed a woman of similar age and build to Mr Williams.

'I just asked one to help me open the closet door. Mr

Williams appears to have had an accident.'
'Silly old bugger. Broken our seat again?' said the
woman. 'Wanted a shit myself, shortly. Been waiting all
day, and now me guts are bubbling. Done this before he
has.'
'Can I help?' said a young man, just entering the yard, a
short wooden ladder under one arm.
'Just the job. I need to get the door open. Mr Williams
has fallen into the closet.'
The young man laughed, bringing the ladder up against
the upright post on the outer edge of the door, climbing
up and leaning over. Shepherd could hear him retching,
instantly.
'Jesus, the stench is bad. What you been eating Walter?'
addressing the trapped man.
The door came open, revealing the full humour of the
man's plight.
Shepherd and the young man reached in to the confined
space, and grabbed an arm each, pulling, gingerly.
Slowly the man began to rise from the closet, and with
every inch, the stench got worse.
A woman came and stood alongside the door, with a
large bucket of dirty water. Before either man could say
anything, the water was thrown, unceremoniously, over
the man's filthy body, fortunately missing both helpers.
'You dirty old bugger. Busted the plank again? You can
get yourself cleaned up and put it right before you do
anything else. I shall be late for church again, you dirty
old sod.'
The man, now stood upright, his shirt fouled and wet,
and offering him very little dignity, started cursing. The
woman grabbed him by the scruff of his neck, pulled
him into the centre of the yard, and tipped a further
bucket of cloudy water over him.
'He's alright now. His old lady has him sorted,' said the
younger man. 'Thanks for that. My dad and me had to

get him out last time.'

'Are you Mr Allardyce, by any chance?' said Shepherd.

'That's right, the younger one. And who are you?'

'I am Constable Shepherd. I need to speak to you and your Father about a recent burglary.'

'Poor Mr Paget, I assume? Father and me do the windows there. We were there last Tuesday. Always the same day that we call and do them.'

'Is your Father about?'

'He should be having tea, about this time on a Sunday, if he's got any sense. Keeping out of the way of what's been going on out here.' The man looked towards a low ground floor window in the yard, with dirty curtains pulled partially across. The curtains twitched as the men looked on.

'He'll have been watching. Bugger he is. Don't like the Williams. Wouldn't help if their hovel was on fire.'

Entering the hovel, just a single room with a small door in the corner, leading to a short flight of stairs and, no doubt, a similar sized bedroom. It reminded Shepherd of Cock Muck Hill. It smelled lived in. Dampness and coal prevailed, even though it would have been some time since a fire was last needed.

A middle aged man was sat at a small table with an opened newspaper laid out upon it. A small pair of spectacles that had seen better days was resting on his nose. The man traced his index finger across lines of small text.

'Struggles to read at the best of times,' said his son. 'I don't know why he bothers. Blind as a bat without the spectacles.'

Shepherd wondered how he could see that a window had been cleaned, given his demeanour, reading.

'Mr Allardyce?' said Shepherd.

'Mr Allardyce Senior, that's me.'

'I am Constable Shepherd, and I need to talk to you and

your son about the recent burglary on New Walk.'
'So you're one of these detectives that we have been reading about in the Chronicle, costing the borough more money, I understand?'
'I'm only out of uniform temporarily, helping the detectives.'
'We thought someone would be round. He died, I hear. Didn't think it would be a detective,' said the Father, who seemed impressed.
'What exactly do you want to talk to us about, Constable?' said the younger man.
'I understand you were the last two people to clean the Paget's windows, last week?'
'Suppose that's right. Never said they have anyone else go round.' said the older man.
'I would like to look at your hands, your fingers in particular, if I may?' said Shepherd.
Both men looked puzzled.
'Why's that?' said the younger man.
'I think I am looking for a man with an unusual scar or mark on his hands.' Shepherd reached into his jacket pocket and brought out his notebook, pencil and short ruler. 'Like this,' said Shepherd, pointing to his drawings.
The men went outside with Shepherd, back into the yard, to where the sun lit them, sufficiently, to view their hands.
'I've got scars,' said the son, 'but so has most of the working population I would imagine.'
Shepherd slowly examined the hands and fingers of both men. Each had scars a plenty, but nothing resembling the crescent moon, in either size or shape.
Shepherd felt a strong sense that the scar would be found on one of the Henson brothers, and nowhere else. It was important, and he was now confident that the window cleaners had nothing obvious to do with the

crime, and would be eliminated in due course.

A trip to the circus

Beddows strolled around Barker's Ground, absorbing the noises and smells of the circus, whilst seeking out Eibhlin MacCormack.

He had sensed her shock at Hatter's determination that Michael Lenihan was, without doubt, a murderer. He had also noted Shepherd's doubts regarding his impartiality, and pondered whether he had in fact been swayed by Eibhlin MacCormack.

Her confidence, appearance and obvious flirting, which he had to admit had been rather entertaining for a man with his current disposition, impressed him, probably more than a free ticket to the circus.

He reassured himself that he could remain impartial and maintain his reputation as an honest and forthright detective, and could bring a murderer to justice. But Eibhlin had left her mark. Above anything else, he needed to know a lot more about both Eibhlin and her son, Michael Lenihan.

Beddows found her, just as she was about to head off to the main arena for the late performance. This was the performance that she hoped would get people talking, and bring in the numbers she needed through the week in order to make the business pay.

She was already distracted, and had spent most of the day toying with giving the whole, complicated, business up and trying to find her way to Michael.

However, she recognised that it would be easier for him to get word to her if she stayed put, and at least he knew where she would be for a few days.

She had bitten off more than a few loyal heads during

the last hour or two. People who cared for her, who saw her distress and realised the implications of the rumours circulating around the campsite.

Nobody believed that Michael Lenihan was a burglar, let alone a murderer. The Henson boys, perhaps, who were young, self-confident, hungry, full of lust for living. Now, they could be tempted, but not Michael.

The more people tried to reassure her, the harder she found it to contain her anger and distress, hence the head biting. She would apologise in her own way when she was better able.

As she descended from her caravan, Beddows stepped out, some yards in front of her.

She briefly made eye contact, before casting her eyes down, and avoided Beddows as best as possible.

'Miss MacCormack, can I speak?'

'I thought you had already, you and your unpleasant colleague from London. What more is there to say?'

'I am not of the same mind as Mr Hatter. Neither me nor Constable Shepherd share his views. I said I would come back.'

'Well now is not the best time, as you must have been aware. The performance starts shortly, and I am really busy.' The tone of her voice cut cold, sharp, like an icy wind.

'I hadn't realised the time, to be honest, it has been a rather long day already.' said Beddows, humbly.

'Have you somewhere else to be?' said Eibhlin, her eyes making contact with Beddows', fleetingly.

'I am in no rush.'

'Have you seen a circus before?'

'No, never had cause.'

'Then come along with me. I will sit you down and get the show started. We can speak as best we can through the performance, and then afterwards, I will have more of a chance.' A brief smile made Beddows feel better.

He took time to observe her. She looked so much taller in her circus uniform. A bright red thigh length coat over a very lacy black skirt and riding boots. A white blouse, and a small, scaled down top hat, painted with an American Stars and Stripes flag. Her hair had been plaited and wound into a tidy knot.

White circus makeup made her hair stand out even more, and bright red colouring enhance the fullness of her lips. She was an exceptionally fine looking woman, Beddows considered. Even the more attractive local girls seemed pale and grey, in comparison.

'What's the story of the outfit?

'What if I was to tell you, we got our hands on a load of British Army tunics that were abandoned after the war, and somebody thought they would make a fun addition to our wardrobe?'

Beddows was still working out if she was mocking him, the British, or both, or just having fun with him, when she touched his arm, gently, and reassured him.

'Only joking, Sergeant. One of my team was asked the same question and that was his answer. Thought it might come in handy, one day.'

'Not the little man we bumped into on Saturday. Henry Pensylva?'

'How did you guess?'

'He seemed a funny man, with a wry humour.'

'He is a pain in the butt, Sergeant. A man who likes the ladies, and a man who likes the good life. Sadly he has upset a lot of husbands along the way. But he does have some great little stories to tell, and he keeps me laughing, which is good in this business.'

'You look very smart, may I say.'

'Why, thank you Sergeant Beddows.'

'Why don't you Call me John, or just Beddows. I would prefer that.'

'I thought you were here on business?'

'I am, but I find that sometimes it pays to be a little more easy going.'

'Well, let's see how we get on then, Beddows. Now, sit yourself down over there, and enjoy the show. I'll get back to you shortly.'

Beddows sat down in a small stall, by the main entrance to an arena, marked out with small barrels, and covered in sawdust.

For one horrible, fleeting moment, he found himself back in the dungeon beneath The Stoker's Arms. The darkness of the tent; the flicker of oil drum lights; the smell of sawdust and animals. How could smells and feelings instantly trigger such memories?

Beddows considered that this was a first rate seat, as he had the best view of the performance and performers. The slick transition, managed by bands of labourers, of one type of artist to another was impressive. From high rope swings with safety nets, to cages holding Lions, each change was done safely and with precision.

As the elephants were brought in for the crowd to observe, Beddows was shocked at their size and how difficult they were to handle. He wondered what the borough would do if one was to break free. Probably need to be shot. He looked around at the circus hands for evidence of a musket, but saw nothing. The noise from the crowd, many seeing such beasts for the first time, was a thunderous mix of shock and awe.

The whole performance lasted for about one and a half hours, during which he had only a brief chance to talk to Eibhlin, who was constantly talking to performers, stroking or consoling small children who cried at some acts, and shaking hands with happy customers.

As the last public slipped away from the large tent, Eibhlin walked back to Beddows. She looked hot, and the white makeup had run in places, leaving flesh exposed in oddly shaped lines. Her hair had started to come adrift, and she looked comfortable as she removed her tiny top hat, and shook loose the mane of red hair.

'Goodness, do I need a drink!' she exclaimed. 'Just need to have a word with my right hand man, who will make sure everyone is safe and the animals are okay, and I shall be with you.'

Beddows considered how confident and assertive Eibhlin came across compared to most English women he encountered in his daily life. Perhaps running a business gave her such self confidence. She was nobody's fool, no shrinking violet. English women were still really just chattels, and apart from the Monarch, played a bit part in a male society. Not so with this lady!

On completion of her business, Eibhlin led Beddows towards her private caravan. Her red coat had now been removed and was casually thrown over her right shoulder, as she strode across the worn grass. Small birds sat along the edge of the caravan roof, and birdsong filled the air, which was warm, and pleasantly fresh, considering the proximity to the slaughterhouses and yards of Humberstone Gate, and the tips along the Belgrave Road, behind them.

Eibhlin's black lace skirt flowed, even with the large bustle, and Beddows watched the sway of her hips and the length of her stride. Such a willowy frame. A narrow waist, accentuating her bust, and athletic shoulders, she cut a fine figure of a woman. Captivating, in fact.

At the caravan, the summer sun was still bright enough to allow Beddows a view of the sumptuous interior. Eibhlin picked up a packet of lucifers and lit a series of ornate oil lamps, which flooded the van with warm yellow light.

Probably not much smaller than the parlour in his house in Tower Street, the van had a comfortable looking bed across the full width. A small table appeared fixed to one side, and a chair sat beneath. A cupboard opposite with clothes hanging. Assorted china and glassware on shelving around the walls gave a cosy impression. He had anticipated a scattering here and a scattering there, and piles of all sorts, as would likely follow a transient existence. He was pleasantly surprised. Everything had a homely, feminine touch, in contrast to the dull, functionality of Mrs Beddows' parlour.

Eibhlin opened a small cupboard at the foot of the bed, and took out a partially consumed bottle of liquor.

'Whiskey?' Beddows enquired.

'Bourbon,' Eibhlin replied, gathering two small glasses which she pinched between two fingers, placing them on the table, next to the bottle. 'I take it you will join me, Beddows?'

'Not for me,' Beddows replied. 'There's a story there, but not for now, but please, don't let me stop you.'

'Never seen the inside of a caravan?' Eibhlin asked.

'Not like this. I am impressed with how tidy you keep it. Very cosy. Very lady like.'

'I have an untidy mind, Beddows. I need order to survive. As for lady like, I am shocked.' She raised an eyebrow and laughed. The brogue of her Irish upbringing rang through.

'You like a drink?'

'After a day like today, I need a drink. I don't drink all the time, don't get the wrong impression, but I can't afford to drink too often with everything going on. Dulls my senses,' Eibhlin explained.

'I used to drink, but the demons took over, and caused me a lot of grief. Now I drink tea.'

'I have tea, can I make you a pot?' as she opened another cupboard and pulled out a small box. Inside was a tiny teapot, a tea caddy, and a cup and saucer. 'A wedding present,' she said.

'I didn't think you were married?'

'I'm not, nor ever have I been. It was bought for me by some sweet ladies, some years ago, when Michael's Father was in my life. What might have been, but never was.'

'Something happened to him?' Beddows enquired.

'He preferred card rooms and bourbon, to bedrooms and me. He didn't stay around long when he found I was with child. He runs a gambling house in a place called New Orleans, now, and makes a lot of money. Doesn't offer us a bean.'

'Sorry, I didn't mean to pry.'

Eibhlin stepped down to the foot of the steps to her van, and took a small metal pot which she filled with water from a jug, before placing it over the campfire which folk from nearby tents were also utilising.

'Won't take long to boil.'

'That's very kind of you, I'm parched. It was so hot in your arena.'

'It always is. Did you see what it did to my makeup?' she laughed, nervously, almost embarrassed at how she thought she must look. She reached for a small mirror at the side of her doorway.

'You look fine, but I don't like the heat.' Beddows responded.

'What about you. Do policemen get married in England? Lawmen in America have a history of not living long, and marriage is a dying tradition in their community.'

'I am married. That being said, not happily so. My job has taken its toll on my relationship, and my wife is only my wife by law. She despises me and the job, and I her.'

'Why stay with her then? It's a changing world and you have divorce here, I take it?'

'Divorce is not an option for most folk. Very complicated and expensive I understand. Cheaper to get on with life and wait until one of us curls up our toes.'

'Such a funny saying - curls up our toes. What does that

mean?' she smiled as she asked, tilting her head to one side, mouth open and running her tongue along her bottom lip.

'As in what happens when you die, and the body contracts. Your toes curl up.'

Eibhlin laughed. 'I love some of the quaint English sayings.'

'I'm meant to be asking you questions about Michael and why you don't feel he's our burglar or murderer.'

'And I thought we were getting there, but in a nicer way.'

'We got as far as Michael's Father. You say he is in New Orleans, and you said earlier, that if Michael was panicking, he might try and get to him.'

'He hasn't seen his Father since he was a baby. He may have taken his name, but that is his only attachment. New Orleans is in the deep south, a long way from where we originated from, amongst the Irish in New York.'

'So why say that?'

'You mean, was I trying to deceive Inspector Hatter? You bet I was. He might be scared, but he wouldn't run far. I suspect he is with someone he feels safe with in London. Your Inspector Hatter seems a very unpleasant man.'

Eibhlin filled one of the small glasses, which she had placed out, with the honey gold coloured liquid, which she tipped back and drank in one gulp.

'Boy, you drink bourbon like that?'

'Old Irish heritage is never far away, Beddows. My Grand-Daddy was the man, and everything was always 'straight down the hatch'. Mind, I needed that. A lady would have waited until you had your tea, but excuse me... I sometimes forget myself,' She laughed, wiping her lips on the back of her hand.

'Not a problems for me. Enjoy. You look like you work hard.'

'Did you enjoy the performance?'

'Very entertaining, and a privileged place to be seated.'

'I thought you might like it there. I was keeping an eye on you. You looked like the kids with their parents at times. I like to see a man laugh.'

'I laughed?' said Beddows, somewhat surprised.

'I caught you laughing, several times. The clowns with the bucket of paper that they threw over your local mayor seemed to amuse you, particularly.'

'Shame it wasn't water. His worshipfulness the Mayor is a bit of a pain in the backside, to us.'

'The lady he was with looked like she was sucking lemons.' Eibhlin laughed louder, rolling backwards slightly, on the edge of the bed. 'That's the problem with Bourbon. I get a bit loud, very quickly.'

'She is a bit of an old dragon,' said Beddows. 'She is much like Mrs Beddows.'

'I'm sorry to hear that. You seem a nice man.'

'You have hardly met me.'

'I am normally a good judge of character,' Eibhlin said, waving a finger at him. 'Stop putting yourself down, Beddows.'

'Is that the kettle boiling?' Beddows suggested, remembering the water she had put on to boil.

'Are you trying to change the conversation, or are you just thirsty?' Eibhlin looked hard for a response. Beddows felt his face flush.

'You're a bit of a sweetie, Beddows. I like a man who reacts, naturally. I can trust you.'

'You can trust me. I can assure you of that, but you must also be aware that as a constable, I must be impartial in my enquiries. If Michael is involved, I must find him and question him.'

'You can be as impartial as you wish, Beddows. My concern is for Michael. If I know he will be treated fairly I will do everything in my power to prove his innocence.'

'That tea would be very welcome,' said Beddows, running a finger around under his warm collar, loosening the brass stud, 'and then, you can tell me about you and Michael.'

Last jobs of the day

Ten o'clock, and dusk setting in, Shepherd wandered back through the long grass and along the worn tracks at the rear of the workhouse, seeking the lair of the scavengers, illuminated in shimmering silver, the moon as large as he had seen in many a year.
Rumour had it that they had access to a tunnel that led into a cave under the workhouse, and which came out in the rocks above the railway line to the east of the station. Shepherd had never found such a tunnel, nor had anyone else. Legends of tunnels and caverns underneath the borough had abounded in times gone by, going out from the Abbey, to Stoughton fields in the south eastern edge of the county.
The smell of something cooking began to fill Shepherd's senses, and the glow of a small fire could be seen in the shadow of the grim institution, off to his left.
'Fish,' Shepherd thought.
A whistle broke the air. 'It's only the copper' a small voice could be heard to call out, appearing from a branch in the tree canopy above Shepherd, some yards away, before dropping to the ground, delicately.
The young boy led Shepherd by the wrist, down a small cutting into a spinney beyond the trees, which many would have walked past, oblivious of any occupants.
Sat around a small fire made up of brushwood, was the group of 6 young scavengers, including Queenie, their tomboy leader.
She was busy sucking in a deep lung full of something rather aromatic, from a short clay pipe. A small bag on the ground below her was filled with dried vegetation of

some sort.

'You lot are too young to smoke. Filthy habit!' Shepherd suggested.

'Bugger off, Mister. In this place you're more likely to die of hanging or overwork in the poorhouse than bad habits, even drinking the town waters. Anyway, it puts hairs on your chest, a bit like the gin, they say.'

'But you're a girl. Do girls end up with hairy tits, then?' said a young boy, very similar looking, but smaller, who was hunkered down next to her on a small tree stump. The boy laughed, and was promptly smacked around the ear by his bigger sister.

'Where do you get your baccy from?' said Shepherd.

'D'you really think we're going to tell you that? You'll be thinking we go around lifting it, and next you'll be back accusing us.' said Queenie.

'Amazing what you can find laying about in this borough,' said one of the bigger boys, sniggering. 'Just the other day, a package fell off one of them new steam trains, down the hill. Some books of some sort. Kept the fire going for days, they did.' The boy laughed.

Shepherd realised how one thing to one man was something completely different to another, and he supposed, a book would be something of pleasure to read, whereas to the scavengers they were just fuel for the fire. A strange, sad world, he thought.

'What's cooking?' said Shepherd, looking at something impaled on a long stick over the small fire.

'Just some old fish,' said Queenie.

'You have some fish in ponds around here, or down at the river?'

'This one swam out of somebody's throw aways. Rich buggers get rid of good food when it's still fit to eat. A couple of maggots or a bad smell never hurt anyone.'

The group laughed. Shepherd saw a few small potatoes cooking in the embers, under the fish. The scavengers had learned how to survive on scraps. They probably had more nourishment in their humble scratchings than the poor in the workhouse.'

'I take it you didn't find our men?' said Shepherd.

'We'd have found you if we had,' said Queenie. 'Got as far as the gibbet post on the Aylestone Road. Someone said he thought they might be camped down on Aylestone meadows, by the river. We are going there early in the morning, as soon as the sun is up.'

'Some diddikos told us we were wasting our time as they were already dead. She frightened us to death. Mad woman she was, ranting and drunk,' said the younger brother.

'I think we might have met the same woman. Don't believe everything they tell you. It's probably just the drink talking.'

'Don't you believe it, Copper. My Mammy was told by one that she would be knocked over by a horse and cart, and would be dead by Christmas. Bloody well was, down Granby Street, just like she was told. Mind, she was drunk as a judge,' another youngster declared.

'Well don't let the story stop you looking. There's still that coin to be earned. We need to find them, even if they are dead.'

'Wanna bit of fish, mister?' said the young brother, getting a smack off his sister.

'Doesn't look like you have that much. You kids enjoy it.' Shepherd thought about the smell, gagged and declined the invitation, before walking off towards Northampton Street and back towards the centre of the borough.

Disclosures

Beddows sat at the small table, sipping the warm tea, transfixed on Eibhlin's every word. A picture was now being painted of her son. Born in a remote farmstead on the edge of New York, young Eibhlin had been alone throughout the birth, and after a long and difficult labour, the boy was delivered. It was only at an age of three or four that she realised Michael was not like other children of his age. Tall for his age, but stooped. He was quiet and often sat alone, avoiding even contact with his mother. Slow to start to talk, and clumsy, she soon realised he had some difficulties, and a local physician made the connection with the difficult birth. As the family circus toured, he began to show an interest in the animals, and befriended both them and their trainers. A trapeze artist had tried, once, to get Michael involved in an act, but he froze at the top of a rope ladder, and two artists had to rescue him, climbing down holding on to him. He displayed dizziness, whenever he encountered heights or sheer drops, wherever he went. He became more use to Eibhlin as a helping hand with labouring and animal care - feeding and watering. He developed a strange, lonely stare, which made many uncomfortable in his presence. He was however, a caring and gentle man, taunted and used by many, including the Hensons.

Beddows was more confident that the man was neither a likely burglar, nor a likely a potential murder suspect for Edward Paget, and his attention must focus on apprehending the Hensons. He could not rule out, however, that Michael was not involved in some minor way, which might still lead to his undoing.

As a result of Michael's vulnerability, he would be easy prey in the hands of the ruthless Inspector Hatter, and should be located and isolated as quickly as possible. He would need to seek guidance from Head Constable Charters.

'Well, Beddows, you now know lots about Michael. Tell me about yourself.'

Eibhlin settled back, confidently reclining on the bed, as Beddows opened up to her.

*****

Shepherd's final task of the day was to make a few calls into public houses along the route back, to catch up with a few snouts. A policeman's lot...

Crossing Granby Street, Shepherd walked up and into the rear door to The Stockdale Arms, on East Street. This was an old established inn, favoured by some of the old frame knitters, a few of whom Shepherd knew well. Then it would be on to King Street and Wellington Street, before heading back to the station.

The Stockdale was a small, cosy inn, where Shepherd was well received, as were most constables. It was one place that he had occasionally 'visited' for a quick ale with one of the sergeants who might wish for a wet on the round of checking doors and windows. The licensee was sound, and trustworthy to boot. An alley through to Calais Hill gave an easy escape route, if ever compromised.

Many of the drinkers had been forced to take employment in factories like those owned by the Paget family, the Harrisons and the Corahs. Bitterness at the changes to frame knitting and the effect of working in large factories, some now with new fangled machines, made them valuable sources for what was going on that police or other borough departments often sought. They would talk freely, and information was often instantly tested around the table or in a corner, by more than one source. Shepherd's instinct told him this was the most likely place to start, and a chance of an early result.

Shepherd spotted Ernest Longbottom, a reliable snout, who had lost a hand courtesy of one of the earliest 'new' machines, and who now could only find work as a 'sweeper-upper' in his old employers' factory. Ernest was sat around a small round table, with three legs of different lengths, that rocked as each tankard was lifted or replaced. All the men sat around were smoking short pipes, and a thick, sweet smelling haze visible above the men at Shepherd's eye level.

The man nodded and waved Shepherd over. 'Evening Mr Shepherd, not seen you in for a while.'

'Evening Ernest. How's the hand?'

'Bout the same as the top of your ear, Mr Shepherd.' All the men laughed.

'Not joining us?' said Ernest.

'Not got too much time, tonight. Looking for any gossip that might be going around about the burglary and murder that happened on New Walk?'

'Paget, you mean. There'll be no love lost there. Miserable, tight bugger an' all,' said Ernest. 'Skin a flea for its blood, would Paget. Him and his Father-in-Law, Harrison. Both as bad as each other. Turn out high quality stockings and cotton goods, but only by breaking many of their workers. The kids are worked to the bone and would be better off in yonder workhouse, truth be told.'

'Who might want him dead, then?'

'How many does he employ? Count them up, and then add on the parents who care about their young uns, or at least the money they bring in. Then you might have a

realistic number.'
'Bloody hell. You paint a picture of an unpopular employer. The families all seem quite decent sorts.'
'Don't mean a thing Mr Shepherd. Don't be taken in by their manners. Money is all that drives them and they don't mind killing folk off themselves to get it.'
'Any rumours been flying around?' said Shepherd.
'Only recent, there was word that he was up to his eyes in debt. Buying more than he could afford, and to the anger of Mrs Paget's Father. Had to bail him out at a personal cost, more than once that we know of.'
'And Mr Harrison's reaction?'
'Tales tell that he was summoned to the big house on London Road, where the shouting could be heard for an hour or more. Paget left, head bowed. Told him to sort it out or he would have his posh house and factory took off him, and that his daughter would divorce him.'
'I thought somebody here might be wise as to goings on,' said Shepherd.
'That's why you come here, ain't it? You know you get what nobody else will dare tell of. Don't cost you a sight either, does it?'
'It's worth an ale for each of you at the present. More, if anyone can throw any more light on the crime.'
'The ale will do for now, and we'll see what we can pick up for you,' said Ernest, waving him stump.
'What talk of him having lots of money last week?'
'If he did, he's had it off some bugger else. Probably what got him killed,' Ernest suggested.
'Anyone heard of any other burglaries like this one, within the new factory businesses?'
'Not that I've heard of. Are you sure it was really a burglary, lad?
'That's what we need to find out. We have some suspects, but why they picked on him, as yet is a mystery.'

'Have you tried in The Globe? The men with the money are often to be found mixed in with the new businessmen, listening for opportunities. Apparently, loans on offer up there at higher rates of interest than a man could stomach, a poor man at least. We hear tales of hundreds of Guineas being loaned and handed over, and payback at double the banks' rate not unusual. Our moneyed owners are always hanging around in there, doing their dealing. No hope for the frame-knitters looking to grow.'

'Who would I talk to in order to find out how these loans are arranged?'

'I hear that one of the revenue men is a bad bastard and he picks up on what he earwigs. Offers money at high rates for keeping quiet to his Lords and Masters. Also hear it's not wise to cross him or his like.'

'Rightly so, Ernest. Ale all round I suppose?' Shepherd put his hand in his pocket, brought out a couple of shiny coins that he kept for his snouts, and bid goodnight.

*****

Eibhlin wiped a tear from her eye, sitting upright, as Beddows told of his earlier years in the job, and his life after frame-knitting.

'God, it was a lonely and thankless job. Night after night, venturing into alleyways and yards that nobody would normally dare venture, to shake door handles and windows.'

'What drove you to do it, Beddows?'

'Life as a frame knitter was done for. I heard tales of horror, of folk working in factories, and when they posted for people to become coppers, it seemed an honourable opportunity.'

'And were the fears as bad as you suggest?'

'We all had many a beating from hard men, and the odd

hard woman, too, for poking our noses where they weren't wanted.'

'Surely your judges backed you up?'

'Our magistrates hated us, and originally, openly mocked us. Poor old Samuel Simpkin had his truncheon taken off him, and was half beaten to death with it. He hung on to his prisoners, but the magistrates accused him of creating the situation himself, and that policemen should mind what they interfered in.'

'My goodness, why did anyone want to be a policeman?'

'It had its perks. It was better than the workhouse for a start. And some folk liked us. Landlords plied us with booze to turn a blind eye to the clock. Ladies of the night and lonely widows often had a warm pie or a warm bed, which some took advantage of. My mistake was to get too friendly with our publicans, and it nearly cost me my job, and that was the start of the marriage going cold.'

'You drank a lot?'

'The more I drank, the less afraid I got. I didn't feel the pain of beatings, and learned to take punishment and more importantly, to dish it out. It toughened me up, but at a cost.'

'Your wife turned against you?'

'My wife; the job; Frederick Goodyer; Robert Charters; they all played their part. I had been promoted early on, and I lost my stripes for my drinking, and a bob or two a week off my pay.'

'So what broke the situation?'

'We had a bad time here, some years ago, with the Chartists. Some saw them as the people's lifeline, but there were bullies in with them, brought in to dish out beatings. One of my best mates, George, Shepherd's uncle, was beaten to death one night in rioting. Nobody was ever brought to justice, and as a man who had stood by me through all my bad times, I vowed to find the man who killed him, and I will, one day.'

'And now?'

'Now, I have worked my way back. I am a good copper, and work with some good ones alongside me. I don't like bad people, people who are greedy or evil at a cost to others, and I am good at catching them. Sadly I spend more time doing that than I do with my wife, and she hates me and hates the job.'

'You poor man. Sounds like lawmen here are much the same as lawmen back home.'

'Life is destined to be hard, Eibhlin, and we have little choice but to grit our teeth and get on with it. Anyways, you've told me a lot about Michael, but not that much about you. Your turn now.'

'I think I need another refill, Beddows. Would you fill my glass , whilst I get you another tea. How much time do you have?'

*****

Shepherd was finding the weather and the pace of the investigation challenging. He was hot and bothered, and looked forward to an hour or so with Sally, and a chance to take off his boots and socks. He was aware he was soaked in sweat after the walk back across to Town Hall Lane, but that being said, so was everyone else in the borough that worked hard. He smelled better than most, or so Sally had assured him.

The station was quiet, and the 'late turn' Charge Sergeant, Joseph Wright, had only one or two in the cells for the morning courts.

There was no sign of Beddows, and he had not been seen by anyone else. Mr Charters was in the yard at the rear of the buildings, where his wife had some pretty flower tubs, which they were found to be watering as Shepherd stepped out.

'Ah, Shepherd, back into the office if you would.'

Charters placed his small watering can down on the floor and left it for his good lady.

'Good night, Mrs Charters.'

'Good night, Constable Shepherd.'

Shepherd held the door open and Charters followed him in.

'What do we have, so far?' said Charters.

'We now have most lines of interest started. Sergeant Kettle and his team were still up on the junctions earlier. Have they come back yet?' Shepherd enquired.

'Only just. The light has faded and we'll gain nothing more tonight.'

'We have some scavengers assisting. They are young, fast of foot, and sneaky. They've helped me before, and will start on the fields towards Aylestone in the morning. We heard tell from the Romanies that in a dream, yesterday, the elderly woman up there saw them killed by a tall dark haired man.'

'Romany myth and folklore doesn't sit well with me, Shepherd. I doubt that a dream will solve our dilemma, but see how your runners get on in the morning. And nothing else?'

'I have just been talking to a reliable snout, who says that Paget has been borrowing more than he can afford, and his Father in law has recently made veiled threats to him. But it sounds equally likely that he may have borrowed from a man in The Globe recently, possibly one of the revenue men who sneak about in there, and runs a loan business at high rates of interest.'

'Another possible interesting line of enquiry, if the burglary was to recover an outstanding debt, and get to it whilst Paget still had his hands on cash. Had Paget let it be known he was about to buy some machines with cash?'

'That's what I was pondering, Sir. The Globe may be the place where Mr Paget has made a mistake, one way or other. Do we have any contacts with The Revenue?'

'I have a contact, but I don't know what good it will do me, if one of their men is doing something underhand. They are like Masons, Shepherd. A secretive bunch. But leave that one with me. Talking of underhand dealings, I take it Inspector Hatter is no longer with us?'

'No, Sir. We saw him off first class, on a train to the Capital.'

'Thank goodness for one small mercy. What does Sergeant Beddows think of your information?'

'I haven't seen him since early evening, when we divided the outstanding tasks. I came into the borough, and Beddows headed for the circus to see Miss MacCormack.'

'Well he's not back yet.' said Charters.

'Perhaps he's still busy.'

'So it appears, Shepherd. Back here at six in the morning and we'll see what Beddows has to say then.'

Doubts and suspicions

At five forty-five on the morning of Monday, 5th of July, Shepherd sat impatiently, awaiting Beddows' arrival at the station. Unusually he was not there before him. He could not recall one single occasion when Beddows had been late for duty.

St. Martin's Church clock struck six, as Robert Charters walked into the small office at the rear.

'Where is Sergeant Beddows?'

'I have no idea, Sir,' Shepherd replied. 'I've never known him be late, before.'

'I recall days when he was late, Shepherd. I hope for his sake that he is not slipping back to those days. Get him found. I will get the early shift to look out for him.'

Shepherd set off at a brisk walk, across the top of the Market Place, along Belvoir Street, King Street and into the small, compact streets now surrounding the county gaol. It was six-thirty when he knocked on the wooden door at the front of number 36 Tower Street. People milled about, and there were the normal comings and goings at the gaol.

Shepherd heard a key rattling, and then a bolt being pulled, before the door slowly opened. A woman who he assumed was Mrs Beddows appeared in the opening, her hand shielding her eyes from the early light.

'Mrs Beddows, it's Constable Shepherd.'

'I know who you are. What do you want?'

'I need to speak to Sergeant Beddows, rather urgently.'

'Well he's not here. To be honest, it has been the best night I have had in years, so when you find him, tell him I would rather he did not return.'

'He has not been here, overnight?'

A short and solid looking woman with prematurely white hair, tied back and pinned. A round, haggard face, and chunky solid neck. Her face wore the scars of some pox, no doubt in a younger time. She wore a dowdy grey dress in some coarse fabric, under a heavy grey shawl, which seemed odd, given the current weather. Plain and harsh in appearance, her face was set in a grimace. As she crossed the room to allow him in, he noticed that she walked very slowly, painfully so, and the pain showed in her face, adding to the impression he was getting.

The room reflected her mood, dark and plain, with dark stained walls, dark furniture and a strange number of clocks. Musty, Shepherd considered, and unloved. It seemed so strange as the houses were still comparatively new, compared to many in the borough, including his Aunt's, across Oxford Street.

A small fire had been lit in the leaded grate, with a kettle above it.

'I haven't seen him since yesterday morning, early. I assumed he was still at work as he often has been over the years, but clearly not.'

'Is there anywhere else he might stay?'

'I am not his keeper, Constable Shepherd. He and I hardly speak any more. I don't go anywhere to know anything. He doesn't give a thought to me. Now, please leave me alone.'

The woman pushed the door shut, and the lock closed securely, once again.

Shepherd now appreciated why Beddows may have been so angry, of late. Mrs Beddows had hardly looked at Shepherd. She looked old and haggard, and her words were not only abrupt, but bitter. She must be hard to live with, and Shepherd could, perhaps, sympathise with Beddows. She appeared more like a mother than a wife.

So where might Beddows be? He knew what was intended to be Beddows' last call of the previous evening, thus set off towards Barker's Ground.

*****

At the same time as Shepherd walked to the circus, along the edge of the High Fields to the south of the workhouse, the young scavengers were awakening, setting off to the fields beyond Raw Dykes towards Aylestone, to where the rivers Soar and Biam ran away from the borough and off into the countryside.
It was a perfect area to camp, with fresh running water, and copious fish to tickle, in the streams. Shallow beaches and dense copses and spinneys for as far as the eye could see. The young scavengers still thought it was somewhat strange that anyone who had just murdered someone would want to hang around. They had decided that if it had been one of them, they'd have been off on their toes and probably to some other town where they could be lost. Birmingham was nearby and would easily hide a criminal, they considered. However, the Romany woman had also made them think warily. Bodies could not run away.

*****

Shepherd's arrival at Barker's Ground was not un-noticed. The campsite was awake, performers and followers already up and about, feeding and cleaning animals, practicing, washing clothing, cooking.
The ever cheerful Henry Pensylva saw Shepherd and made a direct line towards him, standing between him and Eibhlin MacCormack's caravan.
'Ah, Constable Shepherd. You are an early bird today. How might we help you?'

'I am trying to find Sergeant Beddows, who I believe may have called here last evening.'

'Ah, and so he did, Constable. So he did. And why do you think he might be here now?'

'He has not turned up for duty, this morning, which is out of character.'

'And you think he is still here?'

'I need to ask Miss MacCormack whether he said anything when he left.'

'I thought you said you thought he was still here? You seem confused, or am I sensing, a little on edge?'

'I need to speak to Miss MacCormack.'

Shepherd was becoming frustrated at the man's untimely attempt at humour, and delay. He stepped aside the small man, and approached the steps to the caravan.

'You'll be sorry. She ain't so good first thing in the morning.'

'That's the least of my worries. You haven't met my Head Constable.'

Shepherd knocked on the small door, noticing how white and dainty the flimsy lace curtains inside appeared in the morning sunshine.

Shepherd could hear nothing. He waited, briefly, before gently pressing down, trying the handle. The door came ajar, rather easily.

Slumped on a small chair, head resting on his arms, was Beddows, snoring quietly. Asleep on her side on top of the bed, still dressed in her circus regalia, was Eibhlin MacCormack.

Shepherd coughed, loudly.

Beddows woke with a start, looking around, clearly disoriented. Eibhlin began to stir, stretching her arms above her head, and her eyes slowly opening.

'Shepherd, what are you doing here?' barked Beddows, gruffly, coughing to clear his voice.

'It is gone seven o'clock in the morning. Charters is furious and wants you back at the station, now. Your wife is none too happy, either.'

'Seven? God's teeth, we must have fallen asleep.'

'Must have been all that talking,' said Eibhlin, looking unconcerned that Beddows had been found in her caravan.

'Talking?' Shepherd's voice suggested he had some doubt.

'Talking!' Beddows asserted, the strength of his anger articulated in just one short word. He glared at Shepherd.

Eibhlin attempted to reassure Shepherd. 'We had a lot to talk about Constable Shepherd, and I fear the bourbon had some effect on a lack of awareness of time.'

'Shepherd, get out of here and go back to the station. Tell Mr Charters I will be with him, shortly.'

Shepherd closed the door behind him, and set off for the unavoidable encounter with Mr Charters. He needed time to think about what he should say, and how much he should tell.

'Not going to be a good day,' he thought out aloud.

*****

Shepherd walked through the doors at Town Hall Lane, to find Charters pacing, anxiously.

'Where is Sergeant Beddows?'

'He is on his way, Sir. He should be here shortly.'

'And why am I still waiting for him, this late in the day? Why is he not with you?' Charters eyes were locked on Shepherd's face. He reached into his waistcoat, and removed a gold hunter, which he opened and examined, shaking his head.

'Sergeant Beddows will no doubt wish to explain,

himself,'
'Where was he, Constable?'
'I would rather Sergeant Beddows be allowed to explain for himself, Sir.'
'I don't care to wait. Tell me.'
'I'm sorry Sir, but I owe it to Beddows to allow him to explain for himself.'
'Constable. I shall ask you once more.'
'I feel that I cannot answer, with any certain knowledge, and that Sergeant Beddows should explain.'
'Get out of my sight, Shepherd. Go and find your scavengers.'
Shepherd needed no second bidding.
Just inside St. Martin's West, he came face to face with a furious looking Beddows.
'What have you told him?' Beddows snarled.
'I have told him nothing. Nothing at all. I have no idea what you were doing, or had been doing, and I am making no judgement. Trust me.'
'Does he know where you found me?'
'No, I told him nothing. Not my place to, is it?'
'And you think that I would start drinking again. I have no desire to drink bourbon. That is Miss MacCormack's preferred tipple.'
'You don't need to justify anything to me Beddows.'
'And where are you off to, now?'
'Mr Charters has sent me off to find the scavengers. He is not happy with me as I told him nothing.'
'Did you, or did you just protect your own arse?'
'I neither did, nor said, anything to your detriment.'
'That's so noble of you, Shepherd. We will speak later, if I am so inclined.'
'I'm sorry you feel that way, Beddows. You told me to stand up, and I did just that'
'I don't know what to make of you anymore. You seem to judge me rather a lot, of late, such as with my

relationship with Mrs Beddows.'

'I didn't know, Beddows. You never told me.'

'My private life is, or rather was, private, but now it seems It may no longer be so.'

'Mrs Beddows was rather abrupt and hostile. I understand why you may have been so angry about her.'

'You know very little, Shepherd. Your Uncle George realised my situation. I don't know what he would make of you at the moment.'

'Who is judging who, now?'

'Go and find the scavengers, whilst I face the wrath of Mr Charters.'

'Good luck, Beddows.'

'Good luck? Charters will have made his mind up already. His pompous, bible bashing background. He will have made up his mind that the 'Old Beddows' is back. One small mistake and I shall suffer because of it.'

Judgements

Beddows was unceremoniously ushered into the small rear office. Charters followed him in, slamming the door behind them, for the second time in as many days. All noise within the station stopped instantly, as the shockwave rattled through the ancient walls and flagstones.

'Tell me, Beddows, why you have arrived so late for duty?'

'I went on my enquiry with Miss MacCormack, rather later than I had anticipated, last evening. I realised that she was of considerable importance in respect of the man Michael Lenihan, her son, and a potential murder suspect. I had rather a lot of information I wanted to establish.'

'So late last evening, you went to see the mother of a murder suspect, all on your own?'

'Yes, Sir. With the shortage of resources and the lines of enquiry, Shepherd was given some tasks last night, and I followed up others. Together we could not have completed them all in the one day.'

'And why did that result in you failing to turn in this morning, knowing the importance of the enquiries you are currently undertaking?'

'As I said, Sir, I went rather late. I wanted to know as much as I could about her son. We spent a considerable time going through his upbringing, his impediments, and his demeanour, which took rather longer than I thought.'

'I sent Shepherd to find you. Where were you?'

'I would rather not say, Sir.'

'Why?'

'Personal reasons, Sir, As you are aware, things are not good at present at home, and things must have caught up with me.'

'So you slept over?'

'Yes, Sir.'

'Are you drinking again?'

'I knew you would bring that up. Can't a man ever be trusted again. I made a mistake many years ago, and vowed never again. Never again, and I meant it. No, Sir, I am not drinking.'

'Why did Shepherd have to go to Barker's Ground this morning?'

'Barker's Ground?' Beddows echoed.

'Don't mess me about, Sergeant. You know what my eyes and ears are able to pick up in this borough. Isn't that where he found you, at the circus?'

'He told me he hadn't said anything to you.'

'Nor did he, Beddows. He is a fool, trying to stick up for you. It is a foolish man to cross me, particularly when I have a murder ongoing. You are both fools. Leaving yourself alone with the mother of a murder suspect. Are you without your senses?'

'I beg your pardon, Mr Charters, but what are you implying?'

'I hear that Miss MacCormack is a rather attractive and unusual woman?'

'She is attractive, intelligent and good company. Is that a crime?'

'In my book it is when it distracts one of my Detective Sergeants from catching a murderer.'

'Well let me put you right, Mr Charters. I was with Miss MacCormack. Having completed my enquiries, I spent some time with her socially. We talked, we laughed. She made me feel better about myself. And then I committed a cardinal sin of falling asleep. Perhaps if we had more men, and the work was shared about more fairly I wouldn't have fallen asleep.'

'Perhaps you shouldn't be doing such protracted detective duties. Perhaps you would prefer to put your uniform back on?'

'Perhaps I might prefer not to have nothing further to do with police work at all?'

'Perhaps so, Beddows. Perhaps you have forgotten why we have to keep a distance between our work and our private lives, and a line which you have clearly just crossed?'

'I was doing my job. I had been up and asking questions, all over this borough, for well over sixteen hours, yesterday. Having completed my enquiries I took an opportunity to be a person for a while. I haven't been just a person for a long time. I quite liked it.'

'In that case, Beddows, perhaps you should consider yourself on some unpaid gardening leave, until you come to your senses. Sergeant Kettle will take over your duties as of now. Stay away from Miss MacCormack. Stay away from the enquiries. Come back and see me when you can prove to me that you have come to your senses.' Charters pointed to the door, picked up his pen, and began to write, head still shaking.

Now Beddows slammed the door, on his way out.

'How dare he?' Beddows muttered. Being told who he could see or not see was a step too far. Nothing would stop him seeing Eibhlin MacCormack, certainly as he was now on unpaid gardening leave. Once Charters had got over his anger he would be sending for him, realising the borough could not manage without him.

'*Damn Robert Charters. Damn this bleeding job!*'

*****

Shepherd walked dejectedly towards Aylestone Road, beyond the infirmary and onward towards the county.

His mind was spinning, after defying Head Constable Charters.

He was angry with Beddows. Shepherd considered he had done nothing wrong, personally, but felt like he was unfairly held accountable for Beddows' actions.

By the time he reached the earthworks left behind by the Romans at Raw Dykes, at a point opposite the site of the old gibbet cage, he had walked past god knows how many people, many of whom may have said good morning to him, but he couldn't remember a single one. The earth works had always fascinated Shepherd. Apart from the Roman occupation, it was said that during the English Civil War, it had been the site of an artillery battery held by the Royalists from where they had pounded the old town. He sat and dreamed for a while. Rupert's Gateway and Roundheads, scurrying for shelter. Now he sought shelter from Charters' barrage.

Aylestone Meadows was part of what had been enclosed land belonging to the Manners family, the Dukes of Rutland, but until recently, Aylestone Hall had been given to a purpose as a ladies boarding school. The Meadows surrounded the land to the rear of the hall and back towards the borough. It was here he pinned his hopes that the scavengers might find sign of the suspects.

*****

Back at Town Hall Lane, Sergeants Smith and Haynes had turned up from their covert work. Charters called them into the office.

'We are in a temporary mess, but a mess none-the-less, gentlemen. What I have to tell you is in confidence. Much of it will become the main topic of chatter, quickly, but other stuff I need to make you aware of must remain between us alone.'

'Sounds serious, Mr Charters,' said Tanky Smith.

'I have just ordered Beddows onto unpaid gardening leave.'

'Bugger,' muttered Haynes, looking up and across at Smith. A puzzled look apparent on both faces.

'Beddows may have become too close to the mother of one of our suspects for the Paget Murder. He was late for duty and was found in the woman's caravan. He says he fell asleep, but he has also been acting strangely of late. I do not want a return to the Beddows of old, and can't risk losing a suspect through personal distractions.'

'Gardening leave sounds a bit harsh, if I may say so, Mr Charters,' Smith suggested, politely.

'It may be harsh, but it was clear from his demeanour that there is more to this event than one late duty.'

Smith looked shocked at his Head Constable's actions.

'And what is it that requires our involvement?' said Haynes.

'Sergeant Kettle will take over Beddows' enquiries, immediately; those in Leicester, that is. Unfortunately we have a complication with this suspect, a rather dangerous and determined detective from the Capital to contend with.'

'I heard Joseph Keetley was none to impressed with the visitor?' Smith chuckled.

'Not a laughing matter, Smith. Irrespective of Beddows' thoughts about our suspect, he should be arrested, interviewed and justice seen to be dispensed fairly and lawfully.'

'And you think there is a risk of that not occurring?' said Smith.

'I am concerned that if the man is in the Capital, and Inspector Hatter finds him first, we may not be allowed to see justice done, fairly, at all. He is adamant the suspect is the killer, albeit we have two stronger suspects who may still be nearby the borough. But, I smell a rat, and Inspector Hatter is trying too hard to get this man hanged. However, I want you two to go to London and use your resourcefulness to find the man first. Bring him back here.'

'Won't the Metropolitan gaffers be well narked with us?' said Smith. 'if they have a murder as well, and he is their main suspect, surely they would have first crack at him?'

'Only if they find out, and I trust you two not to put us at risk in seeking him out. You must use all your guile and resourcefulness.'

'How and where do we start?' said Haynes.

'First task may be to locate and observe our Inspector Hatter. He will have his eyes and ears, and it may be useful to see where he is asking questions. That may give you an area to focus on. Rumour has it he may seek passage to America, if that can be believed. I prefer to think he has gone to ground in London.'

'So who is this man?' said Smith.

'His name is Michael Lenihan, and from what we know of him, he should not be too difficult to identify once you get close enough to him. Here is the information that we know of to date,' said Charters, handing Smith two sheets of handwritten notes, covering the suspect and also Inspector Hatter.

'And how long should we expect to be away?' said Haynes.

'As long as it takes. Do you have any contacts in London?'

'I have a contact who runs a lodging house in Paddington. A bit shady, but he will allow us to fit in. He is an old sweat and is sound. If you need to leave word for us, this is his address.' Smith wrote his own note for Charters.

'Draw some expenses money from the duty Inspector,

enough for a few days, and get what you need, then be off as quick as you can. Take whatever transport will get you there the quickest. Don't mention this to anyone. Hatter has influential contacts and is ruthless, as no doubt will be those same contacts. Bring me back receipts for anything you spend, of course.'

Gertrude Beddows

Beddows wandered through the dry and noisy streets down to his home on Tower Street. The door was still locked and bolted, so he banged hard.
'Who is it?' His wife's voice called out.
'It's me. What are you bolted in for?'
'To keep you out. Go away!'
'Open the door. We need to talk. Do you want to tell the whole neighbourhood of our woes?' Beddows leaned his forehead against the door, frustration setting in, and the realisation that his life was spinning out of control.
The sound of the lock opening and latch being lifted. The door opened.
Gertrude Beddows stood back from the door, and shuffled back, uncomfortably, to the small hearth, allowing Beddows room to enter the tiny room. Their two small wooden chairs remained empty as the couple stood face to face, initially in silence. A small bowl of dark coloured chrysanthemums the only colour in the drab dark ochre coloured room. The onions for today's stew, heating on the grate, now scented the hot, musty air. The sound of his wife's clocks filled the room, the variety of ticking movements drove him to distraction, as always. She was obsessed with time, or watching it drag past.
'I've had more than enough of you and the stupid job you do. Life was better when you were a frame knitter. What has happened to you, John Beddows?' said the angry wife.
'We have grown so far apart, that it is painful to watch any more. You don't ask me about anything. I may not

175

sleep in the marital bed anymore. We eat alone. What am I supposed to think?' Beddows looked out of the window through fraying nets, shaking his head in disbelief.

'I have stood by you for sixteen years in this job. I have watched you come home beaten and abused. I have cleaned up after you when you drank to forget what you dealt with. I held you when you cried yourself to sleep. But you changed, and then it was just you and your current investigation. Some gory description, some sad life spoiled. Is that all what you want of me? Someone for you to talk at? You never once considered what it was doing to me. Look at me. I am broken from carrying you. My pain and illness is for me to deal with, as you are too busy with your work. '

'What do you want?'

'I want the marriage over. We aren't a couple. You are more married to the work than to me.'

'What if I don't agree?'

'Where were you last night?'

'Don't you start. I have enough of that from Shepherd and Charters. I was working, simple as that.'

'You expect me to believe that? I know when you have worked all night and I know when you are lying. Why should they send someone to find you if you were at work?'

'I fell asleep on a job.'

'A woman or a public house?' she asked, spitting out the words.

'It's not what you think,' Beddows attempted to reason with her.

'I don't care anymore. I don't want this life. I would sooner be dead. I suspect I'm not that far off, and I am racked with pain, but what do you know?''

'That would make life so much simpler, but in the meantime we are stuck with each other,' said Beddows.

He had no sympathy for the woman. He could not even remember when she had changed.

'No we are not. I want you out. Go and live with one of your friends. Move into the station. Just leave me alone.'

'This is my house,' Beddows bellowed, his fists tightening, his words more clipped, 'and don't forget it's my wages that pay for it.'

'It was our house, but what is it now? I don't know anymore. I just know that we are not intended to be together anymore. If you are seeing another woman I shall seek advice. I hear that ending a bad marriage is complicated and unpleasant to redress, but I cannot stand the thought of you, any longer.'

'You mock me and yourself. Who has filled your head with such nonsense?' Beddows rolled his eyes in disbelief.

'It may be nonsense to you. I have a little money saved up, which you would never have realised as you don't have a clue how I keep your house for you. I have some inheritance from my Aunt. I will be rid of you, one way or another. Now get some things and please leave this house. I am in great pain and wish to sleep.'

'What if I won't? My life is falling apart and nobody is interested any more. Why don't you go, instead?'

'With my illness? I can hardly walk the width of this room, as you well know. Me move out? Over my dead body.' said his wife.

'You know that could be arranged,' said Beddows, no longer prepared to hold back the pent up anger. 'Who would miss you? A lonely and dried up old woman? You don't know how often I have wished for you dead, just to make one part of my life less painful.'

'You don't know what pain is John Beddows. You don't know the pain I carry daily, and have done so for many months now, but you care not. I think you have said enough.'

'I'm on unpaid gardening leave. I turn in late, once. I have had a clean slate for so many years and now it is all being thrown back in my face.'

'Well think about what it is that you have done. Why should Mr Charters do that unless it is serious?'

'Is there nobody who can understand?' Beddows voice crumbled. His head bowed.

'I suggest you go and find solace at the place you preferred last night. I shall send a message to you when I have sought advice about how we can end this charade.'

'You are a policeman's wife. A common skivvy. Our kind have no rights. You have to apply to the Government to be rid of me. Do what you have to, but I pray for a quick end to this purgatory.'

'I hear that a law may come soon, that will easily allow for women like me to be rid of bad husbands, and not before time,' she said, handing him her wedding ring.

'I realise I may have to wait, but patience is a virtue. I will make sure it is more painful a separation for you than life presently is for me.' A chill ran through Beddows' parting words.

'Mr Charters will hear of your threats, John Beddows. If anything ever happens to me, be warned!'

Skinny dippers

People were milling about all over the fields. Those who had to work were hard labouring on the fields, or moving livestock. Those who didn't have to work were either seeking the free resources the area sometimes gave up, or contemplating a rather leisurely summer's day.

'Giz a ride, mister,' Queenie's younger brother yelled from the stony canal towpath.

One or two small rowing boats were attracting onlookers as their occupants explored the navigable part of the Soar.

One small boat contained a well dressed gent, rowing rather leisurely, and a posh lady in her Sunday attire, a parasol shielding her from the sun. The woman ate grapes from a bunch she held, and a picnic box filled the floor of the boat between the occupants.

'Chuck us some scoff,' Queenie shouted, salivating at the thought of posh food.

'Be away with you, you rascals,' the rower called back, chuckling at their impudence.

The response was met with one or two carefully thrown, heavy stones, which splashed water up from the canal and over the occupants, and dampening the contents of the basket.

The scavengers, roaring with laughter, scampered further into the fields, seeking not just the wanted men, but any more mischief they could create.

Some fishermen sat along the banks of both the Soar and in little sheltered holes along the Biam, the smaller river running parallel with the main waterway, seeking out an odd small trout or cunning pike for the table. 'Got a big worm, mister?' Queenie teased an elderly man, sitting with a young child at his side, their makeshift fishing rods no more than willow branches with string and peacock quill floats, bobbing in the ripple.

The rivers this side of the borough were fresh water, the foul and noxious mix within the borough fading beyond Leicester Mill, and the canalised section of the river. The scavengers split and were now working their own separate areas. Two were walking the length of the Soar, including the section that incorporated the Grand Union Canal, down to the Biam. Two more walked the section between the Biam and the edge of the fields at the railway, and two more between the railway and Rowley Fields.

The agreed plan for the day was to walk as far as the fields bounded by Aylestone Church, unless anybody saw or heard anything. Anything strange or any danger was to be announced by the customary (and unique) gang whistle that each could blow at ear shattering levels. Failure to be able whistle was reason for immediate rejection at the gang initiation.

Queenie insisted that as she had been leader when Shepherd had originally set the challenge to find the two men, that honour should remain until they received their reward. If anyone disagreed, she had suggested she would punch their lights out. Nobody disagreed. She chose the section between the Biam and the railway, which she particularly fancied.

The Biam had some well known skinny dipping spots, and she had previously come across some naked lads, pinching their clothes and running off with them. They had sworn to get their own back if ever they saw her again. Today was a good chance for a return encounter, which would add some additional fun, instead of the

daily drudge and hardship in the heart of the borough.
They had yet to realise that what they were doing was
denied to many of their age, who life passed by, daily in
factory or workhouse.

However, scavengers were instinctively scavengers, and
each had been briefed to nick anything worth nicking,
discarded skinny dippers' clothing included.

The thought of a swim, naked as the day they were
born, appealed to many.

In bygone years, it was a frequent occurrence along the
River Soar between The railway terminus at West
Bridge, and along Bath Lane, opposite where the Roman
baths had originally stood at the Temple of Janus.

Apart from the objection of the god-fearing, non-
bathing public, the river was now so polluted within the
old town, it was a dangerous place and the water now
vile and noxious.

Queenie had deliberately chosen one of the older
scavenger boys, Robbo, a painfully skinny 15 year old, to
accompany her. He was a bit reclusive and shy, and she
had a bit of cruel fun planned, opportunity permitting.
His clothes were so thin, that they had holes in them,
and how they stayed on his scrawny bones, she had no
idea. That being said, he looked cooler than she felt in
her newly acquired jacket, tied around her waist.

The pair wandered through the fields, climbing over
fences or through holes in hedges. They waved
occasionally to their fellow scavengers, if they caught
sight of each other. Occasionally straying into private
land, and working fields, they were chased off by
labourers.

Eventually they reached an area on the Biam known
locally as Pebble Beach, halfway between the Canal and
Rowley Fields.

Pebble Beach was a shallow hollow, where the water ran
sparkling clean, and deep enough to swim if you were

fortunate to be able, or to paddle and bathe, otherwise. A few local lads were already skinny dipping. Splashing and laughter obliterated the song of hundreds of birds, including some skylarks, directly above.

The sun was hot and Queenie lead the way, Robbo tagging behind. She reached the long grass at the edge of the pebbles which gave the area its name, and quickly threw off her jacket and breeches, jumping naked into the cool flowing water. An enormous splash erupted as she entered, surprisingly so for her build. She knelt with just the top of her roughly cropped hair exposed, relishing the feel of cold running water over her grimy body. She began to scrub, unconsciously, at the areas that itched the most. She could not recall the last time she had chance to clean herself.

'Come on Robbo, it's bleeding marvellous.' she yelled. It wouldn't be long for the other scavengers to hear her yells and join her. She whistled, in any event, as she had pre-arranged with the other five.

Robbo stood on the bank, arms crossed. 'I ain't taking my rags off for nobody.'

'Well get in as you are then, dumb nuts.'

'I ain't getting in. You can't make me!'

Before he could say another word, he was unceremoniously grabbed from behind as the other scavengers crept up on them, pulling his rags off over his shoulders and from his writhing legs. They were falling apart in the scavengers hands as Robbo screamed like a girl, in Queenie's opinion.

Once stripped of his meagre rags, Robbo was held by his ankles and wrists, and swung, unceremoniously before being released, dropping into the water alongside Queenie, the splash further soaking her. Coughing and spluttering, Robbo bobbed up, scrambling desperately to find a foot hold. He couldn't swim.

The rest of the scavengers quickly disrobed, casting

their dirty rags onto the grass at their feet, before joining their friends in the water. To passers by, the change was probably more noticeable, as layers of ground in dirt began to disappear from the unfortunate youngsters. Months of foul dirt and stench washed away in minutes.

This was like Heaven, fun in the sun. No clothes to inhibit them, and laughter instead of miserable drudgery.

The other swimmers wisely ignored the scavengers, happy with their own pleasures.

The only person not soaking up the relief was Robbo, acutely embarrassed and not happy that he had been stripped and soaked.

'You're a prat, Robbo. Why d'ya think Queenie chose you, of all people?' said Queenie's young brother, flicking water in the boy's flushed face.

'Bastards, all of you. I hate you all.' The boy stood upright and rigid and held his hands over his 'privates'.

'Show us your Dick, then,' Queenie teased him, rushing towards him, creating a wave which nearly knocked him over again in her haste.

'Bugger off, tomboy,' Robbo bleated, realising as soon as he had said it, what the consequences, undoubtedly, would be.

'Who are you calling tomboy?' Queenie spat, face contorting and fists clenched.

The other scavengers laughed, as Queenie chased Robbo through the water and out onto the bank, her bony legs gaining good ground as she ran.

'I'll show you tomboy,' she laughed, grabbing the back of the boy's hair, pulling him to a stop, before knocking him flying and jumping on him as he fell.

Robbo landed on his back on the small, hard stones, and felt the wind leave his lungs as Queenie landed on top, straddling him.

Queenie was so skeletal, her breasts were barely evident, like two poached eggs, but smaller, but she liked being the dominant one, especially being a girl. She felt like a girl, so she thought, and had girl's 'needs'.

'D'ya like 'em Robbo? Don't ya want to give them a good feel?' Queenie giggled wildly, noting the boy's embarrassment. 'D'ya want to give me a good diddling? I can feel it, you can't hide that thing you've got,' realising that Robbo had become aroused.

Robbo was starting to panic. Queenie's emaciated body was pushing against him, as she tried to impale herself on him, and he gagged.

'Fuck off, tomboy,' he cried again, working out that she would sooner fight him, for calling her names, instead of risking his virginity.

He anticipated the first punch, pushing hard against her barely developed breasts as she swung a poorly aimed fist.

Robbo wriggled out of her grasp and ran for all his worth, noticing a thick spinney a few yards away and a tiny, narrow gap in the hawthorn that edged it. He anticipated he could get through but Queenie would prefer not to - not without getting scratched to bits, anyway.

He dived through the gap, listening for the heavy breathing, heavy footsteps, and laughter following not far behind him.

He felt the thorns tear, momentarily, at his right flank, but it was a small price to pay for getting the deranged tomboy off him.

Looking back through the gap, he could see Queenie and the other boys seeking a suitable entrance to get to him. He looked around in the mottled half-light for an escape route, conscious that he was still naked.

As his eyes adjusted to the broken shadows from the

hawthorn, he became aware of the fact he was not alone. At his feet, not far behind him lay two men. Blond men, stripped naked and with guts spilled out. A dense swarm of flies had already settled all over them. Vomit filled his mouth and nostrils. Robbo threw up and then screamed out.

Queenie broke through an opening on the far side, rushing in, hell bent on beating the shit out of Robbo, but stopping dead in her tracks at the sight before her. 'Jesus,' she cried out to the scavengers. 'Get your clothes on, and go and get the coppers. I think Robbo just found who we've been looking for!'

*****

Shepherd was already on the meadows, on a track that crossed from Cow Lane, near the Roman Raw Dykes, to where the canal joined the Soar. He realised that it was always hard to work out where the borough ended as the size and shape of the area changed, almost daily. He saw the two youngsters, one of whom was familiar to him from the scavengers, running his way at a good sprint. The boys were almost out of breath, and both were over-talking each other. Fast, rambling and unintelligible words, tangled together.

'Slow down and take a breath. What's wrong?'

'We've found them blokes, Mister. Robbo nearly fell over them. Dead they are, butchered. Guts everywhere.'

'Where abouts are they?' Shepherd asked.

'In some bushes alongside Pebble Beach. Queenie and the others are still there. It's gruesome they reckon.'

'I want one of you to run into town and report this at the police station. Who is the fastest and fittest?'

'I'm the best,' said the smaller boy. 'I can run into town and be there in ten minutes.'

'Here, take this note, and hand it over. Tell them what

you know. Ask for Sergeant Beddows.' Shepherd scribbled a short note in a page from his pocket book, his pencil slippery in his fingers. The paper was warm and damp from his body heat.

'You take me to where the bodies are,' said Shepherd to the second boy, setting off at a brisk walk back into the fields.

It took only about ten minutes to reach the site, and around the bushes a small crowd had gathered. Some were the remaining scavengers, including Queenie and Robbo, and others were the skinny dippers, farm workers, and a few walkers, attracted by the screams. Queenie was still holding Robbo around his shoulders, as he continued to vomit into the bushes. He was as white as anyone Shepherd could ever recall, and looked like a bony corpse himself.

'Where are they?' Shepherd asked Queenie.

'I ain't going back in there. It stinks and it looks bleeding terrible. Blood and guts everywhere.'

Shepherd identified a break in the bushes, large enough to enter the area without too great a risk of risk of personal injury. The Hawthorn looked vicious, with their large, barbed thorns hidden within their dense dark green foliage. It was evident that the bushes were covered in insects, and small caterpillars crawled everywhere, on shimmering webs.

It was a good place to hide a body or bodies. The bushes formed almost a perfect ring around a patch of barren earth, and with only one main break in the foliage, would also have been an ideal place to camp relatively unobserved.

Inside the bushes, laying almost side by side on their backs were two white males. Their overall appearance was of young adults, stripped naked to the waist. The blond hair, which would have looked white, in normal circumstances, was dishevelled, matted and heavily blood-stained. Each man had his belly crudely cut open, exposing their guts. Marks on their bodies suggested they had already been gnawed by rodents. Wildlife was quick to feast on free offerings. Shepherd's immediate thought was back to the St.Clair killings, two years back, in terms of the savagery.

The men looked to Shepherd as if they had been placed, rather than killed in the exact spot that they lay. Both showed signs of having been dead some time, in the current heat wave. It was clear they were similar in appearance and could well be related. Shepherd could just about make out the pale eye colour, but in the half light, and insect activity, and a skin that seemed to be forming on each pupil, he could not be sure. Sweat trickled down from his forehead into his eyes, making observation even more difficult. He brushed his face, feeling the small insects that dropped onto him and crawled over him and the corpses at his feet.

He thought about the Romany woman's vision or dream, and shuddered at what she described, now unfolded in front of him.

The hands would need further scrutiny, later, but Shepherd was confident that he had the Hensons. The only problem now was who killed them and why? Who was the tall, dark haired man in the vision? Michael Lenihan fitted the description, but so did a great many other men.

Shepherd stepped outside and started to question the onlookers whilst he waited for reinforcements.

*****

Gertrude Beddows sat in the cool of the main office, courtesy of a chair produced for her by Sergeant Roper, the Custody Sergeant. She waited to speak to Mr Charters - who did not appear to be in a rush to talk to her. It had taken all her resolve, and her physical strength to walk to the station.

She had sat, rather uncomfortably, owing to the activities of a rather obnoxious drunk in the cell facing the raised desk of the Charge Sergeant.

The man's language was obscene, and the Sergeant had already spoken quite sharply with him, but he continued to put his face to the hatch, and leer at the woman.

'Is there not somewhere less public that I could wait?' she asked, abruptly.

'When Mr Charters is free I am sure he will take you elsewhere, but we haven't much space here, as you probably know.'

'Why should I know?'

'Hasn't Sergeant Beddows told you all about the place?' the sergeant enquired.

'I have never asked, nor has he told me, or I have not listened when he has rambled on in the past.'

Sergeant Roper sensed this was not a happy lady, and decided to keep quiet.

The drunk peered through the hatch again, making strange, grunting noises.

'Oi, Horace, cut it out,' the Sergeant bellowed at him.

'Dirty old bugger, can't help himself,' he tried to explain. 'Suppose his cell will need cleaning, once he's gone.'

Gertrude Beddows wretched at the thought.

Robert Charters appeared at the rear corridor, and beckoned Mrs Beddows.

'How can I help you, Mrs Beddows?'

'I want to talk to you about Sergeant Beddows. What is going on with him and what are you doing about it?' she asked, a clear bitterness in her voice.

'That is for Beddows to explain to you, Mrs Beddows, not I.'

'Why is he on gardening leave?'

'So, you have spoken to him?'

'Briefly, only to tell him our marriage is over. He has become a stranger because of this awful job. He is married to it, not me anymore.'

'Things aren't well at home, either, then?'

'He openly admits he would sooner see me dead, and knows people who would willingly help. What do you think of that?'

'I cannot comment. People say things in the heat of a moment. Has he actually threatened you?'

'Not a threat, but he has been openly hostile, and wishes me dead. Should a woman put up with that?'

'That is for you to decide, Mrs Beddows.'

'Will he return to work, Mr Charters, as I shall still require money to live?'

'That is Beddows' decision alone. I cannot offer you any more hope than I already have. Police work is difficult and takes its toll on men, differently, as you have already experienced. Something is clearly amiss, but *he* must decide if he still wants to be one of us.'

A woman's charms

Beddows stood at the foot of the steps to Eibhlin's caravan.

He felt dirty and confused. He was just trying to do his job, and was now being punished for doing so. The fact that he was always deemed to be on duty, had always struck him as grossly unfair, but he had tolerated the rules since 1839.

Why had Charters not just given him the ear bending he had anticipated?

He was not a bad copper anymore and was in the midst of a most serious and important enquiry.

Why could Shepherd not understand that they had just talked and fallen asleep?

What would Eibhlin say when he told her?

A host of thoughts flooded his mind, thoughts that overwhelmed his ability to make sense of anything.

'What are you doing, John Beddows? You look like you have the worries of the world.' Eibhlin was standing in the doorway, brushing her long red mane.

'How long have you been there?' Beddows asked, somewhat embarrassed at the situation.

'Just a couple of minutes. I was intrigued, just watching you. Are you okay?'

'You don't want to know.'

'Come on in. The kettle is on the campfire.' Eibhlin held out her hand and stepped back into the caravan.

'Sorry. I hadn't realised you were there,' said Beddows, head bowed.

'My goodness. What has happened?'

'My Head Constable didn't understand what had

happened and why I was late for my duties. We argued, and for some reason he has put me on what we call gardening leave.'

'What does that mean?'

'Unpaid leave. I've been told to stay away from you and to stay away from the enquiry.'

'How can he do that, or say that to you?'

'Oh believe me, he can. He is a tough man and has the highest morals and expectations. My past indiscretions have clearly been taken into account, and he must believe he can't trust me, presently.'

'Oh Beddows, don't be so silly. I trust you. It will blow over. Would you like me to go and talk to him?'

'Thank you for the offer, but I need to find another way of resolving this.'

'And what is in the bag?' Eibhlin enquired, noting a large canvas holdall in Beddows' possession.

'To add insult to injury, my marriage is effectively over. As I didn't return home last night, the woman I once married has thrown me out of my own home.'

'Can she do that?'

'She has. I can't go back whilst she is there. One or the other of us would end up killing the other.'

'Oh, Beddows, I can't believe this has just happened, and because of this one investigation?'

'It's not your fault, nor is this particular investigation. It is just the culmination of a number of bad things. I am not in a good place at the moment.'

Eibhlin laughed, walked forward and took Beddows face in her hands, planting a gentle kiss on his forehead. 'You poor man. We both seem to have some unexpected and unpleasant days to contend with.'

'Even Shepherd seems to thinks we were probably doing something untoward.'

'Let him think what he wants. You and I know what happened. If you believe in God, he knows what happened,' Eibhlin giggled.

'But your reputation, Eibhlin?'

'I have the reputation of a hard, callous, circus owner, who pushes men around and has no husband, but a man in every other town. Will another one, perceived, indiscretion make much of a difference?'

'It's the assumption that people jump to,' said Beddows, shaking his head.

'Let them make assumptions. If that is the best they have to offer, then they don't deserve respect.'

'I think Shepherd tried to protect me, to some degree, but I saw the look on his face.'

'Tell him, Beddows. If he is truly your friend, he will listen.'

'And how am I going to tell him, if I have to stay away from everyone?'

'You know where he lives, go and see him.'

'You have such straightforward ideas of how I can resolve this, Eibhlin.'

'I don't have the bad thoughts going round in my head, not your bad thoughts, anyway.'

'But it is your son that is being pursued, both here and probably in London, as we speak.'

'My head and heart tell me that Michael will be somewhere safe. He is slow but not stupid. I have good friends, including family, around London. We will find him, Beddows, and you will make sure of his innocence in the end.'

'You have more confidence than me, at the present.'

'Beddows, I trust you. I told you, I am a good judge of character.'

Beddows stood up and Eibhlin place her arms around him, holding him tightly. 'These may be dark days, Beddows, but truth will come out - for you and for Michael. Mark my words.'

Beddows held her tightly. The smell of her scent. The

softness of her hair and face alongside his. The softness of her womanly curves pressing against him. He had not been so close to a woman for such a long time. He savoured the moment.

The Hensons

A hive of activity followed the arrival of the scavenger at the police station. The note from Shepherd was handed to Charters, in Beddows' absence, and Charters had started to direct his constables to attend the meadows.

As there was doubt as to whether this was the borough's jurisdiction, or Mr Goodyer's for the county, word was sent to county Headquarters in the Market Place for the attendance of Goodyer's officers.

Freeman's Common and part of the meadows was in the borough, to a point where it divided into either the Braunstone or Aylestone 'Lordships' which signified the start of the county. In view of the borough connection, and enquiries already undertaken, Frederick Goodyer might be glad to leave it within the borough in any event.

Herbert Kettle was advised that he was now the detective in charge of the investigation and should go to the scene and take charge. He also authorised for a horse and cart that would be required for the recovery of the bodies. The Coroner, Oliver Mitchell was also to be made aware, as he covered both Borough and South Leicestershire, and yet again, he would be responsible for establishing a verdict, after examination and Inquest.

Charters cursed to himself, realising that with Smith and Haynes on the way to London, sending Beddows on gardening leave may have been a premature and an excessive reaction. He was getting shorter of quality officers by the minute.

'Damn that man. He gets my hackles up every time he does something wrong,' slamming his fist down on the small desk, to the shock of Kettle and the small group of assembling men.

'Who is that, Sir?' asked Kettle.

'Beddows, Sergeant. Why does he always push me too far?'

'He is an excellent detective, Sir. He has always been challenging, but he is far from the Beddows of old.'

'Well it's up to him to prove that he can still be a good detective and to come back and show me.'

'What if he doesn't come back?' said Kettle.

'He will, I hope. But for now we have to make do without him. Damn him. Damn him!'

'Do we need a surgeon to the scene, Sir?'

'Call in at the infirmary. Either Buck or Hamilton would no doubt be the Coroner's choice. See if one of them can accompany or join you there.'

The idea of taking a surgeon to a crime scene, rather than the victim to the surgeon, was somewhat of a novel idea, but Charters had seen the benefits in this last three years, and Buck and Hamilton had both been happy to oblige.

The horse and cart was sent to what was known locally as the Canal Street entrance to the meadows, mid way to Aylestone, where it could get over the canal and, probably, make the carriage of the bodies a little less onerous in the heat. A number of canvas sail cloths that had been adapted to secure and carry victims were sent with it.

*****

Fortunately, Herbert Kettle realised that he would likely find both the Coroner and Thomas Hamilton together, as the inquest for Edward Paget was taking place at midday at the infirmary and then onwards to The Turk's Head. The inquest had just finished and the juror's had not long dispersed, when Kettle entered the inn and broke the news of more bodies.

Coroner Oliver Mitchell confirmed that a verdict of murder had been recorded and that he had released the body of Edward Paget for his family to dispose of.

Mitchell and Hamilton accompanied Kettle on the walk down to the meadows at Pebble Beach.

Mitchell was in possession of a long walking stick, and was annoyed that his midday lunch had been interrupted. He huffed and puffed as he tried to keep up with the younger men. He looked for a passing cab, to relieve the indignity.

Inspector Chapman completed his record of payments for the jurymen that had attended, before setting off to the police station to inform Mr Charters of the result, and the attendance of Oliver Mitchell and Thomas Hamilton.

*****

Beddows and Eibhlin MacCormack walked around in the early afternoon sunshine, chatting, whilst Eibhlin confirmed that the performers and animals were prepared for the evening performance. Eibhlin cooled them with a little lace fan, which she had acquired on her travels. The heat was draining, and Beddows felt beads of sweat trickling down the small of his back.

He felt a strange sense of both relief and disbelief, not working or having to be accountable to anybody. It was a new experience.

'What will you do?' said Beddows. 'The circus is only here for a few days. Where is it off to next?'

'We are meant to travel to Nottingham, in the meadow fields beyond the fifteen arches bridge into the borough, shortly after the last performance on Sunday, next.'

'Have you any thoughts about changing your plans?'

'The circus must travel on. It is the receipt money that allows me to keep it going. Whether I go, or whether Henry Pensylva manages it for me for a few days. He's more than capable. I know he comes across as a humorous and lecherous rake, but he has good business sense.'

'Is he as bad as he makes out with other people's wives?'

'He has had his share of other people's wives. There were some of the new Pinkerton men at the port when we left the states, last. He evaded them, but understands that one or two husbands would likely shoot him on sight, if ever he went back.'

'Not what you expect of such a little old fellow,' Beddows chuckled.

'What is the typical gigolo then, John Beddows?' Eibhlin responded.

'How do you mean?'

'Are you a ladies' man, strong and quiet?' she smiled, resting her head against his shoulder as they walked.

'Are you joking?' said Beddows. 'I'm a rough and abrasive old copper, and offer nothing appealing to the fairer sex, I quite imagine.'

'Don't be so sure, Beddows. Some women like strong, rugged, interesting men.'

'You flatter me, Miss MacCormack, but thank you for trying to cheer me up.'

'What can be done about getting you back into your Head Constable's good books?'

'I don't know that I want to be back in his good books. I get tired of dealing with other people's problems and tragedies. Perhaps I should do something else?'

'Like what?'

'I quite fancy running a tea and coffee house. I can imagine myself behind the counter, an apron tied over my breeches, surprising everyone with my knowledge of tea. A bit like my friend Joseph Keetley. I should introduce you.'

'That would be nice. Perhaps we could have supper there?'

'I will make the arrangements. How about tomorrow?'

'That would be nice. How will we get to know what is happening about Michael? Will Shepherd keep you updated?

'That still worries me. I was actually thinking that perhaps I could go to London myself. Now I am on unpaid leave, Charters couldn't stop me.'

'Would you really do that for me, John Beddows? I could come with you.'

'You should stay here. They may be more interested in watching you, and anyway, you need to be here if Michael appears.'

'That makes sense, but why should you do that for me?'

'You would have to agree to have supper with me when I get back. I could go later today. The overnight coach is often empty, or an early train would get me there by tomorrow. I don't need to get a bag, I have everything with me.'

'I can give you one or two names that might help you in London,' Eibhlin added, looking excited at the thought of Beddows proposal.

'How will I find him?'

'One of the names I shall give you is a relative. He is very discreet and Michael would likely contact him at some point, if he was in trouble. You could stop with him, I'm sure. I have a small pendant portrait of Michael, which was completed for me last year. It is small, but a good likeness. It's in the caravan.'

'I don't know how long I will need to be there. I have no

knowledge of how big a task it may be. Staying with your relative may not be such a good idea. Inspector Hatter may already have eyes upon him.'

'How would he know we were related? He is only a cousin, but he is respectable, and has good business links. I must give you some funds, then, to help cover your costs.'

'That would be very helpful, given the circumstances. You never know, one day there might be an opportunity for such independent detectives. I could earn my keep without the drawbacks of police duties and rules.'

'You never know, John Beddows. You could become famous.'

'What if I'm not back before the weekend?'

'I shall either have left a message for you or I shall still be here. Where is your friend's inn?'

'It is opposite the police station, The King and Crown. Ask for Joseph and tell him I sent you.'

'Thank you, John Beddows.' She kissed him on the cheek and squeezed his nearest hand, pulling him closer to her. 'Please find my son for me.'

*****

By Three o'clock, the area around Pebble Beach remained the centre of attention for many. Aside from quite large numbers that had been moved back and who were watching from a distance, around the ring of hawthorn bushes stood an assortment of constables, The Coroner, Surgeon Thomas Hamilton, and the scavengers. Frederick Goodyer had sent a county Inspector, Richardson, and four county reserve constables, just in case it turned into a county matter.

However, there was agreement, once Herbert Kettle had taken charge, that this was well inside the borough borders and therefore a borough crime - and likely part of the wider investigation already in hand. Richardson was only too pleased to wash the county's hands of any longer term involvement. Coroner Oliver Mitchell had no objections.

Shepherd was by now both surprised and confused. When Kettle explained what had happened to Beddows, Shepherd felt both guilt and anger. John Beddows had started this investigation, and should be finishing it. For Charters to have removed him on unpaid 'gardening leave' shocked him. He recalled talk of Charters doing something similarly some years ago, and getting into trouble with the Watch Committee. Herbert Kettle was a good detective and a nice bloke, but he was not Beddows.

'What do you think, Shepherd?' said Kettle. 'Do you think these are your two suspects?'

'I would like a better look when we have more light, beyond the bushes or at the infirmary. I have not found any belongings, such as their tent or any baggage, either. Certainly there is no property evident from the burglary. Perhaps the killer took that with him?'

'I will not gain much more in here, Shepherd,' said Thomas Hamilton. 'I have had a good look around and I think they were killed elsewhere and concealed here.'

'Why is that?' said Kettle.

'The wounds they have sustained are brutal and they would have bled massively. If you notice, as much as there is blood on the ground, under them, it doesn't seem enough for two healthy young men. More like residual blood that has drained as a result of a slight slope below them. The main blood loss must have occurred elsewhere.'

'But we've not seen anything outside,' said Shepherd, 'we've had a good look around.'

'What if they were at the river. Look at their heels, Shepherd,' said Hamilton.

Shepherd saw that both men had scuff marks on their heels which were also grazed.

'I think they were killed at the river, where they would have bled freely, almost undetected, and then moved here and concealed.

Kettle and Shepherd walked back along the short track to Pebble Beach. Along the way, there were signs of something being dragged, and a trail of what might be dried blood, apparent, leading from the stones at the water's edge.

Signs of a small fire and animal bones again suggested a recent campsite, nearby to the beach, that might also be connected. The fire contained some cloth within the debris.

'Perhaps somebody burned their belongings, to destroy evidence?' suggested Shepherd.

'Not sure, lad. Mr Hamilton should have been a detective,' said Kettle.

'He is in his own way,' said Shepherd. 'A medical detective.'

'He is damned good, though, Shepherd. We are lucky to have the likes of him and John Buck in Leicester.'

'Can we move the bodies, Mr Mitchell?' Kettle enquired. 'Surgeon Hamilton?'

'As far as I am concerned. I want the bodies back at the infirmary. I will examine them both there.'

Kettle called over four hefty constables, who had been detailed to assist in recovering the bodies. They unfurled the sailcloth, large enough pieces to wrap a body in, and carry it in straps.

The bodies were recovered to Oliver Mitchell's satisfaction, and carried to the cart at Canal Street, to be taken onwards to Thomas Hamilton's operating room at the infirmary. There, they would temporarily join the body of Edward Paget, who was yet to be collected by his family.

'What is it with you and murder, Shepherd? You are like Jonah, the tragedy follows you around,' said Hamilton. 'This is the second time in three years. It's hardly a plague of biblical proportions,' said Shepherd.

'Not far off though, Constable Shepherd, or should we call you Jonah from now on, as Surgeon Hamilton suggests?' chuckled Coroner Mitchell.

'Ere, Constable Shepherd, where's our coin?' Queenie demanded, stood at the front of the onlookers, and still holding on to a very sickly looking Robbo.

'Come to the police station at nine o'clock tomorrow. I need to take a report from each of you. I will give you what we promised.'

'What about today? We're starving,' she replied.

'Who are these urchins?' enquired Oliver Mitchell.

'They have been my most useful eyes and ears, and came out looking on our behalf. It was they that found the bodies. I promised them some reward for their toil.' Mitchell reached under his jacket, and into a pocket of his waistcoat, taking out a Florin coin.

'Take this for now. You look like you could do better with a good feed and some sturdy clothes. Come to my offices at 10 New Street, when you have been seen by Constable Shepherd. I might have something else for you.'

'Thanks, Mister,' said Queenie, shocked at the size of the reward already, and the prospect of more. 'We'll see you tomorrow then.' The scavengers ran towards the town. The money would buy some bread, baccy and a good bottle of gin for the gang, and a good night would be had by all. The tent and clothing they had found concealed nearby would serve them well. They wouldn't mention that, as after all they were scavengers.

*****

By six o'clock, Kettle, Shepherd, Coroner Mitchell and Thomas Hamilton were stood at Hamilton's small operating room at the infirmary once again.

'Are these the men you were looking for, Shepherd?' asked Kettle, mindful of Shepherd's earlier comment.

'I want to have a look at their hands, before I make further judgement. I am confident they are, and we will need somebody from the circus to confirm it, officially. I am more interested in whether one of these was the man in Paget's house.'

'What are you looking for, Shepherd?' said Hamilton.

'A scar or mark, with the appearance of a crescent moon, like this,' reaching into his coat pocket and producing his notebook, pencil and ruler, and his earlier sketch and measurements.

'Meticulous thinking, Constable Shepherd,' Oliver Mitchell observed.

'I have a strong case that the scar will connect one of these men to the inside of the house, and thus the killing.'

Hamilton took a small bowl of water and carefully cleaned the dead men's hands, following a thorough visual examination for evidence, to allow for a better view of marks and scars. The first man had scars and what looked like old burns on his hands, but no crescent moon.

'Look likes rope burn to me,' said Hamilton. 'I have seen it before with sailors and navy men.'

'That makes sense,' said Kettle. 'circus performers, probably use ropes in their performance.'

Examining the second man's hands, on the inside of the right thumb, Shepherd saw what he had been hoping for. A scar in the shape of a crescent moon. Hamilton took measurements and they were exact to Shepherd's original notes, and the scar matched the sketch faultlessly.

'This looks like what you were hoping for?' asked Hamilton, optimistically.

'This looks like our killer, Mr Mitchell. The same mark was visible on a cleaned glass on a table lamp used by the killer, and on the inside of the window that had been lifted to make his escape.'

'Very impressive, Shepherd. Finger marks. I feel I have read something recently of such practices by the judiciary in France,' the Coroner remarked.

'What colour are his eyes, Hamilton?' said Shepherd.

Hamilton lifted the dead man's eyelids. In the improved light, it was clear that they were the palest blue.

Shepherd was content that they had their man.

'What we need to know now, is what the other man was doing, and was he involved, and why they have been murdered themselves? said Kettle.

'My job is to tell you how they died,' said Thomas Hamilton.

'And your job is to tell me who killed them, gentlemen,' said Oliver Mitchell.

'Mr Hamilton, I think you have the first part to play, although the wounds look pretty conclusive to me,' said Kettle.

Hamilton set about his examinations, concluding that both men had been killed by a long bladed weapon and had been cut from belly button to sternum, severing several key blood vessels and organs along the way, and subsequent blood loss.'

The small pile of coffins in the mortuary room began to grow again. The grave-diggers at Welford Road would be busy soon.

'Who can identify the men for us?' asked Oliver Mitchell.

'I will get somebody from the circus,' said Herbert Kettle.

'I know somebody that will probably be glad to see at least one of them dead,' said Shepherd.

'Inquest to be held tomorrow at The Turks Head, after viewing here, again. Can that be arranged quickly enough?' said Mitchell.

'If we can get identification done tonight, and Mr Charters has somebody left to sort out a Jury in the morning, I would suspect so, Sir,' said Kettle.

'And we need to start to think about finding Michael Lenihan as an even greater priority,' said Kettle. 'He could still be our tall, dark haired man that these were last seen with.'

'Or not... as the case may be,' said Shepherd, thinking of Beddows.

*****

Herbert Kettle and Samson Shepherd were feeling the stresses and strains of a long day that had no apparent end in sight, as yet. Having updated Head Constable Charters (who never once even acknowledged Shepherd's presence) and arranging for tomorrow's duty Inspector to yet again convene Mr Mitchell's inquest, the two men set off for the circus. No doubt the evening performance would be in full swing.

On arrival the performance tent was illuminated and performers and animals were constantly changing. About nine-thirty, Eibhlin MacCormack came out of the arena and noted the presence of the two men.

'Constable Shepherd, can I help you?' The greeting was frosty.

'We think we have found your missing performers. We are looking for somebody who will identify the bodies.' said Kettle, holding out his hand to introduce himself.

'And that is how you generally break sad news to people? They have friends and family, Sergeant ... Kettle.'

'I am sorry if you prefer more pleasantry, but we are rather busy. Who can assist us?'

'I was thinking that perhaps your contortionist, Annie. She seemed to know them better than anyone,' suggested Shepherd.

'If Annie is prepared to do so, I don't see why not. She will be out shortly.'

'Thank you, Miss MacCormack.'

'Constable Shepherd, may I speak to you, privately?' said Eibhlin.

Shepherd looked to Kettle who nodded, approvingly. Eibhlin walked over to some cages and out of earshot of Herbert Kettle.

'What have you to say about Sergeant Beddows' current situation?'

'All I have been told is that he is on unpaid leave. My Head Constable won't even talk to me, even though I refused to say anything to Beddows' detriment. Sergeant Kettle has been put in charge.'

'Beddows is very distressed. He may seem otherwise, but he is. His wife has also refused to let him back into his home.'

'I know she was very angry, but I didn't know that she had thrown him out. Nobody has said anything. Is Beddows here, and may I talk with him?'

'I don't know where Beddows is. He left here early this afternoon when he had finished his enquiries. I have no idea where he might have gone.'

'Enquiries? I thought he was off the case?' said Shepherd, picking up on the odd comment.

'He is off the case. In fact he is considering whether he ever wants to come back. But, he is very disappointed in you Constable Shepherd. You were his closest friend, and even you doubted him. He had done nothing wrong. We have done nothing wrong, as we tried to tell you earlier.'

'I really could do with speaking with him. Please tell him so. If he needs me he can always leave a message at my Aunt's house.'

'If he mentions you, and, should he choose to contact *me* again, I will tell him.'

'Has anybody from the station spoken to you about your son?' said Shepherd.

'No, why?'

'You still have no idea where he might be?'

'As I told you before, I suspect he is in London and may be trying to get passage back to America. Why do you ask?'

'He may have been seen here, as late as Saturday evening, with the Hensons.'

'He can't have been in Leicester. Trust me, whoever was seen with the Hensons, it was not Michael.'

'You are his Mother, and you are bound to be protective of him. Now the two men look like they are dead too, we really do need to find him.'

'So find him, Constable. No doubt your Inspector Hatter is doing his best already, back in London. Perhaps you should join him?'

'Thank you for your help, Miss MacCormack. Please let Beddows know what I have said. Now, if you would, we need to speak to Annie.'

Eibhlin went off to the area behind the performance arena, where the tents and small enclosure was filling up as the performers closed down for the night.

'What was all that about?' said Kettle.

'She is angry with me because of what Mr Charters has done with Beddows.'

'A woman scorned?' said Kettle, smirking.

'I somehow get the feeling that she is, as much as she denies so. She says she does not know where Beddows is, and I also suspect that she is lying about that.'

'What about Lenihan?'

'She says she has still heard nothing, and suggests we should concentrate on London,' Shepherd replied.

'But if he was here after she had already stated he was in London, we have a problem,' said Kettle. 'We need to see if Mr Charters is prepared to have somebody looking out for him, down here, covertly.'

'But what if the tall, dark man wasn't Michael Lenihan? We still have the rumours about The Globe and a revenue man. I think Mr Charters will want us to concentrate on that at present, and that London will be down to Inspector Hatter and his colleagues. what do you think?'

'There are a lot of loose ends up here, and tonight our job is to identify the Henson bodies. Here is your witness, I presume?' noting a woman walking back alongside Eibhlin MacCormack.

'That is Annie, who went out with the elder brother, Henry. Peter is the smaller of the two.'

'The infirmary then, Shepherd. Times like this I wish we had a carriage, like our county colleagues. I hope Annie is up for a long, humid walk?'

*****

Well after midnight, Samson Shepherd walked through the door at his Aunt's house on Twizzle and Twine Passage. His Aunt would be long retired to bed, but Sally was sat under a bright lamp, reading a well thumbed copy of her beloved 'Mansfield Park'. Shepherd noted how brown the pages had turned, and so quickly.

'I am surprised to see you still up and about,' Shepherd professed.

'I hate it when you're late home. I know it is a murder enquiry, but I always wonder where you are and that you are safe. Jane Austen is keeping me amused.'

'It hasn't been a particularly good day, today. Beddows has had an awful fall out with Mr Charters, and sees me as part of the problem. I think he actually hates me. He has not been himself of late.'

'Poor man, he must be very distressed, to hate you?' Sally's little tongue in cheek was missed by Shepherd, completely.

'I have left messages for him to contact me, but he has been suspended from duty and to add insult to injury, his wife has thrown him out. I don't know where he is.'

'Suspended? What has been going on?'

'I know he and his wife have been having a particularly bad time. He warned me not to let the job destroy what we have, like it has done to his marriage. But it's more than that. He is so angry and so not himself. I don't know what to think any more.'

'And why has he fallen out with you?'

'Over the last day or so, he says I have doubted him. He has found friendship with the mother of one of our suspects and I thought he may have taken a drink. Twice he has been placed in the way of temptation, and I am not sure that he is not weakening. Charters fears the old Beddows is returning.'

'Until you sit down and talk with him, you won't find out. It's never the best time to talk, honestly, when you are distracted by a murder. Wait until the right moment and I'm sure you will sort it out.'

'I hope so, Sally. He has been a true friend and a knowledgeable mentor. I do not go out of my way to offend him, but at present, he is clearly offended by me.'

'Give him time to think things through. He will find the truth and things will restore themselves. I have made you a small platter of cold ham. Come and eat, and then off to bed with you. I assume another busy day tomorrow, and yet another early start?'

'You know the demands of the job so well. Perhaps this is what Beddows is warning us about. What would we do if the job soured our marriage?'

'You're stuck with me, Samson Shepherd. Rest assured.'

Pink eyes

Tanky Smith and Black Tommy arrived by train at Euston terminus in the early hours of Tuesday morning, not long after Kettle and Shepherd had finished at the infirmary and the bodies of the Henson brothers formally identified by Annie.

The journey had been long and hot, and the basic wooden slats of the open seating had made the trip most uncomfortable. Neither men had used the train before, and had ended up sitting with their backs to the engine with coats cloaked over their heads to protect them from what seemed like an endless stream of hot cinders, and to prevent loss of their precious headwear. Black Tommy thought it was like being transported in an old cattle wagon, and it was the price to pay for new modes of transport. They were glad to get out at the end of a six hour trip.

If they had travelled by coach, albeit more comfortable, they would still have another ten hours or so of journey remaining. Neither could see Robert Charters putting his hands in the borough coffers for first class covered seating.

Tanky suggested that taking a cab would lead to questions or conversation that they didn't want to risk, so agreed to take a slow walk via Marylebone and on to the contact in Paddington. The lodging house was in Praed Street, off the Edgware Road, close to the wharf overlooking the Grand Junction Canal, and predominantly the lodging of navvies and boatmen.

It was a rough area, considering how close it was to Hyde Park and the City, a short walk away. It was only half an hour walk across the parks to Whitehall and the likeliest lair of Inspector Hatter. Far enough away to remain safe from prying eyes, they anticipated, at a good ninety minutes away from the cheapest and roughest inns and lodging houses along the Thames and its docks, where Michael Lenihan might, most likely, be secreted.

The walk was pleasant in the cooling air.

Surprisingly to the men, many of the streets of London were still bustling. Some of the green areas were exposed and warnings of footpads and highwaymen still abounded, a danger to even hardened coppers.

One or two uniformed constables were noted along the walk, drunkenly staggering across side roads, and like the constables they had left behind in Leicester, a walk between grog spots seemed common practice. Clearly no interest in passersby, just personal agendas to fulfil, and staying safe.

Tanky and Black Tommy split up at intervals and took turns to step into a doorway or alley and ensure they were not subject of any speculative followers.

Tanky had heard tale of a group of men who were known of, unofficially, as the *'Special Branch'*, which, according to the Metropolitan Police didn't exist, and thus vehemently denied. Tanky suspected that this was where Hatter actually operated. This shady group had likely evolved from The Alien Office, which had been formed and, subsequently, expanded under William Wickham, the Country's earliest spymaster, since 1792. In recent times, it was rumoured that Palmerstone was tasked, personally, by Victoria, to oversee the security of the state using *all available means*.

They were reputedly bad buggers, mean and ruthless, and had direction from above and beyond the Police. Peel's rules did not apply in this department. Anything subversive or out of the ordinary, particularly potential enemies of the state, were their target.

Charters was not surprised to hear such tales, with Hay holding such power, but It did beg questions about Hatter's interest in a divisional murder and burglary. Sat on the corner of Praed Street was a very new and ornate pub, The Fountain's Abbey, which was now in darkness, but both men could hear voices inside. No doubt 'friends of the landlord' enjoying out of hours libation.

Hearty singing could be heard from the rear.

I went to an alehouse I used to frequent,
And I told the landlady my money was spent
I asked her for credit, she answered me, 'Nay',
Saying, 'Custom like yours I can have any day'

And it's no, nay, never!
No nay never no more
And I'll play the wild rover,
No never no more

Smith and Haynes could have murdered a tankard of ale of two after the uncomfortable journey.

'Tommy. I bet there's a few in there, trying it on with the landlady, just as the song suggests,' said Tanky, chuckling.

'Is your mate going to welcome us with some well deserved libation, at this unearthly hour?' asked Black Tommy.

'He should be up and about,' said Tanky.

'You sound confident. Hope he has got a brew in, or knows the landlord, here. I'm gagging for one.'

'He is a night owl. He rarely sleeps at night, and will be up, I'm sure. So long as he isn't out.'

'So, he'll be up but he might be out?'

'That's about right.'

'What is he, a burglar or the night soil man?'

'I knew you were good, Tommy. Didn't take you long to work that out.'

'You're joking, tell me you are,' said Tommy, anxiously.

'He's a lamp lighter. He walks around the streets of Paddington lighting lamps, and then when everyone is waking up, he goes around and snuffs them out. He used to be the local knocker-upper but he couldn't be guaranteed to get his sorry arse out of bed, so it was a sensible life change.'

'You had me worried there for a minute. I had this horrible vision of shit developing, and feared the worse.'

'It's still a doss house, and he was never the cleanest bloke I knew,' said Tanky.

'What do I call him?'

'His name is Trinder, Edward Trinder, but they call him Torchy, because of his job. He answers best to Torchy. Loves playing with fire, he does.'

Tanky led Tommy down into a small area at the front of a grubby looking lodging house. The smell of stagnant water drifted through the air from the canal wharf. The house looked damp, and green mould covered many of the area windows below the level of Praed Street. The steps were similarly mouldy, and Tommy momentarily felt his hobs lose their grip, and he grabbed Tanky, bringing about the usual foul response.

Little pink eyes could be seen in dark recesses, as the local rats watched the new arrivals.

Tanky gave three loud raps on the front door. A few seconds later, a further three raps. Movement came from inside, and a flicker of light from a candle or small lamp could be seen in the narrow glass panel above the door.

'Who's there?' a gruff voice called out.

'A ghost from your past, you old bugger. Tanky Smith.'
A moment passed, as very odd noises, including what sounded like multiple chains, could be heard, and the door opened enough for a nose and eye to be seen, inside. A pale, withered fellow, with slim, sallow face, and piggy eyes, set deep in black recesses, scruffily unshaven. He had a look of 'not long for this world' about him, Tommy considered.

'Bugger me, Tanky Smith. What you doing down here? Changed your mind at long last and joined the coppers down here?'

Black Tommy looked puzzled.

'I need a favour, and I decided it was time to call it in,' Tanky replied.

'Favour?' said Black Tommy?

'Cor blimey. Who's your minder? Handsome bugger, if trees are your thing,' Torchy looked up and down at Black Tommy's menacing frame.

'This is my partner in crime. Detective Sergeant Tommy Haynes.'

'Two coppers at the same time. Don't sound good.'

'Nothing for you to get worried about, Torchy. A little bird tells me you're still at the fire lighting business?'

'When are you two going to tell me what went on in the past?' said Black Tommy.

'Some things are best left, Tommy. Let's just say he owes me a large favour. Family and bad pennies. Saved him from the old devil's claws.'

'Are you going to invite us in, or are we going to walk round with you on your rounds?' said Tanky.

The door opened, and Torchy stepped back to allow the two men in. The smell of the rooms was rank, but both Tanky and Black Tommy were accustomed, and spent many an hour tucked away in similar hovels in the Rookeries, but still wondered how people lived like it, day in and day out?

Dark stains permeated the bare walls, evidence that water was gaining access from street level, and as the light of Torchy's candle passed, shimmers of light reflected from wet areas. The floor was thick with old rags and paper, probably as an attempt to soak up the water, but had been left and had formed a soggy mat, which still squelched under foot, in places.

'Got a bit of a damp problem, I'm afraid. Can't do much about it being this close to the cut,' Torchy explained, shrugging his bony shoulders. 'Should have me own boat really.'

In a smaller back room, a leaded grate was lit, and a well used kettle simmered over the flames. An oil lamp weakly lit the small room, and a square table with four roughly hewn wooden chairs filled the centre of the space. Piled on the table were an assortment of old mugs and tankards, most of which were unwashed, amidst half empty bottles of something or another.

'So what brings two of you to my neighbourhood?'

'We need somewhere to doss for a few days. Out the way, so to speak, whilst we try and apprehend a suspect,' explained Tanky.

'Sounds rather strange. Thought you would have found an inn more suitable?'

'We don't want the local constables to know we are anywhere nearby. This is far enough away from our area of interest, and rumour has it you have a stream of people coming and going, so we shouldn't be that obvious. Got to keep this to ourselves, though, Torchy. Not a word to anyone. There's some ruthless coppers that are looking at the same problem, and we don't want our paths to cross unless it's on our terms.'

'Quiet as a mouse, me, Tanky, as you well know.'

'There's a few of them around, by the look of it,' said Tommy, noticing the droppings and little piles of shredded papers around the room.

'You want to see the rats. That's what you worry about down here. Big buggers they are. You want to see my cat?'

Torchy walked back into the front room, pointing out a mangy looking ginger tom. The cat's hair was falling out, and it's face was a mass of scars. One eye was white over, and obviously blind.

'That's what rats do, down here. He's my ratter, but he's lost as many fights as he's won with the buggers. Keeps going back for them, though. Not bad for twelve years old.'

'I know a few bruisers back in Leicester that look like that,' Tommy laughed. 'Some of them at Tanky's expense.'

'I recall his reputation as a hard copper. Have to be up in them Rookeries of yours, I hear tell. You want to pop in to some of ours down here. The streets round the back of the canal wharf here are like that, but get up to Whitechapel while you're here, or better still, around Seven Dials, St. Giles and Tottenham Court Road. Scares me shitless when I've been dragged over that side on 'business'. Apparently the coppers in St. Giles don't last long, not the straight ones, anyhow.'

'How many you got dossing here at the moment then, Torchy?'

'Trade's rather poor at the moment, Mr Smith. Just two navvies working on the canal extension. Irish navvies, real piss heads. Not come back yet. Probably out shagging, or collapsed unconscious, somewhere.'

'Our story will be that we are waiting for a tobacco man that's been delayed into port. Waiting on news and then we'll be working our passage,' said Tanky.

'Thanks for telling me,' said Tommy. 'I hate ships. Get queasy on the thought of it.'

'Fancy a grog?' said Torchy.

'What you got?' said Tanky.

'How about some nice Barbados Rum. Got a bottle or two tucked away, that fell into my hands. Don't like it much, personally, but it's great for starting a good fire.' Torchy grinned through what were left of his blackened teeth stumps.

Torchy picked up three small glasses, and wiped them with his thumb, before filling them with the dark ruby liquid.

'Fancy some nosh, soak up the grog?' said Torchy.

'What is it?' Tanky enquired, as a strange smell sifted from the hearth.

'A bit of mutton broth.'

'Smells more like bow-wow mutton to me,' said Tanky. 'Where is your old mutt?'

'Good to see you haven't changed a bit, Tanky. Still a dry old sod. Here's to getting your man. Wouldn't say that to any copper down here, normally!'

Feeling rather the worse for the bottle of rum that they had managed to consume, Tanky and Tommy inspected the two beds that Torchy had provided them with. These were for his best guests, and in the second room of his private quarters. Threadbare sheets and blankets that smelled like they had not seen soap or water for some years. God help those in his poorer accommodation.

'Jesus, Tanky. We need danger money for just sleeping here. My bed's alive, by the look of it.'

'When you're asleep you won't notice it, and I don't reckon it will take us long to sleep tonight by the feel of my head. It'll look better in daylight.'

Loyalties

Herbert Kettle had allowed for a slightly later start, given the time they had finished at the infirmary the previous evening, and Shepherd, forever the early bird, was sat in the small rear office at the station when he arrived, around six forty-five.

'Mr Charters wants to see you before we do anything, this morning. He should be in shortly,' said Kettle.

Shepherd half expected Charters to walk in, as if by magic, but not so today.

'Any idea what for?' asked Shepherd, anxiously.

'Two and two suggests something to do with Beddows.'

'Shouldn't be surprised. I must have annoyed him terribly by not saying anything when asked. I just thought it was right for Sergeant Beddows to explain for himself.'

'And so you did, Shepherd,' came the gritty voice from the corridor, as Charters entered the building.

'Can you give us five minutes Sergeant?' said Charters, not that it was really a question, nor that Kettle had an option.

He stepped out into the courtyard to inspect the flowerbeds, lovingly tended by Mrs Charters. Gardening was also his passion, and he had thought a spell of gardening leave might do him and his vegetables a bit of good.

Charters closed the door behind him and sat himself down, back to the window onto St. Martins West.

'Constable Shepherd. I admire your loyalty to Sergeant Beddows, and understand why you chose not to speak out against him. I must admit I was not best pleased, but we have to move on. Lesson learned, I hope?'

'I hope so, Sir.'

However, at the same time Shepherd was thinking that he would not do anything differently, if pushed. Friendship and loyalty were vital in this job, albeit Beddows had not seen fit to respect his efforts.

'You probably know Beddows better than any man in this job, Shepherd. What's going on with the man?'

'I now know he has problems at home, as he has made clear for a few days. I didn't know how bad it was, until I spoke with Mrs Beddows yesterday and was shocked at her bitterness and hostility towards Sergeant Beddows, and this job.'

'She did come across as a harsh woman.' Charters half smiled, raising his eyebrows and his glaze at Shepherd. 'What about this woman, Eibhlin MacCormack?'

'She is the mother of one of our suspects. She is a very assertive and unusual woman in my estimation. However she also seems honest and sincere. She also does appear to have taken a shine to Sergeant Beddows.'

'Women and policemen are not a good mix, and many a constable has come unstuck as a result. Remember that, Shepherd. '

'Yes, Sir. That being said I don't believe that Sergeant Beddows would be so foolish as to fall for her just like that, nor jeopardise the investigation of a serious crime by doing so.'

'So, when you discovered him in her caravan, what were your first thoughts, honestly?'

'I was shocked, to be honest, even to find him there. But he was asleep on a chair against a table and she was clearly dressed and asleep on top of her own bed. He has been terribly tired, of late.'

'But to be shocked, there must have been something that made you so?'

'It was not what I had imagined he would do. We had

been offered a drink by the Romanies, earlier, up on the racecourse. Beddows didn't take it down, but suggested that we would offend them if we didn't *appear to* take their offerings. He spat his out, which made me realise that he still has a dislike for the stuff.'

'And what did you do, Shepherd?' Charters gave him a lingering look.

'As with Sergeant Beddows, I spat it out, Sir, Wouldn't want to get tarred with any reputation of drinking on duty.'

'A wise decision, Shepherd, as it is truly the Devil's brew. Have you spoken to him since?'

'No Sir. I left message that if he wished to speak, I would like to speak with him. I have always considered him not just a colleague but also a friend.'

'You must think I was overly harsh with him?'

'You have to keep 50 odd men in order, Sir,' said Shepherd, diplomatically.

'If he had not been so stubborn and pig-headed, I may have not reacted so harshly, but he made it clear that he is disenchanted with his work, and I had little option. I am a harsh man, and I do question his present ability to make wise decisions.'

'Sir, I understand.' Shepherd didn't really understand at all. In the midst of a murder? He suspected this was more about Charters' iron will and reputation, else Hatter's sudden intervention.

'Sergeant Beddows must make his own mind up, now, as to where he sees his future. If you do cross paths with him, please make sure he realises that.'

'I have no idea where he is at present, Sir. Miss MacCormack states she has not seen him and knows not of his whereabouts. He is not at his home address. Would Sergeants Smith or Haynes have better knowledge of where he might be found?'

'Both Sergeants Smith and Haynes are otherwise

engaged, until further notice, and cannot be of assistance to us.'

Shepherd gave a puzzled look.

'Do not ask,' said Charters. 'Beddows whereabouts is not a priority at present. Leave him to his own devices, and hopefully he will come to his senses and return to us with his tail between his legs.'

'And in the meantime?' Shepherd enquired.

'Sergeant Kettle and yourself must carry on with the investigation. We now have three dead bodies, and we are missing Michael Lenihan. If he is our tall, dark haired man, he may still be closer to us than Miss MacCormack might lead us to believe, and I want him here, for us to question.'

'And if he isn't?'

'I want to know who that third man is. You still have the information about the revenue man at The Globe to explore?'

'We do, Sir.'

'Then Lenihan and The Globe must be the Leicester priorities. Fetch Sergeant Kettle in, and I will confirm what I want of you both.'

*****

John Beddows had sat huddled on a bench at Wigston railway station. Very aware of his visibility within the borough, he had acquired transport from the circus, hiding under the tarpaulin covering a small cart which had been driven by one of Eibhlin's trusted colleagues. He had left the borough under cover of darkness, and dropped off on the bottom of the hill below Wigston All Saints spire, from where he had made his way down to his current location. He had given some thought to taking the night coach from within the borough, but considered it too open to view. His trip to London was between him and Eibhlin, and not for any of Charters' prying eyes and ears. Spying wasn't confined to the capital, he reckoned.

The station was unmanned overnight, and he had kept reasonably out of sight of any passing county constable. That being said, if he was to be approached, he had a plausible story worked out and by the time news got back to borough colleagues, he would be on his way by train to Hitchin, where he could connect on to the capital.

By eight a.m. he had paid for his fare and was on his way to London, with cash in his pocket and his head full of information from Eibhlin to assist him at the other end.

By tea time, he would be there, and then he would have to think quickly on his feet, looking for one man in a City of over two and a half million people, compared to Leicester's seventy thousand. Nor would he have the resources available to Inspector Nimrod Hatter to call upon. Beddows thoughts of needle and haystack sat prominent.

The angel of death

Nearing ten a.m. Kettle and Shepherd walked around
the edge of the racecourse and sought the Romany
gathering once again. The description of the tall, dark
haired man, was in need of clarification, and any
further 'insight' would be welcomed.

Before they had left Town Hall Lane, Queenie and the
scavengers had collected their dues, and a further florin
had been handed over, from their 'informants pot',
courtesy of Mr Charters.

The scavengers had then gone on to see Oliver Mitchell,
who had acquired an assortment of clean and
comfortable clothing for them to share out. They did
not tell of their finds, the previous day, and had enjoyed
the shelter of the tent and shared out the other things
they had scavenged, including some strange looking
shoes, soft soled and very comfortable, from the edge
of the Biam. After all, they were scavengers, first and
foremost.

Shepherd was keen to learn whether the old woman had
any more dreams of which to tell. What could she offer
that hadn't been considered?

Kettle was more robust in his response to the offer of
poteen from the Baro, and made it quite clear that it
was a very kind gesture, but against their regulations,
and refused for both he and Shepherd.

His wife was amused, and sat puffing on her pipe,
blowing smoke from her nose, and laughing like
somebody more akin with the asylum, across the green,
which left Kettle feeling somewhat disturbed. He had
dealt with his fair share of mentally deranged, during

his time in the borough, but this woman was stranger than anyone he had ever previously encountered.

'Constable Shepherd has told me about your vision, and we have found the bodies of the two men we were seeking, much as you say you foresaw. We need to ask you more about the other man in your vision.'

'The angel of death? Pure evil to be sure,' the woman replied.

'When you saw him, what exactly did you see?' said Kettle.

'A tall man. Dark haired. Very upright and thin. He carried death in his head and in his hands.'

'What do you mean by that?' said Shepherd.

'His intention was to kill them from the start. He made them feel safe, and then mullered them. He had his weapon in his coat, ready for a chance when it came. A strange curved knife, from foreign lands, with which he was to despatch them, and the river flowed red.'

'That's very interesting,' said Kettle. 'Do you see him now, or are you relating what you saw earlier?'

'The river has just shown itself to me, again, as has the knife. It has killed many, but not here. I see red sand and smell spices. I feel heat and dust.'

'Are the man and the knife connected to other killings then? Is that what you are telling me?' said Kettle.

'The knife is connected to two men. Both are tall and dark. Both have killed with it. Both men are dark and menacing. One controls the other. The elder man holds a Bible.'

'In the original vision, you said the man was tall, dark haired and scruffy,' said Shepherd.

'He wears shabby clothes. Drab. Not how he would be seen, normally. Killing clothes. I see him bathing in a river and blood coming off his hands, and clothes burning nearby. I see him carrying a bag away across his chest. '

'And?' said Shepherd.

'He is gone, the angel of death. I can't see him anymore. We are now in danger, too much danger. You be careful as you are all in danger because of this, too. Death is close at hand, I am being told, and closer than you may realise.'

*****

'Well that was all very peculiar,' said Kettle. 'I've heard tell of these Gipsy women and their visions, but never seen one working, before. Most bizarre.'

'If we can believe her,' said Shepherd. 'However, she came up with the river flowing red, as Surgeon Hamilton had suggested, and we did find a small fire, which wasn't really a surprise, given they were camped by the river. But she said that they had been gutted, and the knife had killed many before, by more than one hand.'

'She said a strangely curved knife,' said Kettle. 'I had a relative in the Afghan wars, and he brought one home with him. Got it off a native soldier, as I recall. Called it a Kukri.'

'Well, it certainly doesn't sound like Michael Lenihan. This man is cold and calculated, if you continue to believe the woman.'

'If he is in London, as Miss MacCormack has always stuck by, then he is at the peril of Inspector Hatter. We can't do anything about that, and it is in the lap of the gods. However, we need to establish who this dark haired man is, if he exists at all, and who controls him. Mr Charters may not be keen to have us following up on an angel of death from a Romany vision.'

'But if he is real, what does she mean by death being close at hand? Somebody here in Leicester that is a real danger to us, perhaps? We need to talk to Mrs Paget and her Father, again. They may throw some light on the background behind Paget seeking excessive loans. Perhaps we need to look harder at The Globe and talk of corrupt revenue men.'

'And that is where we should head to next, Constable Shepherd, Mr Harrison's factory and then The Globe. I could really do with a cold lemonade to wash away this dust.'

Special Branch

Tanky Smith and Black Tommy Haynes took a long slow stroll. After a shared bowl of clean cold water, and a welcome wash, they had dug into their bag of disguises, and had surprised even Torchy himself when he walked in on them.

Tanky had gone for the boatman look, and beneath a woollen hat, he had donned a dark beard, and a scruffy looking canvas top and breeches. His clogs echoed on the stone floor, and were so uncomfortable he changed into some soft canvas shoes in anticipation of a long walk along the Thames. Tommy had gone for a soft shirt and apron, and wore a long dark wig, tied in a pony tail. His hobnails were tried and tested, and were amongst his favourite means of personal protection, having brought many a big man down after a toecap in the crown jewels. A stubby pipe poked out of his teeth. They truly were masters in the art of disguise, as many of Leicester's hardened crime gangs had found to their cost.

Tommy slapped at his neck, and in between his thumb and forefinger, squeezed a fat flea, which had come to his notice, despite the wash and change. 'Bastard crawling with 'em,' he grunted, looking towards the bed he had slept surprisingly soundly in, no doubt helped by the rum.

'Don't start scratching. That's all I ask,' said Tanky. 'You know how it makes me start and my rash comes out.' Tommy casually started scratching his armpits, and Tanky threw one of the discarded clogs towards him with some force, striking the bed, a myriad of little black specks bolted for cover.

London was as hot and smelly as Leicester, but busier. Very busy. There were people everywhere, and the roads were noticeably congested, with dozens of carts and carriages of all shapes and sizes plying their trade too and from the docks along the river. Noise was overwhelming. It was also crawling with foreigners, of every colour and tongue you could imagine, probably merchantmen and traders.

'Give it a few years, Tommy, and this is what Leicester will be like, mark my words.'

Their first stop was 4 Whitehall Place, or more accurately, Great Scotland Yard, at the rear, the headquarters of the Metropolitan Police. They needed to locate the offices of Inspector Nimrod Hatter, and some cautious observations would be the most likely source of success. He would no doubt venture in or out at some stage, to the beck and call of his masters. Smith would take up a position in Whitehall, itself, and Haynes in Northumberland Avenue. With no line of sight, whoever identified Hatter would have to follow him on his own. The contingency was that they should meet up under Charing Cross, just to the north of Whitehall, at six o'clock, unless their follow (should it take place) took them past one or the other, which would be more favourable.

The streets around Whitehall were crawling with Military men of all description and ranks, and those with the biggest hats and medals gravitated to the buildings along and around the Police Headquarters.

Election tensions were high, with voting due in just a few days, and Derby was busy, rallying his supporters. Politicians and their guardians rode in shiny growlers and made grand entrances at their ports of call.

Tanky imagined who they might be, and what plans they were scheming. Tommy wondered what they were filling their fat bellies with, and suspected this was more like a fancy dining club than a real working hub of the country - all brass and hot wind.

Whitehall and Westminster had far too much going on for Tanky and Black Tommy to become of interest to anyone, Tanky had anticipated, optimistically.

A nosey Metropolitan uniformed sergeant with a barrel chest, full of war ribbons, walked towards where Tanky was sitting, and stood in front of him, leaning against an impressive looking pace stick, topped with an ornate silver metal handle. A useful and handy little cudgel, Tanky thought.

'What are you doing, cluttering up our streets of power, you scruffy toe-rag?'

'I'm enjoying the sunshine, Constable. My ship ain't in yet, and I have time on my hands.'

'Sergeant, not a bloody constable!' he bellowed. 'I know blokes like you, waiting for some gent to pass by, and no doubt turn him over, one way or another. Piss off, or I'll cart you over the road. Mr Disraeli is due here any minute, and he don't like people loitering. Very nervous he is about loiterers. Thinks someone might take a pot shot at him. Can't think why?'

'Used to study law, I did,' said Tanky. 'That was before I decided that a life of travel and adventure was more for me. What powers are you anticipating carting me in with?'

'Got a smart arse, have we? How about if I was to say the Vagrancy Act? That would do nicely, then, wouldn't it?' said the sergeant, getting angry and loud, pointing and prodding with his pace stick.

'What do you know about Special Branch, Sergeant,' Tanky enquired, menacingly, 'and what if me and my mates were to take objection at your manners?'

'Special Branch? Don't know what you're talking about my friend.' A look of concern crossed the large man's face.

'I think you do Sergeant, and I think you know it is most unwise to cross us, so hurry away and let me alone to do my job, looking after the likes of Mr Disraeli,' Tanky snarled. 'We're all over the place, today, so behave. And a word of warning. If you ever raise that fecking stick at me again, I shall shove it so far up your lardy arse you will never sit down again! Savvy?'

A long nervous silence, and then a hasty salute, thrown up reluctantly, and a sudden realisation that perhaps even a salute was a giveaway, the sergeant turned tail and scurried off, apologising, pathetically.

Tanky considered whether it had been a wise ploy, but as well as getting rid of the nosey man, he had reaffirmed that word was out that such a branch actually existed, and the reaction suggested they were feared. He was also confident that it was unlikely to be reported by the sergeant for fear of reprisal. A result, Tanky considered, grinning broadly. He hoped that Tommy would not get similarly challenged on the other end of the street. He would have his own ruse, no doubt, if challenged.

What's a life worth?

Kettle and Shepherd climbed the stone steps to the first floor of the factory. The air was thick with dust and the smell of oil, and both noticed how the structure of the building seemed to vibrate with the hum of the machines.

'Where do we find Mr Harrison's office?' said Kettle to a passing worker.

'At the end on the left, me duck, can't miss it. Fancy indoor windows with his name all over them in big letters.'

Sure enough, very fancy windows they were indeed, all frosted glass and engravings, where, sat at a large desk looking out over the street, was the man they desired to speak to.

Knocking on the glass, Harrison beckoned them in.

'Yes, gentlemen, can I help you? Oh, Constable Shepherd, I didn't recognise you.'

'Is it a convenient time for Sergeant Kettle and me to ask you a few more questions?' said Shepherd.

'No time is convenient, where money is either to be made or squandered, but as good as any, I suppose. Not brought Sergeant Beddows along with you?'

'We have heard tales that your son-in-law may have had some financial difficulties?' said Kettle, not beating about the bush.

'Tales? Malicious and scandalous tittle tattle more like,' Harrison replied.

'It doesn't come across like that to us, Sir. In fact, it opens up all sorts of possibilities regarding what the motive for Mr Paget's murder may have been,' said

Kettle.

'Motive? It was a burglary, man. He was damned unlucky, and that's the top and bottom of it.'

'We have reliable sources that say you have personally bailed Mr Paget out recently, and that not only did you threaten to put him out of business, that you would see fit that Mrs Paget would leave him,' said Shepherd.

'That's rather off the mark. Look, he had a bad run on some of his speculation, and yes, I have settled a few accounts for him and his business, as I don't want my daughter to end up known as the wife of a disgraced fool with no money.'

'Several people heard the threats,' said Shepherd.

'So I may have raised my voice in the wrong place, but nothing more than that. You surely don't think me a suspect?'

'We have to consider all our options, Mr Harrison. When we hear one thing from you and your daughter, and a completely opposite story from independent witnesses, we have to check these differences out,' said Kettle.

'Has he borrowed from anybody else, to your knowledge?' said Shepherd.

'I am not his keeper, as much as you may think he sounds a kept man,' said Harrison, clearly annoyed. Harrison reached into his waistcoat and pulled out a gold fob watch on a matching chain. 'I hope this won't take much longer, I have a meeting with the Mayor, shortly.'

'Why would he go to another for a loan?' said Shepherd.

'If he did, at all? As far as I am aware he is good for credit at present and has money. Ask my daughter, if you doubt me. Anyway, I thought he had lost bank notes of his own?'

'We will speak to your daughter, Mr Harrison, but we wanted your version of events. The money obviously went into the bank, but where from, if it wasn't from you?' said Shepherd.

'There are various means of loans, freely available in the borough, if you know where to ask. If the banks are wary of a proposal, there are one or two very well connected people who offer a loan at a higher rate, not that I would wish to consider such a transaction. However, if there is a chance of a deal being lost and a few guineas more in interest, then they may be considered.'

'Have you heard tell of anyone from Her Majesty's Revenue, that may be offering such opportunity?' said Kettle.

Harrison flinched, noticeably, and hesitated. 'Be careful, gentlemen. I have heard tell of such people, not just one. But dealing with The Revenue is not a wise move, in the current climate. No business wants them on their back.'

'And why might that be?' asked Kettle.

'There are fine margins between profit and wealth, Sergeant. Those of us who chose wealth sometimes have to be prudent about where and how we do business, and *legally* minimise our liabilities to Queen Victoria's tax collectors.'

'Surely they would be as keen to get their noses into businesses that won't do business with them, let alone ones that do go to them? In any event, this sounds more like unofficial loans, and that worries me,' said Kettle.

'Either way, they are bad news, and best kept at a distance. My accountants deal with those at The Revenue - the legitimate ones - once a year, and are much more attuned to what they will accept. My accountants are very prudent as to what is permissible.'

'How far would you have gone with your threats if Mr Paget had let you and your family down?' said Shepherd.

'I would have choked him out of business. I would have made him a laughing stock, once my daughter was removed from his grips, and then I would have taken everything I could that he might have owed me, in money or property. He would never be able to do business in Leicester, ever again. That is probably common knowledge amongst the cotton industry in Leicester.'

'Would you ever have physically hurt him?' said Shepherd.

'If he had hurt my daughter, physically or emotionally I might have considered thrashing him, but wouldn't any man?'

'What about getting somebody to recover your dues, if he failed to repay a debt to you?' Kettle suggested.

'Haven't I just said? I would make him a laughing stock. I would take my time and enjoy the demise. However, that was never the case and he did not owe me anything that I had not given freely. My daughter was well looked after. They had a nice new house in a good area, and things were looking up. If he has deceived me, and deceived her, and this murder has happened because of that, I have no pity for him.'

'What if it transpires that he was up to his eyeballs in debt and your daughter loses the house and her nice trappings?' said Kettle.

'She will never be poor. He had life assurance and when our solicitors sort out all the estate, I am confident that she will be a wealthy widow, even if it is through the assurance company and some astute planning by Edward before his demise.'

'I have never considered life assurance,' said Shepherd. 'What would it be worth to a widow?'

'You can buy a good assurance policy for anything between two guineas and six guineas per hundred guineas assured. Thus, I suspect that she will see several thousand guineas as a result of his death, as I encouraged him to make sure she was well protected.

With cholera and recent epidemics being so indiscriminate, it is wise, Constable Shepherd, *even for lowly policeman.'*

'Thank you for the advice, Mr Harrison, but we have very little spare on our wages,' said Shepherd, noting the cynical tone of the advice.

'Don't leave it too late, Constable. You never know when you will be called.'

'That sounded rather menacing,' said Kettle.

'Menacing? No, I would hazard that with such an unpopular role to perform, the risk to you gentlemen is rather higher than for most, so I would advocate you get some professional advice.'

'Perhaps you could suggest to the Mayor and his colleagues on the Watch Committee, that we should get life assurance as a part of our remuneration,' said Kettle, laughing.

'I am sure they would not see any extra expense on our Constabulary as justifiable, especially when you have so few real friends or support within the borough.'

'But we are a necessary resource, Mr Harrison, as much as we are seen as a nuisance to many. Who else would go after you son-in-law's killer for so little reward?' Kettle looked annoyed.

'Then I suggest you get after the killer, Sergeant. By the way, the gentleman I saw you with at the Railway station, Shepherd. Was his name Hatter, by perchance?'

'Why the interest?' Shepherd enquired, rather abruptly.

'I told you, I thought he looked familiar.'

'How did you come up with that name?' said Kettle.

'I may have encountered him at a dinner in London, hosted by his Father, some years ago. I recall him as a very efficient and assertive man. Perhaps he might offer you some assistance?' Harrison smirked.

'Inspector Hatter is already doing just that, with any London enquiries that may be relevant to the case,'

Shepherd confirmed.

'So you know his Father, also?' Kettle enquired.

'Yes, I also met him the once, and recall him, vaguely. What a very small world?' Harrison seemed to smirk. 'Good day, gentlemen.'

*****

Kettle and Shepherd walked across to London Road, intending to speak with Edward Paget's widow, whilst temporarily residing at her parents' address. Kettle hoped that the widow would be more inclined to expose her dead husband's accurate financial situation, but had a niggling feeling that he may be being rather optimistic.

'Strange that Mr Harrison had crossed paths with Inspector Hatter and his Father, before,' said Shepherd. 'I wonder if there may have been anything more to their acquaintance? Might be something we need to explore further. If Hatter's Father is as ruthless in business, as he was alleged to be in the service of Wellington?' Kettle pondered.

'I wonder what Algernon Hatter imports?' said Shepherd. 'Perhaps we can throw the name in when we speak with the widow,' said Kettle.

*****

Both men felt like they were seen as no better than the tradesmen who scurried in and out of the sumptuous premises, through a scullery door that was only accessible from the alleyway from Prebend Street. That is where they were directed by a rather surly butler who answered the front door and promptly closed it on them.

'We are here to see Mrs Edward Paget,' said Kettle, to a large woman, covered in aprons and flour dust, organising the deliveries and collections.

'Who shall I say is calling?'

Kettle identified himself, and the woman scurried off, leaving both men standing outside on the steps.

'Feel like we're not that welcome, Sergeant?'

'These people clearly don't like prying coppers, Shepherd. You'd think that a widow would want to co-operate closely with us, but the family just seem to close rank, close the doors, and everything carries on as if nothing has happened.'

'If it had just been about *their* money, I suspect they would be chasing us,' Shepherd suggested.

'Too bloomin' right. Money is their life, and this family have it by the bucket load, or at least so it appears.'

The man who had denied them access at the front door now appeared and escorted the two men through the large ground floor kitchen and laundry areas, and up a small, well worn, flight of stairs to a room at the rear of the house. There they stood in anticipation of the widow's arrival, a few minutes later.

'Good morning gentlemen,' said the widow, 'how can I help you, now?' She sounded bored with their persistence.

'We are sorry to disturb your mourning, Mrs Paget, but we have had some discrepancies that we need to discuss with you. We have just come from your Father's works, and he has given us some information. However, we need to check some facts with you, directly,' said Kettle.

'Did you tell my Father you were coming to see me, and if so what did he say?'

'We did tell him we needed to ask you some questions. He said nothing to suggest we shouldn't. Would it make a difference?' said Shepherd.

'He is very supportive, as Fathers should be, and I would not wish to offend his wishes.'

'The nature of our enquiry is about loans that your husband may have had to resort to,' said Kettle.

'Loans? How do you mean?'

'We understand from your father, that in the past he has 'settled' certain financial problems that your husband had run up, in order to protect you and the family reputation,' said Kettle.

'My Father told you that?'

'Yes, he did. He also told us that he would have put your husband out of business and run him out of the borough if he had put you at risk, physically or by reputation.'

'He is a very protective man, Mr Kettle, and a very astute businessman. That is why he is so successful and why he and my Mother have such a comfortable lifestyle,' indicating with a sweep of her hand at the plush surroundings. 'Wealth and comfort such as this doesn't come without hard work and sound financial prudence.'

'So were you aware that your Father settled some debts on his behalf?' said Shepherd.

'He had tried to be a little more ambitious than perhaps he should, but he only wanted to please me and to please Father. He borrowed more than he could pay back, and he was threatened that if he didn't settle, with a huge interest rate, then he would be ruined and ridiculed. My Father paid his debts, and yes, he did tell him that it should never happen again.'

'A loan from whom?' said Shepherd.

'I was never told, but it was not from a bank. Possibly a larger business, friends of my Father, even.'

'No name or other detail was ever disclosed?' said Kettle.

'My Father may have known, but you would need to ask him.'

'And would you have left him, if your Father had implored you?' asked Shepherd.

'I would have had to consider what was in my best interest, and whether it would also reflect on my Father's reputation, as a leading businessman in this community and the wider hosiery industry.'

'What about love?' Shepherd asked, closely watching her response.

'Love is not all that it is promised to be. Reputation, status, wealth and comfort are most important in this day and age, and if I can be assured of that, then I can live without love.' Her gaze momentarily shifted.

'Your eyes tell me otherwise,' said Shepherd.

'What do you mean?'

'You couldn't look at me when you answered about love. Do you really believe that a relationship can endure without love?' Shepherd continued.

'My Father and Mother made sure I understood the importance of *partnership* and that their lives were built on such foundations.'

'Did you and Mr Paget love each other, or not?' said Shepherd.

'We had an initial attraction to each other. It was business interests that drew us together, but it is our strength as a couple and as a family business that allowed us to prosper. I supported Edward as best as I could.'

'You seemed inconsolable when he passed. Surely that is not a reaction devoid of love?' said Shepherd.

'My Father would have seen that as a weakness, Mr Shepherd. Is it not a wife's duty to mourn in such a way?'

'Love or duty aside, has your husband had need to borrow any more, recently, to your knowledge?' said Kettle.

'Why should he? We have money in the bank, and good credit.'

'We understand that he may have had to borrow to buy

his latest intended machinery?' said Kettle.

'He told me that the money was already in the bank.'

'But how did it get into the bank?' said Kettle.

'You would need to talk to the company accountant, or view the bank statements.'

'Would you authorise for us to do that?' said Shepherd.

'You would need to ask my Father. He is drawing together all the legal and financial matters resulting from my Husband's death. We use the family solicitors.'

'Have you ever heard your husband talk of any dealings with somebody from Her Majesty's Revenue?' said Kettle.

Shepherd noticed her gaze drop to the carpet, once again, momentarily.

'I do not believe so. Why, may I ask?'

'We believe that he may have taken out a loan from an unscrupulous source, who may, possibly, be something to do with the revenue men. It may be that the same person has taken steps to regain his loan and interest, which may be motive for your husband's murder.'

'I'm sure he would have told me. He didn't appear worried or anxious.'

'Even if he knew that it might jeopardise not only his business, but also his marriage?' said Kettle.

'I would surely have seen changes in him. He seemed his normal self, and pleased with the prospect of the new machinery.'

'Did he ever use The Globe, Mrs Paget?' said Shepherd.

'Many of the new factory owners do business there, yes, of course. Mr Corah and his family, my Father, Edward, many of them would be in there.'

'Who did he associate with when he went there?' said Kettle.

'I don't know. He would meet buyers and dealers, many out of town enterprises would know that it was the best place to go to source new business.'

'Have you ever heard the name Hatter?' said Shepherd.
'Not to my knowledge. Is there a reason why I should?'
Shepherd saw no signs of deceit in her face.
'We believe that your father has some knowledge of him, something to do with the Cotton trade,' said Kettle.
'My Father has dealings with all sorts of competitors, some helpful, some not so.'
'What about your husband?' said Shepherd.
'Father may have introduced him to one or two, perhaps. Mainly he used the ones my Father had dealings with, as they were likely reliable.'
'Would you give some thought about the possibility that your husband may have taken out a loan. Anything at all that might throw some light on who may be behind it,' said Kettle.
'As I have told you gentlemen before, I would do anything to help catch my husband's murderer. Of course I will think, and I will talk with my Father, and see what he may offer to me that he might be reluctant to disclose to you.'
'He does not seem to have much time for the Police,' said Shepherd.
'His brother was a Chartist, and spent time in prison for his beliefs, after the troubles here in Leicester some years ago. He believes the police were heavy handed and treated the protestors unfairly.'
'My Uncle was a constable and was assaulted and killed during those same troubles. I know he was a just and fair man and he didn't deserve to die. There were no winners and losers, everyone would say they were doing what they believed in,' said Shepherd.
'He never forgives and never forgets, Constable Shepherd.'
'It takes a strong man to forgive, but I understand,' Shepherd replied.

'Have you heard anything more from your house-keeper, Eleanor Skinner, by any chance?' said Kettle.

'She returned yesterday, and is back at New Walk, looking after the house during my absence.'

'We would like to talk to her, in order to eliminate her from our enquiries,' said Shepherd.

'Even though you have these other suspicions?'

'We can't rule out any possibility, but at the moment we have too many to make sense. The sooner we can do so, the better,' said Kettle.

'She will be there all of the time from now on. I am sure you will quickly realise she has nothing to do with this horrible affair,' said Mrs Paget.

'We will try and catch up with her later today or early tomorrow,' said Kettle.

'Do you know how much you stand to inherit as a result of your husband's death?' said Shepherd.

'That is not something I have even considered, Constable. It is a rather tactless question given my loss.' She took a lace hankie from her sleeve and dabbed her eyes, tears starting to well.

'Far from it, Mrs Paget. With a large inheritance, and a large Insurance payout, some people might suggest that you have more to gain by your husband's death, and much more than a bad debt collection. A means to ensure that you never lose what you have, by your husband's financial difficulties.'

'I think it is time you left, gentlemen. I have never been so insulted. If this is what my Father sees in you, it is little wonder he has such a dislike for the police.'

'As my colleague, Sergeant Beddows, told your late husband, we are not here to be liked, we are here to discover the truth,' said Shepherd.

'Even if that means distressing a grieving family? A grieving widow? Is that fair or appropriate?'

'It is necessary, Mrs Paget. If we don't ask, we don't get

to the bottom of things and ultimately, the truth,' said Kettle.

'If you wish to speak to me again, then do so via my Father, or better still, our solicitors. I would prefer that we did not have to go through such a ghastly process again.'

'You may wish that, Mrs Paget, but I cannot guarantee anything. If we need to get back to you, we will, mark my words.' Kettle was developing a dislike for this family.

The Revenue

'What did you think of her reaction when I asked her about Hatter?' said Shepherd.

'She said she had never heard of the name. You read too much into how people look.'

'So what next, the housekeeper, or The Globe?' said Shepherd.

'I could murder a wet,' said Kettle. 'Let's go to The Globe and ask a few awkward questions, and see what we can turn up. Hopefully Mr Charters may have started his enquiry with his contacts in The Revenue, but in the interim, we can make a start.'

The bells of St. Martin's Church struck two, as the men walked into the inn. The place was packed with the usual mix for such a time of day, and tables were covered in papers and coins, passing hands quickly. Cautious eyes picked up on their presence.

Nathaniel Hitchcock gave them a knowing nod, as he poured a tray of small glasses full of gin, taking coins from a large, well dressed man as he did so, sliding the coins into the pocket in the front of his stained brown apron.

'No Sergeant Beddows with you today, Constable Shepherd? Thought you two were joined at the hip?'

'Don't ask, Mr Hitchcock. He is temporarily and otherwise engaged,' said Shepherd. 'Sergeant Kettle is suffering my presence instead.'

'What can we do for you gentlemen?'

'Remember we spoke of revenue men, when Beddows and I were here last? We need to try and work out who they are.'

'I said before, there is always talk of them spying on the wealthy who are dealing in here, but I could not say who was and who wasn't. Some of my regular customers never speak much, other than to buy their ale or gin, but there are some odd folk that come in, watching business, but not buying drink or joining anyone around the tables. Speculators, they call them, hence my ignorance.'

'Nobody has ever talked to you about one or any, in particular?' said Kettle.

'The Revenue are much feared, or at least treated with contempt or suspicion. Don't think anyone would dare identify them for fear of repercussion, let alone talk openly with them.'

'Let's try something different, then. What about loans? Who can people go to, or who do people go to for loans for their ventures, within the inn?'

'That's a different thing altogether. There are a couple of blokes that are known for offering loans that the banks wouldn't consider.'

'How often are they in?' said Kettle.

'Never quite sure. They seem to have a way of communicating within the business community, or the other way around, and turn up when there seems to be a need.'

'Surely, if they were that organised, the last place they would do their business would be within the inn?' Shepherd suggested.

'Many folk don't want to be seen to be doing anything that may affect their standing or reputation, so if it looks like normal business, within their normal day to day dealings, it goes much unnoticed,' said Hitchcock.

'Makes sense,' said Kettle.

'Are these men locals, or do they come from out of the borough?' said Shepherd.

'They aren't locals as far as I am aware, certainly not

from within the borough.'

'Do you know of any of them by name?' said Shepherd.

'I don't, Mr Shepherd. I don't ask, to be honest. If they are connected to The Revenue, they're not folk that a landlord wants on his back. Hard enough to make a shilling as it is. Anyways, other businessmen would not be too impressed if I upset their barrows, so to speak.'

'Who would be the best person to tell us, if we were to ask?'

'Would have thought that gentlemen like you would have a snout in here that you could rely on. Know any Freemasons?'

'Why do you ask that?' said Kettle.

'Freemasons may well be the answer to many, if not all, of the questions you currently have,' said Hitchcock. 'Many of the businessmen in here seem to think you have to be one to succeed.'

'I thought the suspicions about Freemasons was over and done with?' said Shepherd.

'Very powerful and influential men, they are, Mr Shepherd. Look at Sir Frederick Fowke, supposedly the main man for miles around, the Grand Master. Strange bloody lot and they all look after each other. Funny handshakes and secrets are not for me.'

'And why do you think they have the answers?' said Shepherd.

'They don't like outsiders who influence or interfere with their members interests. If the men you are after are not Freemasons, then somebody may wish to see them warned off, and you would be doing the Freemasons a service. If they are Freemasons, then you do have a problem, as it will be secretive and they protect each other, or sort out their own messes.'

'I suspect many of our local dignitaries may fall into that category,' said Kettle, 'and some of our notable Industrialists.'

'Mr Harrison didn't give anything away. Which camp do you think he falls into?' said Shepherd.

'Mr Harrison is without doubt a Freemason,' said Kettle. 'Did you not see some of the paraphernalia around his drawing room?'

'I wouldn't know a Freemason if he stood in front of me now,' said Shepherd. 'What paraphernalia?'

'All those strange images, crossed compasses, all seeing eyes and the like, and that funny jewel on his watch fob,' said Kettle.

'This is clearly a gap in my knowledge, and I have some research to do,' said Shepherd.

'My thoughts now are that Mr Harrison may have good reason not to go into too much detail about any loans that his son-in-law may have solicited. What goes on with these people stays behind locked doors. I bet he knows who Edward Paget went to.'

'And he won't tell us?' said Shepherd.

'We will have to find out for ourselves, Shepherd. Landlord, we may shortly upset some of your regulars, but we need to ask some questions.'

'Mr Kettle, I have a living to maintain. Please don't upset too many.'

Kettle and Shepherd walked slowly through the ground floor, which seemed to be mainly paymasters and hard drinkers. A few stocking knitters were selling baskets of low quality products.

Climbing the stairs to the first floor rooms, it became clear that there was more serious business being done, once again, and bags of coins were quickly pocketed or placed into bags or laps, under the tables. These were not paymasters, and there were no queues of workers. At one of the tables, a well dressed man was a little slow pocketing a small book, which Shepherd noticed, and nudged Kettle. The men around the same table looked caught out and a notable silence had developed.

'Gentlemen, we are policemen. Would you mind telling us what you have been doing?' said Kettle.

'Just some buying and selling,' said the man with the book, now concealed within his jacket.

'You looked like you were calculating something, totting it up in your book,' said Shepherd.

'No, just keeping a tally of my purchases,' said the man, looking flushed. Possibly the heat could be responsible, but more likely the reaction to being caught out.

'May I see your book?' said Shepherd.

'What for?' said the man, nervously.

'To see exactly what you were recording,' said Shepherd.

'You have no cause to ask me,' said the man, confidently.

'Do you work for the Revenue?' said Kettle.

'No, I am my own kept man. I thought you were Revenue men, that's why I put my book away.'

'In that case, what if we suspected that you were defrauding Her Majesty and that this book would be evidence of such an offence?' said Kettle.

The man coughed, and reached inside his jacket, pulling out a book of a similar size and dimension to the one constables carried, handing it to Kettle.

'What are all these columns of figures and names?' said Kettle.

'What I have just paid to each of these gentlemen for their products,' said the man.

'What products?' said Shepherd, noticing an absence of any goods at this particular table.

'Future goods,' said the man, swallowing visibly.

'Gentlemen, I take it you can show us the money that you have just been paid, then?'

The small group looked sheepish, with glances being exchanged amongst them.

'Empty your pockets, please,' said Shepherd.

'We were paying him, Mister, not like he said,' said a scruffy looking man, gaunt and pale.

'Why were you paying him?' said Shepherd.

'Times are hard. Sometimes we borrow against future production. Means we have money when we sometimes need a bit more. Wool and cotton is costly at the moment, and if we can buy more, we can make more stockings, and hopefully pay back what we owe, faster, yet make a small profit for ourselves.'

'So you are offering loans to these gentlemen,' said Kettle, eyeing the smarter man.

'Only small loans, Constable, and I am helping these gentlemen by doing so,' he replied.

'How much interest do you apply?' said Kettle.

'Two shillings for every guinea they borrow, an achievable reward and that most of them honour,' the man replied.

'And you declare all this to the revenue men?' Shepherd asked, loudly, causing a number of men about the rooms to look at the group.

'You'll get me locked up, or worse, Constable. No need to shout about my business. I'm not the only one here who does it.'

'So we understand. Are you a Freemason?' said Kettle.

'What?' said the man.

'What is your name and where do you live?' Shepherd called out loudly, again receiving the attention he anticipated from nearby.

'No, I am not a Freemason as it happens. Don't want anything to do with them?'

'What about the others?' said Kettle.

'The Freemasons deny us the contacts and support we need for all of our businesses to grow. Many were Chartists. You know how determined they are?'

'Why don't you like me asking you loudly?' said Shepherd.

'You don't know who we are up against, Constable. Not all these men are like us and some of them are not very nice about how they do business. They are the ones that you want to be looking at,' said the man.

'Which ones?' said Kettle, scanning the rooms.

The man said nothing, but looked towards a table in the far corner, where a much wealthier looking group of men were sat. Again, anything that had been on the table other than food and drink had been removed, hastily, when the two men had arrived.

'They are the sort of men that people eavesdrop. Big money attracts bigger money, and where I take a reasonable percentage, they attract bigger loans, at higher interest rates. Watch who is watching them,' suggested the worried man.

'How often do these watchers come in?' said Shepherd.

'Honestly, I couldn't say. The only one I have ever knowingly encountered was a really nasty individual, who trod on my toes and threatened me with violence if I carried on my sideline,'

'When was this?' said Kettle.

'Weeks ago. Haven't seen him recently, but if I did I would certainly not be talking loans with anyone.'

'What did he look like?' said Shepherd.

'A tall bloke, very tall, over six feet. Hard faced with a strong jaw and jet black hair. Well dressed he was, and respectable looking. Just hard. Reminded me of some ex army types I've met. Had some very shiny riding boots. Black with spurs. Looked like he had got his own horse. About 40 or so as I recall. Had a nice tan leather case over his shoulder. Quality it was. Had some initials stamped on it, but I can't recall what they were.'

'Interesting. Did he suggest he was connected to The Revenue or was he just another loan merchant?' said Shepherd.

'I didn't dare ask. His voice was chilling and he didn't

need to warn me twice.'

'And you haven't seen him since?' said Kettle.

'No, but I always keep an eye out. Watch in the shadows for men like them, opposite, and he'll turn up, sooner or later.'

'Just watch yourself. You don't want to end up on the wrong side of the law, either with us or The Revenue. I don't understand business, so I shalln't judge what you do. We'll leave you to your work,' said Kettle.

'Thank you gentlemen,' said Shepherd, acknowledging his group, before he and Kettle walked away, and back to Mr Hitchcock, downstairs.

'Times like these, we could do with Tanky or Black Tommy to spend some time lurking in the shadows for us,' said Kettle.

'Not likely at present. Mr Charters suggested that they were on some hush hush job and that I shouldn't ask.'

'Same said to me. I suspect he has sent them to London to see what Inspector Hatter is up to.'

'I did wonder,' said Shepherd. 'At least that's one enquiry we can leave to somebody else. What did you think of the description?'

'Let's not go putting two and two together again and making him fit our tall, dark man.'

'I know somebody else who had a stamped leather case,' said Shepherd.

'Who?'

'Inspector Hatter had a matching baggage set, in tan, with his initials on,' said Shepherd.

'How the other half live.' Kettle laughed.

'Where would somebody like that, prefer to stay overnight, if they were visiting the borough?'

'Somewhere more like Joseph Keetley's establishment than anywhere else, nearby. About the closest with a stable and quality rooms,' said Kettle. 'You go and see Mr Keetley whilst I have another word with Mr

Hitchcock.'

*****

Shepherd entered the King and Crown, to seek out Joseph Keetley. The inn was busy and a coach party was being fed before they set off on their next leg, and Keetley and his staff were scurrying between the kitchen and the tables, carrying plates of baked potatoes and bowls of nourishing stew. Piles of crusty bread sat amongst the travellers and they fed on the warm accompaniment as they awaited their main meals. Jugs of warm ale for the men, and sherry for the ladies, were laid out accordingly. Shepherd questioned such fare, given the current heat wave, and would have preferred a light meal and some fruit.

'With you shortly, Shepherd. Just finishing off the coach party as they need to be away shortly.'

Shepherd bought a glass of lemonade, reminding himself of Charters' warning about drinking on duty and as much as an ale would have been welcome, something cool and wet was the main requirement, and lemonade would do the job.

Alice Bates, one of Joseph Keetley's newer barmaids kept him company, chatting aimlessly about this and that, whilst displaying her ample bosom, which she had found attracted the tippers amongst Joseph's clientele, for some reason, and which she maintained, she couldn't understand.

A pretty little thing, but already showing signs of developing her mother's attributes, more curvaceous around her hips and waist, and a rounder face, but very popular all the same.

It did not take Joseph Keetley long to complete his service, and he wandered over to Shepherd, ushering him to a quieter spot in the corner of the bar.

'What's all this about Beddows?' Keetley enquired.

'What have you heard?' Shepherd replied.

'He came in, late last night, and told me that he was on gardening leave after a falling out with Head Constable Charters. Didn't sound very optimistic about his future, and was angry. Wasn't that happy with you, either, it appeared?'

'He is not himself at the moment, and there are a number of things that appear to have affected him. I actually haven't taken sides, and I think that he felt I should have sided with him, over Mr Charters. I would never betray a friend and he is a true friend, but at present he has a mistrust of me, which I am struggling to understand.'

'Who is this Eibhlin, he spoke frequently of?' Joseph enquired, clearly concerned.

'She is the owner of the circus, currently in situ on Barker's' Ground. She is part of our current murder enquiry. Why do you ask?'

'Beddows spoke a lot of her, like I should know of her personally,' Joseph shrugged his broad shoulders.

'Part of the problem, I suspect. They have formed a strange new allegiance. She is a stunningly attractive woman, and they seem to have a shine for each other.'

'Not like Mrs Beddows at all then?'

'How do you mean?' said Shepherd.

'Mrs Beddows has been a source of pain for Beddows for years. He has sat and poured out his sorrows over many a pot of tea. She dislikes me and my establishment as much as she dislikes Beddows and the police. I met her once, years ago, and she seemed a pleasant lady, but I bumped into her recently in the Market, and she was most rude about drink, publicans and drunken policemen. I bid her a good day and haven't spoken to her since.'

'Beddows makes out he would be better off without her,

one way or another, and that he would not be sad if she passed away. I am sure that is not the case.' said Shepherd, naively.

'Believe me, Shepherd, Beddows speaks the truth. He would be a happier soul without her, but marriage traps him.'

'I hope he comes to his senses. Did he say what he was planning to do?'

'He suggested that he might be out of town for a while, and that he would leave any messages for Eibhlin, here with me.'

'Did he say why he was going out of town?'

'No, he said it was personal business.'

Shepherd's mind began to work overtime. Where might he go? Had Eibhlin given him information about her son? Who would tell him?

'Anyway, Mr Keetley, you are distracting me from my task. I want to ask you about a visitor that may seek a room here, occasionally.'

'Who might that be?' Joseph asked.

'I do not know his name. He may be connected to Her Majesty's Revenue. Does that mean anything to you?'

'Not especially,' Keetley replied. 'I hear tell that they remain incognito, and would probably never give away that was their occupation.'

'He would be about forty years. Very tall, with dark hair. Most likely he travels on horseback, and is always well dressed, wearing very elegant riding boots and spurs. He may have tan luggage with some form of initials there upon.'

'Sounds like Mr Montague. He comes here once or twice a month, perhaps, then goes for months without making an appearance. I thought he was a businessman, up here to trade with our local Industrialists. Always has lots of money and always leaves a large tip for all of our staff.'

'Have you seen him lately?'

'Not for a month or two, now. He is very mysterious. Doesn't say a lot, but watches and listens. He has only spoken once of any substance, when there was difference of opinion between two clients about the war in Afghanistan. He disclosed that he had been out there and had experienced things that these two would never have imagined, and that his view was that war had been just and necessary, but poorly managed. He has a very military presence, and I suspect he has served, as he suggested.'

'Do you have any more information?'

'Wait, whilst I get the guest book.' Joseph went off behind the bar, emerging with a large volume, which he placed on the counter and began thumbing through.

'Here you are. His last booking was five weeks ago. He stayed for two nights, arriving late on a Monday. Tobias Montague, his signature is here, look,' sliding the book around for Shepherd to view.

'Has he ever left an address?'

'No, he arrives when he arrives, and I normally have something to suit him. He has a different fine horse, each time, as I recall. I have seen him with several. The stableman may give you more information.'

'Does he meet anybody here, whilst he stays?'

'Only once, have I seen him with anyone. He ordered a table and he and another man had dinner one night, perhaps three or four months ago.'

'Who was he meeting?'

'I didn't recognise the other man. Allegedly he was some local businessman looking to do some business with Mr Montague. Looked a strained meeting, as I recall, and definitely money was handed over by Montague, but not without some difficulty, so it seemed. Very raised voice from Mr Montague, at times, and hard to ignore.'

'That seems to fit with what we think might be

happening. Thank you, Joseph.'

'Sure I can't tempt you with an ale?'

'I am already in Mr Charters bad books, so I shall say no, sadly.'

Beddows' quest.

Beddows' train journey had been delayed by an incident at Hitchin. The connection with the Wigston train was delayed, and it was nearly five o'clock by the time he arrived in London.

As with Tanky and Black Tommy, he had decided that a coach was a more comfortable, if slower means of travel, and had not enjoyed his journey.

A heavily pregnant woman sat opposite with her husband, a member of Parliament, travelling to Westminster, who had boarded along the journey. She had been continuously sick for the entire route, and the carriage had been awash with her stomach contents. No chance to stop and rest, as a coach would have allowed. Not a pleasant experience.

Kings Cross station was also a new experience for Beddows, with queues awaiting trains that sat alongside its northbound platforms, getting up steam, which curled across the entrance area like a thick, swirling fog. He was in awe at the progress of modern industry and had once spoken, albeit briefly, with Robert Stephenson, himself, at the West Bridge station in Leicester, during a visit by Stephenson and William Stenson, at the opening of the passenger terminus, many years past. Kings Cross made West Bridge look insignificant.

Walking out onto the streets of the Metropolis, Beddows took in the hustle and bustle. His eyes quickly acclimatised to pick out the lurkers and ne'er do wells, from the folk going about their days, genuinely.

Eibhlin had given him a letter for her relative, whom she

had spoken of in some detail, but not before giving Beddows the option of utilising him, or not.

He was of hard drinking and hard playing Irish stock, and had settled in London after the family had fled the law in county Cork, after an 'error of judgement' over ownership of a horse which had been found in his yard. Patrick McNally had a chequered history of scrapes with the law in the 'ole country', but was devoted to Eibhlin, and was a possible port of call for Michael Lenihan. He had worked hard as a carpenter, making and fitting frames and props for shoring up earthworks for the navvies on the railways and tunnels, working down from Liverpool, where he had entered the country, and settling in his present situation.

He had more recently become somewhat 'moneyed' from his hobby of betting and gambling, in any form. He and Beddows were probably as opposite in traits as Beddows could tell, but if he was a potential link in locating Michael Lenihan, and came with Eibhlin's endorsement, he must be trusted. Eibhlin's letter would make Beddows need for help, quite clear, on a family basis.

McNally was most skilled in his craft as a carpenter, and the winnings had taken him out of the dirt and grime of the gutters, and he had set up his own small yard and workshop on the edge of St. Giles rookeries - allegedly, according to Eibhlin, the posh edge. There he made tables and stools for the pub trade, which kept him busy. He had a small delivery cart and Beddows could be a useful extra pair of hands, whilst at the same time having time and opportunity to make his enquiries. He lived in rooms above the yard, which suited Beddows' need for some privacy.

Beddows' only reservation was that as McNally was of Irish stock, and may have a reputation that followed him, he may also be of interest. That being said, there were so many Irish in the capital, that he would have to have been of *extra interest*, to get police attention. Beddows had recent knowledge of the reputation of the St. Giles rookeries, and its occupants, from recent events around Cock Muck Hill, and that it was not an area for the faint-hearted. A long slow walk was the order of the day, and time to get his bearings in his quest for Michael Lenihan. A chance to compare the rookeries of Leicester with those of legend.

Tobias Montague

Just after six, Shepherd walked back into the police station, where he was met by Herbert Kettle who was leaning against the charge desk, talking with Sergeant Sheffield, through a haze of pipe smoke.

'How did you get on, across the road?' said Kettle.

'Joseph Keetley was most interesting to talk to. I think we should speak privately, as I don't want prying ears from within the cells to be wigging. Sorry, Sergeant,' he said, addressing Sheffield, 'Nothing personal.'

The two men walked into the small rear office. Robert Charters walked in behind them, from the yard, and joined them.

'It would appear that our investigation has taken yet another strange turn. Mr Keetley has given me a possible identification for our tall, dark, man from The Globe, as our possible money lender. His has previously registered in the name Tobias Montague, and he seems to fit the description and criteria,' Shepherd explained.

'Tell me more,' said Charters.

'He has met at least one local businessman there, where money was seen to be exchanged, and the other person involved appeared under some duress. Joseph Keetley is familiar with him.'

'And when was this?'

'Three or four months ago, roughly, according to Mr Keetley.'

'And what does this Montague do?'

'Mr Keetley believed him to be a businessman. He says he was always in possession of money and was a generous tipper. He assumed he was involved in the hosiery trade.'

'Do we know where he heralds from?' said Kettle.

'No, he never has said, and nothing is recorded in Keetley's guest books. However, he was seen and heard by Keetley to challenge two customers about the rights and wrongs of the last Afghan war, and he disclosed that he had been there and that in his opinion the war was fair and just. Seemingly an ex military man, in keeping with his dress and demeanour.'

'Did you ask about the revenue suggestion?' said Charters.

'Joseph Keetley is of the same mind as everyone else, that they would not divulge such an occupation. Nobody seems keen to ask too many questions, for fear of their undue attention,' said Shepherd.

'I need to chase up my contacts. It would be interesting to know whether Montague is one and the same man,' said Charters.

'There is also talk of Masonic influence,' said Kettle.

'Not the Freemason paranoia, again,' said Charters.

'The masons are much maligned and afeared in many communities. I am not surprised. Many of our local businessmen and dignitaries are masons, and use their allegiances to favour their businesses. They scratch each other's backs, financially, and have their own networks.'

'Revenue men *and* Freemasons? Whatever and whoever this man is akin to, he is seen by smaller businesses as bad news, and he seems to favour the bigger businesses and to the detriment of those with smaller aspirations,' said Kettle.

'Nothing to say that he isn't associated with both. I would imagine that is quite feasible.'

'Don't suppose you are connected, Sir?' asked Shepherd, realising immediately what a foolish enquiry, given his lack of current favour.

'I come from a hard and proud family of miners and

grafters, Constable Shepherd. I fight for men like you and mine, with our worshipful Mayor and Watch Committee, and have no wish to spend any more time with them than I absolutely need. No, Shepherd, I am not a Freemason, nor do I wish to be one. However, my position does give me an advantage to gain valuable insight into their daily business. I have what you might call, 'an inside man', who can tell me if Montague may have any Masonic connections.'

'I didn't mean to offend,' said Shepherd, 'but Beddows always said if you don't ask, you don't find out.'

'You have Beddows' tact and diplomacy, at times, Shepherd. Just be cautious as to where and when you choose to employ it. So, I will try and gain more about this man from my contacts. What are you two doing next?'

'We are off to see the Paget's housekeeper, who has now returned from her family bereavement, and is back at New Walk,' said Kettle.

'Have we any news of Beddows?' said Charters.

'I understand he may have left the borough for a few days, on personal matters,' said Shepherd.

'What might that mean?' said Charters.

'I have no idea, presently, but can only wonder if Miss MacCormack has more information than she may have disclosed, previously,' Shepherd replied.

'Put her on the spot. I want to know what Beddows is up to and if he has gone out of the borough, where to, and what for.'

Shepherd nodded, but knew Eibhlin MacCormack would not elaborate, further.

Eleanor Skinner

Kettle and Shepherd took a gentle stroll back to 62 New Walk. Dark clouds were rolling in from the west, and Kettle suggested a thunderstorm might be on the way, as it felt heavy and the air was oppressive. Distant rumbles confirmed the opinion.

'Some rain would be so welcome. I love a good thunderstorm,' said Shepherd. 'I used to sit out when I lived with my folks, and just watch the clouds and the lightning, for hours if I could.'

'It certainly would be nice to freshen the air up, as it is unbearable at present.'

The canopy of leaves along the young trees that lined the walk, rustled and added to the coming storm, and the sky darkened and the warm wind swirled.

As they stepped up the short path to the large green door, a flickering light, followed closely by a mighty crash of thunder and the first spots of heavy rain began to dampen the stones in front of them.

Kettle pulled on the brass handle, and the 'cowbells' rang inside. Footsteps could be heard inside, as bolts were moved, and the door opened.

'Can I help, Gentlemen?' said a small, finely boned woman, dressed in black dress and apron.

'Eleanor Skinner?' said Kettle.

'That is my name. I take it you are the constables who have been waiting for my return?'

'I am Detective Sergeant Kettle, and this is Constable Shepherd.'

'Please come in. We will have to go down to my quarters. I have no remit to allow you access to my employers' areas, I am afraid.'

'That will be fine,' said Kettle, smiling.

The woman lead them down a short flight of stairs from a doorway at the rear of the hallway, under the grand staircase. Downstairs was a small, cramped area, about ten feet square. A narrow bed stood in the corner of the room. A table and a two rickety chairs, and a small wardrobe took up the rest of the living area. A small grate sat on the end wall. Adjacent to the room was the laundry, with a dolly tub, mangle, assorted irons and suspended washing lines that took up most of the room. They sat down around the small table. Eleanor sat on the edge of the bed.

'We are sorry to hear of your loss,' said Shepherd. He looked around and realised that being a housekeeper was not as glorified as he had perhaps considered.

'Why should you be sorry for my loss? It was nothing of your doing. Just another untimely and unnecessary death.'

'Who was it?' said Kettle, 'If you don't mind me asking.'

'It was my younger brother, Harold. My parents are both too old and infirm, and not of the sharpest wit to sort out the arrangements, hence my absence.'

'You said unnecessary?' said Shepherd.

'Some disease he picked up from the factory. All that fluff that fills their noses and throats. In the end he coughed and coughed until he bled to death. Just for a few coins, and a subsidised lodging, each week. It seems so unfair.'

'And this was in your home town?' said Kettle.

'No, he worked here, in Mr Paget's factory. That's why they gave me time away, for arranging the funeral, and allowed me to stay away a little longer. I had to take my brother home, once he knew how ill he was becoming, and that is where he passed away.'

'He worked in Mr Paget's factory?' said Shepherd,

looking at Kettle, watching his expression.

'He was just a boy. Started off as a fluff picker, and then Mr Paget allowed him to take an apprenticeship on one of the new machines, but by then he was already ill. His chest was bad, and he knew he was ill, but what choices do we have?'

'You must have been very angry?' said Kettle.

'Angry? No. Sad? Yes. These are hard times, gentlemen, and there was nothing in Welford after the frame knitters had their homes attacked and they were frightened off and into the factories, so he came here and worked for Mr Paget.'

'They hadn't explained. Mrs Paget never said a word. I'm sorry we weren't aware of the circumstances,' said Kettle.

'She wouldn't, would she? They are on the face of it, good people, Mr and Mrs Paget, but he used people like us. Those who have little. We know how much their offer of work means to us, and I know what a roof over my head and a small wage allows me. My brother lived in a small room provided at a penny a night, in George Street, with seven other workers, and thought he was well off. But, it doesn't make what goes on in the factories right. It didn't happen on the small frames at home.'

'Why don't you hate Mr Paget for causing your brother's death?' said Shepherd.

'He would have died of something. Cold; hunger; hard work in the workhouse. It was ordained for him.'

'But the fact it was in Mr Paget's factory? Surely you must have felt blame lay within your employers' business?'

'There are three or four in the factory, all living in that same little house, all of a similar age to my brother. They all have the same illness, from years of fluff picking under the machines. They will all die soon, but today they are alive. They get paid, and they can live whilst they are able.'

'That's a very forgiving viewpoint?' said Kettle.

'What could I do, even if I hated Mr Paget for killing him? We are devout Christians and forgiveness is a virtue.'

'Mr Paget is now dead. Somebody may have wanted him dead. We need to be sure that person wasn't you.' said Kettle.

'The bible also says *"an eye for an eye"*,' said Shepherd.

'Do I look like I could kill someone, even if I wanted to?'

'Have you any connection with the circus on Barker's Ground, or anyone connected to it?' said Shepherd.

'What a strange question.'

'We believe that a man from the circus may have been in this house, and killed Mr Paget. Whether it was intentional, or whether, as it was made to appear, that it was for money, we are not yet sure.'

'No amount of money would put right what has happened to my brother, and no, I do not know anybody from any circus. And no, I am not involved in Mr Paget's death.' Her reply was crisp and confident.

'Do you know anybody that might have wanted him dead, or wanted his money?' said Shepherd.

'Or both?' she replied.

'Why do you say that?' said Kettle.

'Mrs Paget's Father hated him. You must promise me that you will never divulge what I am about to tell you, because it would leave me in a terrible situation.'

'We can try, but until I know what you have to tell us, I cannot say whether we can keep it to ourselves,' said Kettle.

'Mrs Paget, originally, thought the sun shone out of Mr Paget's bottom, if I may be so rude. He could do no wrong as she was besotted with him. When I used to work for Mr and Mrs Harrison, before the marriage, she had to beg for permission for Mr Paget's hand. Mr Harrison could not stand him, and thought him a poor prospect. Too much of a reputation as a fool with his money, allegedly.'

'So how was it resolved and permission given?' said Kettle.

'Mr Harrison gave him twelve months to prove himself. To show him that he was a sound risk as both a businessman and as a husband to his daughter.'

'And?'

'And over the twelve months, Mr Paget's business grew. He made lots of money and attracted business, to Mr Harrison's satisfaction, and bought this house as a result of it, or so it seemed. They took him to America and he brokered some good business, and Mr Harrison gave in. They then married.'

'So it sounds like he did just what Mr Harrison had asked?' said Shepherd.

'Only after the wedding did Mr Harrison find out that Mr Paget had borrowed excessively large sums of money from these new 'backers' and was actually unable to repay many of them, completely. There were some blazing arguments. Mrs Paget took Mr Paget's side and threatened to disown her parents if they did not help him out.'

'So Mrs Paget forced her Father's hand in paying off some of the debts?' said Kettle.

'He swore that nobody would ever take his daughter away from him. 'Over his dead body' was what he said, more than once.'

'And when did they last argue?' said Shepherd.

'A few weeks ago. Everything had gone quiet and I thought things had been resolved. Mr Paget had arranged a business meeting, and invited some people to the house, with a view to setting up some business in New York. Mr Harrison got word of it and went mad. He told Mr Paget to stop his dreaming, and to get his business interests in Leicester sorted. He said he would be better suited to thinking like a real businessman and to buy some new machines and invest more wisely. He reminded Mr Paget of the consequences of taking away his daughter.'

'How did you hear all of this?' said Shepherd.

'I should think half of the borough would have heard Mr Harrison. I was stood in the kitchens, sorting out dinner. He sent the visitors away, very embarrassed they were. None of the people Mr Harrison deals with, I understand.'

'What did Mrs Paget have to say about that?' said Kettle.

'She was very upset. Mr Paget was frightened though. I heard him saying that he had found out where he could buy new machines, but they were more expensive than he thought. She had told Mr Paget that he should not take any more risks. She would do anything for him, but for money, not for love. She liked the lifestyle that went with the marriage. She thought her Father too controlling, and preferred to be the independent lady.'

'But we know he intended to buy some new machines, and it was the money for those machines that appears to have been stolen, along with some family jewellery,' said Shepherd.

'That is very strange. Mr Harrison wanted him to buy new machines. But if they were more expensive, where did he get the money from?' Eleanor asked.

'A very good question. Would Mr Harrison have given him the money, or underwritten borrowing it?' said Kettle.

'Mr Harrison wouldn't do anything for Mr Paget, in my opinion. Those threats stick in my mind,' she replied.

'And how can we be sure that you are telling us the truth?' said Shepherd.

'You asked me a question, earlier. If I had wanted him dead, I would have done it myself. I would have poisoned him, slowly, just like he did to my brother. It was all too swift, for my liking. Justice, but not fair justice. He should have had a lingering death, just to know what it feels like, but as a Christian, I am wrong to even think such a terrible thing,' she replied.

New acquaintances

Tanky and Black Tommy drew a blank in their quest for Inspector Hatter. No sign of him at either end of Whitehall Place, suggested that the elusive and clandestine 'Special Branch' might have a less obvious base to which they reported. That was unless the two men had failed, miserably, in a task at which they considered themselves experts.

A slow walk back from Charing Cross, where they had met as arranged, at six o'clock, and back to Praed Street. Rumbling stomachs and a dryness that goes with sitting doing nothing all day, caused both men to agree that a meal and an ale or two was the order of the day. The prospect of refreshment at Praed Street and the canal basin did not appeal to either, and an alternative, out of the way, suited them more.

As neither would likely be recognised in their present disguise, it was felt safe that they should venture towards the river and a find a hostelry where they could check on the comings and goings of the vessels bound for America, just in case finding Hatter, first, failed.

A passing sailor had stopped and spoken with Tanky near to Scotland Yard, and made talk of American skippers frequenting the 'Prospect of Whitby', on the river. He also thought that such a likelihood may also attract Nimrod Hatter, if it hadn't already.

*****

Beddows finally reached Hogg Lane, at the end of St. Giles High Street, the abode of Patrick McNally. As for it being within the 'posh' edge of St. Giles, it was, initially, reminiscent of Edward Pawley's yard, off Short Street, dark and grubby, but out of the way. What had Eibhlin sent him to?

The yard was accessed through large double gates, which were ajar. An old grey mare stood tethered in one corner, its nose in a forage bag, and a large bucket of water, half full, stood alongside. A well maintained cart, which appeared solid, stood to one side. The yard was surprisingly well swept and lengths of wood stood in piles around the walls. The interior of the yard was at odds with the exterior of the rookeries.

'And what can I do for you, squire?' came a loud Irish voice.

Beddows looked up and saw a large, stocky figure of a man, with curly black hair and a thick beard, leaning against a rail, atop a flight of wooden stairs.

'Might you be Patrick McNally?' said Beddows.

'And who might be asking?'

'My name is John Beddows, and I have been sent by Eibhlin MacCormack. She has sent a letter which explains my visit.' Beddows walked up the steps, holding the letter out in front of him.

'I smell a policeman,' said the man, straightening up to reveal his full height. Beddows noticed the tattoos that covered his arms.

'An ex-policeman, or sort of, but not a threat to you.'

'And why should Eibhlin MacCormack be sending an ex-policeman to see Patrick McNally?' The man's emerald green eyes scoured Beddows face as he responded.

'To seek his help in finding Michael Lenihan, before a really devious London policemen does so.'

'Michael is a gentle big lump. Why should the police be looking for him?' Patrick seemed amused at such a thought.

'Because the London policeman thinks he has killed somebody, and is keen to see him hanged.'

'Let me see this letter you talk of.'

Beddows reached the top and handed over the paper. The light was poor, but the man scanned the writing, shaking his head.

'Well, John Beddows, if you're a friend of Eibhlin's, then you are welcome. Patrick McNally, at your service.' The man held out a huge hand.

Beddows took the offer and winced at the strength of the man's grip. A huge hand, with fingers like vices. A very manly grip, indeed.

'Years of hard graft, John Beddows. And a good grip in return. A hard man yourself?'

'I have a reputation, or rather, had.'

'A bad boy, hey. Drink or women? That's the normal demise, I believe.'

'Allegedly, both, but actually, neither, but my Head Constable does not believe me.'

'They didn't believe me, when I said I was taking the horse back after I had been found with it.' The man grinned. 'A drink. You must be thirsty?'

'Tea if you have it.'

'You're fecking joking, right? I mean a real drink. Irish.'

'I don't anymore. I used to, once, but it got me in real trouble.'

'As it happens, I like tea. I'll put the kettle on. Come in John Beddows.'

'Please, just call me Beddows, everyone else does.'

'Sit down and tell me how my favourite cousin is. Is she still as lovely as ever?'

'I have only met her in the last few days, but in my humble opinion, Eibhlin seems a lovely and warm woman, as you suggest. However, she is struggling with these accusations. That is why I have offered to help her.'

'Eibhlin is a tough lady, Beddows. She runs that circus of hers with a rod of iron. She wanted me to work for her, but we would have clashed, like thunder and lightning, we would.'

'So I gather. But I admire what she has done, and I want to help her through this mess, particularly as something seems amiss with the London interest.'

'So what has Michael done, allegedly?'

'People are saying that he may have been involved in a burglary where a man died. He fits the description of a man seen. He is also wanted in London for a similar burglary, where his name has, *allegedly*, been given. That is the one that this London detective wants him hanged for, more so than for our burglary.'

'Michael wouldn't harm a flea, and I should know. He is soft, Beddows, and harmless. Somebody is playing dirty.'

'Eibhlin thought that he might try and make contact with you. She was worried he might try and gain passage to America, and get to family there, if threatened.'

'Well I haven't heard from Michael in ages. A year or more I last saw him. What was he doing in London?'

'The circus was here for a while. It was during that time that a burglary took place and a man died. The London detective came to Leicester looking for Michael, only to find we had just had a similar offence.'

'And what, exactly, can I do for you, Beddows?'

'I need a place to stay, where I can make my own enquiries to try and locate Michael, and get him back to Leicester and proper justice. I need to do so without attracting the Metropolitan Police's attention.'

'There is such a thing in this world as proper justice?' McNally laughed, cynically, raising a heavy eyebrow.

'More so than here in London. I hear justice here is swift, and at times ill considered. I assure you we are thorough and fair, and I already have huge doubts about the evidence with which we have been presented.'

'What if he contacts me. Do I tell him? Do I stop him going to America if that is what he wants? You are putting me in a very difficult situation, Mr Beddows.'

'You have read Eibhlin's letter. Her words. You can see what she wants me to do.'

'And that is what I must consider, also. Bugger of a place to be, no?'

'We can help Michael. We must get to him before Inspector Hatter, or I fear he stands no chance.'

'I have heard that offensive name before.'

'How?'

'I have strong Irish *political* roots, Beddows, as Eibhlin may have hinted. Many of my Irish friends are quite bitter and angry at previous English interventions in the ole country, and have a reputation as politically a threat to the government of Her Majesty. There is talk of a small group of police and their agents, who are very dark. They work in the shadowy world of spies and activists, dissidents and trouble makers. That is where I have heard his name. My question is, why should some detective from such a murky world be looking for Michael Lenihan?'

'That's a question that, as yet, I have no answer for. Michael may be implicated in something that is of such a nature. Perhaps the man who died in the London burglary was a politician or influential in some way, or something sensitive may have been stolen?'

'These men are feared in the communities that have settled in London. Ever since the Cato Street raid, some years ago, the Irish, Jews, Polish, all have tales of similar early morning raids and of people 'disappearing' after their involvement. Not even a head left for public viewing, these days. Hatter is supposedly a ruthless man, and uses extreme violence, even torture, I have heard. They have their spies, everywhere, or so we have been told.'

'Then we need to find Michael quickly, as I suggest.'

'I have a widespread network of friends who can help

us, Beddows.'

'We must be very careful not to alert Hatter that I am down here. I must be very careful as it would not be good if Hatter's seniors thought there was a policeman from other than London, poking his nose in their business.'

'I thought you said ex-policeman?'

'It's complicated. I have had a disagreement with my Head Constable and been sent on gardening leave. So, I am not actually a serving, or paid, policeman.'

'Well there then. No problem. My contacts are discreet, and they may know of Michael's whereabouts. Is it worth the risk? I trust them. Good men and loyal.'

'Their ears may be more valuable than their deeds, thank you. Just warn them not to ask too many questions and make no mention of me.'

'To be sure, Beddows. Now then, that tea must be about ready. Come on in and let's get you settled in. My yard is a bit cosy for two, but you are more than welcome for a few days.'

'Your yard appears uncannily tidy for a working yard?'

'I am a very tidy man, Beddows. I love wood and the feel of it. I work tidy and I live tidy. Not a typical bog trotter, as you may be accustomed to in your neck of the woods. Be warned, as I tolerate no mess from guests, either.'

'People might even think that the yard is a front for something a lot less messy than wood turning and furniture making. Doesn't that cause you a problem?'

'What might a poor Cork man be doing in London other than carving out a few pounds for his keep?'

'I hear you are fond of a little betting and gambling. Not that I am averse to such enterprise.'

'A little flutter on the gee gees. A hand of cards. A little light relief. But not here, Beddows, that's for the heart of the rookeries, where I am safer doing so, and amid the mugs and punters. Let me show you around.'

The two men walked through a small door at the top of the staircase, and a neat workshop came into view. A small lathe, a bench and a wall full of craftsman's tools. At the far end, a small collection of three-legged tables, in need of polishing.

'My latest job. A few tables for a local inn.'

'Nice looking work. You have the tidiest workshop I have ever seen in my life.'

'A tidy workspace, and a tidy mind, Beddows. I need order. I would make somebody a good wife, much like Eibhlin, who is similarly obsessive.'

'And where do you live?'

McNally led Beddows past the piled wood, and through another door. A small room, already lit with a hanging oil lamp. A table and chairs, and what looked like ship's hammocks, hanging above them.

'Hammocks?'

'Clean and dry, Beddows. Some of the buildings around here are less than savoury, and when I have guests, I like them to be clean and away from little visitors.'

'Never slept in a hammock before.'

'You'll have fun, Beddows. Until you've fallen out you haven't lived. Make yourself at home, and then I'll take you for an exploration of the rookeries. You might be a little shocked.'

'I have heard of these places. We had a gang in Leicester, recently, who had moved from the place and thought our own rookeries were more civilised.'

'This is an awful place, Beddows, but the people are the salt of the earth, and look after their own. It's a fortress within the Capital, and very rarely do your colleagues venture inside. Not a wise place to get lost.'

'And Hatter's men?'

'They are sneaky, Beddows. They will have turned one or two weaker ones. That is what we need to be aware of. They will have eyes and ears in the rookeries, too, but will not venture in themselves.'

'We'll have to see, then, won't we. We must be discreet.'

'Discretion is my middle name, Beddows.'

*****

The Prospect of Whitby stood on the north shore of the Thames, upstream at Wapping, beyond the parishes of Whitechapel and Poplar. It had stood since 1520, and had originally been called 'The Pelican', then 'The Devil's Tavern'. It stood very close to the Metropolitan Police's Wapping station, where their river division were accommodated.

Tanky had heard tell of days when it was a favourite venue for public executions, where pirates and traitors were hung from gallows over the river at the rear.

By the time the two men had followed the river and arrived, it was full, and people were spilled out onto the cobbled wagon ways at the front, and on decks at the rear. Black Tommy observed that it had the look of an old galleon at the rear, over the river, and bars at two levels added to the impression of decks.

A mix of voices, some local and some foreign, and skins of many different colours and races mingled. The noise was deafening, and rum and ale flowed freely. New faces would bring suspicion, so their story had to be plausible and researched, at which Tanky and Tommy were well prepared.

Bumping into River Police was not something they needed and were sure that there would be at least one or two lurking, picking up scandal and crime in the planning. The good thing was that they were hugely unpopular with all river users, and had regularly been attacked and beaten for their troubles. No doubt the regulars would be sniffing them out already.

Finding a spot by a large leaded window overlooking the river, Tanky pulled at the sleeve of a small, well dressed man. Talk had indicated he was something to do with the Port's Authority, and would be in the know. It always amazed Tommy how quickly Tanky picked up on who was who. 'Any news of the Christiania, do you know?'

The Christiania was an American owned package vessel, plying trade between America, the Indies and London, and was known by Tanky to be due in London in the forthcoming week.

'You blokes looking to join the crew?'

'We are meant to work our ticket on the return passage. Got in a spot of bother last time around and owe the company, so it won't even be worth our pay.'

'There is another ship at Tobacco Dock. The Spirit of Boston. She is due out on Friday's early tide. I hear they have some need for crew. Where are you headed?'

'Easily pleased. New York, preferably, else we would have sought work from Liverpool to Boston. Both have opportunities for us. Any other package vessels due in or out?'

'Not until next week, at the earliest. I thought you were working men?'

'We are, but we have some friends who might want to pay for a passage.'

'Your skipper will take them, won't he?'

'Should do, if he has space. Only fifteen cabins and they are normally pre-booked. Mind, he won't be best pleased with us. We had a little disagreement with some Frenchmen in a pub in Bow, and got thirty days. Had to go off short-handed the last time out.'

'You could try the Margaret Evans. Captain Barrington's vessel. If he's not on board, he sometimes stays in the Mayflower, or The Town of Ramsgate. That's Ireland bound on Thursday then on to New York after it has traded. That's moored in St. Katharine's Dock, presently.'

Tanky and Black Tommy moved to a quiet corner and supped on warm ale. They ordered bread and cheese, and an elderly woman sliced and served them at the end of one bar. The bread was on the hard side, and the cheese was meagre, but nothing touched the sides, as both men hungrily devoured the offerings.

'So, there are a couple of ships that might be worth keeping an eye on. Both could offer Lenihan passage. We perhaps need to split up and watch both,' said Tanky.

'Sounds like a plan. If we know that, so will Hatter. Probably more chance of finding him and his men snooping around in the two areas than in Whitehall, if we can't find him there,' Tommy agreed.

'Lets just have a listen and watch, tonight, and we will make an early start tomorrow. It's your shout!'
*****

By ten o'clock, Shepherd and Kettle had sat down in the office at Town Hall Lane.

'This case gets more complex with every enquiry,' said Kettle. 'It seems that both Mrs Paget and Mr Harrison have been lying to us, and things between them both and our dead man were more strained than they had earlier admitted.'

'They have told us a little, but not as much as we should have been told. Mr Harrison's threats seem much more realistic than he would have had us believe. Mrs Paget had not suggested that she and her husband were ready to move to the Americas, which would have given her Father even more of a motive to want Paget harmed.'

'But to die at the hands of a burglar, that still beggars questions. If it was a burglary, and the Hensons committed it, who was the third man? Who had the proceeds? Was it Michael Lenihan?' said Kettle, still struggling with alternatives.

'And what is the relevance of the man in The Globe? Are we making more of it than we need to, or could it be that we have stumbled on some form of conspiracy? Could Harrison have been involved, and did it just go wrong?' Shepherd pondered.

'We need to find Lenihan, either through Inspector Hatter's endeavours, or if, as we suspect, that Tanky Smith and Black Tommy have been sent to London for that purpose. I wonder if Mr Charters would confirm that bit of the puzzle?'

'No he would not,' came the booming, Geordie voice. 'Some interesting questions, gentlemen, and ones that I too am pondering. Lenihan is, I am sure being actively sought. I need say no more than that. Also, I am meeting with a contact of mine, early tomorrow, to find out more about our Mr Montague and links to The Revenue and our Freemason community.'

'What about the jewellery?' asked Shepherd. 'If it was an act of retribution, and the money was the target, why take jewellery? That is identifiable and more likely to convict somebody in possession of it?'

'Interest?' suggested Kettle. 'A return on their investment?'

'Or a return of family jewels?' said Shepherd. 'Might Mr Harrison have wished to regain control of family treasures?'

'An interesting thought, Shepherd,' said Charters. 'Do we know exactly what it was and where it came from?'

'We know what it consisted of, and its value, but I don't believe we ever identified who had given it or bought it,' said Shepherd. 'We also need to get back to Paget's Bank. Those notes will be presented somewhere, and we need to find out where and by whom, unless it is more about Paget not spending the money?'

'So, we still have several main lines of investigation. Mr Tobias Montague and business loans. Mr Harrison and family honour, and Michael Lenihan and a burglary gone wrong,' said Kettle, in summary, 'not forgetting who killed the Henson brothers.'

'And not forgetting some familiarity between Harrison and the Hatter family. is there something there that we are missing, or is that yet another coincidence?' said Charters.

'We need to be harder with Mrs Paget and Mr Harrison. We might even need to consider arresting each of them, and apply more pressure,' said Kettle.

'A lot of unanswered questions, gentlemen, and none we can actively pursue, effectively, tonight, so time to go home. I will see you back here at 7 o'clock tomorrow morning, and we will start afresh.'

A general election

Wednesday 7th July 1852 was a significant date across the Country, with the first day of polling in the general election, and those who wished to do so, were making plans for casting their vote. A split in the Tories, between Derby and Peelites, and growing pressures from the Whigs, the country was in uproar, and voters confused.

Politicians would be making their last speeches, touring their constituencies, and, hopefully, a distraction for Inspector Nimrod Hatter and his men, providing protection and dealing with 'unpleasantries' that may arise within the Capital from the activist opponents of Derby.

Tanky and Black Tommy had woken early, and bid Torchy farewell, as they set off for the docks. As had been suggested the night prior, in the comfort of the Prospect of Whitby, Tanky set off to seek out 'The Margaret Evans', moored in St. Katharine's Dock, whilst Black Tommy sought out 'The Spirit of Boston', moored at Tobacco Dock.

Thunder storms of late evening, yesterday, had passed through, and the air was more humid than in previous days.

Both ships were described as smaller package vessels, but the most likely means for Lenihan to reach America more quickly.

Both men retained similar disguises to the previous day, which had been accepted within the community that they were infiltrating, and should continue to do so. Finding suitable vantage points, they sat, their eyes scanning the passing pedestrians and carriages for Michael Lenihan.

A few miles away, on the edge of St. Giles rookery, Beddows untangled himself from the netting that had formed his bed the night before. He had become trapped and he cursed as he fell out, hanging desperately by the errant arm, standing on tiptoes as his eyes focussed on extricating himself.

Patrick McNally chuckled, quietly, before bursting into laughter at Beddows attempt. 'Told you that they were an acquired taste.'

'I know how cod must feel, now, tangled in the fishermen's nets. Bleeding thing. Must have tossed and turned a bit too much.'

'You were swinging at one point. I lay watching you, and the noise was annoying me, creaking away, backwards and forwards. You'll get the hang of it.'

'Either that or I'll sleep on the floor.' Beddows mumbled to himself.

'Fancy some eggs with your tea?' said McNally.

'Just the job! What do you suggest I do today to start the search for Michael?'

'A little tour of St. Giles is in order, and a word with a few contacts. Discreetly, of course. Hatter's mob will be busy today with the voting, so you have a head start.'

'He's had a couple of days already. He might even have him in custody.'

'If Michael was in custody, I would have heard by now. Fear not on that one, Beddows.'

'Then I am in your hands, Patrick.'

'For feck's sake, call me Paddy. I should have said last night. Patrick is what me ole ma calls me, god bless her, especially when I'm due a thick ear. Lets get some scran and then we can get going.'

As Charters had directed, Shepherd and Kettle reconvened in the police station at 7 o'clock in the morning. Both hoped that Charters' meeting with his contact, later, would throw some light on Tobias Montague, but there was little they could do, immediately.

'What chance of the jewellery turning up in the hands of any of our fences?' said Shepherd.

'Not a lot, I suspect. This whole affair seems to step outside the county, and I reckon that the jewellery will be miles away, if fenced, or out of sight, somewhere its rightful owners would wish it to remain, if it is closer to home.'

'You mean like in Mr Harrison's grasp?'

'I'm starting to think more like that, Shepherd. I am struggling to get my head around the most likely motive. Until we hear more from Mr Charters, we are stuck. That might open up our next move.'

'What about popping down to see Miss MacCormack and seeing what she might tell us about Beddows?'

'Beddows will have sworn her to silence. Not going to gain much there. I reckon Beddows will call upon us if he needs us.'

'What have we missed?'

'I hear that the family are burying Edward Paget, tomorrow morning, up on Welford Road, after the service they have planned. Might be interesting to see who turns up to pay their respects. But that's tomorrow.'

'And today?' said Shepherd.

'We have a lot of odds and ends, so lets follow our noses and see where they take us, starting with some of our snouts, fences and the trail of that elusive jewellery.'

Robert Charters left Town Hall before Kettle and Shepherd, and directed that they should see him back there during the early afternoon. A working breakfast was Charters' plan, and his contact would hopefully have had a good night's sleep at his Leicester home, having spent, no doubt, a busy day on the hustings and persuading undecided voters on behalf of his master, Derby, and his cohorts.

The cab took Charters over West Bridge and out beyond Westcotes, entering the gates to the fine house, and rattling along the long driveway to the front of the hall, before dropping him at the main portico.

Before Charters had paid the cabbie, a well dressed man-servant intervened, and settled the account.

'Sir Henry's best wishes, Mr Charters. He eagerly awaits you, and breakfast will be served promptly.'

Charters was escorted through the fine wooden doors and into the large hallway, where his trusted contact awaited him.

'Good to see you, Robert. Too long since we last dined.'

'Very kind of you to see me, Sir Henry. How is the first day of voting to be?'

'Hot and difficult, I expect. Some very disenchanted people amongst the population, and I fear Derby may be facing a nervous wait. But elections are long winded and tedious, and my personal position is quite safe, so hey ho. Ready to eat?'

The men entered a long, narrow room, bordered on one side by floor to ceiling windowed double doors, which opened out onto the extensive grounds. The air seemed so much fresher than in the heart of the borough,and the gentle breeze made the room comfortable, early in the day.

'A working breakfast, I am afraid, as I must show my face in the constituency, sometime this morning. The Chronicle are watching our every move through this process, and will no doubt report all the things we aren't seen to do.'

Laid out on a sideboard that seemed to fill the opposite wall, were silver salvers, neatly covered, which staff opened for the two diners.

The finest breakfast Charters had seen in a long while, was laid out before them.

'Dive in, Robert. A hearty breakfast sets one up for days like these.'

Charters selected poached eggs, sliced ham, and warm, fresh bread, before sitting down next to the head of the table. A man servant poured tea from a silver pot.

'So, what is all the mystery about?' said the host.

'I appreciate how difficult this may be, but we have three bodies lying in the borough, presently, from crimes of murder. All three appear connected, and have links to a mysterious man. We have a description, in two cases, and a possible name that may also be connected. The rumour has it that this may be the work of a man who works for Her Majesty's Revenue, or a man possibly connected to the Freemasons.'

'The name?'

'Tobias Montague is the name that has come to light.'

'I shall need to ask, you realise,' said the host.

'Naturally, Sir Henry. I did not expect an immediate response.'

'Why do Freemasons get such a bad name. You know that I am connected, of course?'

'I was aware, Sir Henry, and with your Civil Service connections, I thought you might be a good point of reference for both lines of enquiry.'

'Some might see your inference as impertinent, Robert.'

'I appreciate that, Sir Henry, but assume that your agreement to see me over breakfast indicated that you were open to my impertinence.'

'I can assure you that I do not know of the name through local masonic circles. Why the suggestion?'

'The death of the first man, Edward Paget, is being

viewed by people locally as possibly stemming from business transactions between Freemasons that may have gone wrong, else a renegade revenue man, or both.'

'Her Majesty has some rum chaps working in some of her shadowy departments. Many are ex-military and are put to use between conflicts to deal with the unpalatable business, whether criminal, civil or financial. Spies, basically, who needed to be kept busy. They have assumed powers that you would find somewhat disturbing, I am sure, Robert. However, our Field Marshals and Generals, Lords and Masters, have a National interest to ensure, that most of us have little idea of. Dirty work, but somebody has to do it.'

'So I hear, Sir Henry, but in The Revenue?'

'This Country is built on taxes, and tax avoidance is not on Her Majesty's list of acceptable behaviour. Consider the window tax. Imagine how that would impact on this room alone. It used to be bricked up, Robert, or I should have been fleeced by these people.'

'You would never have known, Sir Henry.' Charters viewed the building and could see no signs of any renovation or restoration. One law for the rich, he mused? 'These men have a reputation for offering large sums of money for investments or developments, at a loaded rate of interest above those of the financial institutions.'

'You think somebody is using Her Majesty's money for their own ends?'

'It would make sense. Collect on one hand, loan it out before it goes through Her Majesty's books, and take off a nice, fat profit along the way.'

'Robert, that would not go down well with Her Majesty. Leave it with me. I shall send a message to you as soon as I hear anything, possibly later today or more probably tomorrow. I have a friend, locally, who looks after Her

Majesty's books within the county.'

'Thank you, Sir Henry.'

'How is Mr Harrison taking his son-in-law's loss?'

'You know of Mr Paget and Mr Harrison?'

'My Masonic head, now firmly on, Robert. They are, or rather were, both involved locally, as you no doubt suspected.'

'Mr Harrison does not seem overly upset at the loss. His daughter appears quite beside herself, but my men have some doubt about the grieving widow.'

'A good businessman puts his personal feelings aside where money and profit is concerned. As with our military friends, any sign of weakness is a sign to your enemies as to your vulnerability. Mr Harrison is an exceptionally respected businessman. Mr Paget, on the other hand, not so, as I was to understand. Mrs Paget thinks with her heart and not with her head, and her father has to keep a close eye on her. His only daughter, if you know what I mean?'

'Murder is murder, Sir Henry, and my responsibility is to bring any offender to justice. I care not for his business acumen, unless it was his undoing, at which point identifying who saw his vulnerability would be my priority and interest, hence my impertinence.'

'As one of our Head Constables, I would expect nothing less, Robert. What I can say, is that it has made many of my Masonic connections a little nervous. I suspect the answer, therefore lies beyond the local lodges and I can assure you of that, at least. These are basically honourable men, acting in the spirit of the Knights Templar and protectors of Christian values.'

'Can spies and the like retain both sets of values, doing dirty work and yet maintaining Christian values?'

'We will have to see, Robert. Perhaps there are renegades who are not as God fearing as you and I?'

'On that note I will take my leave, and allow you to

return to the duties of your office.'

'I take it this meeting is off the record and not for sharing in any form?'

'You can be assured, Sir Henry. My sources always remain confidential.'

'Do you want one of my coachmen to drop you back in the borough?'

'Thank you for the kind offer, but I shall enjoy a leisurely stroll back and take in the morning air for a change.'

Old acquaintances

By Midday, Beddows was touring St. Giles Rookery, led by Patrick McNally. A long sleep in had refreshed him, and whilst he slept, McNally had been out on 'private business'.

In the heart of the narrow winding lanes and alleys, at the end of a very pokey yard, stood the Rat's Castle. For a few minutes, McNally had insisted Beddows wore a blindfold. When they came to a stop, in an echoey yard, where the sounds of humanity in all forms screamed, shouted, cried, fought, and by the sounds of it, gave birth and died.

'Guess where we are, Beddows. Feeling nervous?'

'So,' said Beddows, 'this is the infamous Rat's Castle, I take it? We had a gang settle in our own Rookeries who set up a similar den, and named it after the one they had left behind, and lo, here it is. They told tales of a fearsome place, Hell itself, in the heart of the capital.'

'A fearsome place, indeed, Beddows. There have been a few Runners and Peelers over the years that foolishly dared to venture in here, and were never seen again. Stories tell of ghosts wandering the alleys in the dead of night, shimmering white ghosts, all still wearing their stovepipe hats and crying for their mammies.' McNally grinned, enjoying the little tale. 'Woo,' he mocked.

'I can imagine that it would not be a wise place to venture without somebody like you, Paddy.'

'You are confident that I didn't lead one or two of them in myself? There have certainly been one or two that merited a trip down here.'

Beddows watched McNally's face for signs of humour,

but none showed through with that last remark.

'What are we actually doing down here?'

'I have a meeting with a few friends. They know who you are, but I told them that you are a relative's man. A little white lie never hurt anyone, did it?'

'And the purpose of this meeting?'

'You want to know how best to find Michael? You want to know where to find Hatter? These are the most influential men in the Rookeries. Unfortunately, it is not the King Rat himself, that we are meeting, today, with his long nose, sharp eyes and ears, and sharper teeth. He has some business out of the area. His associates will be your scouts, and will get you where you need to be the quickest,' McNally assured him.

'Why the blindfold?' said Beddows.

'You try and find your way out of here with the blindfold off. I bet you struggle. Then imagine, if you can't get out, how we have an edge if we need to move you to a stronghold for your safety. Even Hatter would think twice of following us into here, not without an army.'

'You think he wouldn't?' asked Beddows.

'He won't bother you in here. Or the rats, for that matter. We probably won't even have to come back, but it's my plan if you do get identified.'

Beddows felt much reassured. It seemed strange to be in the heart of the most notorious and dangerous criminal heartlands in London, and not to feel the usual nerves he had, venturing into the heart of Abbey Street or Green Street, back in Leicester.

'A friend of mine asked me to pass on his regards to you,' said McNally.

'A friend?'

'He says you have a history. Sean Crowley says you are a hard bugger and hopes you find the Rat's Castle agreeable.'

'You know of Sean Crowley, and you have spoken

already?'

'Mr Crowley is a well known businessman in these parts, and a good friend to the King Rat. Doesn't take long for word to go around. Bumped into him earlier, while you were snoring.'

'That really does worry me. Sean Crowley would betray me at the drop of a hat if he could. Now I am concerned. That little white lie won't hold much water with Sean Crowley's knowledge of me.'

'Sean Crowley may be a pain in the arse, and a hard bastard to boot, but he will cause you no grief whilst you are with me and ours in St. Giles. He also knows Inspector Hatter, and would prefer to see somebody get one up on him - even yourself. Crowley says if you can get one over on Hatter, he would be eternally happy. Hatter has had a dampening effect on recent Irish business, he has.'

'Strange. We have an understanding, back in Leicester, but I would have put money on him seeing me done down.'

'You might bump into him, if you are here for a few days. He pops in for a game of cards with a few of us from the ole country, every now and again. Probably be in The Bowl, later this week. A big fight coming up. You can buy him a drink if you're still with us.' McNally laughed at Beddows anxiety.

The Bowl was a notorious drinking establishment, along St. Giles High Street, near to Dyott Street. It was a half-way stop off point for prisoners heading from the condemned cell for execution at Tyburn, where they were permitted a last drink, and was one of the only inns and taverns on the fringe of the Rookeries that sensible people would consider entering. It was thus seen as respectable, compared to the others, deeper into the fortress.

It was, however, a cleverly managed premises, with 'the

fancy', bruisers and the likes of Sean Crowley plying their more legitimate business from the busy rooms. Pugilists fought bare knuckled in a large yard at the rear, with access only by invitation, and from the rear of The Angel which sat next to it, a rougher house altogether.

The least legitimate business was generally brokered deep within the fortress.

Beddows felt those nerves starting to twitch. The thought of Sean Crowley and on strange turf, well away from the Borough Boys who would normally be watching his back. His confidence in McNally would be tested to the limit, and he hoped Eibhlin's assurance and recommendations, and McNally's word would true.

'What have I let myself in for?' he thought to himself. 'Do my feelings for a strange woman, who I hardly know, draw me into something out of my depth? Or is it my detective instinct that won't let an innocent man hang?'

'Come on in, Beddows, and meet some of my brethren.' The numbers of folk filling the small rooms was beyond Beddows' belief, and the two men had to squeeze between the tightly packed mob. Men, women and children, many of whom were smoking their traditional pipes, and a stench of dark ale and gin, and something sweeter and stronger filled the air.

'Don't wander in that room to our left. Some of the idiots have discovered some of that Chinese rubbish that everyone seems to be smoking these days, and the smell of it from here makes me feel disturbed. They have a glazed look, worse than a really bad night on mother's ruin or poteen. Have to give out the odd slap when they overstep the mark,' McNally explained, spitting towards the room. 'Idiots!'

The floor felt uneven, and the usual straw and dust left a thick cloud to knee level as they walked. A youngster of no more than seven or eight, clutching a green glass bottle, no doubt containing poor quality gin or poteen, threw up in front of them.

'Taking after her ma, she is. Another year or so and she'll be trying to get you to pay for a knee trembler. Child prostitutes down here are a terrible price for the Rookery to pay, but pay it does, and you'll find lots of them. And mind your purse, as light fingers are always about. The great Charles Dickens himself was keen to spend time with us, some years ago, and you may encounter an odd one or two of the characters from his books in these dark alleys. Rumour has it that Bill Sykes might even have been old Sean Crowley himself in his younger years.'

Beddows sensed how much closer people had to live, and contact, which in Leicester would be a trigger for a slap or a grab of somebody by the neck, was unavoidable in the tight confines of the Rat's Castle. He could have lost his purse already, and been none the wiser. Fortunately, he had a concealed money belt, and his shortened truncheon. Very few would have the audacity to feel that out, so his money felt safer already.

In a corner was another room and two very large men filled the doorway. As they saw McNally they acknowledged him, and moved aside, letting him into the room. As Beddows followed behind, they refilled the gap and blocked him.

'It's okay fellas, he's with me.' The gap opened.

Inside were about twelve men, sat around a large square table, which was festooned with glasses and jugs, and the men drank freely.

'Mr McNally. This is your guest then? Welcome Mr Beddows. Any friend of Miss MacCormack and Mr McNally is a friend of ours,' said an older looking male, at the head of the table.

Beddows tension eased as he was sat down alongside

McNally, and a young girl placed two small glasses and a jug of clear poteen in front of them.

'Not for me thanks,' Beddows responded, placing the flat of his hand over the glass. 'Poteen again,' he thought of the Romanies and the second offer of the vile stuff in a few days.

Strange looks from around the table.

'I'm fine at the moment. Haven't taken a drink in years, and don't wish to do so again, but thanks all the same. I appreciate the offer.'

'Gentlemen, Mr Beddows here, needs to find my cousin Michael Lenihan, and he needs to do so before that fecker Hatter does so. Hatter has a head start on my new friend here. We don't want Hatter to get his hands on Michael, as it may bring about his untimely end.'

'Why should we let anyone take him?' shouted a small, wiry man, with pince-nez glasses perched on a very pointed nose.

'He is alleged to have killed a man. We all know that is untrue. If Hatter gets him he is as good as dead. Mr Beddows here, will secrete him away and back to safety until the truth is out, isn't that right, Beddows?'

'Very true, Paddy. Inspector Hatter has made it clear to me that he does not care if Michael Lenihan is innocent. He has his name and that is enough to hang him.'

'Why do you think he is in London?' said another man.

'He has not been seen since the circus run my Miss MacCormack left London for Leicester. She thinks he will have gone to ground down here, and the worst scenario is that he is scared, and will try and seek passage to America, to his Father,' Beddows explained.

'And do we know whether there have been any sailings since then, or if any are due?'

'I have not had time to find out as yet,' Beddows responded, already feeling inadequately prepared.

'Well I can tell you. There are two package ships in the

docks at the moment, and another due in any day now. They all sail to New York, one way or another. I work at the docks and was only unloading 'The Margaret Evans' as recent as yesterday, in St. Katharine's Dock,' said a hard looking stocky man, wearing a dark smock and a matching woollen hat. Scars on his face suggested a fighting man. Beddows looked at his hands which were enormous, and thick fingers again. A working man.

'Any passengers on board, as yet, Joe?' McNally asked.

'The skippers don't normally take the passengers on board until just before they sail, perhaps the night before. He wants the ships emptied and loaded, depending on what they trade. The Margaret Evans brings cotton in and takes finished goods out. The Americans have great cotton but lousy factories as yet.'

'And the other ship?' said McNally.

'The spirit of Boston is in Tobacco Dock, with a load of tobacco ready to unload. She sails at the weekend.'

'And nothing left?' said Beddows.

'Not since last Friday.'

'So we have a chance if he is here and intending to seek passage.'

'I will make sure any sight or sound of him around the docks gets brought to your attention,' said the docker.

'Does anyone else know Michael and where he might be, now?' said Beddows.

'He's not in these Rookeries,' said a young man at the door. I know Michael, and if he was in the rookery I would have heard. He might come to me if he couldn't get to Mr McNally.'

'Who are you?' said Beddows.

'The name is Kearney. Brendan Kearney. Remember my name, Mr Beddows as I am going to be famous one day.'

'And why might that be?' said Beddows.

'If you stop around to see me fight, you'll see. I'm the best boxer this side of the Irish Sea.'

'Cocky young pup,' said McNally.

'Confident young pup, my big friend. If Michael is anywhere near here, and knows I am fighting, he will be here.'

'How can you be so sure?'

'He always comes to my fights when he's in the area, and stays with me Ma. He knows he's safe here.'

'And by here, you mean in the rookery?'

'A safe house.'

'So, we just need to keep him away from Inspector Hatter,' said Beddows.

'And that will be our joint responsibility, Beddows,' said McNally. 'We need to actively seek him out, between the docks and here. But more importantly we need to keep Hatter away from him, so some mis-information might not go amiss.'

'I hear tell that he and the spies and assassins are busy minding our Government big-wigs, and his other duties are taking second place for a day or two. We need to stretch that out or give him something else to worry about,' said a well dressed man, back to the door. A little goatee beard hid a badly burned chin and mouth.

'Mr Collins, I do believe you're correct,' said McNally. 'An excellent idea. A diversion that Inspector Hatter would not be able to resist.'

'He hates us Paddies, Beddows. Would see all our heads flying off masts along Westminster embankment if he could. He's already seen the end of many a good man.'

'I like the idea of a diversion,' said Beddows.

'You're with the best criminals and military planners in London, Beddows. We have our own skills and getting one back on Hatter would go down very well.'

'Well, sounds like I'm in good hands. Just promise me that what you have planned is not going to get me or anyone else hanged, transported or locked up. Not what I want along the way.'

'We will try our hardest not to compromise your plans, Beddows. I'm sure we can do something annoying enough to distract these people for long enough to save Michael,' McNally grinned.

Some things he said left Beddows feeling uneasy. Did Eibhlin know what Paddy McNally was really all about?

'Get your thinking heads on then, my laddos. A pint at five o'clock for the man with the best idea,' McNally threw them the challenge.

'Let's go and show you the sights, Beddows. It's a nice walk to Tobacco Dock and back via St. Katharine's Dock. Finding Michael is now going to happen, I'm confident of that, if he's anywhere in London.'

'I didn't anticipate a tour of the Capital as part of my search for Michael.'

'You have to see the sights, John Beddows, and what our taxes really pay for. The rich and the Royals have some shabby abodes and workplaces, and I'll show you a few along the way.'

To catch a thief

Shepherd and Kettle sat in the kitchen at the rear of the station, as St. Martin's clock struck one.

'Have you blokes seen Mr Charters?' shouted the Charge Sergeant, from his raised desk inside the public entrance.

'Not since first thing,' Kettle shouted back.

'I have a gentleman here with a dispatch for him,' came the reply.

Kettle walked through to the public area and received the envelope. 'Can I say from whom this was received?' A smartly dressed man, in formal uniform, a houseman or similar, stated that Mr Charters would know who it was from, but it was for his eyes only.

'All very secretive?' said the Sergeant. 'Wouldn't give it to me.'

'I'm sure it wasn't personal,' said Kettle, 'but detectives do give added confidence, it seems, these days. I'll go and knock on his door, else Mrs Charters will know, I'm sure.'

Mr Charters was actually in the yard, near to the door to the Mayor's parlour, talking with Mayor John Manning. Kettle caught his eye by waving the dispatch, at which point Charters ended his conversation and walked back to his small office with Kettle.

'What have you got for me?'

'Just been delivered, by hand, Sir. All very secretive. Wouldn't say who it was from.'

'Good, better safe than sorry. Secrecy is sometimes essential, Kettle, and the least you know about this, the easier for me to protect my sources. Wait in the front, with Shepherd, and I will update you shortly.'

Kettle walked back and resumed his mug of tea, keeping Shepherd at hand, for Charters' next instructions.

'Gentlemen, come in please,' called Charters. 'Shut the door and sit down.'

The two men sat facing him.

'Well, it seems that our Tobias Montague is indeed associated with Her Majesty's Revenue. He is not local, and he is not known to have Masonic links.'

'Where is he from?' said Kettle.

'From the capital. He is another of the ex-military clique who seem to have found employ across many of Her Majesty's departments, including the Police, and who have a reputation of ruthlessness.'

'Ruthlessness?' asked Shepherd.

'There appear to be a band of former army officers who are being kept employed in an enforcement capacity, across a range of Government offices, allegedly, protecting our National safety and best interest. Montague is another of them.'

'Do we know what he does within The Revenue?' said Kettle.

'My source suggests he is responsible for recovering monies allegedly owed to Her Majesty. Not the odd guinea, here or there, but large sums of money, and when all other means have generally failed.'

'And how does he go about that?' said Kettle.

'Any way he gains a successful settlement. Whole or part, but ultimately, whole payment, and he is not averse to using fear or threat of violence to achieve his task.'

'So demanding money with menaces or even....'

'Even seriously harming somebody?' said Charters, interrupting Shepherd, 'Yes, if it resolves the debt.'

'So if all else has failed, a burglary or a robbery might achieve such a result?' said Kettle.

'But how far would a man like that go?' said Shepherd.
'Goodness knows, Gentlemen,' Charters replied, 'but quite clearly, we need to speak to Tobias Montague, and we need to know who else may have been subjected to his recovery methods.'

'Who does he report to?' Shepherd asked.

'How do you mean?' said Kettle.

'Somebody must be his master. Who would he report back to, or receive instructions from? Shepherd added.

'He takes directions directly from somebody within Somerset House. The place houses all sorts of people, including The Revenue hierarchy and some of the Army and Admiralty's darker services. Taxation is seen as the building blocks of Victoria's empire, and The Revenue take the taxes, and the Admiralty condone legitimate piracy on occasions, when it suits, and taxes wealth from otherwise non-taxable sources,' Charters explained.

'So even though he may be using what would be seen as criminal methods, he might actually be sanctioned to do so?' said Kettle.

'That sums it up pretty nicely, Kettle,' Charters concluded. 'That being said, it does not stop us investigating crimes and I want him in here, and to answer some robust questions, if he is involved in any way.'

'But how are we going to find him?' said Shepherd.

'If he was involved in Mr Paget's demise, did he get what he came for? If not, where would he go to get that debt settled?' asked Charters.

'Mrs Paget? Mr Harrison?' said Shepherd. 'Can we establish if Edward Paget did indeed owe Her Majesty's Revenue?'

'I am already ahead of you there, Shepherd. Edward Paget owed nothing, according to my sources. However, his Father-in-law has a rather poor history, and owes Her

Majesty a rather significant debt. He was confronted some two years back about his tax avoidance, and some skilful accounting suggests he is in default for several thousand pounds.'

'So, is Montague in the wrong place at the wrong time, and looking at Harrison, not Paget? said Kettle.

'What if Harrison saw Paget as a sacrifice? His assets, if you took his business and his money, would pay off that debt. An Insurance claim, on the other hand, might also settle the whole debt, leaving Paget's assets as a bonus,' suggested Shepherd.

'An interesting thought, Shepherd,' said Charters, raising his hand to his chin, and stroking it, gently.

'But still, possibly, a mere co-incidence,' said Kettle.

'To add a little further colour to the situation, would either of you care to guess who Montague's Commanding officer was in his Military service?' said Charters.

'Wouldn't know where to start, Sir,' said Kettle.

'Not Inspector Hatter's Father?' said Shepherd.

'Why, Shepherd, we may make a fine detective out of you yet. Montague served in Algernon Hatters' intelligence corps in Afghanistan.'

'So would he know Inspector Hatter?' said Shepherd.

'If these men are all doing similar work across Her Majesty's departments and within the Police Service, and Montague served under Hatter senior, I would think there is a very good chance that they know each other,' said Charters.

'So Hatter's haste to get Michael Lenihan named and hanged might be to protect Tobias Montague's efforts?' said Shepherd.

'Gentlemen, we seem to have inherited a very noxious, odorous puzzle to solve. Inspector Hatter is a dangerous man, which I know personally, of old. If Montague is of a similar disposition, then we have a formidable task, as their plans will probably be meticulous, and may have

Her Majesty's sanction, albeit unwritten,' said Charters. 'What about the crime in London that Hatter was investigating?' said Kettle.

'That is something we may need to examine, further, if we can make connections at this end,' said Charters.

'And what about London?' said Shepherd.

'Gentlemen, two of your colleagues are in London, as you probably already suspected, and doing their very best to find Michael Lenihan. We need him alive and well, to eliminate him. Then everything else becomes possible. If he is dead, Captain Hay will close the books and claim he has cleared up our crime along the way, and we are not going to allow that without a fight.'

'And we don't know where Beddows is, presently,' said Shepherd. 'I have a horrible feeling that he may also be heading that way.'

'I thought as much, Shepherd. If he has developed an attachment to this woman from the circus, he may see his efforts as a sign of his determination, and to see Lenihan safe. Not much we can do about it, but I hope if he is, he is not going to put our reputation at risk,' said Charters.

'He is a dedicated detective, Sir, and if he has gone to London, I suspect it is to find Lenihan, not to appease Miss MacCormack,' said Shepherd.

'I hope you are right, Shepherd, for all our sakes.'

'What about up here?' said Kettle. 'How do we set about finding Montague?'

'We need to keep an eye on Mrs Paget and Mr Harrison. Montague may still have unfinished business.'

'Mrs Paget is staying at her parents' address, presently. So we only have the house and Mr Harrison's factory to consider.' said Kettle.

'And tomorrow is the funeral, and they will be out and about together,' said Shepherd.

'Would he be so audacious as to come back for more,

assuming he is involved?'

'I want you two to turn over every stone you can between now and tomorrow. Tomorrow I want you to watch the funeral and the mourners, just in case.'

'Mr Keetley already knows we would be interested if Montague returns,' said Shepherd.

'Good,' said Charters. 'I have a positive feeling about this. perhaps things are swinging favourably for us at last?'

For whom the bells toll

Shepherd and Kettle stood under the gateway to Leicester Castle, the glare from the early morning sun avoiding them in the shadows, affording them the best vantage point to observe people attending Edward Paget's funeral.

Shepherd had been surprised that Paget was to be 'seen off' at the church of St Mary de Castro, off Castle Street, rather than in one of the smaller, less significant places of worship in his parish.

Charters had advised that this was the prestige church for Leicester's upper classes and, no doubt, William Harrison's influence had been brought to bear, with reputation highest in his mind.

King Henry VI had been christened in these hallowed walls in 1426 and John of Gaunt, amongst others, had been patron in times gone by. It was the highest church in the borough, without doubt.

It was still unusual, Shepherd considered, that whereas a working man would be laid out and remain at rest until the first convenient Sunday after his death, here he was on the morning of Thursday 8th July 1852, awaiting the service and later, the burial, of a wealthy man.

A mournful note rang out from the bells, high in the Tower above them, the slow and regular toll announcing the service to the borough.

They had watched as many of Leicester's rich and important, had arrived in their carriages, that now lined the cobbled street, and entered the church.

The Corah family comprising of the late Nathaniel

Corah's sons, Thomas, William and John arrived, separately. Kettle seemed surprised that they all chose to represent the family. John Biggs, of course. Robert Walker, of the Wolsey factory, and George Loveday from Wigston all represented the biggest hosiery employers in the borough and nearby villages. Mayor John Manning arrived with several of the Aldermen of the borough. Head Constable Robert Charters, in his finest uniform, represented the borough police, and Frederick Goodyer, the county.

Following closely behind came the families, or more accurately, the Harrison family. Edward Paget's own parents had died some years previous, and he had no siblings. No Aunts or Uncles were present, and probably had not been invited.

Shepherd had earlier noticed a number of staff from the Harrison household arriving, but was surprised to see Eleanor Skinner close by her mistress and senior family members, William and Mrs Harrison.

Finally a shiny glass panelled hearse arrived, pulled slowly by four fine black horses, bearing the coffin of Edward Paget. This was an elaborate funeral, and the family had left arrangements with the good Samuel Ginns and his *Fleur de lis* funeral company, which he ran from the rear of the inn of the same name on Belgrave Road, the most dignified undertakers in the borough. Shepherd had never seen such an elaborate coffin. His experiences had been of cheap plywood caskets, in the main, which rotted and fell apart as the deceased decayed, often before the funeral, and the best that many could afford.

However, this was a sturdy elm construction, with the finest burnished nails adding decor, along with brass angels and ornamentation, and a brass plate on the coffin lid.

Three pairs of brass handles extended along the length

of the coffin, affording handholds for the hired bearers. The coffin suggested that the occupant was loved by someone, but Shepherd was not that sure.

Once the party was inside the church, and the doors closed, Shepherd and Kettle strolled across to the large tree that stood in front of the Church, separating it from the cobbles of Castle Street, and leaned against a large bough which had grown, conveniently, parallel with the grass beneath, and thus a regular seat for many.

Shepherd had sat astride the same bough, many times, painting the area leading to the Castle.

'No sign of anyone we might consider to be our tall, dark, man,' said Shepherd.

'Seemed to be the finest and the best of our Hosiery society and family, in the main,' said Kettle. 'I never did go with the consideration that any suspect might want to show their face at such an event. A bit of a risk if you ask me,' he continued.

'But, we have seen it before, so I can understand Mr Charters suggestion that we watched proceedings.

'I reckon we have a while for a leisurely stroll up to Welford Road cemetery, and to find a similar vantage point up there, for his nibs' burial,' said Kettle.

The two men had a final look around for strangers, then set off for the cemetery, along the Knighton mile, beyond the county Gaol, and before the asylum along Occupation Road.

'I was surprised to see Eleanor Skinner accompanying the widow, rather than coming with the staff,' said Shepherd.

'I suppose she is like a companion to her, at her time of loss,' Kettle replied.

'I know she was Mr and Mrs Harrison's housekeeper, before joining the Paget household, but very informal for such a formal funeral, in my humble opinion.'

'Don't go making more assumptions, Shepherd. Haven't we got enough conundrums presently?'

'Beddows always told me to have confidence in my hunches, and my gut is screaming at me.'

'You and Beddows. He was a good detective, but don't pin everything on what he has advised you.'

'He *is* a good detective, Sergeant Kettle, and I do have every esteem for what he has taught me. My guts are becoming much more reliable, thanks to his patience with me.'

'What if he doesn't come back?' said Kettle.

'What do you mean, if he doesn't come back? Beddows will be back, and with a weight off his back. My guts also tell me that, for sure.'

'Well, Mr Charters may have something to say about that. He is not a man to be crossed, and Beddows has now done it more than once.'

'I think Mr Charters has a silent liking for Beddows. He may not be as 'by the book' as Charters would like, but he gets some sound results. He does it his way, Sergeants Smith and Haynes have their way, and you have yours.'

'You are a good copper, Shepherd, and probably will join the detectives in due course, but gather evidence and then build your case. Miss Eleanor Skinner may have good cause for wanting Edward Paget dead, but where is the evidence?'

'Perhaps we have yet to recognise it, Sergeant, but she has moved up my list of suspects, after today.'

*****

At the top of the Knighton mile, Shepherd and Kettle turned left through the two, ornate, carriage gates, that hung between stone piers. A very grandiose approach to those seeking a memorable final resting place.

Originally intended as a paupers burial ground, the cemetery now also contained as many of the borough's well to do residents, and ornate memorials were springing up across its lawns.

'Where is today's burial for Edward Paget located?' said Kettle, accosting one of the grave diggers he recognised of old.

'Over yonder, Sir,' said the labourer, pointing towards a large pink marble monolith stood alongside a mound of red earth. 'That's the Harrison family plot, and Mr Paget will become is its first resident.'

'I wonder how long he'll stay there after the burial?' said Shepherd.

'What do you mean by that?' Kettle replied.

'Mr Harrison and his daughter did not strike me as wanting to maintain relations with Mr Edward Paget after his death. Sham tears? What's the betting Harrison will have some cheap 'earth bath' dug near the paupers' graves and after the service, have the burial completed there?'

'You're starting to sound as sceptical, or should I say cynical, as Beddows, these days, Shepherd. You don't think much of this family, do you?'

'To be honest, no. Business and money stands head and shoulders above love and respect with them. The grieving widow about to inherit a large house, a sizeable insurance settlement and whatever else Edward Paget left behind. There is no love in her for the deceased.'

'He's really got to you has our Beddows.'

'He has made me look at life differently. I see the bad that before I naively ignored, and recognise the good where it really exists. Call me a realist these days, Sergeant.'

'Can you stop calling me Sergeant. I know you and Beddows are rather more informal when Mr Charters is not about. Kettle is fine with me. It's as if you don't trust me the same way as him.'

'Not at all, Sergeant, but I know you less well, and feel less comfortable being so informal with you. I'm sure things will change with time.'

Both men became aware of a familiar odour drifting from a far corner of the cemetery.

'The paupers could do with a little more topsoil, Shepherd.'

'Poor sods. Cheap boxes or just a cheaper shroud in which to meet their maker. No work on their grave until Sunday, I'm sure. Bet the old mourners will have need of their hankies over their noses, today, else they will be chucking up all over the place,' Shepherd observed.

'I hear tell that Mr Ginns provides mourners with delicately fragranced handkerchiefs, or vinaigrettes, ' said Kettle. 'Looks more dignified and they take them away as a token of appreciation for their attendance. Mind you, the Harrisons will be paying a fortune for his services. Did you see the hearse? Now that's posh.'

'More money than sense, I reckon. I have to question making money out of somebody's death.'

'Well, Mr Ginns seems to do very nicely out of it. I hear tell he is eyeing up some rather grand premises along Highcross Street, just for his funeral business. When I pass away, I suppose it won't matter to me, as I won't be settling the bill. The missus will be upset if the bill is too big. God help me if she catches up with me on the other side.'

The two men walked towards the bushes and shrubs edging Occupation Road, where they could look down across the cemetery at the mourners, once again.

The invitations had some attending the service only, whereas others were invited to both service and burial. Shepherd thought it would be a non-invited guest that they should be aware of, and scanned the grounds. Shortly after the two men had established themselves in a well hidden vantage point, the horses and hearse appeared, followed by the flagging band of mourners, walking slowly behind.

'That will teach them to choose St. Mary de Castro,' said Kettle. 'Bloody long walk in your finest togs, on a day like today.'

Shepherd smiled at the slightly cynical comment.

'Perhaps he isn't so bad,' he thought to himself.

The Clergyman stood at the head of the freshly dug grave, and a smaller number of people, mainly family and Harrison's staff, stood around.

Many of the business associates had gone, no doubt to start the planned celebration of the deceased's life, and a good feed at Paget's expense, which had been laid on at Devonshire Place. A much more pleasant event than the traditional wake, stood over the deceased, lying in situ, just in case they 'awoke'.

Shepherd saw a movement in between memorial stones beyond the group. He touched Kettle's arm, catching his attention.

'They have another guest, Kettle.'

A tall, thin figure, sombrely dressed, closed in on the group, removing his stovepipe as he did so, and nodded courteously towards the primary mourners, before taking a position slightly away from the group.

Shepherd and Kettle split, each going in the opposite direction, to cut off the options of escape. Slowly but deliberately, they closed on the figure, who Shepherd noticed was considerably taller than any other mourner. A male, with dark hair tied back in some manner, and well dressed in black tails. As Shepherd got nearer, he could see that the man appeared tanned or swarthy skinned, compared to the Lily white skin of the locals. Kettle and Shepherd stood back awaiting the end of the burial.

The group broke up after the final words of the

clergyman rang out. Maria Paget lingered over the grave and wiped her eyes with a small lace handkerchief. Shepherd considered this more of an obligation, and thus expected, than genuine.

Briefly, her eyes met those of the tall man, and a subtle nod was observed from the widow, before she turned away with her Father, as Eleanor Skinner followed close behind with Mrs Harrison.

The tall man turned to walk back towards the path from which he had originally emerged, leading down towards the railway line on its straight line into the station in Campbell Street, less than a mile away.

Whether he was already aware of the two men, or one or other had caught his attention at that moment, the man broke into a determined run.

Shepherd wondered why he should choose to run, after the risk of turning up. Likely, he did not expect to be identified or challenged, which suggested he might not be so bright as they had anticipated.

Kettle was catching up with Shepherd as the man broke through a gap in the hedge, before scurrying down the steep embankment and onto the stones and tracks below. Shepherd followed not far behind, and Kettle followed a few yards after.

The three men now ran towards the tunnel crossing below the London Road, leading to the station. Darkness replaced bright sunlight, and Shepherd and Kettle found their vision suddenly impaired.

Slowly and steadily, cautiously, they continued into the darkness.

'Be careful, Shepherd. I think I hear a train.'

The two men moved to one side of the tunnel, away from the tracks. Not far into the tunnel, they would appear as silhouettes to anyone further in, against the bright light some yards behind them.

A sudden crack, which was louder in the confines of the

tunnel, a momentary flash, and what sounded like a very fast insect buzzed close by the two men. Shepherd had heard such a sound before, at Cock Muck Hill.

'The bugger's got a pistol,' Shepherd shouted.

'Unless he has two, he has to load and is more likely to run. After him, Shepherd,' Kettle yelled.

Without any further hesitation, the two men ran into the darkness. Now they had the advantage, as the daylight broke through in the distance, and now they had the sight advantage, as a single figure could be observed about fifty yards ahead of them, running towards the daylight, beyond the tunnel.

Shepherd was gaining on the man, and before the tunnel finally ended, flung himself at the tall figure, bringing him to ground.

A short but ferocious struggle was brought to an end with Sergeant Kettle joining the fray, and a torrent of punches from Shepherd, which finally overpowered their man.

Kettle reached into his jacket pocket and fetched out his Darby handcuffs, which he swiftly used to secure the man's hands behind his back.

The man was roughly ushered into the daylight of the station to the horror of several public, stood beyond, awaiting their transport to Rugby.

Shepherd stood the man up and quickly ran his hands up and down the man's body. He could now see his adversary, clearly. He stood taller than Shepherd, about six feet five or thereabouts, tall. He was slim but sinewy, with strong arms and a rugged face. Olive skin gave the impression of someone who had spent more than his fare amount of time in warmer, sunnier climes. Inside the man's coat, just under his left armpit, Shepherd felt a small, hard object, inside a leather holster. Further inspection revealed a very small silver coloured single shot pistol. Shepherd could smell that it had been recently fired. In another pocket a small pouch containing charges and small lead balls.

Beneath the man's breeches, he wore long, well polished riding boots. Shepherd found a similar piston in the top of the right boot. This was loaded and unfired.

'Bloody hell,' said Shepherd, 'he did have another one. He could have killed one of us.'

Shepherd's heart raced and he thought, momentarily, of Perkins, once again.

'But he didn't, Shepherd. We got him, thanks to you and your man handling skills. Very courageous, I must conclude. Mr Charters will hear of this.'

Shepherd and Kettle looked each other up and down. Shepherd, particularly, was sporting some new grazes and a bloody nose, and his best suit was looking rather dishevelled from oil and grease which coated the gravel and tracks on which he had battled. Kettle looked remarkably intact, probably due to the sole contribution of locating and fitting the cuffs.

Their prisoner, on the other hand, no longer looked the picture of sartorial elegance he had presented at the graveside. His hat now lost, somewhere along the tracks or in the tunnel, and his coat, torn and soiled. His riding boots were somewhat scraped and would take some repair and time with a large amount of polish to return them to their former glory. Cuts and grazes adorned his face and knuckles, accompanied by a rather fat lip from one of Shepherd's better right hooks.

'What is your name, Sir,' Kettle asked.

'That is for you to find out,' said the prisoner, spitting blood onto the platform, and subsequently a tooth that had become dislodged. Shepherd smiled at his ability to subdue even the most skilful of adversaries, and this was a dangerous man, he believed. As much as he still despised his father, the pugilistic talents had come to serve him well in his chosen career, once again.

The man carried no papers or identifying marks upon him. Shepherd, however, was taken by Joseph Keetley's description of Tobias Montague, and he was confident they had their man.

'Mr Montague, I assume?' said Shepherd, confidently. The man gave no obvious reaction. Stony faced and hard, he had probably been trained to resist far harsher questioning, probably physical violence, too, which neither Shepherd nor Kettle considered appropriate in any event. *Not with this man.*

'A long day ahead of us, Sir?' said Shepherd.

A cold stare was the only response.

'No doubt the folk at the burial who were acquainted with you will be pleased to help us,' suggested Shepherd.

'What burial?'

'A long day, indeed,' said Kettle, shaking his head. The two men began a challenging walk to Town Hall Lane, their new prisoner manhandled and handcuffed before them, and far from passive in his detention, to the amusement or consternation of the population through which they passed.

All very Hush hush

Whilst Shepherd and Kettle had been busy observing the funeral, Tanky Smith and Black Tommy had been equally busy in The Capital.

A little more time than anticipated, and a few more drinks to loosen tongues amongst the riverside inns of the Thames, had actually paid dividends, and the men now had some vague reference to where and how Inspector Hatter and the secretive 'Special Branch' might be located.

With whispered talk of the wider organisation of *The Aliens Office* and the importance of revenue to her good majesty, Queen Victoria, comments pointed the men towards the 'Legal Quays' around Customs House, on Lower Thames Street, and the associated warehouses The Revenue and their associates controlled along the river between London Bridge and The Tower of London. Comings and goings here continued day and night, and safety of the valuables the quays held, was a logical reason for accommodating the more secretive protectors of the realm, within their walls.

Access to the river meant they could use small boats to reach most of the capital, and more and more of the threats to the Nation had come along the river.

The two men found suitable vantage points, savouring the smell of fresh fish coming off the boats on the river, and conveyed into the recently completed Billingsgate market complex, adjacent to the quays.

One particular building stood out, and it was a visit by none other than Captain Hay, himself, who Tanky had recognised from an earlier visit to London with Charters, that focused their attention.

Not long after Hay had left, a number of hard looking men had left the building and split into obvious pairs, heading in different directions.

One man looked promising. Very thin and upright, and seeming taller than he probably was, and with a long leather riding coat which seemed out of season, and shiny riding boots, he stood out from the rest, and was clearly their commander. Tanky suspected the coat hid at least one weapon of choice. His dark hair was visible under a very tall, thin, stovepipe hat. Tanky was confident that he had found Inspector Nimrod Hatter and his lair.

As much as these men should have been actively protecting their Lordships and Ministers, with the election only in its second day of voting, Hatter and a colleague who accompanied him were not heading in the direction of any obvious parliamentary business.

The second man was shorter, and nearly as wide as he was tall, but clearly muscular, with large spade like hands. He looked more of a navvy than a policeman or spy, in his working clothes and thick soled boots.

Tanky and Black Tommy followed the two men in time honoured ways they had honed in Leicester, splitting up, one holding back, and occasionally passing one another with a new lead, split across both sides of roads along which they walked.

The men wandered purposefully along until they reached Drury Lane, along Shaftesbury Avenue, and towards Seven Dials, the confluence of seven major roads.

Along the way, stops were made at The Red Lion and Still, on Drury Lane, The Grapes, on Sardinia Street, The Fountain, in Neal Street, and The Crown, in St. Giles High Street, where several conversations were held in dark corners, no doubt with trusted informants.

At The Crown, Black Tommy watched, as Hatter and his colleague escorted a scrawny looking man with bright red hair, through a door and into a yard at the rear. Screams and cries failed to turn any head within the pub. The locals knew what this meant. Hatter and his man returned but the red haired man did not. Tommy waited until the two men had walked past, and returned to Tanky.

'Someone's just had a real good hiding out the back, there. Didn't have time to go and see, but I didn't want you wandering off on your own with those two in that mood.'

'They're obviously getting nowhere using conventional means, so a punishment beating may be the leverage they have needed,' said Tanky.

This was now taking them into the heart of the place which Torchy had warned them about, the St. Giles rookeries and the notorious Rat's Castle. Strange to think that such squalor could exist within the wealthy heart of London's theatre land, around Covent Garden and Drury Lane.

Even given it was a bright summers day, these narrow streets that they now encountered, sucked the light and life out of everything. Grime and stench became the prevailing conditions, as an ever increasing number of poor, sick and destitute filled the cramped lanes and yards that they passed through.

It was getting 'a bit dodgy' as Tanky described it. This was home to the hardest and most ruthless gangs of old London. What with that to consider, and proximity to two very determined men with unsavoury business themselves, this was a risky place to be.

Children and old folk pulled at the men's clothing, holding out their hands, or soliciting sexual favours for coins or gin.

Light began to appear again, as the men followed their

foe out along side streets, and onto Holborn Hill, where they turned into a small alleyway, the sign of which announced their arrival at Union Court.

Number eleven had a swinging wooden plaque, painted up with words *The Philanthropic Lodging House*. This reminded Tanky of Pork Shop Yard and the squalid lodging house run by Abigail Hextall, back home in Leicester.

The Philanthropic Lodging House offered accommodation at 2 or 3 pennies a night, exclusively to single men, within what was a tight Irish community. This was an area well known to Sean Crowley and his bruisers, and they would be equally well known in the area.

Hatter and his colleague strolled in, ignoring two large men who attempted, briefly, to stop them. Tanky heard the words 'Special Branch' from Hatter, and that obviously had the desired effect.

Tanky and Black Tommy stepped into a nearby doorway, attracting curses and kicks from a litter of scruffy youngsters, hunkering down, playing in the thick layers of dirt.

'What is that place?' Tanky asked one of the ragged youngsters, a boy of about ten.

'Cost you a halfpenny for me to tell,' the young boy replied, in a thick Cork accent, familiar to Tanky from around Green Street and Abbey Street.

Tanky slipped his hand into his breeches and gave the child a small, dark coin.

'That's the local safe house, so it is. When you're in trouble with the coppers, that's where you go,' said the child, knowingly. 'Only the coppers don't normally dare come in this far.'

'Is that right?' said Tommy.

'So it is, mister. Are you with them others?'

'What others?' said Tanky, winking.

'Don't think I'm fecking stupid. I can smell coppers a mile off.'

'If we were coppers do you think we would come in here, after what you've told us?'

'Probably not, I suppose.' The boy looked confused, and scratched his dishevelled mop.

'Well there then...' said Tanky.

The kids ran off, shouting.

'Think we shouldn't hang around much longer,' said Tanky. 'I suspect this place will be flooded with bruisers any time soon.'

Tommy nodded in agreement.

A chair flew through cheap stained glass at the front of the lower floor of the lodging house, closely followed by a stout middle aged man, now well blooded. Shouting and screaming came from inside. A second body was ejected through the adjacent window to the first, as loud voices shouted out, 'Who next?'

'A bit like being outside the Admiral Rodney, at chucking out time,' Tommy chuckled.

'Sounds like Hatter and his man are closing in on our man Lenihan,' said Tanky. 'Let's get back onto Holborn Hill and watch from outside. The natives won't like this. If Lenihan is in there, there's not much we can do now, but out there is a different matter.'

The two men retreated to a safe and wiser vantage point in the busy street beyond.

A few moments later, and two men ran from the Courtyard, chased by a larger band of heavy set and large men, many bearing cudgels. Hatter and his man came close to a kicking themselves, by the look of it.

'That's a shame,' said Tanky, 'it would have been fun watching those two get a good hiding off the Irish.'

However, they were still without Lenihan, so all was well for the time being.

*****

Tanky and Tommy walked back down towards the river, taking the reverse route that they had followed to the Rookeries. Both were now hot from their ordeals, and ready for some refreshment.

They chose to stop at The Crown, which was now somewhat busier, and walked through to the bar. The place was packed with a strange mix of rich heading to the theatres, and Irish from across the roads around Seven Dials, just doing what they always did, and drinking to excess. Both groups seems happy, side by side.

'Probably a bit of an adventure for these posh folk, slumming it, for a change,' said Tommy.

'Probably good pickings for our lighter fingered friends,' said Tanky, watching a young boy of about thirteen slip a wallet out of a man's coat and running off before the victim was even aware, and then slipping it to an accomplice beyond. 'Not our business, today. Good luck to them all.'

Tommy looked around the pub, picking out the red haired man that had been dragged outside, earlier, by Hatter and his colleague. He sat on his own, head in hands, the remnants of stale ale in the bottom of a battered tankard in front of him.

The two men made their way through the drinkers, and put a fresh tankard full of frothy ale in front of the man.

'Looks like you've all the woes in the world on your shoulders, Cully. Here, have a drink on us,' said Tommy.

'You don't want to know, and had better not ask, if you have any sense.'

'Sense is not something my friend and I are well blessed with. We have a habit of listening to peoples' woes.'

'It's a dangerous practice around these parts,' the man replied. His face was starting to swell, and his right eye was almost closed.

'You picked a right pair to cross there, you did,' said Tanky.

'Fecking murderous bastards, those two, and never is enough enough for either of them. Both hold a candle to the Devil.'

'You know who they are?'

'I've had the displeasure before, but never like that.'

'What have you done to deserve that?' said Tommy.

The man looked around, sheepishly, sipping slowly through his damaged lips and swellings.

'It's what I haven't done that got me that.'

'I take it you are a snitch, and that's why you're sitting on your own?' said Tanky.

'You two are coppers, I can smell it on you.'

'Your community seems to have a nose for coppers, or you have a vivid imagination. We are just visitors to your fair city, and saw the harsh treatment you were on the receiving end of.'

'And they're supposed to be the law. They have no rules, them boys.'

'Aliens Office or Special Branch?' asked Tommy.

'Don't mention any of that stuff in here. People will kill me if they thought I was a tout for them lot.'

'People are probably thinking just that. They're probably also wondering what it is they want so badly,' said Tommy.

'They want a man. They do want him badly, dead or alive. I failed in their challenge to find him. This was my reward.'

'Michael Lenihan?' said Tanky.

'How would you know that?'

'Let's just say we have Michael's safety at heart.'

'How do I know you aren't with them? If I tell you anything and not them I get the same again or worse still?

'We are not with them, nor do we have anything to do with them. We have people in common with Michael, and his Mammy wants him with her.'

'If I knew where he was I would tell him, but the only place I thought he might be is where those two were off to next.'

'The Philanthropic Lodging House?'

'That's right. How do you know?'

'They went straight ,there after leaving you, and tore the place up. Threw a couple of folks out through windows, they did,' said Tanky.

'Fecking Special Branch. They get away with murder. That one in particular tells everyone he already has, and I have no cause not to believe him.'

'Which one is that?' said Tommy.

'They call him Mad Hatter. He has a frightening way of persuading people. There are a few friends of mine who just vanished overnight, after he and his sort had been around.'

'Why don't you report him?' said Tommy.

'To who? This lot are not ordinary police. They are seeking out enemies of Victoria herself, and they hate the Irish. We're all enemies of the Queen if you ask them, so we're fair game. If the police can't control them, who can?'

'Fair point,' said Tanky. 'Perhaps you had better enjoy your beer and keep out of their way for a while.'

'I'm off to stay at a friend at the Rats' Castle for a while. Even them boys won't go that far to find me.'

'Let it be known that we are asking after Michael, and that he should get in touch with his Mammy,' said Tommy.

'Who shall I say is asking after him?'

'Just tell him he is not safe in London.'

Tanky and Tommy got up and left swiftly, out onto St Giles High Street, merging with London's crowds, once again ensuring they were not followed.

Favoured weapons

Tobias Montague was safely secured in the smaller cell in Town Hall Lane, overlooked by the Charge Sergeant, standing at his desk. An extra constable had been pulled in to add some extra security at the public door.

Charters rubbed his hands, appreciative that they had one of their more elusive suspects in custody. He could not resist a peep through the hatch in the thick door at the mystery man.

'And he had the audacity to try and shoot you?' Charters shook his head.

'Only one shot was fired,' said Kettle, 'and it clearly missed us both.'

'That's not the point, Sergeant, as I distinctly heard the damned ball whizz past my ears, like some devilish insect. He had a good thump coming to him,' said Shepherd.

'Very courageous of you, young Shepherd, and I hear you subdued him rather effectively?' said Charters.

'A rather lively struggle, but one good blow stopped him in his tracks, and then Sergeant Kettle got his cuffs on him.'

'You both did well. The fact that he made off as rapidly and was so determined to avoid capture, speaks for itself. Guilt written all over his face. A job well done.'

'Guilty he may be, Sir, but at the moment we are not sure of what,' said Kettle.

'Perhaps after a robust interview, he will be more forthcoming as to what he has done, to cause him to run from you both.'

'I saw eye contact between Mrs Paget and our prisoner.

A subtle nod, but she clearly knows him, or recognises him,' said Shepherd.

'Interesting,' said Charters. 'I hear there were more weapons when you arrested him?'

'A second pistol in one of his boots. Still loaded,' said Shepherd, showing Charters the two pistols.

'I have seen pistols of that type before. Derringers. Very easy to conceal and very useful at close quarters,' said Charters. 'Damned American gunsmiths will be the death of so many more. No signs of any knife, I take it?'

'Not on him, when we detained him. We need to find out where he has stabled his mount, and where he may be staying over. There may be evidence there,' said Kettle.

'Talk to him first, and see what he might tell us.'

'He has been very quiet so far, and won't even tell us his name,' said Kettle.

'Keep trying, and then we will consider what to do next,' said Charters.

*****

Following some serious assaults on constables that had occurred, Charters had recently sanctioned a metal chair to be bolted into the floor, in the small office adjacent to St. Martin's West.

Shepherd manhandled the prisoner into the room, where Kettle unlocked the handcuffs, before feeding the man's arms behind the chair where he was shackled yet again, preventing assault or escape.

'Let us try and start off on the right foot,' said Kettle, introducing himself and Shepherd, formally.

The man stared at the wall behind Kettle. His face was calm and gave nothing away. He was probably an excellent card player.

'What is your name, Sir?' said Shepherd.

'You seem to think you know me, Constable.'

'Are you Tobias Montague?' Shepherd responded.

'Am I?'

'What are you doing in Leicester?' said Kettle.

'Is it an offence to be in Leicester?'

'What were you doing at a funeral this morning?' said Kettle.

'What funeral?'

'Have you ever stayed at the King and Crown, over the road from here?' said Shepherd.

'What if I have?'

'What details have you given to the Landlord, previously?' said Shepherd.

'You obviously have the answer to that.'

'Have you ever been in the Globe, just further down the street?' said Kettle.

'Where?'

'Have you ever told anyone in there that you were a member of her Majesty's Revenue?' said Kettle.

'Have I?'

'Have you ever met Edward Paget?' said Shepherd.

'Who?'

'Or Maria Paget?' said Kettle.

'Who?'

'Or William Harrison?' said Shepherd.

'Who?'

'Why did you run off from us, earlier?' said Kettle.

'As I said, I thought you were trying to rob me. I shall have to lay a complaint with your Head Constable.'

'Why did you shoot as us?' said Shepherd.

'You were trying to rob me.'

'Do you customarily carry two loaded pistols?' said Shepherd.

'Leicester can be a nasty place, so I'm told. Full of robbers and cut-throats.'

'Did you kill Edward Paget?' said Shepherd.

'Did I kill whom?' Shepherd thought he noticed a slightly longer eye contact from the man.

'Edward Paget,' said Shepherd.

'Never heard of him.'

'Did you kill Henry and Peter Henson?' said Kettle.

'Who?'

'Have you ever been in Her Majesty's Army?' said Kettle.

'Have I?'

'Have you ever met or served under Algernon Hatter?' said Shepherd.

'Have I?'

'Have you ever met Nimrod Hatter?' said Shepherd.

Kettle looked puzzled.

'Who?'

'This is going to be a long day, Shepherd, and our friend is clearly intending not to tell us anything.'

'In that case, given what we already have, I think we should just write statements in which he admits everything, and hang him anyway.' said Shepherd.

'Probably come to that,' said Kettle. 'Don't think his friends will be able to help him, then.'

'You really have no idea who you are dealing with, do you?' said the prisoner. 'You are stepping foot into a world that does not involve you, deliberately. A murky world that ensures that you and your family sleep safer in your beds. I shall not be here that long, mark my words, and do not expect me to hang. I would hate to disappoint you both. You would do well to save your breath for somebody else.'

A knock at the door rang out. Shepherd stood up and opened it. Stood there were Mr Charters, and alongside him, Joseph Keetley.

'Do you know this man?' Charters asked Keetley.

'Good afternoon, Mr Montague. Good to see you again,' said Keetley. 'Chosen not to stop with me this time?'

Montague gave Keetley a contemptuous glare.

'The fact it says Montague in the book, and that I have previously used that name, means nothing. Who am I? You clearly haven't any confidence, and really are out of your depth.'

Shepherd placed Montague back in the small cell, under the watchful eyes of Sergeant Sheffield.

Nothing was going to provoke Montague, without evidence. Charters was happy to leave him rotting in the cells for as long as necessary. There was enough to charge him with attempting to murder his constables, and evading arrest. If there was nothing else forthcoming, he would not be walking away freely.

Mr Kelly

Beddows and Paddy McNally had been summoned to a small yard off Phoenix Street, where a small group known to McNally had gathered, hastily.

This was deep in the Rat's Castle stronghold, and a safe place for the discussion that was about to take place.

'Why the rushed meeting?' said Paddy.

A very hard looking Irishman, taller and wider than Beddows had ever seen in his life, sat at the head of the small table, a glass of Irish in his hand, and bottle before him.

'Who is this?' said Beddows.

'This is the man who is trying to help a fecking ex copper sort out some business, that's who. Danny Kelly is the name, Mr Beddows, and I am the man who runs the rookeries. The king rat. Sorry I missed you, earlier, but other *Family* business needed resolving, which at the time was most important.'

'Relax, Beddows, you're our guest here, and Mr Kelly, if anyone, can be most trusted,' said Paddy.

'The reason we have called upon you, is that there have been visitors in the last hour or more. Your Inspector Hatter and at least one of his minders has been causing upset around the area. He really doesn't like Michael Lenihan, by the sound of it.'

'What have you heard?' said Beddows.

'He has been flashing very large amounts of money, and has dished out two or three good 'anointings' across the yards from St Giles High Street, through to Holborn Hill. Word is out that he wants Lenihan, dead or alive. He is talking of a very big reward. Both money and anointings are big enough to turn one or two of our less reliable sorts, and we know he must have a tout or two close by.'

'Where is Hatter now?' said Paddy.

'He nearly ventured too far in Union Court. Smashed the Lodging House up, well and truly, and broke a few bones throwing the occupants out of a couple of windows. By then, word had gone round of Special Branch in the yards, and some of our bruisers got there just too late. They made off, tails between their legs as the muscle arrived.'

'Will they come further in, looking for him?' said Beddows.

'Hatter is mad enough to do anything, but he would need an army to come to the heart of the Castle, to breach our stronghold.'

'So, apart from putting the frighteners out, what has he achieved?' said Beddows.

'He has made a point, and money around here turns people from our cause. Your Queen Victoria dishes out money to her spies and coerces weak souls to work for her. Michael Lenihan is now on borrowed time, should he come into the rookeries, alone.'

'That makes my job almost impossible,' said Beddows.

'If he doesn't try and get word to Paddy, here, then one of the packet ships may be his only other consideration.'

'To make things really interesting, two other men were watching Inspector Hatter from a distance, and also asking questions about Michael Lenihan,' said Kelly.

'Any idea who they were?' said Beddows.

'My man says they were coppers. Not ones he had seen before and not from around these parts, although they denied it. Told my man that Michael should be told his Mammy is looking for him, and he would be safer out of London.'

'I have a funny idea I know who they might be,' said

Beddows.

'Who?' said Paddy.

'They're likely two of my former colleagues, both good men, and good at their job. They will be treading carefully and deliberately, though, if they have Hatter in their sights.'

Beddows started to wonder whether it might actually be Tanky and Black Tommy. It would be well suited to their skills, but a dangerous gamble on Charters' part to send them down to London.

'What now then, Beddows? Have any ideas?' said Paddy.

'Where the hell is Michael Lenihan? Where else might he go?' said Beddows, thinking aloud.

'What will your friends be doing?' said Paddy.

'I should expect them to be watching Hatter, by day and by night, now that they know what he is up to and where he is looking. They will use him to find where Michael Lenihan should be looked for.'

'What might they know about Michael's whereabouts that we don't?' said Paddy.

'If Hatter is looking elsewhere, they would have that in mind. We are in a strong position where if Michael were to come here, or make an approach to somebody here, we would know, quickly. They have eyes and ears beyond the rookeries,' said Beddows.

'So between our community and your two friends, if Michael comes to light, we have two opportunities to find him. Let's leave it to them to find him outside our yards and alleys, but do we offer them safe haven if they need to protect him further?' said Kelly.

'How will we know where they are and what they are up to?' said Beddows.

'We have had them followed since they left Union Court, probably by unlikely eyes. They will get back to me if there is anything we need to know,' said Kelly.

'Somebody must know where Michael is,' said Beddows.

'Those that do will be very cautious, if they know who is looking for him. They may be biding their time for a safe opportunity to get him to safety,' said Paddy. 'Michael is a bit slow and would need guiding.'

'In the meantime, we sit and wait. I have a source who may tell us why Hatter wants him dead or alive. Some of my friends are persuading him to talk at the moment, but he is a resilient so and so,' said Kelly.

'Persuading him?' said Beddows.

'Don't ask, Mr Beddows, don't ask,' said Paddy.

'By the time the rats have had a good gnaw he'll be ready to talk,' said Kelly, grinning widely.

'By rats you mean your men?' said Beddows.

'No, Beddows. Presently he is in a small holding cell beneath a courtyard. His only contact will be the rats that scurry and bring our diseases. They will be hungry for a while, and he will squeal when he's had enough.'

'That sounds rather severe,' said Beddows.

'Touts is touts. If he has taken Hatter's shilling, he can tell us what we want, and then I will allow him passage from the rookeries,' said Kelly.

'You would let him go, and have him run back to Hatter?'

'That's not how touts get safe passage down here, Mr Beddows. We don't risk or tolerate touts. The only safe ones are dead ones, if you get my meaning.'

Beddows had no cause to suspect that not to be the case, and stopped asking questions.

A late call

Before Shepherd was to get home to his young wife, he had one more call to make. A note had been left for him with the Charge Sergeant, to pop into the King and Crown where somebody was waiting for him.

He was not one for spending time in watering holes, late at night, and had no desire to sit or stand drinking, when he had a wife waiting.

The inn was crowded, and the normal fog from the smokers gave a strange haze across the room. Joseph Keetley caught his eye, and he pointed towards a corner of the room and a small table.

Sat alone, Shepherd saw Eibhlin MacCormack. She was drinking a golden coloured liquor in a small glass.

Eibhlin looked like no other woman in the inn, with riding boots, light breeches, a very flamboyant frilled shirt, and her hair was braided and plaited. She wore no makeup and was, indeed, naturally stunning.

A woman, drinking alone, was not a usual sight in Leicester, and she was the talk of many of the customers, watching her every move. Only some of the more flamboyant totty from Manky Lil's might ever been found alone, whilst waiting for a gentleman to pay for a few minutes of their time and pleasure.

'Why Mr Shepherd, I didn't know if you would come.'

'Good evening Miss MacCormack.'

'Eibhlin, please.'

'How can I help you?'

'I was wondering if anybody had heard anything from Beddows?'

'I certainly haven't, and must admit, I am concerned as

to where he is and what he may be up to,' said Shepherd.

'I thought you had already guessed that he had gone to London to look for my son?'

'It did cross my mind.'

'He didn't have to go, but kindly thought it might help.'

'Where did he say he would go?'

'I provided him with details of a relative of mine, who Michael might be trying to get to. He would see Beddows safe. He has some unusual contacts within his community, but is very discreet and the community would look after Beddows, also.'

'I hope so. You know we have the Metropolitan Police making enquiries, also.'

'That Inspector Hatter made me very nervous, Mr Shepherd, and I somehow don't trust him. That's why Beddows offered to make his own enquiries.'

'I suppose that no news is good news?' said Shepherd.

'Would you tell me if you heard anything?' said Eibhlin.

'I will do my best.'

'Can I offer you a drink, Mr Shepherd, rude of me sitting drinking as I am?'

'Thank you but no thank you, I have a young wife who is sitting wondering where I am and when I am coming home. I will say goodnight, Miss MacCormack.'

Shepherd walked briskly out and off, in the direction of home.

Revelations and questions

The hours of legwork, yesterday afternoon, had proven fruitless. Visit after visit to the most prominent establishments around the borough to locate Montague's horse, and thus probably his lodgings, had unearthed nothing.

The word had gone out from one or two carefully chosen and trusted informants that Shepherd and Kettle needed to find both, and quickly.

Hotels, inns, livery houses and coach yards had all been checked, and very little of the old town remained to be searched.

'It would be just our bloody luck to find that he is being put up by some posh individual with their own stables,' said Kettle, 'and not to say it isn't outside of the Borough walls.'

'He must have made good contacts with his earlier business, if the talk in The Globe is anything to go by. What concerns me is that where in the past he has been content to use The King and Crown, for once he clearly has not,' said Shepherd.

'Possibly too close to home, if he is our tall, dark man. But then again, if he is, why risk coming back at all, especially so close after the crime, and to turn up at the burial?' said Kettle.

'Perhaps he is still to be paid off. Either that or he is cock sure of being rescued by his Masters. He is supposedly a ruthless man and feared in the Globe.'

'A conundrum, Shepherd, and until we find what we are looking for, one we may never get to the bottom of. He isn't going to talk, freely, based on yesterday's performance.'

'If he has been in the army, and he has been trained to resist questioning, even under brutality, then he will be a devil to crack.'

'And that's without the possibility of somebody from Her Majesty's Revenue coming up and bailing him out as he suggests.'

'Even if he is suspected of murder?' said Shepherd.

'If there really are men who work in dark and mysterious worlds, amongst us, who knows?' Kettle shook his head.

The two men walked down Belgrave Road, towards the north-eastern edge of the old borough. The next stop on the list was Samuel Ginns' Fleur de lis Inn, from where he also ran his funeral and livery services.

Turning in through the carriage gates to the rear yard, two young lads were busy washing down the hearse that Shepherd and Kettle had seen at yesterday's funeral. The horses would have been washed and brushed after the event, and were probably enjoying a quiet day in their horse boxes, in the large sheds at the rear of the yard.

Samuel Ginns was not on the premises, but a young manager, William Bates, announced himself to the men.

'How can I help you, Gentlemen? Looking for anything in particular?'

'We are trying to locate a horse that may have been stabled in the borough over the last day or so, and whether the rider may have a room booked here?' said Kettle.

'Do you have a name?'

'We are looking for a Mr Tobias Montague,' said Shepherd.

'We have a Mr Tobias staying with us, although he has not been in since yesterday. He has been with us for most of the week. Mr Harrison has booked him in once or twice lately.'

'Not William Harrison, by any chance, the man whose son-in-law you buried, yesterday?' said Kettle.

'The very same, indeed. Mr Tobias is a business associate of Mr Harrison, I understand, and has been conducting some business on his behalf.'

'We will need to see his room, and also his horse and horse box,' said Shepherd, feeling a tinge of relief.

'He is a very tidy man, gentlemen. Carries everything in his saddlebags and in one travelling bag. His room is always immaculately left when he leaves it.'

'May we start with his room?' said Kettle.

'This way, please.' Bates took the constables up a short rear staircase to a room overlooking the stable block. 'He likes this room, as he can keep an eye on his favourite mare.'

Room two was a small, but tidy room, with a single bed, a bedside table with an oil lamp, and a small chest with a functional but sturdy wash-stand and bowl. No personal effects were evident on or in any of the drawers or furniture. A quality leather bag, stamped TM, hung from a peg on the side wall. A couple of silk shirts and a cravat. Clean white riding breeches. a razor and soap in a small wash bag. But no papers, anywhere.'

'Have you seen Mr Tobias this last few days, and if so, what was he wearing?'

'I only saw him, briefly, yesterday, and he was in mourning dress and topper, and I assumed he was dressed for the funeral.'

'Do you know if he knew the dead man, Edward Paget?' said Shepherd.

'I don't know. I only know he was acquainted with Mr Harrison.'

'And now we would like to see his horse and horse box,' said Kettle.

The man lead them back down the steps, across the

yard, and into one of the boxes in the main stables, towards the rear.

'Has Mr Tobias been down here since he arrived?' said Shepherd.

'He often comes and tends to his mare. He has had different horses the last two times he has stayed.'

'Does he keep anything down here?' said Shepherd.

'The feed is charged with the room and stable fees, as is grooming. He doesn't pay for grooming and looks after it himself. He has a small kit in his saddlebags, which we look after in our office at the back.'

'May we see his bag?' said Shepherd.

The man unlocked the office and pointed to a tan leather bag with two pouches, big enough to secure across the horse in front of the saddle. Initials TM were stamped in the fine grade leather.

Kettle opened one of the pouches and removed a bundle, wrapped in cloth. Just a horse brush and some small tools for the animal's hooves. In the other pouch was nothing at all, other than a cloth, which seemed to be oiled for the leather on the saddle and equipment.

'Is that all he has?' said Kettle.

'To my knowledge,' said the manager.

'I would like a look inside the horse box,' said Shepherd.

The manager took him to a stall with a fine grey mare stood inside. The horse looked over the gate to the box, and seemed content with new company.

'Do you like horses, Shepherd?' said Kettle.

'I grew up with them,' Shepherd replied.

'Well, in that case, you go in there and look. I can't stand the damn things. Make me ill, they do. I come out in hives and sneeze for England.'

Shepherd opened the gate and patted the horse, stroking its nose and neck, before closing the gate behind him and beginning a search of the hay and feed that filled the floor of the box.

'I've got something, here,' said Shepherd, reaching deep into a far corner, under some sacking. He felt a bundle and pulled the obstructing sacking and hay away. Something curved and heavy, wrapped in layers of coarse cloth, Shepherd observed, walking back to the daylight at the front of the shed, to where Kettle remained.

Removing the layers carefully, Shepherd revealed a large knife with a curved blade. The blade and handle were tarnished, and the cloth layer nearest to the knife appeared heavily soiled.

'Blood,' said Shepherd.

'Those Gypsies spoke of a curved blade. This is a Kukri, as we have spoken of, and I would suggest that this is what could have killed the Henson boys,' said Kettle.

'Bloody hell, Kettle. So we have our man. TM - Tobias Montague. A man who is staying here courtesy of Edward Paget's Father in law. And now a possible murder weapon connecting him to two other murders. Perhaps this may loosen his tongue?'

'Has anybody else had access to the horse box since Mr Tobias arrived here?' said Kettle.

'Anybody could get in to it. It would be easy to climb into the shed and open the box.'

'What day, exactly, did Mr Tobias arrive?'

'He is signed in since Tuesday evening,' said the Manager.

'But they were dead by Monday morning, Kettle,' Shepherd whispered, out of the hearing of the manager.

'When had he been here before?' said Kettle.

'I would need to check in the book, but I believe it was the week before, or two weeks at the very most.'

The men returned to the inn, and the guest book retrieved.

'Here we go. He was last booked in on the 20th June, and stayed for two nights.'

'He definitely wasn't here on Sunday the 4th of this month, or Monday the 5th?' said Kettle.

'It's definitely not shown in the book, no. And then he signs back in here on Tuesday evening, the 6th.'

'Thank you, good Sir,' said Kettle. 'I am afraid Mr Tobias is somewhat indisposed at present. Is his horse and room safe for the time being?'

'Mr Harrison has yet to settle the account, so until we receive notification and the bill is settled, I would assume so.'

'Then we would bid a good day to you, Sir.'

'There is something amiss, here, Shepherd. No paperwork, no personal content in any quantity, but an easily found, concealed weapon. I suspect we are going to have more questions than answers with this one.'

The tout

Beddows woke early, and found himself feeling remarkable refreshed, and he felt he had finally acclimatised to his hammock.

His nose gave early indication of eggs and meat cooking, and he wandered through to find Paddy McNally, with a small pan on the stove, and some thick fatty bacon frying, and two large eggs bubbling away merrily.

'I have a good feeling, Patrick McNally, that we are close to Michael Lenihan in one way or another, and with the possibility that two of my friends might also be watching out for him, an even better feeling.'

'We just need to get to him before those bastards in Special Branch.'

'I wonder how well fed the rats were overnight?' said Beddows. As much as the law was often cruel, and to many often excessive, there was something satisfying of seeing how the truth could out when no rules had to be applied.

'A wander over to see Mr Kelly is on the cards, once we have fed, ourselves.'

The lanes and courts off the narrow, fetid alleys of the Rookeries were humid and the whole of poverty could be smelled by those who dared venture down them.

Many would stop at the better lanes, put off by the stench. What went into the Thames, and had been subject of complaint by those in Westminster, was always underfoot, to these poor folk.

Yet, many would choose never to venture out of them, as a sense of safety, and a sense of community prevailed.

Paddy guided Beddows to a new area, where he had yet to venture. However, Paddy had blind-folded Beddows, firstly, as this was part of the rookeries in which very few were actually allowed to venture.

Had this been a real Castle, these were the dungeons and 'oubliettes', where those who crossed the community met their fate.

Dark, slow moving drains, already carrying remnants of carcasses in one form or another from backstreet butchers and sausage makers, together with those of the very large rats that grew fat on the remnants, allegedly formed the means of disposal of those who merited such an end.

The law of the rookeries was something they all lived by, without complaint.

Nobody complained, and nobody was really missed.

Beddows was ushered into a very noisy room, clearly with several men already inside, and only then was his blindfold removed.

Mr Kelly and some very large men stood around a man who was hanging upside down from a heavy beam, suspended by rope, tied around his ankles. Kelly and his bruisers were bare chested and had clearly been 'encouraging' the hanging man.

Beddows noticed what appeared to be raw bite marks on his extremities.

'The rats fed well, last night,' said Kelly, 'but they may have fed on this man's tongue, as he has been annoyingly silent, until the last few minutes. He now has something to tell us about Mr Hatter, don't you?' Kelly struck him violently around the side of his head, and he span on the rope, spitting blood.

'Why don't you just kill me and be done with it, because that's what will happen to me when Hatter and his henchmen get hold of me,' the man said.

Kelly struck him again, spinning him back the other way.

Beddows felt that he should do something, but he was no longer Sergeant Beddows, and was in a different world.

'Just tell us why Hatter wants this man Lenihan dead.'

'These men are Her Majesty's bad men. She condones them using whatever tactics they see fit to rid the state of its enemies,' said the man, grimacing as he spoke, his jaw swollen. Beddows suspected it was already broken. 'Hatter has killed men himself, and used the powers they have as justification. Michael Lenihan has papers, given to him by two of Hatter's spies and 'getters', that would cause Queen Victoria and Mr Hatter himself, amongst others, some serious embarrassment.'

'When was he given these papers?' said Beddows.

'A few days ago, after a murder was committed in Westminster. The men who did it made a mistake and realised Hatter would have their guts for garters, and they left London in fear of their lives. They gave Lenihan the papers to hand in to The Times newspaper, if anything happened to them. Lenihan must have got scared and turned and ran. He can incriminate Hatter, and is a dead man if Hatter gets him.'

'Little wonder he's keeping his head down,' said Paddy. 'Poor bugger must be shitting himself.'

'The papers also incriminate several big names around London, and rumour has it they will have anybody that threatens them silenced. Aliens Office is in uproar and questions are being asked by Wellington as to who sanctions their actions to this level,' said the inverted man.

'And how much does Hatter pay you for touting for him?' said Paddy.

'Pay? that's a joke. Very funny. I don't have many bones that haven't been broken and I don't want many more. He beats the shite out of most of his touts. I have seen one or two who have actually been branded, a trick he learned from his Father, one of the big wigs in the Aliens Office.'

'And what should we do with you now?' said Kelly.

'Whatever you do, make it quick. For I can be certain that Hatter will make anything he does long and painful. Shoot me or something, for feck's sake, please.'

'Cut him down, boys, and give him some Brandy. We'll sort out what to do with him later,' said Kelly.

*****

'Poor fecker must be shitting himself,' said Paddy.

'He already had by the smell of it,' said Beddows. 'What will Mr Kelly do with him?'

'We are not privy to what Mr Kelly does, Beddows. It is safer not to pry. He is a fair man, and may even take pity on the man and send him off somewhere as a tout for our cause. Touts with feet in two camps have their uses, subject to who pays better.'

'How often does he become charitable?'

'Do you know how many people live in these few square miles, Beddows? Thousands, many of whom, nobody knows and nobody will miss. I have met one or two that have been turned to our cause and have served Mr Kelly well. On the other hand, I have also seen others being 'encouraged' and then never seen again. It's a war, Beddows, a fecking secret war, but war none the less.'

'How do you mean?'

'Ireland has been the subject of so many wars and invasions over the years. It is vulnerable at the moment, with so many running after the famine. Your Majesty wants it all in her name, but one day the Irish uprising will come. Probably not in our lifetime, but one day. In the meantime, Inspector Hatter and his Special Branch will try and eradicate every possible one of us who shows Irish allegiance, and we disappear at a faster rate at his hands than we do at Mr Kelly's.'

'Bugger. Hadn't realised how bad it was down here. I hear stories from Sean Crowley's folk, back in Leicester, but nothing like this.'

'Believe me, Beddows, these bad buggers are in Leicester, somewhere, mark my words, and Sean Crowley will have crossed swords with them. He may not admit so, but they have eyes and ears everywhere, and are not opposed to making folk disappear wherever they go.'

'It was interesting to hear what the tout had to say. I know we were interested in two brothers who knew Michael, and my colleagues will be searching for them in Leicester, if they haven't already found them.'

'Michael will be scared, Beddows. He is slow but not stupid. He must be close by with somebody he trusts, and won't go to a paper on his own. But where?'

'Waiting is still hard for me, Paddy. I want to be out there knocking doors, but in this case, I know how dangerous that is in itself. I hope my mates are aware of the danger they face.'

Dirty tricks?

Kettle and Shepherd walked back to the police station, and immediately sought out Robert Charters, who was about to take lunch with his wife.

'You look like two happy constables,' said Charters.

'Not necessarily what you will wish to hear, Sir, but intriguing, none-the-less.'

'Go on.'

'We located our man's horse and lodgings, earlier this morning. You'll never guess where we found them?' said Kettle.

'Just get to what I need to know,' said Charters, who seemed easily irritated.

'He has been stopping at the Fleur de lis, under the name Mr Tobias, paid for in advance by none other than Mr William Harrison.'

'You jest?'

'I jest not,' said Kettle. 'He arrived on Tuesday evening and has been staying there ever since. Not the first time either, as he was there at Harrison's expense back in June.'

'Young Shepherd, here, was never keen on Mr Harrison, is that fair to say, Shepherd?'

'I did have suspicions, after the story of his threats to Edward Paget.'

'What did you find?' said Charters.

'This is where things become a puzzle.' Kettle opened the package he held, layer by layer, until the Kukri came into view.

'Is that what I think it is?' said Charters.

'Yes Sir, the Gypsies spoke of a curved knife, which we

thought may be a Kukri. It appears heavily stained, probably blood, as is the cloth in which it is wrapped.'

'And the man has served in Afghanistan?' said Charters

'That was one of the rumours. But then again, so had Inspector Hatter's Father, before him.'

'But these things can be picked up in any market place or pawn-brokers shop. There must be many that were brought back by Soldiers and now in circulation,' said Charters. 'So why a puzzle?' said Charters.

'If the man did not arrive and check in until Tuesday evening, where was he over Sunday and Monday when the Hensons were killed?'

'That is something you will need to establish in interview, gentlemen, else we will need to try and locate that information by other means.'

'The problem I see is that these items were not in his room, but hidden in the box in which his horse is stabled. Anyone could access that.'

'What are you suggesting?' said Charters.

'If he denies any knowledge of the knife...' said Kettle

'Don't create problems until they are created for you. He might now admit it and everything else,' said Charters.

'There are a lot of strange and conflicting issues we need to resolve,' said Shepherd.

'And that is what we are paid to resolve,' said Kettle.

'What about Harrison?' said Shepherd.

'We will wait and hear what Mr Tobias Montague, or whatever his name really is, has to tell us. Mr Harrison can wait, but he will face his time here, sooner rather than later,' said Charters.

'Have we had any attempt to have him released by people in London?' said Shepherd.

'I don't suspect we will, Shepherd. It is very early, yet, since he was arrested, and the drums may not yet have reached the right ears. Also, if he is doing dirty work, they will not want to acknowledge that he really is. In my experience, men like that will be thrown to the wolves, if there is any truth in that at all. Queen Victoria would not want any dirty washing on display.'

'What if he admits that he is up to dirty work?' said Kettle.

'We keep it to ourselves, and I will follow that up with Sir Richard Mayne if that is the case. For now, we really don't know whether these stories are just to put you off, so stick with it and do what you normally do.'

'I wonder if our illustrious surgeon, Thomas Hamilton, could offer us any extra information if he was to examine the knife and rags?' said Shepherd.

'You live in your own world, at times, Shepherd. Blood is blood, and a cut is a cut. What do you think a doctor will be able to do for us?' said Kettle, shaking his head.

'If you don't ask, you don't find out. Science is a wonderful thing, like nature, and one day it will solve many things that we cannot presently,' replied Shepherd.

'I suggest you let Surgeon Hamilton examine the knife, Sergeant, to see if it is feasible that the gutting that the bodies underwent is consistent with the blade, but I want you two to concentrate on being good coppers for now. Being a copper is complicated enough without science,' said Charters.

Shepherd felt elated that Mr Charters had agreed to his suggestion.

'By the way, Sir, I bumped into Miss MacCormack yesterday, on the way home. She confirms that Beddows is in London seeking information on Michael Lenihan.'

'I suspected as much, Shepherd. I hope he is being sensible. Keep me informed if you hear anything from her.'

The Bowl

Beddows had just bought Paddy McNally a jug of ale in the Bowl Inn to wash away the midday dust and grime. A fine pie from Betsy's eel and pie shop, opposite, would set each man up for the day. Paddy said these were the best pies around for miles, and Beddows presently would not disagree.

The inn was busy, and always attracted people visiting London, for its macabre connection with the hanging trade.

Beddows could not help but sit with his back to the wall, affording himself best view of people passing through. Any violence offered could be seen coming, and the lessons learned had served him well, over the years.

Paddy McNally laughed at his anxiety.

'A scrap's a scrap, whether it starts in front or behind you...'

'The scars on the back of my head warn me otherwise,' said Beddows.

'And whilst you've been looking out for somebody who might want to bash your head in, tell me, who is the man who has been watching you from the doorway opposite?'

'What man?' said Beddows, looking into the sunlight towards the shadows.

'There was a man. Looked like a merchant man. A French Breton cap, and canvas top, and a fine ginger beard. Anyone you know?'

'I can't see anyone,' said Beddows.

'You can't now, but he was there. A pound to a pinch

that when we set off, he'll not be far away. If it's one of Hatter's fecking men, I'll lead him a merry dance. When we go, just stay very close to my heels, as they will not want to take the route I will take us.'

'Shall we test your supposition?'

'After I have finished my pie and pint, Beddows. If I am to die, it will not be on an empty stomach.'

A few minutes later, the two men stepped into the sunshine, and after a cursory scan of the doorways and lanes around them, Paddy crossed the road, briskly, with Beddows hard on his heels.

Beddows recognised the odd road, as alleyways ended and the way forward widened, briefly. At Church Street, Paddy stopped, sending Beddows across the road on his own, to stand in the next alleyway entrance. Beddows saw this was an alleyway that took him through to Ivy Street, and the dense and foreboding yards and courts in the stronghold.

Paddy gave it a minute, and then crossed, walking past Beddows and taking lead.

'We are being followed, Beddows, but my friends here know the signs. In a few yards we come to a very tight yard to the right. We enter there and wait.'

'Why?' said Beddows.

'Cat and mouse,' said Paddy. 'Let's watch the cats become mice.'

The numbers of idle people in these never-ending maze of alleys, continued to surprise Beddows. It became quite claustrophobic.

'It takes somebody with exceedingly large crown jewels, or minute brains, to follow the likes of me into this part of our stronghold,' said Paddy, 'but these seem very determined. They are about to get a harsh lesson in rookery rules.'

As Beddows followed Paddy into the turn, Paddy grabbed him and they turned to face the alley they had just negotiated.

A disturbance became audible, and several burly men appeared from nowhere, manhandling two foreign looking men into the small yard.

'Bloody hell, Beddows, it is you,' came a familiar voice. 'We half expected to get grabbed, half a mile or so back. Realised it was the only way we could get in touch, safely.' The man wore a Breton cap and a vivid ginger beard, which he carefully peeled away, revealing his well worn face.

'Back off lads, these are friends of mine,' shouted Beddows, preventing some serious rookery justice being dished out, summarily.

'Paddy, let me introduce you to two of Leicester's finest, Sergeant Francis Smith - Tanky to his friends, and Sergeant Tommy Haynes - Black Tommy to his.'

'So which is it?' said Paddy. 'Large crown jewels or minuscule brains?'

'We have both,' said Tanky, 'but sometimes you just have to trust your intuition, and if Beddows was safe, we reckoned you were decent blokes.'

'Mind, I nearly shit myself when I saw the size of the blokes forming up behind us as we came through your cosy little yards. Reckon old Sean Crowley could do with a few to beef up his muscle in the borough,' said Tommy.

'Oddly enough, many of them are Sean's men,' said Paddy, 'and he has told me about the legends of Tanky Smith and Black Tommy, over an odd glass or three.'

'You know our Sean Crowley?' said Tanky.

'You mean, you know our Sean Crowley, Mr Smith?' Paddy grinned. 'He was ours long before he found a soft spot in Leicester.'

'What are you two doing down here?' said Beddows?

'I was about to ask you the same thing,' said Tanky. 'Charters said you were on gardening leave, but a little bird suggested that you might come to the capital. Young Samson Shepherd will be pining for you.'

'Mr Shepherd and I were not on speaking terms when I left. I am trying to help a friend out.'

'Looking for Michael Lenihan, perhaps, just like your friends in Special Branch?' said Tommy.

'Have you any idea how many people are looking for him?' said Beddows.

'Have you any idea how few people know where he is?' said Tanky, a wide grin breaking.

'You know where he is?' said Paddy.

'Who is your friend, by the way, Beddows, you haven't introduced him?'

'This is Patrick McNally. Paddy to his friends. A relative of Michael's.'

'And are we safe with Mr Crowley's boys about?'

'I suggest you say nothing until we move to somewhere a little more secure.' said Paddy, leading the men off to see Mr Kelly.

Sacrifices

Shepherd fetched the prisoner from the holding cell, and pushed him through into the small office, once again. The process of securing him to the fixed chair seemed quicker this time.

Kettle sat directly opposite the man, and Shepherd alongside Kettle.

'This is a noisy place,' said the man. 'Drunks and harlots, all night long, shouting and screaming. I could do with a lunchtime snooze.'

'You'll have plenty of time for that when you have your room at the borough gaol, and then, possibly, the sleep of the dead, shortly after that,' said Kettle.

'You seem confident?'

'For all your efforts to avoid our earlier questions, we now have more than enough to connect you to the murders of Edward Paget and the Henson brothers,' said Kettle.

'You have been busy then.'

'Many questions have now been answered for us. The staff at the Fleur de lis have been very helpful. Now is it Mr Tobias, or Mr Tobias Montague?'

'Take your pick.'

'Well, assuming that the lettering on your leather bags is correct, we will work with Tobias Montague,' said Shepherd.

'Observant boy.'

'We asked you several questions yesterday, and you avoided an answer to many. I am going to ask you them again, and to give you a further opportunity to tell us your version of events,' said Kettle.

'I don't answer questions, not to you, anyway.'

'When Mr William Harrison and his daughter are arrested, next, they will be very keen to tell us the truth. They will still probably hang, but they will squirm and try and talk their way out of it,' said Shepherd.

'He will not be impressed with having an extended bill to pay for you and your horse after all this,' said Kettle.

Montague smiled, but said nothing.

'They will convict you of the killing of Edward Paget, and their words will then connect you to the murder of the Hensons,' said Shepherd, 'well, that, and your hidden weapon.'

An apparent look of puzzlement appeared across the face of the prisoner.

'Ah, have we hit a nerve. You assumed that we wouldn't look for it?' said Shepherd.

'You are trying to trap me with falsehoods and prevarication. I'm not swayed.'

'Your service history is already suggested, and the weapon we have found will support the service you have done for the Country, but it will also hang you,' said Kettle.

'You have my weapons. You took them off me at the Railway station.'

'We are not talking about your Derringers,' said Shepherd.

'What then?'

'What do you think?' said Shepherd.

'Something is afoot here. You are still trying to implicate me in crimes I have no knowledge of.'

'Why should we do that, when we have evidence to hang you for crimes we know you have committed?' said Kettle.

'I think it is time you contacted my handlers, who will sort this out without all this ridiculous questioning.'

'And who might they be?' said Kettle.

'I work for a very specialist organisation. It is something that is essential for a Country like this to exist. If you get a telegraph to the person in directions I shall give you, they will ensure my release.'

'And who shall we tell them we have in custody?' said Shepherd.

'My field name is *The Fisherman*. That is enough for you to know and for them to respond.'

'And mine is Napoleon Bonaparte,' said Kettle. 'I don't believe you and give me one good reason why I should?'

'Because it is the truth. I haven't killed anyone, and I have done nothing that isn't sanctioned by my Organisation.'

'What is the name of this organisation you claim to be working for?' said Kettle.

'Imagine a Country where foreign powers undermine Sovereignty with their spy networks. Imagine a Country where the money that should be paying for our war chests and national security is held back or stolen by rich individuals. Her Majesty seeks to restore the financial stability of the country and to use that revenue to pursue those who wish to see and end to our Sovereignty.'

'Very interesting. Spies; Revenue; Sovereignty; I have read tales of such a nature,' said Kettle.

'It is the truth. Contact them, and you will see.'

'Are you sure they would be interested in a renegade, who uses his position to gain personal wealth, and offers his services to highest bidders for criminal services?' said Shepherd.

'You have a narrow minded viewpoint as to what, or rather, what is not acceptable to further the needs of Her Majesty.'

'I should think her Majesty would not wish to hear of a murderous felon, using her name to justify his criminality,' said Kettle.

'You keep talking of the murder of three men. Why do you consider that I am responsible?'

Shepherd recognised that the prisoner was intrigued.

'I do not wish to answer any further questions until you have made contact with my Lords and Masters.'

'Then rot in hell. Farfetched stories and delays will not save your neck. Tell us what we want or face your maker alone,' said Kettle.

'I ask you to honour my request. I am a servant of Her Majesty the Queen, as are you, as constables, and I reserve the right to return to my duties.'

Kettle laughed, loudly. 'Nobody walks out of this station having committed murder, unless through the yard and the condemned cell. No deals. We don't believe you.'

'Send a telegraph, as I ask. Send it to *'Saint Paul'* at the address I shall disclose, and you will see that I am telling you the truth.'

'Attempting to kill two constables is enough to hang you. Your time is running out, and there can be no justification for that,' said Shepherd.

'Your word against mine.'

'And this?' said Kettle, showing the prisoner the package recovered from the Fleur de lis.

'And now the trickery.' said the prisoner, 'what is that, and what has it to do with me?'

'That is without doubt, the blade that killed the Henson Brothers. And where do you think we found it?'

'Where do you allege you found it? No doubt planted somewhere to add weight to any confession that you will purport to come from me.'

'Do you deny that it is yours?' said Kettle.

'I have never seen it before in my life.'

'You know what it is?' said Shepherd.

'It is an Indian Army Kukri, favoured by Nepalese troops, and there were hundreds brought back with our army from Auckland's Folly.'

'And you have one of your own, somewhere?' said Shepherd.

'I learned that close combat was far too risky at times. You have seen my preferred weapons. Guns are much more efficient if you are in numbers.'

'We recovered this a short time ago from the stall in which your horse is presently resting, at the inn. Not very well hidden for a professional,' said Kettle.

'Well it is not mine, nor do I have any knowledge of it.'

'So who would choose to put it there?' said Shepherd. 'Who would want to incriminate you?'

'Apart from you two?'

'Isn't it time you had a little think about your present situation?' said Kettle.

'What do I have to think about?'

'Are you a God fearing man?' said Kettle.

'God? I have no faith in any God. When you have seen what man can do to man, can any man believe in God? Why do you ask?'

'Some people would wish to make their peace with God and admit their sins,' said Kettle.

'I have no sins to admit, that are of relevance, here.'

'If you have done nothing, why should somebody wish to incriminate you?' said Shepherd.

'You are spinning us a web,' said Kettle. 'You have told us nothing, not even your own name. You have shot at us and fought us when arrested. You deny any knowledge of anything or anybody. You tell us of secret organisations and murky and dangerous men, and wish us to send a telegraph to *Saint Paul*. I am starting to wonder whether you are actually a mad man, and treat you as such.'

'Your questions would be answered by one short telegraph. Send it, and see what the response brings.'

'I think you need time to work out what is happening here. What have you done that is so terrible, that somebody is prepared to sacrifice you? Perhaps this is the work of your Lords and Masters and you have served your purpose?'

'If they have thrown me to the wolves, then so be it. If they will deny any knowledge of me, but I shall still say nothing more at this time.'

Having placed Montague back in the cells, the two detectives sought out their leader.

'I'm not keen on the idea of a telegraph, as he asks,' said Kettle.

'I have heard of strange names and codes being used by these people,' said Charters. 'Many of the former military men I worked with in London had such communication networks, in respect of issues of National Security. *Saint Paul* is already familiar to me, as a pseudonym for somebody at high level.'

'Do we humour him and send such a telegraph, then?' said Kettle.

'I will instruct two to be sent. One as he has asked, but I shall also send one for Sir Richard Mayne, seeking any information he may be able to furnish us with,' said Charters.

'And what about Tobias Montague, or whatever his real name is, in the meantime?' said Shepherd.

'He stays in the cells, Constable Shepherd. One way or another, we have potentially capital offences against him, if he chooses not to speak to us. That is his problem. In the meantime we have other enquiries to pursue, which may throw further light on the truth. I think it is time we spoke to the widow and her Father, officially.'

'Mr Keetley has identified him as using the name Montague. Is it worth us bringing the Gypsies in to see if they recognise him. We still have the 'tall, dark man' to resolve,' said Shepherd.

'It won't do any harm, not that I am a believer in their mysticism, of course,' said Charters.

A trio of Borough Boys

Patrick McNally led Beddows, Tanky and Black Tommy, blindfolded, through the maze of lanes, one further time, to seek out Danny Kelly.

Kelly was sat in a large leather armchair, with several newspapers scattered around him, and a cup of tea in his hand.

'Good afternoon, gentlemen. I take it these are your friends from Leicester, Mr Beddows?'

Beddows introduced the two men, now removing their blindfolds.

'And to what do I owe this pleasure?' said Kelly.

'My friends know the whereabouts of Michael Lenihan, but clearly we did not wish to disclose it with Hatter's eyes and ears lurking. We need to find a way to approach him, and then to get him safely back to Leicester.'

'So where is he, Gentlemen?'

'We very quickly established from a very drunk and talkative bruiser in the Bowl Inn, that he had seen a man answering Lenihan's description, with a local boy called Brendan Kearney, a bit of a boxer. He says they were off to visit Kearney's Mother, somewhere around Seven Dials,' said Tanky.

'We spoke with Brendan Kearney, the day I arrived,' said Beddows. 'He said he thought that Michael might come to him if he could safely enter the area, but he never let on that he was already with him.'

'Brendan Kearney is a bit of a hot head, gentlemen,' said Paddy. 'He is a man who trusts very few, and has a very short fuse. He is very close to your Sean Crowley.'

'Would Sean not have let you gentlemen know, if he was aware of Lenihan's location?' said Tanky.

'Sean may be being cagey, if he knows. There may be more to this than he has yet felt safe to disclose,' said Kelly. 'You said that there is talk of some very damning papers that Hatter wanted, and which may be in Lenihan's possession. What if it is those papers that Sean is considering?'

'That would make sense,' said Beddows. 'Would Sean Crowley share such information with you, Mr Kelly?'

'An interesting question, Mr Beddows. I need to be careful how I answer it, with so many policemen in the room.'

'I think there are some safeguards, Mr Kelly. Firstly we are in a city in which we have no powers. Secondly, you gentlemen have been actively helping the three of us. I think it highly unlikely that we would be looking to use anything against any of you,' said Tanky. Beddows and Black Tommy nodded in agreement.

'Mr Crowley and I have differing interests within the Rookeries, and their immediate surroundings. My interest is built on keeping the community safe, and my politics and the people I have at my disposal, are those who have our true home in Ireland at heart. We are the boys who Mr Hatter and his Special Branch are keen to see hanged or disappeared. Mr Crowley is more interested in business and assets, and he and his bruisers assist me to maintain my interests. We have a cosy relationship. He has no interest in my politics, openly, so I let him get on with his.'

'So why might he be sitting on papers and on announcing that Michael Lenihan is safe?' said Beddows.

'I think we need to meet Mr Crowley, and ask him that, personally,' said Kelly.

'How safe is Kearney's mother's house?' said Tanky.

'He will be safe, for the time being. Mr Hatter would

need to come very heavy handed if he wanted to try and take him from there,' said Paddy.

'Will Sean Crowley think it suspicious if you call on him for a meeting?' said Beddows.

'I shouldn't have thought so. He is probably expecting some contact.'

'You don't need to come and find me,' came a booming voice from the doorway.

Sean Crowley and several burly bruisers that Tanky, Tommy and Beddows recognised from his businesses in Leicester, entered the room.

'I heard tell that word might be out about Michael's whereabouts,' said Crowley. 'Bless me, though, what are three of Leicester's finest doing on our hallowed soil?'

'We weren't actually together,' said Beddows. 'These two didn't know I was here, nor I them.'

'Sounds like a little tiff?' Crowley grinned.

'Nothing that can't be resolved, Mr Crowley. What a small world it really is,' said Tanky, acknowledging their old adversary.

'I take it you have been digesting the papers that Michael was trusted with?' said Kelly.

'I have indeed,' said Crowley. 'I was more concerned about them than I thought I might be. Little wonder Inspector Hatter wants them so badly.'

'And why might that be?' said Kelly.

'They were handed to Michael by two brothers, who Hatter has used for some time, to commit political burglaries. Unfortunately they overstepped the mark on the last one and a man was killed. Not only do the papers detail all the dirty work that Hatter has involved these boys in, but they also contain papers from the last burglary, and they would be of huge embarrassment to Her Majesty, if Michael was to hand them to The Times, as he was told.'

'How damaging?' said Kelly.

'Enough to bring down Queens, Kings and Kaisers,' said Crowley.

'Bloody hell,' said Tommy, gulping. 'What have you got?'

'It would seem that it is not only our Majesty who is paranoid, and looking over her shoulder all the time. This details a network of would be assassins and details of routes and vulnerabilities of our good lady, and suggests ill blood across the royal families of Europe.'

'Where was the burglary?' said Beddows

'The home of the German Ambassador to Victoria's court.'

'Bloody Hell. Hatter must be shitting himself if he organised a bodged job. If Victoria knew, he would be off to the Tower,' said Tommy.

'And this is what Special Branch and Aliens Office get up to?' said Beddows.

'And we would not be unscathed,' said Crowley. 'The assassination attempt, three years hence, in Green Park is actually documented, and suggests Irish handlers, here in the Rookeries, who instructed young Mr Hamilton to shoot her for her meddling in the ole country. Some interesting names recorded, Mr Kelly.'

'Feck,' said Kelly. 'We always thought someone was snitching to them. May I see the papers?'

'Better than that,' said Crowley, 'you can keep the papers. I suspect that this is the safest pair of hands for much of the material. They seem to offer you information to use to your political advantage, when the time is right.' He handed Kelly a brown paper package.

'I shall look through this with interest, later,' said Kelly, 'but for now, what about Michael Lenihan?'

'He is safe, as you now know. I am happy to see him safely out of the capital, using my own organisation,' said Crowley, 'if that would help. Not forgetting these gentlemen, of course.'

'How can we distract Hatter and his Special Branch, whilst this takes place?' said Beddows.

'How about that wee distraction we suggested?' said Paddy. 'What if word went out that Lenihan was going to be at a certain place at a certain time?'

'Like what?' said Beddows.

'We need you three to make it look likely,' said Paddy. 'Our young Brendan Kearney is taking part in the fight of the year, tomorrow night, in the yard at the back of The Bowl. It has been well promoted, and a lot of high rollers will be there. The place will be packed with *Fancy* and bruisers from all around the Rookeries, and one or two politicians, perhaps even lesser royalty. Lenihan is known to have acted as a second for Brendan in the past. Hatter wouldn't dare not take the bait.'

'And where do we come in?' said Beddows.

'What better than to suggest that some gentlemen from Leicester who have been looking high and low for Michael will be there?' Said Paddy.

'Can't be done,' said Beddows. 'Nobody must know that Tanky and Tommy are coppers from Leicester. Captain Hay will have their bits!'

'But what about you, Beddows? What if we put you there?' said Paddy. 'We'll make sure you have plenty of muscle around you.'

'That might work,' said Beddows.

'I don't like it,' said Tanky. 'We should be watching your back.'

'I would be happier if you were going back to Leicester with Michael Lenihan and Mr Crowley's boys,' said Beddows.

'We will look after Beddows,' said Danny Kelly.

'And if Michael Lenihan is actually well out of the capital, long before the fight is scheduled...' said Paddy.

'I can have him on his way at the drop of a hat. I have some goods going to Leicester, oddly enough. They are loaded and ready to go. A couple of carriages and several 'labourers' to load and unload, and drivers of course.'

'Is that safer than waiting for darkness?' said Beddows.

'Your Mr Hatter will have men out on the heaths beyond the capital, checking on who moves at night. Special Branch and Revenue men. During the day there is so much routine transport in and out of the capital, daylight becomes a safer option,' said Crowley.

'Even though you and your men are of such interest to the police, generally?' said Tanky.

'The uniform police down here are not a worry to me. Most of them are drunk or bent, or both, and leave me alone. A case of whiskey, or a barrel or two of French Brandy, if ever I'm challenged, normally does the trick.'

'But if they do turn up?' said Tanky.

'They might get a shock, Mr Smith. My boys are all rather useful, if you know what I mean.'

'And what is the cost of your assistance?' said Tanky. 'Mr Charters will be wary of running up expenses.'

'This is a favour, Mr Smith. I think everyone gets something out of this transaction. I am not a bad man. Hard but fair, as I hope you are starting to appreciate?'

'So, do we have a plan?' said Kelly.

'We have a plan,' said Crowley.

Cracks

Shepherd walked up New Walk, passing by the Paget house, on his way to the racecourse and the fields beyond, where the gypsies were camped.

The shadows from the trees that had grown along the route rustled, and the skies had started to cloud over a little, the hottest part of the day over, bringing the smell of impending rain.

He loved this new bit of old Leicester, and thought of the Roman Legions leaving Ratae en route to some southern outpost, along the Via Devana.

It had a romanticism to it that he favoured over the grime and stench of the new industry, behind him to his left.

At the campsite, the families were starting to pack up and break down their fire pits and stow their kitchen wares.

'Off somewhere?' said Shepherd, nodding to the Rom Baro.

'Not as yet, Constable. Rain's a coming, and we are just getting prepared. Wedding's not until Saturday, and we'll be on our way by Sunday. Places to go and all that...'

'I thought I could smell it in the air,' said Shepherd.

'Never lose trust in your senses,' said the old man. 'Your eyes, nose and guts are the best predictors you will ever have. Many forget, and their guts is only used for stuffing themselves, these days.'

'I'm surprised we can still smell rain in the air, with all the soot and dust from the factories,' said Shepherd.

'That's why we live this life. Common ground, fields and

riverbanks is where we are all meant to be living.'

'I want to ask a favour of you,' said Shepherd.

'What might that be?'

'I want you and your wife and son to come and look at a man we have in the cells at the police station.'

'What man?'

'We have somebody who we think might be the man that killed the two blond men. The tall, dark man.'

'Shouldn't do any harm. I ain't walking though, my lad has a trap, and can take us all back to the town.'

After a few minutes whilst the Romanies tethered their horse to a small open trap, the four occupants drove off to the police station.

'How much we getting for doing this?' said the younger Gypsy?

'Did I mention money?' said Shepherd

'Bloody hope there's something for our troubles,' said the Baro's wife.

Shepherd considered that this might not be such a good idea now, or it was going to cost him, personally.

There was no messing about at the station. The horse and trap were made secure, courtesy of Joseph Keetley, who Shepherd spoke to, briefly, before the four entered the station.

'I just want you to have a look in each of our three cells, and see if you can see anyone that looks familiar to you,' said Shepherd.

'I thought we come to see the tall dark man?' said the old man.

'In a way, that's right, but it wouldn't seem right to single one man out, would it?'

The three gypsies took it in turn to view each cell, including the one nearest the charge sergeant, in which the prisoner in question was held.

After all three had looked, there was a unanimous agreement. The man that they had seen, and that featured in the visions later, was not presently in the cells.

'Bugger,' said Kettle.

'Depends on whether they were any good as witnesses in the first place,' said Charters.

The old man turned to the constables and spoke. 'When we said that death was close by you, the other day, it felt like the man was very close to you. My good lady says he was here, in this police station, around the time we spoke, or just after. He really was that close to you.'

The three men shared a puzzled look.

'Thank you all, for your time. When you go across to pick up your transport, make yourself known to the landlord, and there is a drink lined up for each of you, on us,' said Shepherd. Sadly, he has no poteen.'

*****

'I'm not sure about this nonsense,' said Charters.

'Suggesting that the man who they saw, was actually in the police station. Tall, dark, and scruffy, who have we had in custody?'

Sergeant Sheffield looked through the charge book, in which descriptions were entered with all prisoners, even well known ones.

'Nobody who really fits the description. Nobody that violent, potentially,' said Sheffield.

'Well who else could they have seen?' said Charters.

'What about a policeman?' said Shepherd.

'Who?' said Charters.

'Inspector Nimrod Hatter? Tall, dark, and according to you and Beddows, devious and dangerous,' said Shepherd, nervously.

'Are you suggesting that Hatter, himself, could be our killer?'

'Why not? He arrived very quickly, and showed no

interest in the Hensons, when they were suggested as suspects at the circus.'

'I am getting a terrible feeling in my gut, Gentlemen. What with the man in the cells, Saint Paul and The Fisherman, and talk of spies and National Security, what have we stumbled upon?' Charters rubbed his chin.

'Have we had any response from the telegraphs, as yet?' said Kettle.

'I suspect that if we have stirred up or stumbled into something of that nature, there will be some frantic conversations and considerations being made in Whitehall. Sir Richard may give me some idea of whether there is any substance, but I don't expect a response from Saint Paul for some time, if at all.'

'Then should we move on to Maria Paget and William Harrison?'

'Arrest them both, probably Maria first, and see what she says without her Father's influence.'

*****

Kettle and Shepherd arrived at Mrs Paget's New Walk Town House about five o'clock or thereabouts, and were feeling the pressures of yet another long day turning up vital clues.

Eleanor Skinner had just left the house, and was walking down New Walk towards them, a large wicker basket over her arm, and a smile on her face. She was clearly distracted, and had not noticed the constables' presence, and was surprised when they stopped in front of her.

'You made me jump. I don't know where I was for a moment.'

'We were just on our way to see your mistress,' said Kettle.

'She is out, I am afraid to say. She has gone for tea with

a friend.'

'That's a shame,' said Kettle. 'Do you know whereabouts?'

'I'm afraid not, she left a note asking me to collect some orders from Sarson and Simpkin's, on Horsefair Street, and not to wait up for her.'

Shepherd noticed a pretty jewelled brooch that she was wearing on her blouse, which glinted in the broken light under the canopy of trees.

'That's a pretty brooch,' said Shepherd.

'A gift, from Mrs Paget,' she smiled.

'An expensive gift, may I suggest,' said Shepherd.

'She didn't wear it anymore and said it suited me. Cheered me up after I got back from my brother's funeral. She is lovely, like that.'

'The only problem is, Miss Skinner, that I recognise that brooch. It was one of the items she and Edward Paget reported stolen from the burglary,' said Shepherd, his eye for detail working.

'It can't be,' said Eleanor. 'Perhaps she had more than one.' The woman began to fidget. 'I must hurry, else I will be late for the order.'

'Eleanor Skinner, I am arresting you in connection with the burglary at your employers' house, and taking you to the police station,' said Shepherd.

'What are you doing?' said Kettle.

'If this is one of the brooches from the burglary, she has either received it as stolen goods, or if her story is true, Mr and Mrs Paget must have been telling us lies about the original crime.'

'Right then, to the station with Miss Skinner it is,' Herbert Kettle conceded.

'I haven't done anything wrong. This is so unfair,' said Eleanor. 'Mrs Paget will explain everything.'

'Mrs Paget will have her turn, for sure,' said Kettle.

*****

'I thought you were going out to arrest Maria Paget?' said Charters, hearing news of their arrival at the police station.

'And so we were, Sir. Miss Skinner was just leaving the address, when Shepherd, here, spotted the brooch she was wearing as one reported stolen by the Pagets during the original burglary,' said Kettle.

'Is that so, Shepherd?'

'Yes. Sir, it's very distinctive, and matches one Mrs Paget is wearing in a small portrait in her study. Constable Hobbs described it perfectly on the original list of missing jewellery.'

'And what is she saying as to why it is in her possession?'

'She alleges that Mrs Paget gave it her to cheer her up after she returned from her brother's funeral,' said Kettle.

'Well, we have another break through. It always strikes me as strange how your luck changes, and all of a sudden the clues come tumbling out,' said Charters.

'Either she is lying, and she is involved in receiving the brooch, or Mrs Paget has lied from the outset,' said Shepherd.

'Put some pressure on her, and let's see what is really going on here,' said Charters.

*****

A short time later, Eleanor Skinner found herself sat in the small room, facing Shepherd and Kettle.

'I don't wish to frighten you, Miss Skinner, but things are not looking good for you, courtesy of that brooch,' said Kettle.

'I don't know why. As I told you, it was a gift from Mrs Paget,'

'Until we see Mrs Paget, that is your word against hers. What it does mean is that either you have been lying to us, and have more to tell us about your involvement in the murders of Edward Paget and two men suspected of the burglary, or Mrs Paget and her late husband lied to us,' said Shepherd.

'Why should I lie to you?'

'You have already told us that your late brother died as a result of his working conditions in Edward Paget's factory. You have good cause to want to harm the Pagets,' said Kettle.

'Far from it. I love Mrs Paget, she is a lovely lady.'

'What do you mean, you love Mrs Paget?' said Kettle.

'I love her and she loves me. That's why she gave me the brooch. She has had a very unhappy time of recent years, and I think that has allowed us to form a special bond.'

'That's a very strange suggestion, given that a few days ago you were telling us that as much as she did not love Edward Paget, she loved the lifestyle that went with the marriage,' said Shepherd.

'But I knew she had love for me. The brooch proved it. I think I have filled a gap now Mr Paget has departed.'

'What would Mrs Paget say if she heard what you are saying?' said Kettle.

'I'm sure she would admit to having feelings for me. She was very comforting when my brother died, and we share a lot.'

'Would you expect us to believe that a wealthy woman, enjoying the trappings of success, would give it up for love of another woman?' said Kettle.

'She was desperately unhappy with Mr Paget. She let slip that she had realised that she would be better off without him, and that it would appease her Father at the same time, although she made me swear that I should never mention it.'

'What did she mean by better off?' said Shepherd.
'If he was embarrassed, financially, her Father was going to put him out of business. The house is in her name, and there would have to be a huge stipend, whatever the end result.'
'This sounds odd to me. You live in a small area below the mistress's house, and are sent on errands, befitting your position. The allegations you make sound more in keeping with a woman wanting revenge for your Brother's death,' said Shepherd.
'Perhaps out of bad will come good. I shall become her companion and live a better life than I could ever have expected. I know she wanted rid of Mr Paget. Her Father arranged for him to meet with a man intending to tempt him with financial opportunities that he would not be able to resist. Those opportunities would be his undoing. I heard her Father stating so.'
'Who was this man, and when did this happen?' said Kettle.
'I heard her Father say that he had dealings with this man before, and he would ensure that it was a foolproof offer. The whole plan was to make a laughing stock of him and then her Father would run him out of town.'
'You told us some of this a few days ago, and that Mrs Paget no longer wished to be subjected to her Father's control,' said Shepherd, 'But you never mentioned her Father arranging this loan that would ruin him.'
'She had not realised how well off she would be. Her Father told her what she would be worth.'
'How do you know all this?' said Kettle.
'I overheard her Father talking to her. As I said before, he was very loud.'
'And why didn't you mention the missing information?'
'I was worried that you might think she had done something amiss.'
'Why else might she have given you the brooch, if

indeed, she did?' said Kettle.

'Why else but affection?'

'What about securing your silence?' said Shepherd.

'I would never have said a word, if you hadn't accused me of stealing it.'

'And how would Mrs Paget have got the brooch back, had it been stolen in the burglary?' said Kettle.

'I didn't know it was one that had been reported stolen. It was just so pretty, and it would be rude not to wear such a token, don't you think?'

'We will need to see Mrs Paget, and until we do, you cannot go anywhere, so I am afraid you have a night in the cells. Let's hope it is not the first of many,' said Kettle.

*****

'What do you think?' said Shepherd.

'She could be telling the truth, but if she is, Mrs Paget has made a terrible and naive mistake by giving it to her.'

'What about this love thing?'

'A poor girl, in a rich woman's household. A lonely widow with great wealth thrust upon her. She is probably thinking she has a foot in the door with Mrs Paget, but probably has hold of the wrong end of the stick. It certainly is payback for her Brother's death.'

'It was interesting to hear of the man and the business meetings with Harrison. What if that is what our Tobias Montague or whatever his name is, is really up to?' said Shepherd.

'It fits with the alleged man in the Globe, the intimidating Revenue man. It would explain the theory of recovering the money as loaned by means of burglary. It would explain the previous bookings at the Fleur de lis.'

'Something else to put to him, next?' said Shepherd. 'Perhaps he will see sense, shortly. Let's update Mr Charters, and I am going to see if an early start is agreeable with him, tomorrow, to arrest Mrs Paget and her Father.'

The two men sought out their Head Constable.

'I'm glad you caught me,' said Charters. 'I have some news for you from the telegraphs I had sent. What do you have for me?'

Kettle detailed Eleanor Skinner's admissions.

'We will have to see what Mrs Paget says, and yes, make an early start and arrest her as soon as possible. Her Father will have to come in too, as I suggested earlier. He has a lot of explaining to do.'

'What of the telegraphs?' said Kettle.

'Sir Richard Mayne was intrigued as to what we were dealing with. He suggests this may be the work of Aliens Office, which has Revenue men under its structure. He confirms that several branches within Aliens Office do communicate in such a covert way, and, obviously, has knowledge of *Saint Paul*, but cannot elaborate on who that may be. Her Majesty's paranoia and all that, I suspect.'

'And have we had a reply from Saint Paul?' said Shepherd

'Interestingly enough, yes. It acknowledged our responsible action in enquiring with Mayne, simultaneously, so it appears a genuine response.'

'What was the outcome?' said Kettle.

'Saint Paul denies that anybody identifying themselves as 'The Fisherman' has any current connection with his organisation, and is not acting in any official capacity or within the remit of said organisation.'

'Said organisation?'

'Secrets and lies, Shepherd. These are the shadowy people of which our prisoner speaks, but they have clearly no appetite to acknowledge him. He has probably crossed a line and would be an embarrassment to them.'

'That might work in our favour,' said Kettle. 'He was cock sure that he would be freed from our custody and walk away without blemish.'

'He has a lot to worry about, gentlemen, as he faces possible capital charges for attempting to murder yourselves, let alone anything we may connect him to with the Paget business. Saint Paul will probably hope he hangs up here, and keep the name of our good Majesty less tarnished.'

'Mrs Paget and Mr Harrison may well, yet, hang him with their explanations. What did Beddows say, a few days ago? *Radix Malorum est Cupiditas*? Funny how greedy people end up with the opposite of what they set out for,' said Shepherd.

'Don't count your chickens, as yet, Constable Shepherd. Let us see what tomorrow brings.'

Michael Lenihan

In those dreary hours between three and four in the morning, when most of London slept, the three men slid into the small pudding bag, off Neale's Yard, in the heart of Seven Dials. The area matched St. Giles rookeries to the east of the confluence and it was unlikely the Police would venture in at that time of night.

Neale's Yard was a gloomy slum, off Short's Gardens, in the shadow of St. Giles workhouse, famed for its *Crawlers*, the lowest of the low, even within the rookeries themselves, who struggled to find strength to even beg for a pittance.

Beddows followed closely behind Paddy McNally and one of Sean Crowley's larger bruisers.

McNally slid his favoured tool down the door frame and sprung the latch, allowing the three men access to the one up, one down slum.

In the flickering light of the small grate, Beddows could see two men, topping and tailing on a straw mattress. Large hands placed over each man's mouth as McNally woke the sleepers.

A look of terror on Michael's face as he struggled to focus. Young Kearney immediately attempted to move to a fighting stance, but was well restrained by the large bruiser.

'Michael, it's me, your Uncle Paddy.'

Kearney relaxed as he realised they were friends.

'How the feck did you find him?' said Kearney.

'Sean sent us,' said Paddy. 'We've come to take Michael to safety.'

'Why didn't Sean tell me you were coming?'

'And risk somebody tipping off the Special Branch? Even Sean Crowley isn't that fecking stupid.'

'And who is this?' said Kearney, looking to Beddows.

'I am a friend of Michael's mother, and I have come from Leicester to take Michael to safety.'

'He's a good man, Michael, a policeman of all things, but we agree that we need to get you to your Mammy and safety. Get your things together, Michael, we have things to do.'

'What about me?' said Kearney.

'Haven't you got a fight to get ready for?' said Paddy.

'Michael was going to second for me,' said Kearney.

'Not a good idea,' said Paddy, 'but it might actually work to our advantage. We have a plan, and Mr Crowley will tell you what to do, later.'

Leaving Kearney to sleep, the four men slipped into the shadows, threading their way through the narrow alleyways to their safe house.

*****

Whilst Michael Lenihan was secreted, Tanky sent note to Torchy Trinder.

'What are you writing to him for?' said Black Tommy.

'The bloke did us a favour. If we ain't going back, he will be worried, and we ain't got time to get to Edgware and back, by the sounds of it.'

'What about our gear?' said Tommy.

'Do you really want it back?' said Tanky

'I'd prefer to see it burnt, with all those bleeding bugs crawling through it.'

'That's just what I'm telling him, to burn the lot, which is his love after all, setting fire to things.'

'Didn't really get to know much about him and you.'

'You don't want to, matey, you really don't. He's salt of

the earth, but I must admit he's gone downhill since I'd last crossed paths with him.'

'Give us a couple of coins,' said Tanky.

'What for?'

'Least we can do is buy him a farewell drink.'

'Well put yours in first, because I can't see Mr Charters giving us it back without a receipt.'

'You're a tight fecker,' said Tanky, grinning and shaking his head, 'and unappreciative. After all he did for us.' Tanky started to scratch his armpits, just to wind Tommy up further.

How the mighty are fallen

'Old Mr Charters is going soft, Shepherd. Eight o'clock on a Saturday morning to make an *early* arrest of somebody posh?'

'Probably thinks she may have over-indulged, yesterday evening?'

'She must be confused, having left instructions for her housekeeper to fetch an order, yet on return, finding neither housekeeper, nor order.'

'I did ask in the station, earlier, if anyone had reported Eleanor Skinner missing, overnight, but no reports were recorded. She obviously doesn't love her that much,' said Shepherd, *the notion of women lovers still leaving him uncomfortable.*

'Probably more worried that her Sarson and Simpkin luxuries are not available to her, more like,' said Kettle.

'Have you ever shopped there, Kettle?'

'On a Sergeant's wages? You have to be joking. I do call in from time to time, with my good lady as well, if she ventures out with me. The smell of the place is marvellous. We just wander around sniffing and drooling. Tea, coffee, cheese and bacon. I can smell the shop now.'

'Sally says the same to me. Mr Flowers once gave us a basket of some tea and jam from there, and some of their ham for Christmas. I have never had better.'

'This talk is making me hungry, Shepherd. Let's see if we can catch Mrs Paget and then we might get a tea and a wedge when we get back to the station.'

Kettle knocked loudly, forgetting the presence of the brassware which rang the internal bell. Steady footsteps could be hear echoing from inside, and sounds of a key being turned, and bolts pulled.

'Good morning, Gentlemen,' said Maria Paget. 'I am sorry for the delay, but my housekeeper has strangely disappeared.'

'I am afraid to tell you that Eleanor Skinner is presently under arrest back at the Town Hall police station, Mrs Paget,' said Kettle.

'She has been arrested?'

'She has been arrested, yes,' said Kettle.

'Pray, what has she done to merit such action?'

'We called to see you, yesterday evening, and bumped into Miss Skinner leaving. She was wearing a brooch. A brooch that you told us had been stolen during the burglary,' said Kettle.

Maria Paget stood silent, mouth falling ajar, before her eyes rolled and she fainted. Shepherd caught her before she hit the plush carpet on which she stood.

Slowly she came too, flushed and incoherent.

'That appears to have come as a shock?' said Shepherd, rather tongue in cheek.

'I am confused,' said Mrs Paget. 'I need a moment to think.'

'You have plenty of time to think, as we are arresting you and taking you to the station too,' said Kettle.

'Arresting me. Whatever for?'

'Miss Skinner alleges you gave her the brooch. She has also told us of possible motive behind both the burglary and your husband's death. You are being arrested for us to investigate those allegations further,' said Kettle.

'I want my Father advised, that is my right.'

'Your Father will know, shortly enough, as we intend to arrest him next. He is also implicated,' said Shepherd.

Maria Paget's eyes rolled and she fainted yet again.

'I think we are on to something, Mr Kettle.'

'I think you might be right there, young Shepherd.'

After Maria Paget had come too, and had gathered a jacket and parasol, Shepherd had a thought.

'Before we leave, Mrs Paget, I would like to take a look in your safe.'

'My safe? Whatever for?'

'Please indulge me, Madam, and unlock the safe for us.'

For a moment the woman looked like she might faint again. However, rather sheepishly, she lead the men to the first floor bedroom and to the safe that had been opened on the night of the burglary. She produced the key from a chain around her neck.

'You couldn't really say that anyone else had the key, now, could you?' said Shepherd.

Kettle looked puzzled.

The door was opened and a number of jewellery boxes were visible.

'How many more of the jewels that you reported stolen are we going to find back in your safe?' said Shepherd.

'How can they be here, they were stolen. I don't know where Eleanor might have got one from.'

'In that case you wont mind opening the cases and letting me take a look.'

'I wish to explain, it wasn't my idea...'

'What wasn't your idea, Mrs Paget?' said Kettle.

'The burglary.'

'So are we going to find more of your missing jewellery here?'

The woman began to cry, hysterically. 'I am a fool, but nothing else, for listening to my father's stupid idea,'

'How much of the jewellery have you got back?' said Shepherd.

'All of it. It was family jewellery and I could not bear to lose it. Before I say anything else I think I should speak with my lawyer.'

'That might be a good idea. But before we leave, please show us the other items that should not be here, by rights.'

Maria Paget slowly and tearfully gathered the allegedly stolen jewellery.

'Is there any of the money here?' said Shepherd.

'I never saw the money again.'

'You have said enough, already Mrs Paget. Now we have a pleasant walk back to the police station. It's a lovely morning, especially for people watching,' said Kettle.

'You're even starting to sound like Beddows,' said Shepherd, recognising the inference.

Kettle grinned, slightly, enjoying the thought of the walk, and the prospect of Leicester's high and mighty seeing one of their own paraded between two of the borough's finest.

'What will people say?' said Mrs Paget.

'That's the least of your worries, I suspect,' said Shepherd, smiling wryly.

*****

The whispering that was observed by the two officers from amongst the early morning population, must have rapidly reached the houses along London Road, beyond the Railway complex, as before they had reached the station, Mr William Harrison had been made aware of his daughter's demise, and was sending word for the family Lawyer.

Shepherd booked the prisoner in at the Charge desk, whilst Kettle went off to confirm the arrest to an anxious Robert Charters.

From the flap in the small cell door, opposite, Tobias Montague watched as Maria Paget was documented. He considered that things were rapidly deteriorating, and needed to reassess his strategy.

'What should I do with her, Constable Shepherd?' said the Charge Sergeant.

'Please put her in the cell next to Eleanor Skinner, if you have room for two female cells.'

'We have no other females in at present, but I hope you can take one off my hands soon,' said the grumpy Custodian. 'Don't like mixed up arrangements, and we have another of your guests blocking up my favourite cell, opposite.'

'Rest assured, Sergeant, by end of day your cells will look starkly different. Sergeant Kettle and I will be questioning her, shortly.'

Shepherd saw the eyes pressed to the hatch in the cell door, and smirked.

'Yes, you bugger,' Shepherd thought to himself, 'you must be sweating now.'

Smoke and mirrors

In a smart yard, accessible safely through a series of alleys running just off Drury Lane, two canvas covered horse drawn vans, together with their drivers and labourers, prepared to set off. The carriages each carried several large bales of raw cotton.

Each bale was the standard imported from America, weighing 500 pounds, measuring 55 inches high, by 28 inches wide, by 21 inches deep, and required two or three sturdy men to shift each one.

These were no ordinary bales, as hidden inside one, suitably adapted for concealment, was Michael Lenihan, readying himself for a nervous journey to Leicester, and safety.

Building a bale around a large, lanky man, had been no mean feat, but Paddy McNally's joinery skills had crafted a lightweight box on frame, with tubes to assist breathing, around which raw cotton had been structured.

Each bale would pass as the same, and once out of the capital, some little work would allow Michael out and give him greater access to fresh air.

Cotton would draw little attention from revenue men along the route, and the Midlands, particularly Leicester, was a routine and daily route for such loads. Amongst the labourers were Tanky Smith and Tommy Haynes, suitably disguised, and some of Sean Crowley's heaviest punishers and bruisers. It was also routine for value loads to be accompanied by men with firearms, and several blunderbuss and pistols were secreted if required.

Blackstone's 'Rights of the person' gave the more sensible public the right to carry firearms, albeit the Vagrancy and Poaching Acts of late were reducing their circulation, legally. As much as officially Highwaymen were a thing of the past, there were still many gangs that used similar methods to keep themselves busy. Just after eight, the wagons left the yard and headed into the sunshine. It would be a long journey, and several sets of horses, before they reached Leicester. They had the advantage of several good coaching stops on the way, in which Mr Crowley had a 'vested interest'. The plan was to follow the old Roman route along Watling Street, for much of the journey, deviating only if threatened, with an overnight stop in Towcester. In the morning they would follow the same route until they reached The Gibbet at the turning for Lutterworth. Hopefully they would arrive in Leicester by 2 o'clock on the following afternoon, Sunday.

*****

Beddows and Paddy McNally now sat in a huddle with Dennis Kelly, and Sean Crowley, as final plans for the big fight, or rather the distraction for Inspector Hatter and his secretive companions, continued.
'Both Mr Kelly and I have been sending word out with our feeblest residents, one of whom must surely be in Mr Hatter's keep,' said Crowley.
'The bait is out there, then,' said Beddows.
'He is going to be a very disappointed man, come about ten o'clock tonight. God help us all when he realises,' said Kelly.
'Who has been identified as a lookalike for Michael Lenihan?' said McNally.
'I have an up and coming fighter, who looks remarkably like him, having seen him when we packed him up this

morning. The fighter is the same height and build, and probably a bit slower, given the punishment he has taken to get to where he is at. He is passable, especially in the darkness of the ring and the crowds around it.' said Crowley.

'And what do we expect of Hatter and his spies and bullies?'

'They will probably be armed, and will be up for a fight, so we have to be ready for them,' said Kelly. 'Inspector Hatter will not risk losing his man, so he will either come mob handed, or he will wait until the crowd is ebbing away, and his touts will signal when the risk is less. That's what I reckon.'

'And that's better for us. If he is doing this off his own back, he will not want it to go down as Government messing, especially with the election running. Tidying up his own mess is not what Her Majesty will be paying him for, nor his masters. I reckon he will have a handful of trusted men and they will rush us at the end, and they will be dangerous.'

'And what if Hatter mistakes your man and kills him?' said Beddows.

'Don't let him know, but I have better fighters on the up, so I can afford to lose the big daft lumps.'

'You would sacrifice one of yours?' said Beddows.

'To get one over on Hatter and Special Branch, I'd give up me old ma in law,' Crowley laughed.

'And what about me?' said Beddows.

'We need you to make yourself visible, around the rookeries, later this afternoon. I need Hatter to think you have not yet exhausted your interest in Lenihan, and have word of his presence,' said Crowley.

'And how will he know I am here?'

'He already does, Beddows. Somebody must have slipped it out, don't you know.' said Kelly.

'He won't be happy that I'm here.'

'He certainly won't. But don't you worry, as we will have some back up close at hand should he decide to send you a personal message,' said Kelly.

'I fear a bumpy day for us all,' said Beddows.

'Especially for Michael Lenihan. By now he will be bouncing his way along the cobbles of Camden, on his way to your fair borough, Mr Beddows. A rough ride he will be having for sure.' Crowley laughed.

Confessions

Kettle and Shepherd sat Mrs Paget down in the small rear office, and prepared for her questioning.

'Your lawyer has yet to arrive, Mrs Paget. Perhaps he has been delayed,' said Kettle.

'Has word been passed to him that I am here?'

'I am confident that your Father will have spoken with him by now. However, perhaps your Father is getting his story straight with him, before he is sent to support you,' said Shepherd.

'What do you mean, getting his story straight?'

'Both you and Eleanor Skinner have suggested he is implicated in the burglary. Perhaps he has more to worry about than you do?' said Kettle.

'Perhaps he will say it was your idea, and he will deny your allegations and make you take responsibility for your Husband's end?' said Shepherd.

'I think I should like to tell you my version first,' said Mrs Paget, 'and let you judge for yourselves who is more responsible.'

'What about your family lawyer?' said Kettle.

'If he is representing my Father, I do not wish him to represent me.'

'Do you want us to get you one of your own choosing?' said Kettle.

'Are they expensive?' asked Mrs Paget. Shepherd looked perplexed, that a woman in her position and circumstances would be worrying about the cost of a lawyer.

'I think you have enough wealth to afford one of your own, Mrs Paget,' said Kettle, 'well, for the time being,

anyway. Mr Shepherd will find one of your choice.'
'I would like Mr Allen, from Friar Lane, if he would
represent me.'
Shepherd scurried quickly along St. Martins West, to
enquire at the well known Barrister's address.

*****

Whilst Shepherd was absent, Sergeant Sheffield who had
now taken over as Charge Sergeant, sought out Kettle.
'Herbert, your prisoner is asking for you. He wants to
talk to you about some sort of an agreement.'
Robert Charters was checking the cells when he
overheard the comment.
'So our mystery man wants to save his neck, no doubt,
Kettle. He has had two chances and chosen not to. We
will be up to our necks in prisoners singing, shortly, and I
suggest we leave him festering in his cell, for the time
being. We may choose to talk to him again, later.'
Sheffield and Kettle, together with a passing constable
moved the man, shackled, into the smallest cell, close
enough for him to see and hear the progress that was
being made.
'I shall have to see if Mr Goodyer will let us move the
routine prisoners for the rest of the day to his
accommodation in Market Place. I fancy a walk,' said
Charters. 'I just want the four cells for the four
prisoners I suspect we will have with us in the next few
hours.'
'We still have to get Mr Harrison,' said Kettle.
'He will come with his Barrister and try and take an
upper hand. When he arrives arrest him and lock him
up. Tell his lawyer to come back later,' said Charters,
'when you have spoken to Mrs Paget properly.'
Shepherd arrived back, closely followed by Anthony
Allen, a renowned defence barrister for the rising rich of

the borough, who had, over the last two years, acquired a pleasant town house in Cank Street and offices in Friar Lane, on the back of those who strove for wealth, but at times in a foolhardy manner.

He accompanied Shepherd into the small office, and were joined by Kettle who brought in Mrs Paget. Mrs Paget spoke briefly, in a whisper, and amidst a lot of nodding, Mr Allen announced that his client wished to help with the investigation.

'Are you aware of the full circumstances of the crime that Mrs Paget has been arrested for?' said Kettle.

'Of course, Sergeant, it has been the talk of the town.'

'Earlier today we arrested Mrs Paget's housekeeper, Eleanor Skinner, who was in possession of a brooch, which Constable Shepherd here, recognised as having been reported stolen in the burglary. Miss Skinner went on to say that it was a gift from your client.'

'So I understand, and a gift it was, indeed. My client assures me that Miss Skinner is in no way involved in the crime, and the brooch was a gift given, rather foolishly, to Miss Skinner, as a sign of appreciation for her support since Mr Paget's death.'

'That is honourable of Mrs Paget to confirm so. We will ensure that Miss Skinner is detained no longer than is necessary,' said Kettle.

'I was very foolish,' said Maria Paget. 'I had asked her only to wear it on special occasions and not in public. I am disappointed that she could not respect my wishes.'

'A young woman, with very little of any worth of her own, living below stairs in your house, and envying the things you hold dear as a daily normality. Is it not fair to understand that it would have been very special, and the temptation too great for her?' said Shepherd.

'Perhaps it was my fault. It is academic as to why she chose to wear it, but it has brought about my undoing, and now I wish to tell you everything.'

Mr Allen whispered and after a brief exchange, nodded his agreement.

'Tell us why the burglary took place,' said Shepherd.

'Several weeks ago, we had a terrible argument in the family, about my late husband's business aspirations. In the course of it I brought up the death of Eleanor's brother as a result of the terrible working conditions in their factories.'

'By their, I take it you mean the argument was between you, your late husband and your Father?' said Shepherd.

'Yes, that is correct. It became clear to me that my husband was becoming as cynical and heartless as my Father. I also knew that my Father was having terrible reservations, again, about Edward's ambitions, and that word was going around that he was seeking cheap money to buy more machinery.'

'You yourself told us that you had encouraged him to buy more, when we first spoke to you,' said Kettle.

'I had to admit that, because other people by then knew I had been seen discussing loans in various establishments, with people who might not have offered Edward such credit.'

'Why were you and your Father so keen to find him this cheap money?' said Shepherd.

'As I said to you before, my Father had plans as to how Edward would be discredited and run out of Leicester. I was, by then, becoming tired of this desire of Edward's to achieve greatness, like my Father, at any cost. I saw what it had done to Eleanor, and how she was just one of many people who were losing loved ones, daily, to this horrible Industrial monster.'

'Eleanor has suggested that you and she have an affection that many might not understand?' said Shepherd.

'I am fond of her, as a friend, only. She is mistaken if she thinks more than that. I have sought her services more as a companion, since Edwards death. She is the nearest thing to me as a friend that I think I have ever had.'

The door to the small office was suddenly thrown open, and in walked William Harrison, pulling past Sergeant Sheffield.

'Sorry gents, he just burst past. He asked where you were.'

'Maria, don't you dare say another word until you speak with my lawyer.' said Harrison.

'I have my own lawyer - Mr Allen is representing me - and I have taken advice and wish to tell these constables all about what has happened.'

'You will do as you are told, I am your Father. Do you know what you are doing. Your Mother and I will disown you, you stupid girl.'

Kettle stood up and took hold of Harrison by the arm.

'William Harrison, I am arresting you in connection with the burglary that occurred at your daughter's house, and the death if your son-in-law, Edward Paget.'

'You cannot arrest me, you uncouth man. I do not think you have the right to lay your hands on me or to detain me. My lawyers will make you pay for this stupidity.'

'Sergeant Sheffield, can you find Mr Harrison a room for the time being, away from our other guests?' said Kettle.

'And what about his lawyer? He is blocking up my space.'

'Tell him he can come back in about another four or five hours, when we may be ready to talk to Mr Harrison,' said Kettle. 'If he doesn't like that, arrest him for obstructing you.'

'I'm sorry about that, Mrs Paget. Shall we continue?'

'He is a bully, Sergeant. He has made me do things all of my life which I look back on and regret and this is the most reprehensible. I cannot hide the lies any longer.'

'In that case, tell us about your Father's involvement.'
'My Father advised me that there was a man he had dealings with, in London, who had an agent who looked after his financial business interests in Leicester. He wanted to arrange for me to be introduced to this man, who would be able to arrange Edward's financial embarrassment.'
'And that is what you thought you were negotiating?' said Shepherd.
'I just wanted Edward to stop his stupid expansionism and to be done with him. My Father had explained how in pre-nuptial contracts he had Edward sign, that I would never lose the house, and I would always receive a stipend if Edward conducted business in any capacity. He also made Edward take out a significant life assurance, suggesting that it would one day be in my best interest.'
'Who was the man and what was the secret organisation?'
'I never was told of any names, other than the man I was to meet, Mr Tobias. The only thing I gleaned was that the man in London had been somebody my Father had prior dealings with, and was an advisor to some Government organisation that was all very hush hush.'
'So, how and when did you meet the agent?'
'My Father took me to The Globe, some weeks ago, and the purpose was for a public and thus, safe, place to meet, ensuring that there would be no 'funny business'.'
'Funny business?' said Kettle.
'The man is known in The Globe. As a Revenue man he is not held in high esteem by those that have crossed his path. A meeting would be seen as a business transaction, much as with any other that he has conducted, but my Father wanted to be sure that the man could be trusted, and even turn up.'

'And did he?'

'After a short time, we thought we had been duped, and so we left. Once outside the man approached us, having been watching us inside, and introduced himself to me.'

'And what happened at this meeting?' said Shepherd.

'We asked what services he now offered. He was very assertive, almost intimidating, and spoke of being able to arrange 'almost anything', dependent upon the price. He said he had other associates that he could engage, who were most discreet, and they would come, go, and disappear, never to be seen again.'

'And where did he get his money from?' said Kettle.

'He stated that Her Majesty's Revenue had a fund that could be utilised, and short term, high interest loans, were the usual, but failure to repay within time and interest would lend the borrower open to all sorts of unpleasantries.'

'And was everything arranged at that one meeting?' said Shepherd.

'No, he wanted details. Names, places, guarantors, and he wanted to get back to the man who had sent him, to ensure that we could be trusted.'

'So when was the second meeting?' said Kettle.

'About one week before the burglary. My Father had booked him into a room at The Fleur de lis, and we met near to the river at the Abbey, where we could talk and finalise my Father's plan.'

'What was that plan?'

'My Father explained that he wanted Edward discredited, and he needed a temptation that Edward would be unable to resist. He said he could offer us, or rather Edward, a very attractive loan at a very low interest rate. He would deliberately undercut any similar rates available in the borough.'

'And how would this discredit Edward?' said Shepherd.

'I knew Edward had been made aware of some new

machines, similar to some my Father now uses, from .
He was desperate to find the money, so word of cheap
money in The Globe, was enough to get Edward's
interest.'

'And Edward met the man, where?' said Kettle.

'In the Globe, where all such business is conducted.'

'And what did the man offer Edward?' said Shepherd.

'The full amount for the machines that were available,
at half a percent lower rate than most business lenders.
He bit his hands off.'

'And when was the money handed over?' said Kettle.

'Later that same day. Edward banked it, shortly
thereafter. Oddly enough, he was very anxious about
having lots of money in the house, at any time, even the
wages.'

'And how was Edwards downfall to occur?' said
Shepherd.

'The man said he had two 'employees' who came highly
recommended to him, by another of his secretive
friends, an agent in another department, not the
Revenue. They were used to commit burglaries for
them, and it was suggested a burglary and the loss of
the money would put Edward in a position where he
would not be able to buy his damned machines, but he
would be terrified that he did not have the means to get
the money back, even by instalments at the agreed
interest, and would be ruined and humiliated by my
Father and his circle of business associates.'

'So, no money, no machines, nothing to pay the man
back, and ruination for Edward?'

'So my Father seemed to have covered all angles.'

'But what went wrong?' said Shepherd.

'At no time did I ever solicit or discuss that Edward
should be subjected to violence. I was going to be very
nicely off with a house and a stipend, so why have him
hurt?'

'You say your Father had ensured that Edward had taken out pre-nuptial contracts to that effect, but also taken out substantial life assurance?' said Kettle.

'He was adamant that a husband of mine should make good provision in the event of his death.'

'What would happen to the factory and business assets?' said Shepherd.

'I had told my Father, some time ago, that if anything ever happened to Edward, I had no interest in the Factory, so my Father would assume ownership of the enterprise and add it to his portfolio.'

'So your Father would gain, quite nicely, out of Edward's death, too?' said Shepherd.

'I suppose he would.'

'On the night of the burglary what did you expect?' said Kettle.

'I expected things to go as had been proposed.'

'Had you done anything to allow access to the house?'

'I had left the small window above the front canopy on the catch. It looked shut but could be pushed open. I was advised that the men would be very agile, and it would add to the validity of the burglary. It had to look like a burglary at the end of the day, didn't it?'

'When the burglar became violent, what did you think?' said Shepherd.

'I worried for a moment that it was a real burglar, and was starting to panic.'

'You said that he also threatened you, after your husband was hit the second time?' said Kettle.

'I was terrified. That was not in the plan, and I became seriously scared for my life?'

'Why do you think the man used such violence and threatened you, personally?' said Kettle.

'I wondered if it was a message from my father.'

'A message from your Father?' said Kettle.

'A reminder, not to say anything. He is quite a ruthless

man when it comes to money and reputation. A greedy man, but generous, when it suits.'

'When you realised Edward was dying, and again, after he passed, why didn't you say something, there and then?' said Shepherd.

'As I have reaffirmed, my Father would have seen it as a weakness. I would be better off, and he would be better off, so better to say nothing. As things had gone so horribly wrong, we would all have been damned, as now has proven.'

'You clearly had no love for your husband?' said Kettle.

'Not any more. He kept me in good manner, but the love died when he became obsessed with wealth.'

'Some might say that could be said of both you and your Father, also?' said Shepherd.

'I suppose they might.'

'What happened after the burglary?' said Shepherd.

'I was led to understand that Mr Tobias would meet the burglars, and get back his money. Then he met my Father some time later, at the Fleur de lis, and handed back the jewellery.'

'Why was the man at the funeral, or rather, the burial?' said Kettle.

'I know my Father had promised to settle his account, once happy all ends were dead and buried, so to speak, after my Father last met with him. I was quite anxious when he turned up at the cemetery.'

'What did you think he was there for?' said Shepherd.

'I felt quite threatened. It was almost as if he was there as a reminder that he was never far away, and that *we* should remember to say nothing. He made sure I saw him and acknowledged him. My Father saw him, and thought likewise.'

'Foolish, on his part, as we thought somebody might show up at either one or the other. Killers have a habit of wanting to see the fruits of their labour complete.'

'I don't believe he is a killer, he was livid that the burglary had gone wrong, and told my Father that other heads would roll, because of it.'

'But as far as the law is concerned, he may well face the same fate as would the killers.' said Kettle.

'What do you mean?'

'Conspiring to commit such an offence, especially where death occurs, may carry the same penalty as the murder itself. You and your Father may also suffer that fate.'

Maria Paget sobbed, uncontrollably. Her lawyer whispered to her, and then spoke.

'Surely, my client's honesty and agreement to speak from the outset must offer the possibility of some sort of leniency?'

'That is for the courts to decide, Mr Allen. You should well be aware of that fact,' said Kettle.

'What do we do with Eleanor Skinner, now?' said Shepherd.

'She stays where she is until we have spoken to all of the other prisoners. As much as Mrs Paget proclaims her to be an innocent pawn in whatever this game really is, I want no backlash if it turns out she is more connected,' said Kettle.

'Then who do we talk to next?'

'I think after Mr Harrison's little outburst, he and his lawyer can wait. I think we need to have a word with *The Fisherman* once more and break the bad news regarding *Saint Paul*.'

'I saw his face through the flap, earlier, when we bought the women in, and he looked a little more anxious than previously,' said Shepherd.

'Then let's see whether he has changed his tune.'

Having placed Maria Paget back in her cell, Sergeant Sheffield handed the first of the two male prisoners still in his borough cells, to Kettle and Shepherd, and the men returned to do verbal combat.

'We have some bad news for you. You probably suspected it would be the case, but we have validated that Saint Paul exists, but he, or perhaps, she of course, deny any knowledge of you and deny that they have any knowledge of you acting in an official capacity on their behalf,' said Kettle.

'Treacherous lot to work for, I suppose. I am not surprised, as the work we do for them would always be denied, albeit that it is done at Her Majesty's bidding.'

'And you have been keeping a quiet eye on comings and goings overnight. You have seen who we now have detained, here?' said Shepherd.

'I have, and I presume that they are looking after their own necks?'

'We have certainly been enlightened as to your part in our crimes, and thought you might wish to enlighten us yourself, now,' said Kettle.

'I fear that if I don't, what was an act of honour, may be seen to involve me in a capital act, and that is not the case. I have done things for my Queen and Country, but giving my life for something I am not culpable is not for me, so yes, I will answer your questions. It may actually give Saint Paul some food for thought about throwing me to the winds.'

'Firstly, please, confirm that your true name is Tobias Montague,' said Kettle.

'You know that, clearly, and that would have been part of Saint Paul's confirmation.'

'So why do you use Mr Tobias at The Fleur de lis?' said Shepherd.

'Your Mr Harrison and his daughter had a liking for *Mr Tobias*, for some strange reason, when we spoke. I think they found me intimidating. Harrison booked the room, and so it is his mistake, the subservient buffoon. Mr Keetley has always had my true name.'

'What is your reason for doing business in Leicester?'
said Kettle.

'Her Majesty has a dislike for people who don't pay
their dues to the Country. Some of the most successful
businessmen in your borough and county are the biggest
thieves in the country, and think their names and
reputations give them licence to steal. My role is to
encourage prompt and adequate payment back to The
Revenue, often with punitive interest.'

'Your reputation suggests to us that you are quite an
intimidating man?' said Shepherd.

'It depends whether people are being pursued by me
and my like for tax evasion or avoidance, or whether
they are seeking access to money that they could not
otherwise afford.'

'So you are authorised to lend Her Majesty's money as
well as recover it?'

'I am at liberty to make best use of my talents to gain
the maxim revenue for Her Majesty.'

'So where do these talents come from? Why are men
like you tasked to undertake such duties?' said
Shepherd.

'I come from a Military Intelligence background. Men
like me have seen active service for Her Majesty, and
our Lords and Noblemen, such as *Saint Paul*, have seen
fit to use those skills in the defence of the realm.'

'And you saw service in the Afghan war?' said Kettle.

'The folly? Sadly, yes, and I saw too many good men lost
in another fit of political madness.'

'And how long after that service did you begin these
other duties?'

'I was recruited immediately after the return from the
war, and have done so since.'

'And do your duties include the use of violence to
recover assets?' said Shepherd.

'I have never had to revert to force. Fear is normally

more than enough with most of the people I deal with. Many are rich because they have not had their hands dirty, and when it comes to conflict, they are cowards. If I tell them I can name and shame them, publicly and openly, most settle with me, rather quicker than they would have done by choice.'

'And what of your dealings with The Paget and Harrison families?' said Kettle.

'I have had one or two business encounters with Mr Harrison, and it was he who sourced me to execute the downfall of his son-in-law, Edward Paget.'

'To humiliate him?' said Shepherd.

'My role was to create a situation where he would be humiliated. The proposals left the actual exposure to Mr Harrison and Mr Paget's own dear wife. My role was to create the circumstances to allow that to happen, which is something I could accomplish with my contacts.'

'Tell us what happened?' said Kettle.

'I had met Mr Harrison some years ago, when he was a little 'tardy' with tax matters, and we met and the matter was resolved rather easily. I was surprised, then, when I was approached by somebody connected with Mr Harrison, and who I had a working connection with.'

'Who was that?'

'The man who we have in common is named Algernon Saint Paul Hatter. Does that name resonate with you, given my current circumstances?'

Shepherd and Kettle exchanged a brief, knowing glance.

'I seem to have connected with both of you. You have heard the name before?'

'We have heard the name before, but not in this context,' said Shepherd.

'The given names may give you some idea of why I am still in your custody?'

'I think we get the connection,' said Kettle.

'Colonel Hatter was my Intelligence corps' commander, and he was instrumental in my subsequent recruitment to the organisation.'

'The organisation?' said Kettle.

'You hear many names banded about. The Aliens Office is everybody's favourite, but it is not strictly true, as that had very simple targets when established. This organisation is much more, and much more secretive, too. So secretive that it doesn't really have a name, but a number of units that are actively engaged within it, all for the safety of the Nation.'

'And Mr Hatter's connection with Harrison?' said Shepherd.

'Cotton. Cotton is what gives them both their status and living, but on Hatter's part, he has 'other interests'. They met through their import and common supply interest, so I understand.'

'Are you familiar with Nimrod Hatter?' said Shepherd.

'Ah, the prodigal son. Let me tell you, Gentlemen, that Nimrod Hatter is not a man to have any dealings with, if you can avoid him. He has other friends in high places, higher than his Father. He is a very dangerous man, and his little band of merry men are the men who have the dirtiest hands in the secretive world of which I speak.'

'Have you and Nimrod Hatter worked together?' said Kettle.

'I would not have anything to do with the man. I have never worked with him, knowingly, nor would I. Revenue work is one thing, but the work he seems comfortable undertaking is not for the likes of me and mine.'

'Nimrod Hatter did not serve in the Afghan campaign?' said Kettle.

'No, his Father did, but he was not of fighting age.'

'So, back to the arrangements with Harrison and Mrs Paget, tell us more,' said Kettle.

'I was advised to seek out Mr Harrison by Algernon

Hatter, as Harrison had a little problem. I first met him and his daughter to listen to their needs. As it was an unusual request, I needed to check on his current credibility and ensure that what was being requested was achievable. As I would need some additional help, I went back to Algernon Hatter and he stated he would point me in the direction of that additional help. I met with Harrison and his daughter again, and the details were drawn up.'

'And what was the plan?'

'I was to make Edward Paget an offer he couldn't refuse, for a loan at well below any other rate he could get anywhere, that he would be unable to resist.'

'For what purpose?'

'To break him, financially, in order that Harrison could then discredit him, and his daughter would be freed from their marriage. Both Harrison and his daughter were to fare nicely, financially, but Paget would never be able to show his face in the business community in England.'

'And how did you propose to achieve it?'

'I have access to very professional tradesmen in the line of work that her Majesty maintains. I have used burglary as a means of recovering outstanding revenue, before. The 'victims' would never report them as it was apparent from the outset, as to why it had happened. We often leave a little calling card to remind them about being honest and timely with their payments to Her Majesty's Government.'

'And this time?' said Shepherd.

'I was advised that, oddly enough, two of our best burglars were to be in Leicester, a few weeks later, and would offer a perfect resource and if anything went wrong, a justified reason for being in the borough.'

'The Hensons?' said Kettle.

'The Hensons. Yes. They work for a variety of parts of

the organisation and are normally very good at their job.'

'And the plan was to recover the loan from Paget, leaving him unable to repay you, and unable to proceed with his new machine acquisition?' said Kettle.

'Yes, a very embarrassing situation to be in, and not one for one of our calling cards on this occasion.'

'When did you brief the Hensons?' said Shepherd.

'I was advised that they would be in a prominent position on the approach to Leicester, your racecourse, and I met them there the evening of the burglary.'

'What did they understand to be their brief?' said Shepherd.

'To commit a seemingly conventional burglary, get Paget to open a safe where he was keeping the money I had lent him, and get the money back. Normally they take a range of goods to make it look a genuine house breaking.'

'What was their reaction?' said Shepherd.

'They seemed more nervous than usual. Twitchy. They said they had had a problem in London, but that the job was fine. I arranged to meet them after the work had been done, which I did, and they handed me the money and jewellery.'

'Did you not reward them?' said Kettle.

'My Lords and Masters pay them handsomely, for their dirty work.'

'And what was your reward for arranging this all?' said Shepherd.

'An agreement from Mr Harrison to promote my services amongst the more reserved of the business community in Leicester, and a small 'gratuity' he chose to donate. I help him and he helps me. Whether he had an arrangement with Algernon Hatter is between them, old boys and all that.'

'How were the Henson brothers when you last saw

them?' said Kettle.

'They were anxious and angry. They were arguing when I arrived, and they admitted that Paget had threatened violence, so Henry had hit him. Peter had said that was what caused the trouble in London, and Henry was becoming a liability. Peter had said that a few days back in the circus would do them both good, and I assumed that was where they were heading.'

'And what did you do?'

'I had some other business in Birmingham, the next day, so I travelled there, at first light, and didn't get back to Leicester until Tuesday. Mr Harrison was booking me in at the Fleur de lis and we were going to conclude the business.'

'When did you find out that Paget and the Hensons were dead?' said Kettle.

'On the Tuesday. It was the talk of the inn. I was shocked when Mr Harrison arrived and told me what had happened. He was rather nervous and wanted to know what had gone wrong. I told him what I knew, as that is all I had to tell.'

'Did you kill the Hensons?' said Kettle.

'No.'

Did you solicit or direct somebody else to kill them?'

'No'

'So who do you believe did?' said Kettle.

'I have my suspicions, especially after you showed me the Kukri.'

'And who do you suspect?' said Shepherd.

'Nimrod Hatter, or one of his colleagues. They are the men who silence dangerous tongues and tidy up unpleasant business.'

'You are telling us that a Metropolitan Police Detective Inspector may well be our killer?' said Shepherd. 'You expect us to take that seriously?'

'The role is just a front, Gentlemen. Captain Hay's little

unit work for him when needed, but have far wider remit. Queen Victoria doesn't tolerate loose ends and loose tongues, and everything is for the public good.'

'So why are you being sacrificed?' said Kettle.

'The Paget job would be seen as my responsibility. I had been tasked to coordinate it. It went wrong and the implications to our Good Lady Queen would be too much, so they would willingly let me take the blame.'

'Even if it meant that you would tell us the involvement of Her Majesty's secret services?'

'I would imagine that whoever was sent to plant the evidence, the Kukri, would probably have been sent to silence me. You probably beat them to me and now, to incriminate me, is the only way they can save face.'

'How is that?' said Shepherd.

'They would deny me now, rather than terminate me, as it achieves their same goal. Silence. What I can tell you here, may help me, but it by no means can be said in court, and nor would I admit it, but I believe you are fair and just men, and that I have no blood on my hands.'

'And you would stay quiet, publicly, at all costs?' said Kettle.

'As Admiral Lord Nelson, quite rightly said, *'England expects that every man will do his duty'.*'

'Finally, have you ever heard of Michael Lenihan?' said Shepherd.

'No, who is he?'

'Somebody else Inspector Hatter was keen to get to, rather hastily.'

'The Hensons did suggest that they had left something, in safe hands, if in any event they were terminated. Perhaps that is why Hatter wants him so badly?'

'Now that would make a lot of sense,' said Shepherd.

Sowing seeds

The early afternoon saw the Covent Garden and Drury Lane areas fill with London's elite, dining and taking in a matinee. That such wealth surrounded the filth of London's worst rookeries, was both ironic and puzzling to Beddows, as he went about the inns and dens on the edges of the slums, asking obvious questions about Michael Lenihan, or anybody fitting his description.

He made it clear that there was serious coin to be had to anybody with information leading to Michael's location, and some ears appeared much more interested than others.

In the shadowy doors and alleyways, or tiny first floor windows, Kelly and Crowley's men kept a careful eye on Beddows.

Unbeknown to Beddows, it was only a careful eye. The two Irishmen had considered it highly likely that Beddows would be accosted, sooner, rather than later, by Hatter or his henchmen.

This was seen as an acceptable risk, given Beddows' willingness to assist Eibhlin in his 'gardening leave', and would give credibility to the overall plan.

It also gave Tanky, Black Tommy and Crowley's men an extra element of anonymity, if there was still *active* interest in finding Michael, or identifying where he had been thought to be heading.

The two men had only one fear, that any retribution to Beddows might be harsher than he might physically be able to take, but their view, assisted by Crowley's prior knowledge of what a hard bastard he could be, gave them more confidence.

The timing of what to do with the papers now in Kelly's hands, was still debatable, but as a bargaining tool within the dissident Irish community, it may offer them future benefit.

More of a question remained regarding what to do with Inspector Nimrod Hatter and how best to facilitate his demise.

Kelly had an idea, but the cost would be the papers, or at least, some of the more contentious.

Was it a trade worth making? That he still pondered.

*****

The two teams of van and horses had travelled well, and apart from one or two anxious moments on the road up Brockley Hill, north of Edgware, when official looking men on horseback road past them twice, it had been pretty uneventful.

By the time they had reached St. Albans, and the safety of the stables at the Blue Boar Inn, in the Market Place, they were ready for their first change of horses, and a spot of refreshment. This was one of Sean Crowley's 'business interests' and his own men staffed the establishment. The horses in the stables were Sean's horses, and regularly pulled 'goods' between London and Leicester.

The men considered it was now safe to free Michael Lenihan from the confines of his bale.

Whilst one of the minders fetched ale and cheese, with no doubt a large wedge of warm bread, Tanky and Black Tommy engaged Michael for the first time, properly.

'So tell us why Inspector Hatter is so keen to get his hands around your neck, Michael Lenihan,' said Tanky.

The young man had a pitiful look, and a nervous tick, which Tanky had not noticed before. With the look came the impression of a slow individual, as had been described.

'My friends gave me a package. They said they had done something bad, and that I was to look after it for them, in case something happened to them.'

'We understand that they may have killed a man at a burglary, and Inspector Hatter believed you were involved?' said Tommy.

'I didn't do any burglary. That's what they do. They do it for an organisation which includes that man Hatter, and he beats them up if they don't.'

'Have you ever done a burglary with them?' said Tanky.

'No.'

'Were you with them when the man was killed?'

'No. It was afterwards that that they gave me the package. They said that the men would be after them quickly, and they had to go to Leicester, but they were very afraid.'

'And the circus was going to Leicester?'

'That's right. I was going to go up early, but after they gave me the package, I got scared, and I didn't want anything to happen in Leicester, as it's my Mammy that runs the circus.'

'Do you know what is in the package?' said Tanky.

'I do now, and I know why they wanted to get to Peter and Henry, so badly.'

'Do you know where Peter and Henry are likely to be, now?'

'They went to Leicester last Thursday. They had to meet somebody before the circus arrived. Somebody else from the people that Hatter works with.'

'Why was that?' said Tommy.

'They had another burglary to do. They were worried that it was a trap and that it was just to get them both together and kill them.'

'And they still went?' said Tanky.

'London or Leicester, or even staying with the circus,

they were so frightened. They were going to do the burglary for the man in Leicester, and then they were going to try and get passage back to Sweden.'

'Sweden?' said Tanky.

'That's where they came from originally. They thought that they would get money for the next job and pay their way to safety.'

'Why didn't they take the papers to somebody, earlier and use them to bargain for their safety?' said Tanky.

'They had seen Hatter kill somebody, once before. They said he gutted the man like a butcher would gut a beast. They had nobody they could trust, so money and Sweden seemed their only way. They had planned to get to a fishing boat from somewhere and pay their way home.'

'What happened in London that made you stay with your boxer friend?' said Tommy.

'Some of the men, including Hatter, started beating up their informers in the rookeries. Word went round that he was looking for me, last Monday, and I just felt safer with trusted friends. I haven't been out since.'

'Well, you're safe with us and Mr Crowley's boys, and we'll soon have you back with your Mammy.' said Tanky.

'I don't want her put at risk. If Hatter and his men are still looking for me, then they will be close to the circus, for sure.'

'We'll see about that, Michael. Your Mammy was safe and well, the last we heard, and friends in Leicester are making sure of that. If things are really that bad, somebody in London will be looking out for them, too.'

Family values

Robert Charters sat in the small but comfortable sitting room, in his private dwelling. It was unusual to entertain his constables within this private area, but on this occasion it seemed most prudent.

Mrs Charters had just made the three men a pot of hot tea, and dutifully left the room, closing the door to the scullery.

'Saint Paul seems to be exposed, if that is the case,' said Charters.

'It is a strange co-incidence, but it would make sense,' said Kettle.

'And we are happy that this man, Montague, admits to arranging the burglary for Harrison, having been solicited by Algernon Hatter to do so?'

'He does, Sir, but is adamant that he has no blood, personally, on his hands,   and that was never part of the planning. I have to say that his normal practices and demeanour show little evidence of violence or the need, thereof. He also believes that the knife has been deliberately placed at the Fleur de Lis to incriminate him,' said Kettle.

'What do you think, Constable Shepherd?'

'I believe him, as much as I might wish not to. Taking a pot shot at us still makes me wonder why he was so keen to escape us, but his 'duty' to the Queen may explain that. His story makes sense, and the overall picture reflects what outsiders have said about the Harrison and Paget family disharmony.'

'And you still have William Harrison to speak to?'

'Yes, Sir. His lawyer is expected shortly,' said Kettle.

'He must be a very fearful and unhappy man. His daughter has turned against him and by willingly offering us the initial explanation, she has probably ruined him as well as herself,' said Shepherd.

'How the mighty are fallen, Shepherd. It makes you realise that our poor and unfortunate thieves are actually nothing more than a minor nuisance, when you consider the scale of deceit and trickery amongst our wealthy,' said Charters. 'Mr Harrison and his business interests are well and truly in jeopardy, and if the tales we have heard to date are correct, he may well have some dark days ahead of him.'

'There seems little doubt about the burglary and participants, nor of the whereabouts of the proceeds, but we still have no hard evidence as to who the killer of the Henson brothers really is, nor may we ever.'

'I wonder how our colleagues are faring in London?' said Shepherd.

'I hope they are having as much success as we appear to be having with our burglary,' said Charters.

'Montague is of a mind that our killer is Nimrod Hatter. He is stating that the Hensons confessed that Hatter wanted papers from a bungled burglary that would embarrass the Queen and Government. Hensons may have given these to Lenihan and that would explain why Hatter was so keen to get off to London,' said Kettle.

'And he did arrive remarkably quickly after our crime. He may have been here already, and had time and opportunity to kill the Hensons. He also would look tall and dark to onlookers,' said Shepherd.

'The gypsies?' said Charters.

'They have eliminated Montague and said it was not him they saw, physically nor in the woman's dream.'

'I always knew Hatter was bad, but I can't believe he is now a killer for Her Majesty's dark forces!' exclaimed Charters.

'Perhaps the work in London will expose him?' said Kettle.

'I hope it has not exposed our colleagues,' said Charters.

Unbeknown to anyone else, Charters had received a telegraph, not long before, to confirm that Sergeants Smith and Haynes were on their way with 'the package', which he had to believe was Lenihan. There was no mention of Beddows, who Charters had little doubt was still in London. There was a risk to all of them whilst questions remained unanswered.

'Talk to Harrison now, and we will meet up later and review where we are at. If Mr Montague is at risk from his organisation, we need to make sure he remains guarded. I will put an armed man on the cell, for the time being. If I have to go back to Sir Richard Mayne with a 'for your eyes only' report, then I don't want any evidence to be lost, including any one of our suspects.'

*****

Mr Harrison's lawyer spent a few minutes with his client in the confines of the largest cell in the station, and then indicated the readiness of his client to be spoken to.

The four men entered the same, small office, as the other prisoners had now endured.

'One day we will get proper rooms to talk to suspects and witnesses, but this is the best we have to offer, presently,' said Kettle, gesturing towards the two furthest chairs, which included the one fixed to the floor.

'I have instructed my client to say nothing,' said the lawyer, Arthur Baddesley.

'That won't stop us asking him questions,' said Kettle.

'If that is the response we are going to get, he may well

suffer as a consequence, as the courts may interpret it as a sign of guilt.'

'Carry on,' said the stuffy lawyer.

'William Harrison, do you understand why you have been arrested?' said Kettle.

'Because you have taken the word of a recently bereaved and rather confused young woman,' said Baddesley.

'For Mr Harrison's benefit, we also have in custody, here at this police station, Miss Eleanor Skinner, and Mr Tobias Montague, who, together with Mr Harrison's Daughter, have already given their version of events,' said Kettle.

Harrison looked towards his Barrister and whispered exchanges briefly took place. Harrison had appeared shocked when Montague's name was given.

'My client has indicated that the choice of a completely different family lawyer is without his consent, and that his Daughter's interview should be struck from record.'

'How old is your Daughter, Mr Harrison? Is she not an adult, and capable of her own decisions?' said Kettle. Harrison glared and his face reddened.

'Your Daughter has advised us of your attempt to control her every movement and choice, and for that reason alone, she considers she is now in custody and facing serious charges,' said Shepherd.

'That is her problem then, if she disobeys me,' said Harrison.

'Your daughter has advised us that the whole plan for the crime was solicited and negotiated by you, and has gone into great detail as to your part in that planning. Both she and Tobias Montague have told us the same story, and things do not look good for you, Sir,' said Kettle.

'They are lying. They must have conspired to make me responsible for their present predicament,' said

Harrison, his lawyer whispering and putting his finger to his lips.

'And the staff at the Fleur de lis are lying too, in your contractual obligations with them, regarding rooms arranged for Mr Montague, or rather Mr Tobias as you would have the inn believe?' said Shepherd.

'It seems the world is against you, Mr Harrison, and everyone else is telling lies?' said Kettle.

'It will be down to them to prove it, if ever it gets to court,' said Baddesley.

'If Mr Harrison wishes to hang, and to remain silent to the gallows, that is his prerogative,' said Kettle.

'What capital offence are you suggesting?' Harrison shouted.

'The crime that you solicited resulted in the death of your son-in-law, and the subsequent deaths of two young men who actively committed the offence at your solicitation,' said Kettle.

'My solicitation? Humbug!' said Harrison.

'Have you ever had a conversation with a man named Algernon Hatter regarding this matter?' said Kettle.

'I have never heard of him.'

'Mr Harrison, might I ask you to cast your mind back to Sunday morning, when Sergeant Beddows and I were approached by you in Campbell Street?' said Shepherd.

'What of it?'

'Did you or did you not tell us that the man we had been with, looked familiar?' said Shepherd.

'I may have.'

'Did you or did you not tell us that you may have met him at a function in London, and then later, at your factory, tell us that you recalled the man's name as Hatter, the son of a business associate of yours?'

'Did I?' Harrison sought Baddesley's attention, and a further whispered conversation took place.

'I did,' said Harrison.

'How is Algernon Hatter known to you?' said Shepherd.
'He is a business associate through the cotton industry,' said Baddesley.
'Have you spoken to Algernon Hatter in recent weeks?' said Kettle.
'My client chooses to say nothing about Algernon Hatter,' said Baddesley.
'What would he say if we had been told that he approached Hatter, in another capacity that he holds, and that he arranged for Montague to meet him?' said Shepherd.
'He will deny it.'
'What if, ironically, we can demonstrate and prove that the same man solicited the burglars that killed Mr Harrison's son-in-law, and the man who murdered the burglars?' said Shepherd.
Harrison looked stunned. His face went ashen.
'Get the connection with capital offences, now, Mr Harrison?' said Kettle.
'And you still wish to say nothing, with Mr Montague connecting you with the man who provided not one, but three killers?' said Shepherd.
'It was not meant to happen this way,' said Harrison, waving his hand dismissively towards Baddesley.
'What do you mean?' said Kettle.
'I only wanted what was best for my daughter. Edward Paget was a reckless fool when it came to business and he was giving my daughter and I a bad name in certain circles. All I wished was for him to be humiliated, and my daughter freed from a loveless marriage.'
'How is it going to look when not only did you arrange the crime, but you had prenuptial contracts made by your son-in-law, ensuring your daughter's future wealth, but also that you insisted he acquired a significant life assurance, which you were very keen to suggest we looked at,' said Shepherd. 'It might look to a court that

you realised both you and your daughter would actually be better off with Edward Paget dead.'

'That was not what I planned or why I planned it.'

'But that is the inference, or so it may seem,' said Kettle. 'What with that and the links back to Algernon Hatter who provided both the money man, the burglars and the murderer of the burglars.'

'Algernon Hatter is a man who would not admit to such a thing. In fact he is highly unlikely to ever be implicated in any crime, as he is one of Her Majesty's most senior and respected security advisors,' said Harrison.

'So he will leave you, your daughter, and Tobias Montague high and dry, to take responsibility for a contrived burglary and three murders,' said Shepherd. A long pause, and Harrison's face showed realisation of the severity of his situation.

'My God,' said Harrison, 'what have I done?'

'Was it really worth it?' said Shepherd.

'Was what worth what?'

'For your greed, not just for you, but for your daughter's benefit, you have probably sacrificed everything you have ever worked or strived for?'

'In this world, Constable Shepherd, there is no reward without risk.'

'Radix malorum est cupiditas,' said Shepherd, reflecting on Beddows' earlier observation.

'So men may say, but only those who have failed or never achieved great wealth.'

Spiders and flies

Beddows had upset as many people as he felt he could manage in both The Bowl and The Abbey, next door.

He had lost count of the number of times that he had suggested that he was looking for Michael Lenihan, and that he had heard that Michael would be at The Bowl that evening, with some work put his way as a second, at the big fight between Brendan Kearney and Thaddeus Kowalski, a Polish docker who had just come on to the London fight circuit.

Beddows assumed that by now, one of Hatter's snouts would have word back to Hatter that somebody was still, actively, looking for Lenihan. That was also assuming that nobody had disclosed the planned deception, or that Lenihan was already some way to Leicester.

It was an uncomfortable feeling, being alone in a strange city, with only criminals and dissidents offering physical and moral support, and Beddows questioned why he had been so keen to help Eibhlin MacCormack. All the alleyways looked the same, and Beddows hesitated for a moment, as to which one he was best to follow, to get back to Paddy's yard. He was sure this was the one he had walked down with Paddy, previously, and set off, brushing past a throng of small children, drunks and mumpers, the usual occupants of the dark and confining spaces.

Very quickly, he realised he was being followed, and not subtly, either. Two very large men, and staying their distance.

He walked briskly until he reached daylight, and swiftly

turned right, ducking into the nearest recessed doorway. He waited, and waited, until one by one, the two men emerged, one right and one left, scanning the pavements and road, amidst the afternoon hoards. Beddows stepped out and approached the nearer, who had stopped with his back to the doorway.

'Can I help you, you look lost?' said Beddows.

'No thanks, just looking for my mate,' said the man, hesitantly.

'Give Mr Hatter my regards, and tell him that we will no doubt cross paths, later.'

The man tried to look blank. Clearly not one of Hatter's brighter resources.

The two men watched from a distance.

'What is he playing at?' said Hatter.

'Showing out, you mean?' said the second man.

'It's like he knows we are following him, which is hardly surprising. We know he is asking lots of questions about this man, Lenihan. Perhaps he thinks we will lead him to him?'

'Rumour has it that Lenihan will be at the Bowl tonight. There is a big fight on in the back. Lots of money being thrown about already. He has already been in there suggesting Lenihan might be there, and asking where he might be, now.'

'There will be too many roughnecks at the inn. We need to get eyes in there, and if Lenihan does show up, we take him out after the fight is over, and the crowds have dispersed. If Mr Beddows thinks he can stop me, he will wish he had never met me. If only the fool knew who he was dealing with.'

'We could let it be known at Captain Hay's level that there is a copper from Leicester on our patch,' said the second man.

'I don't want Hay knowing anything about this. This stays with us and ends with us. Nobody else must know,' said Hatter. 'Get our best men ready for tonight.'

Waiting

Charters called Kettle and Shepherd to his house, once again, and sought an update.

'All three prisoners have now told us much the same thing,' said Kettle. 'The plan was for a burglary to occur, which would result in repossession of money from Montague, and a chain of events that would discredit Edward Paget for some time to come.'

'What about the fact that Paget died?' said Charters.

'They all seem genuinely horrified by the events, and state it was never in their plan. That being said, I am concerned that the awareness of Paget's worth, alive or dead, was key to the planning, and the life assurance doesn't make things look much better,' said Shepherd.

'What does Montague say about the Henson brothers?' said Charters.

'He is adamant that after he last saw them at the racecourse, they handed over the money and jewellery to him, and were alive and well, but were clearly anxious to move on,' said Kettle.

'What do you think?' said Charters.

'I think they are all telling the truth, and all realise how their lives are crashing down around them. The problem we have is that we are still short of a killer and a definite motive,' said Kettle. Shepherd nodded in agreement.

'That is unless you consider that there are 'dark forces' at work, and Inspector Hatter has some part to play in the killings or the arrangement of the killings,' said Shepherd.

'This murky world that our Queen and Government

seems to condone is worrying to a man like me. I know we have to fight wars, but what can justify such killings in the name of National security, if that was a motive?' said Charters.

'What about Eleanor Skinner?' said Kettle. 'We are happy now that she did no more than receive the brooch from her mistress. She will be a prosecution witness for us, I would imagine.'

'Let her go. She will find out soon enough that her world is shortly to change to her detriment, also,' said Charters. 'That is unless Mrs Paget wishes her to remain as housekeeper whilst she herself, serves her sentence, wherever that may be, and for how long it may last. The rope may change that, of course.'

'And the others?' said Kettle.

'We can't do too much more, until we have something from our efforts in London. Another night in the cells, and then charge them all with conspiracy to commit the burglary, as a holding charge. They can go before the bench on Monday morning.'

'What about Nimrod Hatter and possible connections with Tobias Montague?' said Shepherd.

'We already have a position regarding Montague, and quite clearly whatever part of this murky organisation it is, have washed their hands of him. I never got a proper reply from either Captain Hay, nor Sir Richard Mayne regarding Hatter. I think I need to speak with a contact of mine, again,' said Charters.

*****

By seven thirty that evening, the two vans, their horses and riders arrived at The Brave Old Oak coaching inn, at Towcester.

This was the last stop of the night, and it would be here that the tired and dusty men would rest, overnight, before an early start for Lutterworth, and the final miles to Leicester.

Crowley's teams of horses were of strong Irish stock, and matched the favoured speeds of the best of carriage companies, averaging 8 to 10 miles per hour, and enduring about 30 miles before a rest, or a change of team became necessary.

Michael Lenihan, Tanky Smith and Black Tommy Haynes looked forward to their first night in a comfortable bed for what seemed like weeks, but was, in fact, just days. Hot water, clean towels and a hearty meal was the first priority, and an ale or two.

The trap is sprung

At nine p.m. the rear yard of The Bowl was jammed full. A makeshift arena had been marked out, covered in turf, 24 feet square, marked with posts and ropes, with a scratch line across the centre.

This fight was to be under Jack Broughton's 'London Prize Ring Rules' , which allowed 'seconds' in each opponent's corner.

Brendan Kearney had been the favoured fighter at The Bowl in recent months. A young upstart. However, his challenger was 'arranged' by local Fancy, who had heard of his exploits fighting in the pubs and inns along the Thames, favoured by foreign sailors.

The two men stood on opposite sides of the arena, and it was clear that Thaddeus Kowalski was a beast of a man, standing taller and broader than Kearney.

The locals were exchanging money with dubious bookmakers, illegally of course, many swayed having seen Kowalski for the first time, many others by ale or gin and encouragement from followers.

The crowd was a vibrant mix of Fancy, Bruisers, and other well heeled public, who paid good money to come and see bloodshed. Amongst the crowd were Sean Crowley, Kelly, Beddows and some of the Irishmen's biggest bruisers, for their personal protection.

Beddows received word that Hatter's men were in the crowd, but nobody had seen the man himself.

Crowley and Kelly also had a sizeable contingent of muscle waiting in The Abbey, next door, and readily available closely along the alleys off St. Giles High Street.

Sat behind Kearney, with buckets, cloths, silk scarf and towels, was a man, largely fitting the description of Michael Lenihan. This poor fellow was getting lots of glances from three or four men pushing through the crowd. Beddows considered that Crowley and Kelly had done a fine job, providing Hatter had not met Lenihan before, which he assumed, from Hatter's visit to Leicester, he had not.

The fight started brutally, with both men standing toe to toe, in a fury of fists. Both men were cut, early, and the crowd roared as fresh warm blood was splashed over the nearest of the watching crowd, with each subsequent blow.

London Rules were not to everyone's taste, as holds and throwing were commonly practiced, sometimes to slow the fight or allow a weaker fighter to give himself time to recover.

Kearney was clearly the better pugilist, with fast hands and deft feet. Kowalski, on the other hand, tired quickly, and he began to use his size to grapple with the younger fighter, throwing him and pinning him, before a wicked blow caused him to roll off, grimacing.

It was some considerable time before fitness, skill and speed, overcame weight and brute force, and Kearney landed a beast of a *floorer*, a right upper cut, onto the larger man's bottom jaw, sending him spiralling into a world of temporary darkness.

Kowalski did not come up to scratch, and enormous cheers broke out from the locals within the crowd.

More than the odd 'jolly' between disgruntled seamen and locals had to be quelled by the burly bruisers, before the crowd broke up and slid away, shortly after midnight, and three hours of pleasure. Many felt cheated as recent fights had gone on to the following morning before a result was achieved.

As the numbers thinned, an air of expectation increased

amongst Beddows and his associates, alert to any intervention by Hatter and his men.

The decoy second, was deliberately retained, and spent the time with a large hat pulled over his brow, masking him partially, but his slow and pondering movements fitted those of Lenihan.

As the staff of the inn started snuffing out the many lamps that had been lit, all hell broke loose, as eight large men, armed with cudgels, cutlasses and assorted *Barkers* stormed the arena, from an entrance off the rear alley.

The Irish bruisers who had been deliberately deployed for such an event, waded in, giving as good as they received. Men from both sides wailed in pain, and slash wounds were inflicted, of a repugnant nature, across arms, faces and torsos.

'Get Lenihan,' came a call from the middle of the melee, as Beddows recognised Nimrod Hatter, now dressed in what appeared to be a drab and scruffy leather coat, breeches and riding boots, brandishing a small pistol in one hand and a curved blade in the other.

A large bruiser stood between Hatter and the decoy, and Hatter slashed him across his belly with the curved knife, causing a deep wound.

Hatter reached the corner, where the decoy sat, and raised his pistol towards the man he believed to be Lenihan, and pulled the trigger.

A flash and puff of smoke, and a ball struck the man high on the left centre of his chest, just above the heart. Blood spurted from the wound and the man fell backwards onto the turf.

Beddows leaped on Hatter's back and pulled him to the floor, and Hatter screamed wildly, slashing out with the curved knife. He could not have seen it was Beddows, but his flailing was clearly intended to do serious harm. Beddows felt strong hands grab his shoulders, and one of the men he recognised from earlier, that had followed him in the alleyways, dragged him off Hatter, smashing a large fist into Beddows face, stunning him.

Then came the awareness of something cold and sharp, slashing across his throat, and warm blood on his hands, just before he passed out. Hatter's face was the last thing he recalled, glaring at him, wildly, brandishing gleaming steel.

The omen

Shepherd slid into the cool sheets alongside Sally, tired mentally, from a full day of questioning the three suspects.

Sleep came quickly, and the knowledge of an early start again, playing on his mind.

In the dead of night, and in pitch darkness, Shepherd sat bolt upright in bed, from another dream.

His mouth felt the same uncomfortably dryness. His heart bursting and his head throbbing, he stared, blindly, at his hands, watching Beddows' life blood ebb away.

He called out, yet again waking Sally.

Sally sat upright and cradled him.

'You're having that dream again, Samson.'

'Sally, I'm not. This time it was Beddows, not Archie, and it was Beddows' blood on my hands. What can that mean? I hope that is not a bad omen?'

The lucky man

Beddows' eyes flickered, and slowly he regained consciousness. He was lying down and he could feel something tight around his throat. His arms were tied to runners at the side of the bed with some form of material.

As he looked around the room, trying to make sense, he caught sight of Paddy McNally, sitting at the foot of the bed.

'Feck me, Beddows, you had us scared for a while.'

Beddows tried to talk, but his mouth felt caked and he could taste blood, and his words would not come. Paddy gave him a small cup of water and he sipped, cautiously, sloshing it around his mouth, before spitting it towards a gazunder at the side of the bed, but missing, woefully.

'What day is it?' said Beddows.

'It's only Sunday, you haven't slept that long. There goes my clean floor, you beggar, you,' Paddy laughed, gently. 'Don't try and talk too much as that's a nasty wound that you have there, courtesy of Mr Hatter's wee blade.'

'My hands,' Beddows whispered.

'We had to tie you down as you were trying to tear the bandages off your wound. We had some morphine in our supplies, and it must have knocked you out. Our pet Surgeon is a good man, and very deft with a needle and thread.'

'What happened to the decoy?' said Beddows, now aware of the soreness.

'He will be alright, the big lump. The ball missed anything vital but smashed through him, leaving a big hole. He too has benefitted from our surgeon and will no doubt make a recovery. He's a big, strong lad.'

'And Hatter?' whispered Beddows, drying up again.

'Don't you worry about Mr Hatter and his colleagues. Let's just say they won't be getting up to any of their old tricks again.'

'What do you mean by that?'

'Go back to sleep, Beddows, and we shall talk later.'

The room began to fade and Beddows fell, uncontrollably, back into a deep, deep sleep.

*****

Towcester to Lutterworth was a long run for the new horses, and a longer break would be required when they arrived at The Greyhound, the last stop of the journey. An eight o'clock start in the cooler part of the morning suited, and they would make good time along the homeward leg of Watling Street, up to the Gibbet on the top of the Pilgrim's Lowe, the ancient tumulus at the crossroads to Rugby, above the town, a lasting reminder to those who considered a life of crime.

The men were in good spirit and were relieved that soon they would be back in Leicester and to their routine.

'What will happen to me when we get there?' said Michael Lenihan.

'It depends on what our colleagues have found out whilst we have been gone. Assuming that you aren't involved in any way, then after you have been properly interviewed, you will be free to join your mammy,' said Tanky.

'How will we be protected from the men from London?'

'That, my old son, is what I am hoping our friend Sergeant John Beddows has been sorting out in our absence. With him and your Irish friends and relatives, I reckon there is a good chance that you'll not be bothered again.'

'I don't like the feeling of being hunted. I want a quiet life back at the circus. No more favours for anyone.'

'Let's wait and see what we learn when we get back. Should be there just after two, I reckon.'

*****

It was nearer midday when Beddows came out of the morphine induced stupor, and he shook his head gently, feeling again the tightness across his throat, but now his hands were free.

'God, I feel rough,' he growled, hoarsely.

'But back with the living, so can't be to bad, my friend,' said Paddy, entering the room upon hearing Beddows voice.

'How bad is it?' said Beddows.

'You're fecking lucky. It nicked your throat and just missed becoming a terminal bloodletting. No permanent damage done, other than a very tidy scar for you to display, in days to come. Should be back on your feet in no time. You bled like a stuck pig.'

'So what happened after I went down?'

'There was one hell of a battle. A few of our blokes got smashed up, but nobody got killed. The big lump that you saw get shot is up and asking for breakfast, which is a good sign. One or two of Hatter's men got the biggest kickings of their lives I suspect, and Hatter himself was dragged away.'

'How do you mean, dragged away?'

'Not long after you got cut, another load of fellas poured in to the place. Far more than Hatter had brought along. Very smart in their appearance and actions. All had cutlasses and some new fangled pistols, which they were not afraid to use, and they very quickly restored order.'

'Were they Police, or in uniform?'

'No, but they were very disciplined and clearly there was a commander, who knew what he was doing.'

'Did they lock many up?'

'They weren't interested, so it seemed. They looked around who was there, told two or three to feck off, who we thought were Hatter's men, and they took Hatter away themselves, kicking and screaming.'

'Who the hell could they have been? Who else has Mr Hatter upset?'

'When you move in a dark, murky world, then you mix with dark, murky people. I reckon it was his own, tidying up the mess.'

'That could be a problem. How do we find out? I want to know if Michael Lenihan is safe and if Hatter's lot are still after him.'

'Leave that to Mr Kelly and Mr Crowley. They both have instigated enquiries.'

'Get me some water and a clean shirt, I'm ready to get up.'

'You take it easy for a while yet, we don't want you dropping dead on us. By the way, the other good news is that those few coins we put on young Kearney for you were well spent, and there is a nice little return on your investment. More than you see in a month or two as a copper I suppose.'

'Let's hope the day gets better still,' said Beddows, exploring his bandages, with a small mirror that Paddy handed him. 'Glad they missed the handsome bit.'

'Was your nose broken before yesterday?'

'Once or twice.'

'It looks a fecking mess again, to me, if you look a bit closer,' grinned Paddy. 'I think you might be taking away a few reminders of this little favour for Eibhlin, for a few years to come.'

Loose ends

At about the same time, in Leicester, Herbert Kettle charged William Harrison, Maria Paget and Tobias Montague, with conspiring to commit burglary at New Walk.

All three were remanded into the custody of Leicester Borough Gaol, on Highcross Street, until the next available Quarterly Sessions, due at the end of July. Agreement had been reached with Robert Charters that if new evidence resulted from the London enquiries, that implicated any of them in any of the three murders, they would be further charged to stand trial at the Leicester Assizes in August.

'Word has already spread about the business community regarding the demise of the two businesses. Harrison's lawyers are apparently arranging for his Managers to maintain production, but word has it that the firms will likely fail,' said Charters.

'What do the business community think of having criminals in their midst?' said Shepherd.

'They are a hypocritical bunch, Shepherd. I spoke with one of my contacts last evening, who has Masonic, as well as business links in the borough, and he says they will never see the likes of the support and respect that they have had to date. I wouldn't mind, but from what we have gleaned about them all robbing Her Majesty's Revenue, blind, it's a bit rich.'

'And Eleanor Skinner?' said Kettle.

'She remains at New Walk and will maintain a household until her Mistress' fate is resolved.'

'Will Montague be charged with conspiracy to murder

Edward Paget, knowing that the Hensons were acting on his behalf?' said Shepherd.

'Will we ever be able to prove that he actually conspired to murder them? Probably not,' said Charters.

'And will we later charge Montague with attempted murder of Shepherd and myself on his arrest?' said Kettle.

'I suspect that Mr Montague will be removed from the custody of the borough Gaol and will be interviewed by somebody from Her Majesty's Government, back in London, and we shall probably never hear of him again. Her Majesty would not wish the dirty washing he might present, to be aired publicly, in a court, for example.'

'Even if he is subsequently implicated in any of the murders?' said Shepherd, shaking his head, incredulously.

'Dark and mysterious ways, Shepherd. We do our job, and if needs must, Queen Victoria will be sure to do hers, protecting and defending the realm.'

'And if Harrison and Maria Paget are considered a threat too, will they actually face trial?' said Shepherd.

'I have a niggling feeling that there will be some intervention as to 'is it in the public interest?', Shepherd. Probably a trial, behind close doors, and a conviction and respited sentence, as a lesson to be learned. Perhaps a negotiated short sentence featuring transportation to one of the cotton rich colonies, where they can go about their business, once again.'

'And what about the Henson murders?' said Kettle.

'I suspect that shortly we will be produced a package, gentlemen. A much needed and anticipated package, that may well give us better knowledge of what and whom lies behind the murders. Wait and see.' Charters smiled.

The Prodigal son

Just after two o'clock, two rather dusty vans and teams of horses pulled up in Town Hall Street, directly outside the police station, much to the displeasure of passersby. Clouds of dust took time to settle after their rapid approach.

Stepping down from the first wagon, Tanky Smith was pleased to step foot on familiar soil.

'Welcome to Leicester, Mr Lenihan. This is our final stop for a while, and we need to tidy up a few matters.'

Lenihan, followed by Black Tommy, stepped down from the van, and the three men bid farewell to Crowley's men, who had goods to deliver next.

The door to the station opened, and Charters, who was stood talking to the Charge Sergeant, beamed as he saw his men.

'Welcome home, gentlemen. I assume this is Michael Lenihan?'

'I am, Sir, and glad to make your acquaintance,' said Michael, holding out a hand in response to his greeting.

Shepherd and Kettle appeared from the rear of the building, and looked at the new arrivals.

'Are we glad to see you,' said Kettle.

'Beddows not with you?' said Shepherd.

'We left Beddows in the company of Sean Crowley, and some other Irish gentlemen who have gone out of their way to assist us, these last few days,' said Tanky.

'Let's find somewhere private, and talk,' said Charters.

The six men crammed into the small rear office, which had seen more use in the last week, than for some considerable time.

'We must attempt to pressure the borough to find us somewhere bigger and more suitable, as we are outgrowing this little place, ' said Charters.

'What have you to tell us, Gentlemen,' said Charters, addressing Tanky and Black Tommy.

'We have a tale to tell that you may find unlikely, perhaps even unbelievable, as to why Mr Lenihan here, has been so sought after.' said Tanky.

'Perhaps not so unlikely, as we have been similarly engaged up here, in your absence.'

'Mr Lenihan has, rather unfortunately, through no fault of his own, found himself in possession of materials that would seriously threaten the whole of the royal families of Europe, and a very large number of individuals, personally, in the world of spying and national security.'

'We anticipated that there might be something of that nature,' said Charters.

'These papers were obtained by two men by the name of Henson, from a burglary at the German Ambassador's residence, a few days before our offence. In the course of that burglary a man was murdered, in the Henson's attempts to escape. Hensons allegedly knew that they would be likely killed for messing up their task, which was set them by a unit called Special Branch, part of the wider known Aliens Office, and a certain Inspector Nimrod Hatter.'

'That makes sense,' said Charters.

'Inspector Hatter found out that these papers had been given to Michael Lenihan for security, to be handed to the media if ever anything happened to the brothers. Hatter issued a 'dead or alive' notice amongst his colleagues, to silence Michael and recover the papers, which would bring him great personal pain, having messed up such a task.'

'So you had nothing to do with the London Burglary?' said Shepherd.

'No, the brothers did it on Hatter's orders. The only mistake I made was getting involved by accepting the papers.'

'Rumour has it that Hatter was in pursuit of the two brothers and murdered them or has had them murdered, and thus he only had Michael left to worry about, which is why he was so keen to get back to London.'

'The murderous scum,' said Tanky. 'We have heard some terrible tales of what this lot gets up to on Her Majesty's behalf. Hired killers and spies.'

'And what of Hatter and his men, now?'

'The papers were obviously going to be a problem for Hatter, and he wants them back at any cost. The work he is doing now seemingly falls outside his 'official work' and he and a small, select, bunch of his thugs are terrorising potential informants around Seven Dials and St Giles rookeries. That is what has brought Sean Crowley and his merry men into the process. Some of the associates are Irish dissidents, and Hatter hates them, but they have proved trustworthy and resourceful allies. Beddows is in their care, and they were setting a trap to draw Hatter out, as we left.'

'Why did he not go to Sir Richard Mayne?' said Charters.

'Honestly, Mr Charters, you can't trust anyone down there. For one, we knew you wanted the fact we were down there to remain a secret, and secondly, it would have exposed Beddows to Hatter. They seem to have a plan that they thought would show Hatter to be what he really was, and that he was working outside of his authority, as wide as it appears to be.'

'So Hatter appears to be responsible for the death of our burglars, either with his own hands or at his doing?' said Charters.

'So it would seem,' said Tanky.

'So our work, in many respects, for our offences is done. It would be nice to see some positive outcome from

London,' said Charters. 'I think it is time to reunite Michael, here, with his family. Kettle, Shepherd, will you sort that out for us?'

'Yes, of course.'

'Sergeants Smith and Haynes, I want a full report as to the events in London, before you leave the station, and not forgetting your expenses claim, if you would be so kind. Then, I have another little job for you.'

'I could do with a leg stretch after all that time sat in a van,' said Black Tommy, rubbing his aching backside. 'I couldn't be doing with a job where you sit down all day.'

'Now you might understand why I seem grumpy,' said Charters, looking pleased with himself.

*****

The late afternoon breeze picked up as Kettle, Shepherd and Michael Lenihan walked from the police station. Church bells pealed as afternoon weddings took place across the borough.

Michael carried all his worldly belongings in a canvas bag, thrown jauntily over his wide shoulders.

'How does it feel, to be a free man again?' said Kettle.

'Free? It feels good to think that I have less to look over my shoulder for, but I shalln't rest easily until I know that Hatter and his boys are no longer looking to kill me.'

'We will be keeping a watchful eye over you for a day or two, until we get news from London'

'A watchful eye?' said Michael.

'We have people who will make sure you are safe for the time being. You may not see them and you may not recognise them, but they will not be far away.' said Shepherd.

Barker's Ground was busy, with a big audience from the

afternoon matinee, and the final show of the visit to Leicester.

The three men headed towards Eibhlin's caravan. Walking towards them was the inimitable Henry Pensylva.

'Ah, the prodigal son returns,' said the stocky man. 'Your Mammy is going to be delighted that you are safe and well. You don't know the upset that you have caused.'

'I think that the upset was not of Michael's making, so less of the finger pointing,' said Kettle.

Eibhlin appeared in the entrance to the tent, and scanned the site, looking towards her caravan. Upon seeing Michael she broke into a run, as did he, and they met in a tangle of arms and legs, halfway.

Shepherd and Kettle, respectfully gave them a few moments to get over the evident tears and words, before interrupting them.

'Gentlemen, thank you so much for finding my son and bringing him safely to me.'

'You have others to thank before us. Two of our colleagues who have been actively seeking Michael in London, brought him home, earlier,' said Kettle.

'Beddows?' said Eibhlin.

'Beddows was involved, but he is still in London tidying up some loose ends. We are hoping he is still safe, and is with your cousin and others in the Irish Community, trying to resolve matters,' said Shepherd.

'Loose ends?' said Eibhlin.

'We can't say too much. Michael will fill you in, but it is rather messy, and may be beyond your belief. Whatever happens, please be careful not to speak openly of what you will no doubt hear,' said Kettle.

'Why ever not?' said Eibhlin.

'We are talking about national security, and there are more eyes and ears about than many of us realise,' said

Kettle. 'Talk to Michael, and we will catch up later. Just for your information, as much as we believe the threat to Michael may be over, we will have somebody keeping an eye on you both, for a few days, until we can be sure.'

'We are meant to be going to Nottingham. That was our last performance. Michael will stay with me,' said Eibhlin.

'Do we know where in Nottingham you will be?' said Shepherd.

'Beddows knows, but it is not a secret. We will be on the meadows beyond the fifteen arches bridge over the Trent, before you enter the town. We are there until next Sunday.'

'When will you be leaving, personally?' said Shepherd.

'Tomorrow, early, I would imagine.'

'Well good luck to you both,' said Kettle.

'Will you be in touch with Beddows?' said Shepherd.

'He knows where I will be, and I know how to get hold of him, so we shall have to see,' said Eibhlin.

'In that case, I bid you both well,' said Shepherd.

In defence of the realm

In a small dark room, underground, somewhere close to
The Tower, a man sat strapped to a heavy chair.
The man bore all the signs of a heavy beating and his
eyes were swollen and partially closed.
'What in heaven's name did you think you were doing?'
shouted a very upright and aggressive figure of a man,
dressed in very expensive suit, shirt and cravat.
'I was doing my job, Captain.'
'You have not been doing what you are paid to do for
some weeks, by the sound of it. I am more inclined to
call you a renegade. Gutting men to sort out your own
mess?'
Nimrod Hatter spat at the man's feet, and hissed.
'You lot, sat in your high and mighty, holier than thou
offices of power, rely on the likes of me to do what you
haven't the guts to do yourself. I thought you were
different.'
The man wiped the phlegm off his polished boots, across
the back of Hatter's torn breeches.
'Your remit is to act in the best interest of the Sovereign
and to use only sufficient force or subterfuge as is
necessary.'
'You know we kill, but you haven't the guts to document
that anywhere, have you?'
'It is who you kill, and why you kill that is most
important, and taken into context together. When they
are enemies of the state and a threat to the Sovereign
or National security, there may be special
circumstances. However, your recent killing spree
appears to fall outside of that definition.'

'I did my damnedest to get the papers that I was ordered to secure. I did not instruct my contacts to kill the German. They went renegade on me.'

'And you took it upon yourself to be judge and jury and to eliminate them as a threat to you.'

'No, as a threat to National security.'

'In my eyes you were looking after Nimrod Hatter and nobody else. You knew what would happen when we found out you had messed up. It is ironic that a colleague of yours, just happened to be in the same town as your contacts, doing a job your Father directed him to do, and that he has seemingly been incriminated for your dirty work?'

'What a coincidence.' said Hatter, smirking.

'More than that. You not only exceeded your powers, you betrayed a colleague who was also acting, marginally, outside his remit.'

'He's just a Revenue man. No stomach for dirty work, that lot. Why my Father trusted him, God only knows.'

'Your Father seems to have been helping his own interests outside of his advisory capacity, or so it would seem. He seems to have created a monster in you, and a very dangerous one, to boot.'

'My Father is more of a safeguard to National Security than you have or will ever be.'

'Mr Palmerstone doesn't seem to agree with you, as of this morning.'

'Ah, the Queen's puppet. Should I be surprised?'

'And where are the said papers, that you so aggressively and professionally pursued?'

'I would have had my hands on them last night, if you hadn't intervened when you did.'

'Are you so sure? The man you were chasing had left London hours before, and you were actually drawn into a trap.'

'I saw him.'

'You saw what they wanted you to see. Outwitted by a lowly borough policeman and a bunch of Irish crooks and lowlife.'

'I don't believe you.'

'Believe what you want. How do you think we knew what you were doing last night?'

'I've no idea, but you are clearly going to tell me.'

'We were offered the papers, or, more accurately, the ones that we most wanted, in a trade for a renegade.'

'I was sold out to the Irish. What sort of an organisation is this becoming? What will they fear now of Special Branch?'

'What makes you think that you know better than the establishment, Hatter?'

'Because men like me and my Father are the ones who see the dirty work. The men who look into the eyes of our enemies and stick in the blade, or pull the trigger, because men like you say so.'

'And outside of our orders, also. You are not paid to make this a profitable and lawless role for lining your own pockets. You were meant to be a foot soldier, not a General. You don't make decisions, you follow orders.'

'Well not any more, not after this I won't.'

'You don't know how true your words are, Hatter.'

*****

Monday the 12th of July broke fair, once again. The papers continued to talk of a divided nation and the election rumbled on, with spats between Tories and Whigs, and divisions in the Tory ranks.

A large crowd had gathered on the steps of The Town of Margate, on the banks of the Thames, at Wapping. From here, Captain Bligh had bid for, and purchased 'The Bounty' before his little jaunt to Tahiti.

A small rowing boat from the Metropolitan Police River

Division, with three constables and a sergeant on board had pulled ashore, nearby to the post, to which condemned pirates were once chained, to drown in the rising tide.

Back to back were tethered the bodies of two men. One was considerably younger than the second, but there was a distinct similarity between the two.

The Sergeant saw rope marks about each man's neck, indicating that they had actually hung, not drowned.

'Cut them free, and then off to River Headquarters with them, as we were told,' the Sergeant called to the men, two of whom were now thigh deep in murky Thames water.

Locals who knew the legends of the posts and of the history of the pub, assumed the significance of the bodies.

Here was a message to anyone who may threaten the nation.

The bodies were taken aboard the boat, wrapped in tarpaulin, to be disposed of as instructed.

'Aren't we going to ask any questions?' asked one of the confused constables.

'We're to do nothing on this occasion, on the instruction of Captain Hay.'

Not a single word appeared in the London papers that evening.

*****

Late into the evening, a private messenger called at the Town Hall police station, with a telegraph for Robert Charters.

The telegraph read *'It is with regret that we announce the passing of Saint Paul and the passing of the Grandson of Noah.'*

Robert Charters smiled and rubbed his hands.

'The end of an unpleasant mess. Praise the Lord.'
'What did you say, dear?' said Mrs Charters.
'Nothing dear, just God working in mysterious ways, nothing for you to worry about.'

*****

Beddows was well enough to travel, by the Tuesday morning, and his throat was dressed once more by one of Crowley's pet surgeons, who proclaimed what a fine job he had done with Beddows' stitches.

Patrick McNally had acquired a rather fine silk cravat, which he skilfully tied around Beddows' dressing, hiding the bandages and any staining that might be visible.

Beddows wore a rather nice new suit, which a local tailor had measured and fitted for him, at no cost. That he would have to keep quiet about.

A growler waited outside McNally's yard, and a driver to take Beddows and a few belongings to the Railway station. McNally also sent some gifts for his cousin and nephew, including a case of finest Kentucky Bourbon, which Sean Crowley had sourced.

Mr Crowley had taken the price out of Beddows' winnings, unbeknown to Beddows, who thought Crowley's generosity in purchasing a first class train ticket was very charitable. Crowley smiled and shook Beddows' hand.

'Until we meet again, Beddows, which I am sure we will.'

'Never be sure about anything,' said Beddows. 'Even I don't know where I shall be in the future, nor who I may be with, or what I shall be doing.'

'What would you do without your police duties, and where would your Borough Boys be without you?'

'I can't say for sure. Look at the Hatter family. One day they have the world at their greedy fingertips, and the next day? Did they see that coming?'

'Probably knew they were on borrowed time,' said Crowley, 'and making hay whilst the sun shone.'

'I have some gardening leave to consider, and then I'll see.'

'Goodbye, Beddows,' said Kelly. 'It's nice to meet some honest policemen. Pass on my regards to your colleagues.'

'Thank you for your charitable donation, Mr Kelly, without which I would probably not be here.'

'Not too much of a donation, Beddows. I still have something left for a rainy day in old Dublin Town.'

Beddows realised what had been given up to end Hatter's reign of terror, dissidents or not. Good men with differing politics and values.

Beddows headed off in his driven growler, feeling quite the gent, looking forward to a shorter and more comfortable return journey home than the one down to London.

Beddows

The early train arrived at Leicester, via Rugby, at about five in the afternoon. Beddows was feeling dry and was glad of a canteen of water that Paddy had provided. He shared his first class carriage with one other person, a clergyman, who cared not to converse, fortunately, allowing Beddows time to watch the scenery go by, whilst resting his throat.

He still found it harrowing watching hot embers fly close past his face, but it was definitely a better way to travel.

Walking out onto the forecourt and its splendid columns, into the sunlight along Campbell Street, Beddows considered which way to turn.

Home?

Was there such a place anymore? The bitter and twisted Mrs Beddows would say not, and Beddows had already considered that things had to change on that front.

Eibhlin?

It was now Tuesday, and she would be established with her circus alongside the Trent at fifteen arches bridge. He would wish to go and see her, but probably tomorrow, and an early coach from the Stag and Pheasant. He would be pleased to see her, and no doubt, she to see Beddows, assuming that she had not moved on to 'another port'.

Shepherd?

A tough one, that. He still felt angry and betrayed at Shepherd's doubt, over a week previous. However, he was still more of a friend in the job than he had in anyone else.

Tanky and Black Tommy?
He owed them a debt of gratitude for their assistance in pulling things together, whilst finding and safeguarding Michael Lenihan.

Charters?
He preferred not to, but probably owed him some acknowledgement, and wished to ensure that he was fully aware of how the ends in London had been 'tidied up'. Also he needed to get a feel for Charters' state of mind, and whether a return to his Detective Sergeant responsibilities was credible.

All the people that crossed his mind had information or a purpose that was presently missing, and he needed to get to see them all.

However, his first port of call was to be Joseph Keetley, at the King and Crown. A pot of his finest tea would make a sore throat feel better. Any messages from Eibhlin would have been left with Joseph for him. More importantly, he reckoned that Joseph would have a bed spare, somewhere in the establishment, until he had worked out where to go next.

Admiral of the fleet
A person of such red face that he shows a fondness for strong potations (a heavy drinker)
Abiav
A Romany Wedding
Barkers
Guns
Bow-wow mutton
dog substituted for mutton
Bruisers
Boxers / strong-armed bouncers
Cat-lap
A non-drinker / drinker of tea and coffee
Chavi
Romany for child / in this case, daughter
Congreve's
Safety matches
Crack-a-crib
Break into a house
Crawlers
The lowest of the low, emaciated and exceptionally poor beggars
Dickin
Romany for watching / looking
Devil's claws
The thick arrows on prison uniform
Drabarni
A Romany sooth-sayer / mystic
Earth bath
A grave
Family
The criminal fraternity
Fancy
Those who have an interest in following and betting on boxing / pugilism

Flimpers
Pickpockets
Hold a candle to the devil
To be evil
Jolly
A serious disturbance
Julking
Singing - as in caged songbirds
Kushti
Romany - alright / acceptable / agreeable
Lurkers
A criminal purporting to be a beggar
Make a stuffed bird laugh
Tell a tale that is so absurd or far-fetched
Mullered
Romany - killed or murdered
Mumpers
Beggars or scroungers
Newgate Knockers

Thick waxed sideburns covering cheeks
Oubliette
A cell / chamber where prisoners would be left and often forgotten
Radix Malorum est cupiditas
Cupidity (greed) is the root of all evil
Respited sentence
A Victorian punishment, where a sentence would be manipulated to allow for those convicted to live a more or less normal life, often outside of prison
Rom Baro
Romany - Head man
Salt-peter men
In Victorian times, a common practice was for people to urinate in public spaces / places, and men would dig up the urine impregnated top-surface to provide salt-peter

for explosives / gunpowder.

Satismos
Romany - 'cheers' / drinking salutation

Sell me a dog
To con or deceive somebody

Vardo
A Romany caravan

Other books by this author:

- **Jack Ketch's Puppets** - book one in 'The Borough Boys' series

- **Death lurks in Cock Muck Hill** - book two in this series

Both books are available through Amazon / Createspace in paperback and for Kindle.

36987765R00270

Printed in Poland
by Amazon Fulfillment
Poland Sp. z o.o., Wrocław